The Universe in 3/4 Time

The Universe in 3/4 Time

The Universe in 3/4 Time

Leona Francombe

merle books
brussels

Published by:
Merle Books Brussels
Belgium

First printing 2021

ISBN 978-1-7371600-0-7 (Paperback)
ISBN 978-1-7371600-1-4 (eBook)

Cover artist:
Nicholas Maxson-Francombe

Back photo:
Matthew Waring

www.leonafrancombe.com

For my children,
Eva and Nicholas

Given ships or sails adapted to the heavenly breezes, there will be those who do not fear even that vastness.

—Johannes Kepler (1571-1630)

From Harmony, from Heav'nly Harmony,
This universal frame began.

—John Dryden (1631-1700)

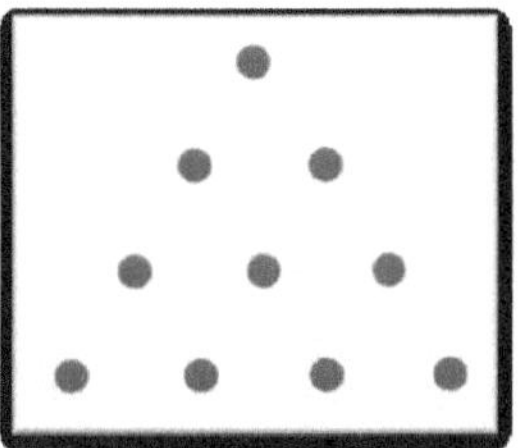

Tetractys

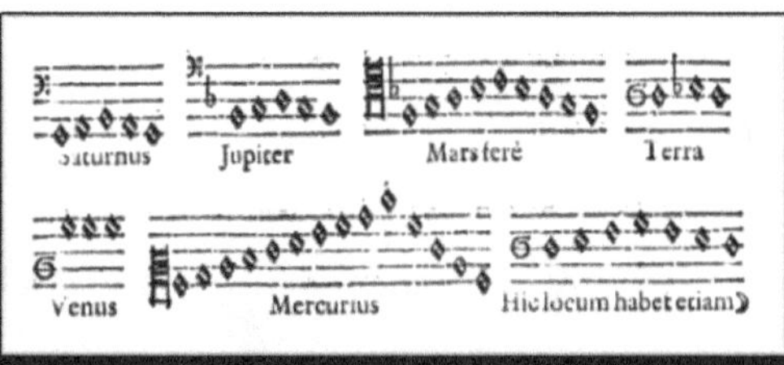

Johannes Kepler's planetary music
(from *Harmonices Mundi*, 1619)

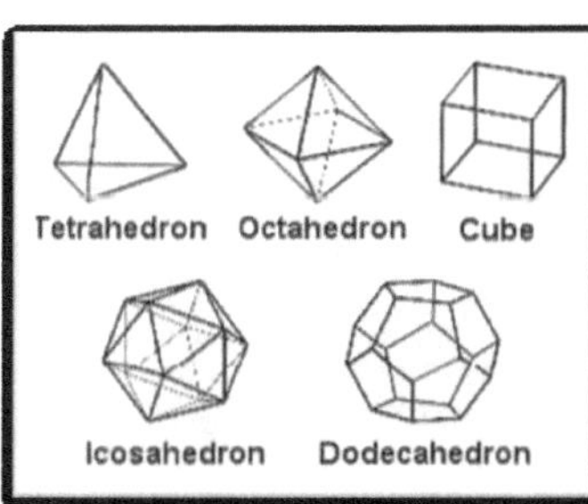

The five Platonic solids

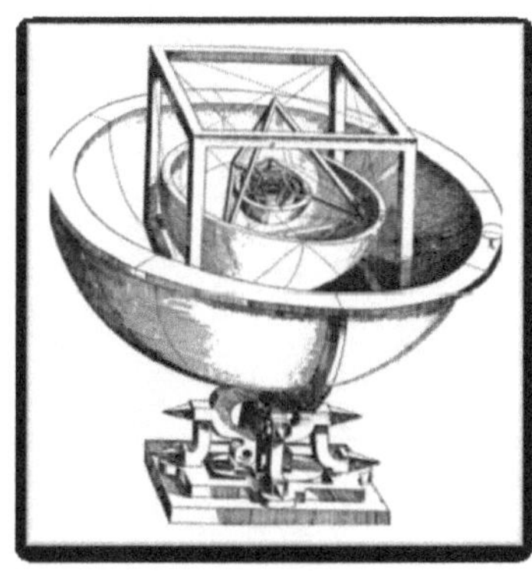

Kepler's Platonic solid model of the solar system
(from *Mysterium Cosmographicum*, 1597)

Pythagoras and the blacksmiths
(from a thirteenth-century manuscript)

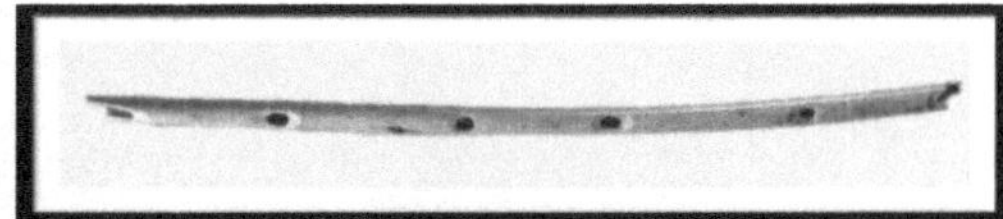

Vulture bone flute, ca. 40,000 years old
(Jensen/University of Tübingen)

PRELUDE

Forty millennia ago, in a cave in what is now southern Germany, some nomads were having vulture for dinner when one of them discovered Music.

It was cold. Spirits flagged. Snowflakes spiraled in through the entrance to the cave and hissed on the fire, creating a sad, limping duet with the wind. Beauty had not yet made herself known to the human soul. But that evening, facing the chasm of another winter's night, one of the nomads felt a peculiar emptiness.

The woman was idly turning over a vulture bone when the wind caught in its hollow and sighed. Her eyes widened: the sound had been purer than the moan of the wind. She tilted the bone again: once more, it spoke. The others stared. Something had quickened inside them, like a living thing. The woman glanced up at the rocky ceiling, for although it was clear that the bone itself had spoken, the sound seemed to have come from somewhere far beyond the cave. Firelight caught on many pairs of bright, hopeful eyes.

It would take more idle moments for the woman to blow on the bone herself; and quite a few after that for her to carve holes in it with a sharp stone. Who knows how long it would be before someone actually played a tune on the thing? Centuries, perhaps. In any case, millennia still had to pass before Pythagoras discovered the building blocks of music, and another twenty centuries or so after that before Mozart took up his quill.

The nomads couldn't have known what raw material they'd encountered that night (the raw material of their egos still being wet, after all). They'd not yet considered, as the ancient philosophers eventually would, that harmony might order the universe and be reflected in every human soul. Or that they, humble cave-dwellers, had tempted Music down from her cosmic cradle with just a hollowed-out bone. But looking up into the darkness as they had, they must have already possessed some instinct—some native spark—that had alerted them to the distant provenance of their visitor.

Perhaps a youthful Fate had been at work; or maybe a still-green god. For had those nomads not been eating vulture on a particularly windy evening; and had boredom not been weighing on them with its heavy winter hand...

Well.

Music might never have been tempted down to Earth at all.

Flutes would never have been invented, let alone pianos.

And certainly the singular events that follow could never have transpired.

PART I

CHAPTER 1

The evening that would change everything began like any other.

Shortly after ten p.m., Audrey Nightingale donned her baggy coat and burgundy cloche hat and started down the six flights of stairs from her garret. She stepped softly, so as not to waken the elderly abbé two floors below, and tip-toed across the front hall, where the landlady mounted guard behind her door, then slipped out into the night.

She felt it at once: the watchful stillness everywhere, quite unlike any other evening. A gauze of icy mist clung to the spires and statues of old Brussels and sent a hush through parks and lanes. Townhouses dozed, century-worn; their cornices brooded like heavy brows.

Audrey pulled her hat down against the cold and stepped up her pace. Someone parting a curtain on their way to bed might have wondered where the petite figure in shapeless clothing was going at such an hour—

and in February, too. They might have seen her of an afternoon, hurrying up and down the cobbled streets from one student to another; or sitting at the window of the café across from the church, drinking espresso and pondering. Most of the time, though, few took any notice of Audrey Nightingale. That she was a pianist, she rarely mentioned; that she was an orphan, she kept to herself entirely, for even she didn't know what lay in the fog of her origins. In any case, the observer on his way to bed could never have guessed that this little woman walked every evening as the city went to sleep, and that, with her gaze set above the rooftops, she was seeking solace in the night sky.

She crossed Place Royale and entered a moribund Parc de Bruxelles. The mist had lifted here, exposing a clear swathe of sky. Audrey wandered along a line of espaliered trees and turned into an obscure alleyway. At last, away from the city lights, she could glimpse a sickle moon through the winter branches, a few stars, and far away in her silvery splendor, Venus.

Harmony could be found in that sky, Audrey knew, reveling in the tranquility. Answers, too—at least for those who still stirred to the wisdom of the ancients. She'd learned these things years ago from her friend, the violinist Florian Lafève. Together with Jonas Liebling, cellist extraordinaire, they'd formed an ensemble celebrated around the world: the Kepler Players, now defunct.

Florian was a Pythagorean, which might have put off some people, but not Audrey Nightingale. He believed, as Master Pythagoras had in the sixth century BC, that music and number ordered the universe; that the heavens echoed with a Great Theme as the planets swept along. Known as the Music of the Spheres, this starry concord resonated in every human soul. *Oh, you can't actually hear this music, Audrey! Because it has always existed. It's like living next to a rushing stream all your life. You don't notice it. But it's part of you.*

Audrey still remembered the expression on Florian's face when he'd said this: like Schubert's, with fresh, school-boy cheeks, and eyes alight behind round glasses. She smiled up at the sky. No one believed this anymore, of course. Maybe not even Florian. He'd far surpassed Schubert's thirty-one years by now, as Audrey had; weariness had probably crept into the fresh gaze. He lived as she did these days, from gig to gig, rent to rent, and with a somber heart she considered that the grinding uncertainty of being a musician could well have dampened his ideals by now—perhaps even snuffed them out altogether.

*And yet...*At that moment, under the glittery dome in which people had always found meaning, Audrey felt sure that harmony must exist there somewhere. She knew the thrill of handling this substance, born of air, yet powerful enough to move multitudes. If someone like Pythagoras had considered music divine, Florian said, there must be something to it. Two thousand years after Pythagoras, Johannes Kepler was the last great scientist to believe in cosmic harmony, which was why, when their trio was founded, Florian suggested that they play under Kepler's name.

A young couple in search of a trysting place startled her. They balked at the odd little figure staring so resolutely through the treetops...at the baggy coat, like a vagrant's, and the strands of silver glinting in the boyish hair. But then a streetlamp revealed Audrey's profile, so finely drawn that the couple halted, enthralled, before veering away.

Audrey wandered deeper into the park. *The Greater is reflected in the Lesser,* Florian used to remind her, which meant that the universe, and a lowly piper, could sound the very same note. It was just a question of scale. *Imagine what power we musicians have, Audrey, conjuring the universal every time we play!*

Every time we play...

She sighed. It had been three years since they'd played together. She hadn't spoken to Florian in all that time. As for Jonas, he'd vanished entirely. The Kepler Players had always been her family—her true home.

Audrey gathered her coat around her and hurried from the park.

Three years already since the disaster.

♦ ♦ ♦

She retraced her steps across Place Royale and felt it again: that watchfulness. It was past eleven o'clock. By this time, she was usually ensconced at Pascal's late-night café across from Trinity Church, sipping Irish coffee and basking in his avuncular fussing. "You really should be more careful at night, chérie," he would say, spooning an extra dollop of cream on her drink.

She knew whom he meant: a tattooed misfit known simply as Nero, with a drunken temper and hair limp with grease. He hurled abuse in his coarse Marseille accent, and drove around at night in a battered white van with a buffalo head stenciled on the door, trawling for discarded items. Audrey, a reluctant gossip herself, would linger at the door of her *boulangerie* for a few tidbits from the matrons: "Did you hear that he escaped from a prison in France? *Non?* Well, it's true! Two *pains au chocolat, Monsieur, s'il vous plaît.*" An excited whisper: "He killed a man, you know! With his bare hands..."

Audrey hurried up Avenue Louise. Nero seemed to be everywhere—and nowhere. She took a chance turning into Rue Nova, as it was deserted, but it was the quickest way to Pascal's. She fell into a stride and the rhythm soothed her, reminding her as it did of a piece the trio had played years ago. She could still hear Florian's soaring melody as if he were beside her, and the dusky voice of the cello played as Jonas spoke, in a warm, guileless rush. Weaving between them was something that danced, and gleamed, and still radiated heat even now, years after her piano had gone silent: the sound of her own playing.

CHAPTER 2

It seeped from the night: a large, squarish object blocking her path. Audrey approached the apparition.

She caught her breath:

A piano.

A jolt went through her at the sight of the instrument she'd pledged her life to, thrown to the elements like rubbish. The upright stood in front of an imposing *maison de maître* without a single light on, though a street lamp gleamed on the cobbled walk.

Audrey peered up and down Rue Nova, as if someone had simply mislaid the piano and would appear soon to recover it. She combed the silhouettes of townhouses, crisp against the city night. Perhaps the perpetrator was even then observing her, wondering what she might do. A chill tingled under her coat at the thought of Nero trawling nearby, on the lookout for just such merchandise.

She removed a mitten and ran her fingertips over the piano's lid. Then she traced the simple coffered design on the front panel. Anguish gripped her: the rosewood veneer, in perfect condition, was already buckling in the humidity. *Who would do such a thing?* No instrument could survive these conditions even for an hour—let alone until morning. The piano had been delivered a death sentence. Yet despite this, it stood proud and steadfast, as if resigned to its fate.

Audrey opened the fallboard and gaped at the creamy, undamaged keys...the impeccably-matched grains of wood. Inlaid bronze lettering read: *A. Náhoda, Malá Strana, Praha.* The make was unknown to her. *Prague.* The Kepler Players had performed many times in that ensorcelled city. *Náhoda.* An obscure Czech manufacturer, she guessed. *What was such a piano doing in Brussels?* The keys were not ivory, but of a sort of cellulose used in some early twentieth-century upright pianos. The instrument could have been eighty years old or more.

She opened the lid and released a wisp of mildew. The hammers were pocked by mold. Mice had gnawed the felts. She was examining the strings and pins when she noticed a curious pattern of dots carved into the wood: a tiny pyramid formed by a line of four dots on the bottom, then three, then two, capped by one dot on the top. Next to this motif, someone had scratched a few crude symbols impossible to decipher.

She closed the lid.

There was something about this piano—an air of nobility...of distant origins. Its lines were almost too clean and elegant. There were no candle-holders, or any of the frippery typical of the period—nothing to detract from the sublime substance all pianos were created to channel. The upright in Audrey's garret was a harlot in comparison, with porcelain cameos of nymphs cavorting; clawed feet; curlicues. Some ancestor of her landlady, Madame Mertens, had hauled it up to the garret before the Second World War, and no one knew if it would ever make it down again.

Audrey's piano had the voice of a harlot, too.

But this...

She depressed a key: a sound leapt forth, pure and pearly. She played a melody: the hammers rattled in protest, but the tones lingered on the air. Audrey swallowed hard. It had been years since she'd played anything at all besides the study pieces of her students, and even those had been half-hearted demonstrations.

She leaned on the piano, overcome. A tear fell on the lid.

You must be strong, Audrey.

The words stung in her memory. They were her foster mother's—an irony, as the woman had had so little moral strength herself. Indeed, she'd been unable to muster the courage to tell the child what needed to be said, so had foisted the task on the school principal, who'd gamely called the girl into his office.

♦ ♦ ♦

"You have a very interesting background, Audrey," he'd begun. It was a coward's way of describing the caprice that Fate had dealt her. He'd been looking out the window with his back to her, for even at the age of nine the girl had possessed that probing gaze, and he hadn't been able to meet it.

She would remember every detail of that office: the dirt trailing on the window; the desiccated plants on the sill; the mustardy walls and piles of documents stacked against them, brown-edged and fungal. Everything except the face of the man himself.

"You were very lucky," he'd said, "that the priest at Holy Trinity Church just happened to go back to his confessional. No one would have found you otherwise." And then: "How blessed you were!", as if most children would have been delighted to start life that way.

Had it really been luck? *Blessed by whom?*

Only later did she learn how close she'd come to the edge of oblivion: that someone had abandoned her in her baby carrier near the confessional on a Sunday evening, just as the parish ladies were locking up the church for the week; that the priest, an amiable tippler, happened to have forgotten a bottle of cognac behind his curtain and gone back to retrieve it. And there she'd been, the infant Audrey. Hungry. Indignant. She'd kicked off her blanket along with the only clue to her identity: a scrap of paper on which someone had scrawled "Audrey Nightingale", that had wafted across the floor of the nave and almost been lost.

No one would have found you otherwise.

♦ ♦ ♦

She stayed late on the day she'd visited the principal—pleaded with the janitor to let her into the gymnasium.

"I won't be long," she said. "Please, Bo." It was what people called him, as his given name was too foreign to pronounce. "It's to see my friend."

The melancholy man who pushed his mop around the gym floor knew which "friend" she meant: a graffiti-covered hulk with all the ivory stripped away—one of Music's ugly stepchildren, though not completely deserted by her, for the wreck could still speak.

Bo unlocked the door. Audrey rushed in and threw her coat on the floor. She sat at the piano, and depressed the rough blocks of wood that passed for keys until she found it: the pulse still animating that sorry carcass. She even managed to eke out a few phrases of Schumann she'd heard on the radio.

Bo let her play. He crossed his hands on the handle of his mop and rested his chin on them. It was a pose he adopted frequently, at any moment of the day, to listen inwardly. His thoughts could not rival the sounds this singular girl was producing, however, so on these occasions, he turned his listening outward.

"Audrrrrey," he said gently, and pointed at the clock. He rolled her name with tropical lushness. "That was lovely. But you must go."

"Just five more minutes," Audrey said.

"*Viens, ma petite.*" Bo wheeled his bucket to the door and switched off the lights. A greenish glow seeped in from the corridor and shone on the wet floor.

Defiant, the girl played on, as if the darkness had only encouraged her. The janitor had yet to discover that in fact, she embraced the night with all its beckoning vastness. He certainly could not have known that just then, as the lights had gone out, she'd seen something that she would never mention to another living soul. It had been so fleeting, after all: just a trick of illumination...of the greenish glow from the corridor that might or might not have been a lady in shimmering robes, passing overhead with a lantern.

CHAPTER 3

She stood in the icy dampness and coaxed the foundling piano to life. One after another, liberated, the tones drifted up, up, through the halo of the streetlamp and far beyond, where Audrey imagined them being welcomed as prodigal children. Were piano-makers aware of this? she'd always wondered, as warmth and energy coursed through her. Had they ever confronted the rogue force they'd caught inside their quivering boxes, and regretted trapping it there?

I've missed you.

It was more of a tremor than a voice. Audrey looked up at the reclining moon. The tremor was familiar, somehow. She'd experienced something like it long ago, playing those rough blocks of wood. A caress, lit from within.

Her hands delighted in their old byways: gestures that in their thousands had made her a musician. Even then, they'd only created a template. What was it that Florian had said? Something about our connection with music far surpassing the mere playing of an instrument.

Yes, that was it! she thought, as the night air embraced her melodies. Florian would surely have agreed that here, under the stars on Rue Nova, she was proving Pythagoras's point: that *musica instrumentalis,* or the playing of a musical instrument, was indeed the conduit between *musica mundana*—the sounds made by the cosmos—and *musica humana*, or the resonance between body and soul.

Remember that ancient legend, Audrey?

She shivered. How could she forget those two Babylonian pillars? On one were carved astronomical discoveries. And on the other...

She summoned a phrase of Mozart.

On the other were carved the secrets of music.

Audrey glanced overhead. *The secrets of music...*She closed her eyes, and even on that wintry Brussels street she could imagine pigment fading on a temple column...sandals on hot stone...a linen robe, rippling in the breeze from the Euphrates...

"Our craft is incredibly old, Audrey," Florian had said. "Even older than religion. The thread stretches back thousands of years." He'd turned his hand over and slowly opened his palm. "And we musicians are still holding on to it. We are the keepers of that mystery."

Audrey smiled as her hands found their way over the keys. "Dear Florian," she whispered. "How right you were."

She opened her eyes and froze.

How long had the man been watching her?

♦ ♦ ♦

He was standing only a few meters away in the shadow of the street-lamp, all limbs and patience. Mantis-like. He wore no overcoat in the crushing cold, only a black suit cut too close that turned his body into a cipher. A fedora sat high on the head. His face was a void.

Audrey drew herself up to her full, unimpressive height. Relief rushed in briefly that this wasn't Nero, only to be replaced by doubt. What if the man was scouting for Nero—preparing to call him at any moment about this treasure he'd found?

"What do you want?" she said. Humidity muffled her words. She could feel the flank of the piano through her coat, pressing against her hip, and found some comfort in this.

The man said nothing; he made no move.

"Do you know whose piano this is?" she ventured.

Silence.

Audrey and her watcher somehow found each other's gaze in the gloom.

"Are you working with Nero?" she blurted. Her hands, so warm and alive from playing, were dead things now.

This seemed to confuse the man. He stepped forward: the move sucked the breath from Audrey. Her exhale, when it came, was now close enough to mingle with his. But as near as he was, she still could not isolate a single feature on the man's face. She studied his hands instead, milky-white at his sides, and recoiled at the thought that he might have followed her here—that he'd been tracking her all along.

A tram sighed as it rounded Place de la Trinité and Audrey turned toward the sound. It was the last tram of the night, and usually her cue to leave Pascal's and go home.

She turned back to the man.

He was gone.

Her heart thudded. She combed the empty streets. *Did I imagine him?*

Emotion welled in her. The evening had been full of illusions...of memories and sensations perhaps better left undisturbed. With despair she noticed that slowly, inexorably, bulges were appearing on the piano's veneer as it pulled away from the wood underneath. In a surge of tenderness she considered staying out all night with this orphan. At the very least, she might be able to prevent Nero from hauling it away.

He killed a man, you know. With his bare hands...

How could she stop someone like that?

Audrey took her cell phone from her coat pocket, then put it back again. It had been a reflex—something she used to do often whenever she'd been in doubt or in trouble, but hadn't done for three years.

What would I say to him after all this time?

She wiped a fresh film of humidity off the piano and took the phone out again.

The moment had come.

She dialed the number. It rang three times only. Someone was there, though: the line was open.

What was he thinking, seeing her name on his screen?

"Florian?" she managed to say. " *Tu es là?*"

No answer.

"Are you there?" she repeated.

She waited.

"*Alors,*" she fumbled. "You see, I've found a...well, something remarkable."

Then, at last:

"Audrey..."

CHAPTER 4

They met at Pascal's.

Most of the cobbled streets in the neighborhood ended up at Place de la Trinité, and anyone who followed them there couldn't miss the establishment across from the church, where candles in colored glass holders winked on every table and windowsill, and the proprietor was a more appealing confessor than the priest across the road.

"I wasn't sure whether to call you," Audrey began, as she and Florian extricated themselves from Pascal's embrace and took their old seats by the window.

Florian reached across the table and squeezed her hand. "I'm glad you did," he said. "*Chère* Audrey...it's been far too long."

For some moments they simply regarded each other, the aging Schubert and resolute woman with graying hair.

Pascal drifted over with his flat-footed sway and put two cappuccinos on the table—their usual order. "How nice to see you together again!" he beamed. His plump cheeks shone in the candlelight. He glanced at the empty chair where Jonas's leather jacket used to hang. "No third one tonight?" he asked sadly.

"No," said Florian, crisply.

"Ah. *Dommage.*" Pascal swayed off again.

Jonas had always been his favorite. The big-hearted German was so much larger than life that most Belgians, unimposing by nature, generally passed through shock and affront before finally succumbing to his charms, which they always did in the end. Tall and disheveled, he would bump through the door of the café with his cello case and call out a general greeting, followed by: "Caffeine! Immediately!" Jonas Liebling was the only customer for whom Hermes, the ancient mongrel sleeping on the doormat, actually bothered to wake up.

Audrey turned the blue glass candle holder on the table and watched the flame bend and buckle. "Florian, have you seen Jonas?" she asked with trepidation, as if the cellist were a ghost.

"No. Have you?"

She shook her head. How she missed that sweet, boorish rake! She ached that Florian had obviously not forgiven him.

"Is he still in Brussels, do you think?" she asked.

"I don't know where he is," Florian said. "Still chasing rich aristocrats, no doubt, and trying to avoid their husbands. He may have gone back to Germany, for all I know." He paused. "Either that, or he's in jail."

Audrey looked up from the candle. "He's still on the run, then."

◆ ◆ ◆

They spooned the cream off their coffees in silence.

"Are you all right?" Audrey asked at length, struck by her friend's pinched, sallow cheeks. A few strands of silver glinted in the dark curls.

"Oh, I'm passably well, I guess," Florian said.

"You're playing at the opera now?"

He gave her a tired smile. "The Monnaie's just one of my gigs these days," he said. "Tonight, *The Magic Flute*. Tomorrow, 'Moscow Nights' at the Russian ambassador's house, for his birthday. You know the drill."

She knew it all too well. Every member of the musical guild understood the price of entry: gigs behind potted plants; cheap quarters; dreary streams of students. Like unicorns in a forest, musicians moved invisibly through a shallow, materialistic world, fashioning the beauties of their art just from shimmers and air.

Audrey studied Florian again, this time to probe his state of mind. He'd hardly mentioned the trio. Was he trying to forget, as she was? At least he was still making music. And though he'd reached the pinnacle of his art and could have been touring the world as a soloist, the reality was less obvious: most of the time, when seeking nourishment, the human soul didn't distinguish much between Mozart and "Moscow Nights", often preferring the latter, which was something that Florian, unlike most musicians, understood and even appreciated.

"And you?" he asked.

"And me..." Audrey stared out at the hulking edifice of Trinity Church. "I haven't played since the trio."

Florian gaped at her.

"Well, I'm not being entirely truthful," she explained. "You see, this evening..."

"Yes!" Florian jumped in. "You mentioned that you'd found something...*remarkable*, I think you called it."

Audrey laughed. "As remarkable as a piano can be!" she said.

He tilted his head, intrigued. "A *piano?*"

It was no easy matter relating the epiphany on Rue Nova. Audrey herself could already feel the events of the night slipping away. A Czech piano...a spidery watcher...the spectral Nero...It all seemed fantastical, even to her. She could only imagine what it must have seemed to Florian.

"A piano on the sidewalk," he mused. "*Extraordinaire!*"

"I think I was meant to find it," Audrey said. She delighted in the color infusing her friend's cheeks.

But he must have sensed that already, she thought. After all, the Kepler Players had spent so much time together that nothing could be kept a secret for long. They'd lived and breathed as one. They'd been able to start a piece together with eyes closed, perfectly. *To the universe and back!* had been their pledge before going on stage, and indeed, once the applause had died away and the music had begun, it seemed as if they'd embarked on the most splendid of voyages.

"Florian, I must save that piano!"

He grew solemn. "But Audrey, what about that man? Not to mention Nero. Isn't he part of a criminal gang? Be realistic." He said these things with a sigh. "I can see that you're as determined as always," he smiled. "Of course I'll help. First, though…"

He took out his electronic tablet from the pocket of his violin case.

"The piano won't go anywhere in the next few minutes," he said. "Let's look up 'Náhoda' online. Ah, here's something:"

Petr Náhoda

A Czech journeyman piano builder active in the second half of the nineteenth century. He learned his craft at the Schweighofer piano factory in Vienna. Náhoda returned to Prague in the 1880s to set up a small workshop in the Malá Strana quarter of the city. Both he and his wife died of tuberculosis in 1915, leaving the workshop to their only son, Antonin. There appear to be no known pianos extant bearing the Náhoda name. It's possible that Náhoda constructed pianos only for special or-

ders, which was the case with many small manufacturers of the time. According to local history, the Náhoda workshop was partially destroyed by fire sometime in 1942.

"That's all there is," Florian said, tucking the tablet back into the case.

"No known Náhoda pianos extant..." Audrey murmured. "How on earth did one turn up in Rue Nova, do you think? It must date from before the fire in 1942, if that guide's to be believed."

"Yes. It must have been a special order for someone," Florian said.

"Oh!" Audrey exclaimed. "I almost forgot. Do you have a pencil?"

Florian rummaged in his violin case again and produced one.

"There were some strange symbols scratched on the inside of the piano. And a little pyramid of dots actually carved into the wood."

Audrey replicated the pattern on a napkin.

Florian stared at what she'd drawn. "Are you sure this is what you saw?"

"Yes."

"A tetractys," he muttered, taking the napkin from her.

"A *what?*"

"It's an ancient symbol—Pythagorean. An exquisite example of hidden meaning."

Florian looked up from the drawing. His eyes shone in the way that Audrey imagined Schubert's must have when the opening measures of the C Major Symphony had first come to him.

"There's a universe of significance here, Audrey!" he said. "Pythagoreans considered the tetractys holy. They actually swore an oath to it."

"It just looks like a pile of dots to me," Pascal said, shuffling over.

"Oh, it's far more than that!" said Florian. "Look." He pointed to Audrey's drawing. "The design glorifies the first four whole numbers. Number one, the single dot at the top of the pyramid, represented unity; identity; the Creator. There are many other interpretations. The two dots underneath it stood for duality: finite and infinite; light and dark; good and evil, etc."

"Ah, yes, I see," Pascal said. He pulled out Jonas's chair and dropped onto it, exhausted from his day.

"The three dots symbolize beginning, middle, and end," Florian went on. "They can also represent harmony: think of the three notes of a chord."

"Of course!" Audrey said. "And the four dots on the bottom of the pyramid?"

"Well, again, there are various meanings: earth, fire, air, and water, for instance. Four was also the number of points needed to construct a pyramid: the simplest of the perfect geometrical solids. And don't forget that all the dots add up to ten, which is the basis of our mathematics."

Florian gave Audrey a charged look. "But carved into a piano...?"

"Yes," she said. "Who would do that? And why?" She glanced around the café and watched the candles in their primitive dance, holding back the darkness.

Florian took off his glasses and rubbed his eyes. "Someone who understood the musical meanings, no doubt. Pythagoras discovered musical intervals, as you know. The intervals we all use today without ever questioning where they came from: the octave, fourth and fifth. Look at the symbol again."

Florian took the pencil and wrote beside each row of dots, beginning with the top of the pyramid:

"Look: 1:1 is the ratio for the single dot, meaning a unison." He continued down the pyramid: "The dots symbolize the frequencies that form musical intervals. 2:1 is the ratio for the octave; 3:2 for the perfect fifth; 4:3 for the perfect fourth."

Pascal struggled to his feet. "You've lost me there! But you two are musicians." He said this with awe. "And Jonas, of course," he added, indicating the chair the cellist had occupied.

Hermes lifted his head from the doormat at the familiar name, then went back to sleep.

Florian let out a cynical laugh. "Jonas never appreciated ancient philosophy very much."

"Please, Florian," Audrey said. She got up and put on her coat and hat. "We must hurry!"

They kissed their host on the cheek, stepped over Hermes, and left.

CHAPTER 5

I t was right here!" Audrey cried. She rushed to the spot. The bell of Trinity Church struck one o'clock in response: a doleful, finite tone.

Florian lagged behind her. "We should be careful," he said, out of breath. "That man might be around."

Audrey stood where the piano had been. She studied the cobbles, as if the instrument might have left a print on them. The feel of the luscious, creamy keys lingered like an aftertaste.

"Oh, Florian, why did I leave it alone?" She could have been talking about a lost child. "I should have stayed with it until morning. I should have…"

"Audrey!" Florian stopped her. "First of all, you would have frozen to death. And second, what about Nero? God knows what he would have done if you'd confronted him"

He wandered over to examine the deserted façade: a *maison de maître* of arresting elegance, even on such an elegant street. The windows, seemingly dormant, nevertheless had a peculiar alertness about them.

"Are you sure this was the spot?" he said. "I mean, you'd need at least two people to carry off a piano. And in the middle of the night…"

Audrey glared at him. "Are you implying that I made it up?"

"Of course not!"

"Florian..." Her voice faltered. "I *played* it!" She folded her arms and glanced away.

He came to her side and observed her profile, which had always filled him with admiration. It was, after all, the view of Audrey he'd spent countless hours looking at when they were playing music together.

"What did it sound like?" he asked.

She hesitated. Then she described the notes she'd released from the foundling—the way they'd glided up into the night sky, as if returning to their origins, and the tremor she'd experienced as she'd played them. She couldn't, however, divulge the childhood memory that the piano had revived—or the possibility that Music herself might have paid a visit after such a long absence, beleaguered though the lady must have been on such a freezing night.

Florian turned to the sky: it was crystal-cut; reverential. "This is just the sort of night where the ancients found their answers," he said, sotto voce.

"Only not so cold," Audrey added.

"No."

They stood side by side where the piano had been and gazed overhead.

"To the universe and back..." Audrey murmured.

"Indeed."

"Florian?"

"Yes?"

"I felt a bit like Johannes Kepler just now, wandering around at night like he did four hundred years ago and coming across a comet. Except, of course, it was a piano."

He laughed.

"I don't think I ever asked you," said Audrey. "But why Kepler?"

Florian answered without turning from the sky. "Because he believed in the Music of the Spheres *and* science," he said. "He used science to construct his notion of cosmic harmonies."

"Ah, I remember now," said Audrey. "He measured the solar system and discovered the ratios of musical intervals in it." She said this light-heartedly, but considering the events of the evening, Kepler's theories didn't seem so preposterous.

"Yes," Florian said. "He constructed intervals from the ratio of a planet's fastest speed, when it's closest to the sun—its perihelion—to its slowest speed, when it's farthest from the sun—its aphelion. Kepler imagined a sort of sliding scale between the two points, like a trombone. He established a bass denominator pitch for Saturn—the outermost known planet. All the other planets sounded in relation to that."

Audrey smiled. "That's quite a symphony!"

"Oh, Audrey. Why is our age so devoid of wonder...so quick to dismiss what we can't see or prove? Modern scientists are embarrassed by Kepler the mystic."

They both spent a moment listening to the soundless street.

"After Kepler died in 1630," Florian said, "the idea of cosmic harmony fell apart and eventually disappeared." He hesitated. "Which was a mistake. Because at the time Kepler died, the Thirty Years' War was in full swing in Europe. If ever the notion of cosmic harmony was needed, it was then." Florian glanced at Audrey. "Remember what he said?"

"Hmm...something about neighing?"

He smiled, and quoted Kepler: "'Let us despise the barbaric neighings which echo through these noble lands, and awaken our understanding and longing for the harmonies.' He could have been talking about wars today, *n'est-ce pas?*"

"Yes," said Audrey. "If you think about it, universal harmony is probably the only thing that could render wars on Earth obsolete." She looked squarely at her friend.

Florian met her gaze. "To think that musicians were once revered enough to be priests in ancient times," he said. "They calculated the calendar; they made measurements of the heavenly bodies. Imagine! They were counselors. They healed the sick. Oh, Audrey..." His words sagged with regret. "Even if we've put behind us what we once were as a trio, we must never forget the divine nature of what we do."

Florian suddenly grabbed her arm.

"Get down!" he hissed, and pulled her behind a parked car.

CHAPTER 6

A man was moving toward them with a curious elastic gait. He stopped in front of the *maison de maître* and rang the bell.

Audrey crept around the car and clasped a hand to her mouth. "It's him!" she gasped. "The man who was watching me!"

"Are you sure?" Florian whispered.

She observed the fedora...the suit clinging to insectile limbs. "Without a doubt," she said. Fear surged in her, but also a bizarre relief, for this man was her only earthly proof of the night's goings-on.

A light came on in the entryway and the door opened. A thuggish silhouette appeared on the threshold.

The gaunt man said nothing. He turned around nervously, as if he'd sensed something in the street.

The light revealed his face. Audrey recoiled: it was a cadaver's. Bloodless. Without soul. She slumped down against the wheel of the car.

"I'm not meant for detective work," she said.

"Me neither," Florian moaned. Sweat glistened on his forehead.

Audrey crept around the car again.

"I don't appreciate you coming by at one in the morning," the thuggish man was saying. He stepped from the door wearing a warm-up suit. His meaty face shone as if he'd been exerting himself.

"So you're living here now?" the gaunt one asked. "That was quick, considering that the old lady died only last week."

"It's my house," snapped the other. "Anyway, I was generous enough. She was months behind in her rent."

The thug slipped up very close to his visitor. It was a hostile gesture. The height of the one, skeletal as he was, seemed hardly an adequate defense against the brawn of the other.

"Where's the piano?" the visitor said without flinching. He didn't cede a centimeter to the thug. His voice had a reedy quality, like a clarinet poorly played.

Audrey flinched, however. She recalled the presence in the shadows—the stalker's patience.

"The piano's gone," the thug said.

The other man stiffened. "You said you'd wait until tomorrow!" His voice cracked.

"The auction house wouldn't take it with the rest of the furniture," retorted the thug. "I'm lucky they offered to move it out of the house. The lady had no heirs. Everything had to be removed."

"A piano isn't furniture!" cried the gaunt man. Then, with sudden, jarring tenderness: "A musical instrument isn't rubbish."

"Well, why didn't you take it away last night, then?" The thug backed off with a swagger.

"Just carry it away, you mean? A *piano?*" The visitor tugged his fedora down against the cold. "You helped someone remove it, didn't you?" His voice had an edge to it. "Who?"

The man from the house ignored him. He took his time drifting back to the door, his shoulders squared with victory.

"*Who was it?*"

The cry sent ice through Audrey's heart.

"Nero," came the answer through the closing door. "And be careful: he's an escaped convict."

The door slammed shut.

The man in the fedora froze in place. His form was just a rune stenciled on the gathering mist. Then a sudden energy seized him. He launched himself into motion, and with the same elastic gait, disappeared.

◆ ◆ ◆

The two friends crouched behind the car for some time

"So it *was* Nero," Audrey said. The brittle cold burned in her throat. She struggled to her feet and started bouncing up and down to get the blood flowing.

"What does the man with the hat want with the piano, do you think?" said Florian. He joined her in the warm-ups, hugging his violin case to his chest.

"I don't know. But he obviously had something to do with the old lady.

"Have you ever seen him around here before?"

"No."

"Did he say anything to you?"

Audrey met Florian's gaze. "Not a word," she said. "I asked him what he wanted. Then he simply vanished into thin air."

Florian clutched her elbow. "Come on, let's check the name on the bell. Hopefully that awful man has gone to bed."

They dashed across the street and ducked into the shadow of the doorway.

Many old Brussels mansions had long since been turned into apartments. It wasn't uncommon for there to be at least half a dozen doorbells, each with a typed or even handwritten name next to it.

This house, however, bore only one name.

"*Nom de Dieu!*" Audrey breathed. They squinted at the small brass plate underneath the bell-pull, on which was engraved, in flowing letters:

K. Náhoda.

CHAPTER 7

They walked through the sleeping streets to keep warm. The city lay mute and lifeless around them, as if a plague had passed over her.

"K. Náhoda…" Florian mulled.

"On the piano it was *A*. Náhoda," Audrey said. Her voice was indistinct through her raised collar.

"They must be related."

"Do you think that K. Náhoda was the old lady who died recently?"

"Undoubtedly."

"Didn't the online article say that the Náhoda workshop was destroyed by fire in 1942?"

"Partially destroyed," Florian said. "It didn't say that anyone was hurt in the fire. Maybe K. Náhoda was a descendant—or married into the family."

"The old lady was Czech, presumably," said Audrey. "What was she doing in Brussels, I wonder?"

"She could have been living here since the war."

Audrey glanced at her friend. "In that big house? Renting for all those years? *Alone?*"

"It's possible," said Florian. His glasses flared in a streetlight. "Maybe she was a widow. There's usually a clause in leases that allows elderly tenants to stay on until they die."

"The man who watched me—he must have known her," said Audrey.

"He certainly knew about the piano. And he obviously considered it worth salvaging."

Audrey sighed. "Oh, it was." She mourned, not only for the orphan she'd been unable to save, but for the music it had briefly summoned—that weightless companion she thought she'd lost forever until tonight.

◆ ◆ ◆

They lingered at Audrey's door.

"How's the sleeping abbé?" Florian asked.

"Still sleeping."

Florian glanced up at the worn façade. "Madame Mertens still hasn't repaired that sagging cornice, I see," he chuckled. "I miss our rehearsals in the garret. How is the old badger, by the way?"

"The same. Nothing escapes her notice." Audrey gave Florian a wry look. "She's also a Pythagorean, you know."

"Oh?"

"Yes. I thought that's why you liked her. She taps on my door three times with her stick to remind me to unload the washing machine. Isn't that one of the holiest numbers since Pythagoras?"

They laughed as they used to.

"Florian," Audrey said at length, watching her breath float out on the mist. "Do you still think about the trio?"

"Every day."

"*Really?*"

"You're surprised?"

"Well..." she stumbled. "I thought you'd moved on, that's all. And..."

"And?"

"And you don't seem to have forgiven Jonas."

Florian set down his violin case, took off his gloves and blew on his hands.

"Audrey," he said. "You know as well as I do that a musical ensemble like the one we had is a fragile marriage. You can't trample on it—let alone engage in criminal behavior like Jonas did and expect your partners to forgive you." He gave Audrey a long, frank look. "The kind of union we had with the Kepler Players only comes around once in a lifetime."

"I know," she said. Her gaze drifted upward, following the rusting downspout to the cornice sagging outside her garret four floors up, and to the milky sky beyond. "But other things come around, don't they?" she said. "Extraordinary things. They cross our orbit when we least expect them." She wondered if this planetary allusion might brighten Florian up.

"It's that piano, isn't it?" he said quietly. "You've fallen in love with it, haven't you?"

Audrey let the questions hang. At length she said, "Old instruments have stories to tell, don't they?"

"Yes, indeed."

"They have souls." And then she thought: *Even the most wretched instruments have souls. Even ones covered in graffiti and stripped of all their their dignity.*

"Of course," said Florian. "Our job as musicians is to let their souls speak."

"Well, then." Audrey turned her most resolute regard on her friend. "I intend to recover it."

Florian stared at her. "But what about the sinister man? Not to mention Nero?"

"I must find it," she said, undeterred. "I sense there's much more to it than we think."

He sighed. "I trust your intuition more than anything else," he said, adding: "How else could we have played such great music together with our eyes shut?"

"You'll help me, then?"

"Well…"

"Tomorrow?"

"I can't. I have a rehearsal in the morning. Then I'm having lunch with Olivia. There's no question of changing it."

Audrey lit up. "Olivia!" she exclaimed, as if he'd summoned something magical.

Olivia Taverner. Peerless mezzo-soprano during the post-war years and widow of the distinguished British conductor, Reginald Taverner. *Soft, scented Olivia.* She also happened to be Florian Lafève's great-aunt, and an enthusiastic admirer of the Kepler Players in their heyday. She'd even organized concerts for them at her home. Olivia had performed rarely during her long life, even in her prime, but when she had, it was often in her own legendary salon in Brussels, where it was rumored that the king himself reserved a seat by the door.

Audrey smoothed the toe of her shoe over a cobblestone. "Florian, you couldn't possibly…"

He laughed. "Oh, all right! I'll call Olivia and see if you can come. I'm sure she'd be delighted to see you again after all this time. I'll meet you there at noon, sharp."

"And afterward?"

"Afterward we'll see about the piano. But don't get your hopes up." Florian picked up his violin, kissed Audrey on the cheek, and wandered off.

He'd only gone a few meters when he turned around and said, "To the universe and back!"

♦ ♦ ♦

The front door boomed shut in the cavernous entry.

"Madame?" Audrey called out softly. It wasn't unusual for the landlady to be on watch at that hour. She recoiled in surprise: Madame Mertens was standing in full view. This was not a common occurrence, as the woman's strength lay in her invisibility, a trait far more powerful than her actual shrunken presence.

"Ah, Madame," Audrey began. "*Bonsoir.* I just have a small question—*une petite question.*" Her attention was momentarily diverted from the lady's badger snout to her scrawny legs, which she wore bare all year long and glowed in the dim hall like phosphorus. "Would you happen to know anything about Nero?"

Madame Mertens retreated a step. "Nero?" The tiny eyes glistened.

"Yes. Do you know where he takes his merchandise?" Audrey was fairly certain that with the landlady's vast mental roster of who was doing what in the neighborhood, she'd be able to answer this question.

Madame stepped forward again. "To Schaerbeek, I believe," she said conspiratorially. "He took an old fridge of mine once. Seems to me he sold it to a Ukrainian dealer." Curiosity flickered. "Why do you ask?"

"Schaerbeek," Audrey echoed. The immigrant quarter used to be Jonas's home. It was a rough place in parts, in others bustling and exotic, where lamb sizzled in corner grills, and roasted cumin and coriander laced the North Sea miasma. Jonas had rented a flat above the Casablanca General Store on Chaussée de Haecht, where Rami, the gentle proprietor, had fallen for his tenant's charms like everyone else, and delighted in the Bach cello suites filtering out over his fruits and vegetables and mingling with tunes on Arabic radio.

"You don't want to go looking for Nero, Audrey," Madame Mertens said. "*C'est un sale type.* He's a bad one. Do you know about him?" Her eyes gleamed. "Do you know what he did?"

But Audrey had already begun the long climb up to her garret. She wished Madame *bonne nuit* as she rounded the first landing.

CHAPTER 8

She lay in bed fully dressed trying to warm up. (Madame Mertens turned off the heat promptly at eleven.) Sleep was an impossibility in any case: she was still awake when the Trinity bell struck three.

Her musician's mind charted the progress of each tone as it jangled forth, vibrated, and rode its sound wave over the tiled roofs into oblivion— each tone followed by a new note refashioned from the same, godly air. Musical notes were alive, she knew. Quite apart from the fact that they contained energy and moved through the air, they came into being, decayed, and were renewed. This was life, after all. Three phases. Like the three dots of the tetractys.

Trinity...How strange, she thought, to live and work so close to the place where she'd been found almost forty years ago. What had the priest made of the hungry infant outside his confessional? Had he considered her appearance a nuisance? *A miracle?* After all, she could just as well have been abandoned at a train station, or in a bathroom on the highway somewhere, or sold by human traffickers. Her keen musical talent could have gone unnoticed, when instead it was discovered in one of her foster homes and nurtured. She'd not only found her soul-instrument, but had been able to spend her life with it. Were these miracles, too?

The cosmos is vast, as Florian liked to say. It can house many possibilities.

♦ ♦ ♦

Jonas visited her dream that night. At least, it appeared to be Jonas at first. But there wasn't a trace of his usual candor or charm. He was inward-looking, this dream-phantom; austere, with distant, mournful eyes. Shorter than she remembered, too. And that scrappy beard Florian was always making fun of...well, now it was fuller, and neatly trimmed in a strange, beaver-tail shape. The phantasm wore a wide white ruff around his neck, pleated and starched. Jonas wouldn't have been caught dead in such a thing.

Jonas?

It was the sort of metamorphosis that only sleep can accomplish: the scruffy, bearded Jonas transformed into the sickly, bearded Kepler. The only thing the two men had in common besides facial hair was that they were both German, and keen on music. The vision could talk, too. (Though hopefully he wouldn't launch into his three laws of planetary motion, which Audrey had never been able to get straight.)

Kepler was addressing someone, it seemed.

In the recesses of her dream Audrey detected another figure: tall, white-robed, though without any solid mass, as if he were simply thickened air. The form stirred in Kepler's presence as an ancient seed, desiccated for centuries, comes alive in the rain

"I wish you could see what I've devised with your perfect geometrical solids," Kepler was saying to the other apparition, although how Audrey understood this she couldn't fathom, as he was speaking in Greek.

"I'm glad to hear you call them *my* perfect solids," said the thickened-air individual. "Plato got all the credit for them in the end."

Pythagoras! The five perfect three-dimensional solids had always been called the Platonic solids, though many thought it was Pythagoras who'd discovered them a hundred years earlier. These polyhedra were unique because each one was comprised of sides identical in size and shape. A cube, for instance.

"Your Greek is very good," said the legendary geometer.

"Thank you," Kepler said, his slight chest expanding with pride. "I studied it at my seminary school."

The two men sat down at a table surrounded by hundreds of winking candles. Maybe thousands. A veritable solar system of them.

Pascal's place?

"So, what did you devise?" Pythagoras asked.

"Oh, you of all people would adore this: my theory is that the universe—which you yourself believe to be ordered by mathematical truths and music—is actually constructed around perfect geometric harmony. According to my theory, the planets move on circular orbits separated by the five perfect solids (though of gigantic proportions, of course!), all nesting one inside the other like huge eggs: the pyramid, cube, octahedron, dodecahedron, and icosahedron."

"The eight-, twelve- and twenty-sided shapes too?"

"Yes! It's a most wonderful discovery, don't you think? But..." Kepler stroked his beaver-tail beard. "I just couldn't get it to work. Because the planets revolve in elliptical orbits. Not circular ones. And only circles will fit inside the perfect solids."

"Ah. A pity," said his companion. "It's a gorgeous scheme, though. I wish I'd thought of it myself. But there's ample evidence of divine harmony in the universe without it. My disciples arrive at this understanding through three years of self-imposed silence, during which they rigorously study arithmetic, geometry, music, and astronomy. Thus spiritual resonance with the universe can be achieved."

At this point, a ghostly Pascal swayed into view.

"What would you gentleman like to eat?" he asked in French. The two anachronisms apparently understood him.

"A nice crisp schnitzel for me, please," Kepler said. Then, to Pythagoras, "I long for the taste of my hometown, Weil-der-Stadt."

"I don't eat meat. Or beans, for that matter," Pythagoras said to Pascal. "Just some bread and honey for me."

"Spiritual resonance with the universe..." Kepler ruminated. "Our human connection with cosmic music, you mean."

"Exactly!" Pythagoras cried. "How marvelous that you are still speaking of this! When did you say you were born?"

"AD 1571."

"AD?"

"Anno Domini," Kepler said. "In the year of our Lord," he added, in case there was any confusion.

But there was some. "Which Lord?" the Greek asked.

"Jesus Christ," Kepler said. "But of course, you were born almost six centuries before him. Anyway, you found your own inspiration in the heavens. Ah, here's my schnitzel."

The men ate their meals in silence, one with Renaissance gusto, the other sparingly, with small, meditative mouthfuls, as would befit a vegetarian philosopher from a hot climate.

At length Kepler said, "I'm a devout Christian, you know. It's only logical that the universe was created by a divine architect—that such an architect would have constructed the most beautiful and harmonic universe imaginable.

Pythagoras nodded, and wiped up the last of his honey with a crust of bread.

"The whole world is governed by number," Pythagoras said. "By Music most of all. She is the true divinity. Music IS number. And the cosmos IS music."

"Ah, yes," said Kepler, turning his mournful eyes to introspection. "There is perhaps a greater freedom—a greater truth—to what you say. Music is indeed divine. What a shame that your disciples scattered into anonymity."

◆ ◆ ◆

Audrey observed the two men through the haze of sleep. She could imagine Pythagoras returning to his arid knoll after dinner to contemplate the sky; and Johannes Kepler going back to his damper, Renaissance knoll, contemplating the same thing, and she marveled at the millennia yawning between them—at how knowledge, though foot-worn, had traversed those two thousand years intact,

She awoke to the bell chiming six. Dawn had swallowed all traces of the mystical Greek. As for the bearded Kepler, he'd left her with the scruffy Jonas again, along with the memory of the last few minutes she'd spent in his company.

◆ ◆ ◆

It had been an evening no one would forget: a concert that had passed into infamy even before coming to an end.

The crescendo of panic...the audience surging to the exits...heads of state bustled away...security swarming through the most secure building in Europe.

She'd found him outside, poised for flight.

"Jonas!"

"Oh, Audrey," he moaned. "I'm sorry...I'm so sorry." His concert shirt hung like a rag from under the leather jacket. Though he spoke to her gently, fury contorted his face.

"Is it true what the baron said?" Audrey's voice was dead with shock. "*Is it true?* That you took all that money? "

"I'll explain one day," Jonas said. He held her cheeks, drained of all color, between his big, moist hands. "Will you make sure to take my cello back to Rami's?" he asked. "I can't possibly go back inside the hall."

"Of course," she said.

Jonas caught her in a tragic hug. He stank of stale pipe smoke, and of sweat soured by fear. "Forgive me," he mumbled, pulling away.

He dashed headlong toward the canyons of the European Quarter, his charming genius forever sullied.

"Jonas!" Audrey yelled over the police sirens.

He called back as he fled: "We never should have named our trio after a sixteenth-century astronomer!"

CHAPTER 9

In fact, naming the trio after Johannes Kepler had paid off handsomely—or so it seemed when they received the invitation from the Kepler Foundation. It would be the crown jewel in their careers: a performance for the inauguration of Harmonia Europa, a continent-wide musical initiative for disadvantaged children. The gala was to take place in the European Council's spectacular new summit building in Brussels, attended by luminaries and heads of state, and broadcasted live internationally.

The Kepler Players were the obvious choice for the occasion. There was their name, of course. But also, they were known around the world as a classical ensemble that had breached the awful severity of their profession. How they managed this wasn't clear. Perhaps it was the blend of casual clothing; talking to the audience; bouts of improvisation and humor. Critics couldn't define what, exactly, drew people to their concerts. Paris Match enthused: *Classical music in the popular spirit!* Wrote The Guardian wrote: *The Kepler Players are blessed to have three stellar musicians, including the genius of Jonas Liebling, perhaps the greatest cellist of his generation. If this group hasn't moved you to tears or made you want to dance, then it's you who've had an off night.*

The fact that Florian was French, Jonas German, and Audrey Belgian was the cherry on this musical cake as far as the Kepler Foundation was concerned. What better way to represent European harmony than with beautiful string music played by those former arch-enemies, France and Germany, united on the piano by their habitual battleground, plucky little Belgium?

♦ ♦ ♦

They convened at Pascal's to plan the performance.

"The program has to be perfect," Audrey said. "European; accessible; meaningful. Gentlemen, this is our moment!" She kindled the same passion in her friends. "We have twenty-five minutes," she went on. "No more, no less, because of TV constraints." She gave Florian a smirk. "You can't do your little spiel about Kepler this time."

Florian's "little spiel" was usually a highlight of their concerts. "Imagine, ladies and gentleman, a time when the skies were steeped in mystery," he would begin, to an enthralled crowd. "A time when people looked to the heavens and found harmony there." Florian's cheeks would shine under the stage lights, and his glasses would flash. He'd ask Jonas to play the tones that Pythagoras claimed each planet made as it glided along, and Audrey would demonstrate the intervals that Kepler calculated between a planet's slowest and fastest speeds. "They're not beautiful sounds in the way that lovers of Mozart and Beethoven might expect," Florian would concede. "But they're haunting. And they have such significance, because they find resonance in *us!*"

"Hermes, *kom!*" Jonas called across the café. The old mongrel limped up to the table, gnawed the morsel of bread Jonas was holding out for him, and waited for his caress.

On the table was a list of the trio's entire repertoire.

Florian glared at Jonas: "Study the list, please," he intoned. "And that dog stinks, by the way."

43

Jonas ignored him, and heaped affection on Hermes.

"I hope your women are sweeter smelling," Florian goaded.

"Friends!" cautioned Audrey. Then, to Jonas: "You'll have to spend more time with your cello in the coming weeks, cheri, and less time with whatever aristocrat you're seeing."

"How did you know she was aristocratic?" Jonas asked with a grin. He chewed meditatively on an unlit pipe and rocked back in his chair until his leather jacket brushed the floor.

"Word gets around," said Audrey. "Anyway, you prefer rich women with titles, don't you? Why don't you ever tell us who they are?" It wasn't jealousy that fueled her remarks, but exasperation that Jonas, in his naïve good will, should be so reckless.

"Mendelssohn's a good idea," said Florian, ignoring them. "The slow movement and scherzo of the D minor, maybe?"

"How about something Czech, since Kepler spent time in Prague?" Audrey suggested. "A movement of the 'Dumky'"?

"Louise Farrenc ticks the French and female boxes," Florian said.

"Who?" Jonas wondered, murmuring to the dog.

"Oh, she wrote great stuff," said Audrey. She searched on her phone. "Here she is: her dates were 1804 to 1875. She was a fantastic pianist, composer, and also professor of piano at the Paris Conservatory, which was no small feat for a woman back then."

"She was alive during the Battle of Waterloo, I see," Florian mused. "That's another European box we can tick."

"How about the first movement of a Belgian trio, to commemorate the capital of Europe—Francois Rasse, maybe?"

"And the European Anthem, of course...we'll have to arrange it for piano trio"

"If we pull this off, maybe we'll finally get a decent recording contract," Audrey said.

"And I can finally publish a book about Kepler and music!" Florian chimed in.

Thus they planned for their glorious future.

CHAPTER 10

Nothing was auspicious about the day they met Baron Aymeric Van Overberg, Chairman and CEO of the Kepler Foundation. Rain lashed in grim, October bursts. They missed their tram, and the taxi soaked them as it cut a corner. They lost their way in the EU district and were six minutes late arriving at the foundation's headquarters.

"The baron will see you now," announced the secretary, bemused by the three dripping bohemians.

Florian whispered to Audrey: "Why did the baroness set up this meeting if she can't be here?"

"It's simply a courtesy call before the concert," she said.

They were led into the cold redoubt of glass and steel that was the baron's office. The occupant, as hard-edged and metallic as his domain, was standing at the huge panoramic window with his back to them.

"The Kepler Players, sir," said the secretary, and melted away.

Van Overberg made no move. He didn't speak. He continued surveying the EU quarter as if it were his own personal fiefdom, a view that included the new Europa building where the trio would be performing. Though wind juddered the glass in front of him, and raindrops raked it like shrapnel, the baron stood impervious at his helm, his gray suit seemingly sculpted to him.

At last he turned.

Audrey perceived it at once: the toxic channel between Jonas and Van Overberg. She made the connection in an instant. *How long has Jonas been sleeping with his wife?* she thought, and could tell that Florian was thinking the same thing.

Oh, Jonas, you idiot! Audrey glanced at her friend and her heart sank. Not because this time, his philandering could embarrass them all, but because the gentle, gullible Jonas was clearly heading for a fall. She could smell his fear even through the leather jacket.

The baron simply nodded to them and sat down behind his desk. He indicated the three chairs across from him, and began thrumming his fingers softly on the polished expanse. Van Overberg's shark-gray hair had been cut with the same precision as his suit, and his black-rimmed glasses corralled his regard not on his visitors directly, but on a point somewhere behind them, as if they didn't merit his full attention.

"We are so happy to be a part of your admirable initiative, Baron Van Overberg," Florian began.

"Here is the program we're proposing, sir," Audrey added.

They did their best to hold up the trio's banner.

For his part, Jonas thrust his hands into the pockets of his jacket and stared at the floor.

The baron barely glanced at the program Audrey slid across his desk. He uttered only a few bland niceties, and seemed relieved when the secretary appeared with coffee.

Aymeric Van Overberg was rumored to be the richest man on the continent. It was said that the twenty million euros he'd invested in the Kepler Foundation was a mere bagatelle, parked there for tax reasons. He had no personal interest in music—or even in culture, for that matter, beyond the necessities of his rank.

Audrey balanced her coffee cup in her lap and observed the baron. A taut current coursed through this man. *Le beau fou.* The handsome madman. It was the moniker the European press had adopted for him—one of those affectionate slights the aristocracy loved to repeat about their own kind, as if they were describing an eccentric relative

Audrey could see the truth in it now. While Van Overberg was, indeed, handsome in a clinical sort of way, whatever madness he harbored had nothing to do with eccentricity or charm; nor was it a harmless consequence of inbreeding. Rather, it appeared to be a well-oiled mechanism entirely under his control.

The baron's attention soon flagged. The musicians explained the European symbolism of each of the composers they'd chosen to perform with barely a reaction from their host; they asked Van Overberg to elaborate on the Harmonia Europa project, for which he referred them to his secretary. Even Florian's passion for Kepler, that one would think, considering the name of his foundation, might have softened this girder of a man, failed utterly.

After a charged silence, Van Overberg pressed a button under the desk and the secretary appeared again.

He stood up, as did the trio.

"We are so grateful for this opportunity to perform," Audrey said. In a show of politeness, she lingered, even though Florian had backed toward the door, and Jonas had already exited.

"This will no doubt be a most important occasion for you," said the baron. It was the longest sentence he'd spoken. His voice was bland; toneless. The black-rimmed gaze was far from uninterested, however. For it was fixed on the doorway: not on an arbitrary point, but on the tall, impatient cellist idling in the waiting room.

As she left, Audrey noticed that despite Van Overberg's immense wealth, there was nothing of material value in his office. His intangible assets were considerable, however, among them a gift for cruelty which, they would realize only too late, could be summoned on a whim.

CHAPTER 11

It was the evening of the concert. Audrey found herself in the ladies' room of the Europa building, changing into the full-sleeved white blouse and long black skirt she would be wearing onstage.

She studied herself in the mirror: the person looking back was different, somehow. This tended to happen around concerts. She'd never been able to put her finger on what, exactly, happened to her on these occasions, except that a heightened version of reality occurred. A musician was handed a unique elixir before performing—of transcendence, and boldness—and having drunk this, the act of offering music to other human souls completed the alchemy, changing everyone in the process.

"This concert is the sum of all our efforts," Audrey whispered, as her heart faltered. She smiled encouragingly at the pale face in the mirror. The boyish hair had no glamor whatsoever, though she'd taken some time with it. She wore no make-up; no jewelry. But it all suited her, somehow. *All the allure of a nun without actually having to be one!* Jonas liked to say, and she took it as a compliment.

◆ ◆ ◆

"This way, please," said the woman in charge of protocol. Her badge swung out as she marched in front of them. "The piano was tuned this morning. You have thirty minutes to rehearse."

The musicians followed her through a bevy of technicians, assistants, uniformed security, hangers-on. A red carpet had been placed at the entrance to the European summit chamber—not for them, of course, but for the heads of state and other dignitaries who would be arriving later: the British prime minister; the German chancellor; the French president; high officials of the European Commission as well as sponsors of the Harmonia Europa project.

Audrey held her breath.

There it was:

The piano.

Sinuous, elegant, it stood at the epicenter of the great circular space. The music stands and chairs had been set out, and the whole stage was ringed with flowers. The desks that normally faced each other around the circle—a sort of Round Table for Europe—had been left in place around the stage, with extra chairs for the audience fanning out behind them.

The Europa building was the newest and most spectacular structure in the European quarter. Symbolism abounded: in the 3,750 restored oak window frames that made up the exterior cube, brought to Brussels from all corners of Europe; and in the polychrome interior, a cheerful design of squares painted on floors and ceilings, lifts and corridors, in the colors of the flags of all the Member States.

And then there was the lantern: a huge glass egg nesting in the center of the cube that towered ten stories high and contained meeting rooms. At night, when lit, the lantern seemed to hover like a ghostly beacon. From the center of the summit chamber on the ground floor, where the piano now stood, one could look directly up into the open base of the egg.

*A lantern...*Audrey stared up into the darkened ovoid while Florian and Jonas were tuning. As they prepared to marshal the most numinous substance on Earth, she fancied what might be lingering in that opening: someone whose business it was to light their way, perhaps.

Not too fast in the scherzo!

Audrey, watch that entrance!

For God's sake, Jonas, you're still too loud!

Do you think we could rustle up some coffee?

The rehearsal was eerily normal considering the circumstances. Banal details caught Audrey's attention: the duct tape holding down a television cable; the drooping lily that the florist had overlooked; a faint smell of disinfectant. The acoustics were vacuous and indistinct. The many voices, and the heels clipping back and forth over the wooden floor, all melded together in a single wash of sound that did not bode well for music-making.

Audrey spotted him first: the tall, gray-suited figure in black-rimmed glasses. He was idling near the entrance with a fawning coterie. Not once did the baron acknowledge the trio. Instead he droned on to his listeners, stabbing the air with his index finger while looking at his phone.

Audrey glanced at Jonas and her morale plummeted. He'd obviously seen Van Overberg, too, which had had the effect of turning the ebullient, incorrigible rake—the Kepler Players' secret weapon—to stone.

♦ ♦ ♦

They were led to a drab meeting room where they would wait until summoned to play. Pitchers of water and orange juice had been set out on a table with a selection of miniature sandwiches.

Florian paced about the room, fingering his violin.

Jonas retreated to a corner and chewed on his pipe stem. It was unusual for him not to attack the food.

Audrey approached him. "Jonas..." she began. Foreboding had been gnawing at her since the rehearsal. "Don't let Van Overberg's presence disturb you in any way." Her voice trembled with nerves.

Jonas gave her a sad smile. "I'll try, Süsslein." It was his special endearment for Audrey. *Sweetie.* It both charmed and irritated her. "You know about the baroness, don't you?" he added.

"I've known since the meeting with Van Overberg," she said. "It was pretty clear to anyone in the room." She couldn't bring herself to say: *Why the hell would you have an affair with such a person?* Not now...not just before playing. As it was, Jonas seemed dangerously off-form.

"Is the baroness coming?" Audrey asked.

"No."

"Are you sure?'

"Yes."

A pause. Then, feeling bolder: "Are you in love with her, Jonas?"

He gave her an unusually penetrating look. "God, no! No one could ever...Oh, Audrey, you are..." He reddened, and looked away.

Whether she was buoyed by the fact that he didn't love the baroness, or by what she thought he'd been implying by his unfinished sentiment, Audrey couldn't say.

There was a soft knock, and the protocol officer opened the door.

"It's time," she said.

CHAPTER 12

Audrey went first. She tucked her scores under her arm, smoothed her moist palms against her skirt and followed their guide. Florian came next, holding his violin by its scroll. Jonas brought up the rear with his cello.

They walked in silence down several long, polished corridors before arriving at the summit chamber. Through the entrance they could make out the Chancellor's bright blue jacket—the blue of Europe—and the lacquered heads of VIPs. The audience preened and puffed like exotic birds. All eyes were trained on the doorway.

The musicians regarded each other without speaking. They continued to do this until each of them had felt it: a shared consonance. *Our cosmic chord,* Florian called it, and even Jonas acknowledged that he could feel it, too. They were more than ready. All the hard work had been done and now, in the long, long shadow of Pythagoras, the only thing left to do was to connect their playing to something greater than themselves.

"To the universe and back!" they proclaimed in unison.

The protocol officer held her arm out to usher them in.

Someone announced: "Ladies and gentleman, the Kepler Players!"

They entered the chamber to excited applause and took their places.

Audrey played an A for the strings to tune. She pulled up her sleeves in the heat of the television lights, blinking in their glare.

The audience hummed, rippled, then grew still.

They began.

Audrey let the familiar lightness sweep her up to that place where all their hours of labor found such sweet rewards. Never had she felt such freedom onstage—such unfettered joy. *This is why we play*, she thrilled. *For these few moments of sublimation.*

Oh, she'd seen him, all right. *Le beau fou*. She'd spotted Van Overberg as soon as they'd made their entrance. He was sitting in the second row not far from the Chancellor. No doubt Jonas had seen him, too. But the power of the moment was all theirs. They could play as they pleased; they could frolic with abandon under that great lantern: Europe's symbolic navel. No one could touch them now. No one could stop them. Such a breach of protocol would have been beyond imagining.

They played flawlessly, as if possessed. The Rasse, Dvořák, Farrenc, Mendelssohn...applause thundered through the chamber after each selection. Even Florian and Jonas lay their grievances aside and achieved a rare union, passing sparks of music back and forth between their bows before letting them float up to the entrance of the lantern as new ones flared.

Who would have dared to break that spell?

♦ ♦ ♦

The baron simply stood up at first.

It seemed benign enough, especially for such a well-known eccentric. Surely he was just stretching his legs.

The trio was tuning for their final number: the premiere of their own arrangement of the European Anthem. Of all the pieces on the program, this was the one that had garnered the most interest in the press.

Audrey took deep breaths and collected her energies. She dried her fingers on the lace-trimmed handkerchief she used for important concerts, then tucked it back into the piano. Anticipation charged the hall. Programs flipped white in the half-darkness. Heads leaned together for a final whisper.

Florian and Jonas lifted their bows to begin.

Audrey poised her hands on the keys, ready to nod the cue.

Everyone assumed that the baron would sit down.

Unease rustled through the crowd: Van Overberg had not taken his seat. Quite the contrary: he was standing tall, facing the stage in a defiant posture. The rustling swelled, and even the Chancellor turned briefly to glance at the man known to everyone in the chamber.

The string players lowered their bows and stared at the elegant madman. Audrey looked up from the score and felt it again: that toxic channel.

For Van Overberg had fixed all his malevolence on Jonas.

Everything happened in an instant. Later, Audrey would reflect on the oddity of this phenomenon: how the moments around which life turns are really very short indeed.

"He's a criminal!" Von Overberg shouted, stabbing the air in the cellist's direction. A wave of gasps crested and fell. Then not a single molecule moved in the hall.

The cameras zeroed in on the disturbance.

"A criminal, I tell you!" the baron repeated, in a low drone this time. "He should be in prison." The silence deepened to capture every word.

Florian shot Audrey a panicked look. *He really is crazy*, he mouthed.

Audrey waited for the absurd blow to hit—for the announcement of Jonas's philandering. But this was not a crime, of course.

"Jonas Liebling embezzled thousands of euros from the Kepler Foundation for his own personal gain." Van Overberg intoned.

Then he shouted: "Arrest him!"

The two words tossed shrapnel through the chamber. Protocol was shredded. Solemnity blown apart. The ensuing din encompassed every possible emotion.

If Van Overberg was mad, he was also clever, for he'd managed to convert all his monstrousness into Jonas's. (Perhaps not such a difficult thing to do when one was pitting a poor cellist against the richest man in Europe.)

Even greater damage had been done, however: one deadly shard of shrapnel had pierced the heart of the Kepler Players.

Jonas gave Audrey a look she'd never seen before—the hopelessness of a doomed man.

There was another collective gasp:

Van Overberg had reached into the pocket of his exquisitely-cut suit.

A muffled yell: *He has a gun!*

Security officers sprang to life. They surged toward the baron. Within seconds bodyguards had surrounded the heads of state and herded them toward a side entrance.

Van Overberg broke free of the melee, defiant. He had no gun, as it turned out. Only a handkerchief. "Detain that cellist, for God's sake!" he spat.

Jonas dashed from the stage leaving his cello behind.

"Jonas! *Wait!*" cried Audrey. She launched herself after him.

"Audrey!" yelled Florian.

Pandemonium reigned.

CHAPTER 13

They arrived for luncheon at the grand Taverner residence just as the church across the pond was chiming noon.

Florian rang the bell.

"Does Olivia know about what happened to us three years ago?" Audrey asked. She took off her cloche hat and smoothed her hair in the shine on the brass knocker.

"Everyone knows," Florian said. "But Olivia's too much of a lady to talk about it. Anyway, she tends to drift off on her own memories these days."

The glossy black door swung open and a diminutive Portuguese maid greeted them. She took their coats and ushered them to the salon.

Audrey sucked in her breath: nothing had changed in the hallowed space. An antique Bösendorfer still dozed in one corner, reflecting on its Viennese youth; pastel brocade, plush cushions and orchids all reduced the imperial space to something approaching cozy...confessional, even. Olivia claimed that no concert hall had ever suited her better than her own living room, and so she'd performed her lieder repertoire almost exclusively here, in this vast *maison de maître* overlooking the Ixelles ponds. Her husband, Reginald Taverner, was always at the piano.

Audrey noticed the handsome gilded chair near the door. "Did the king really come here?" she whispered.

"Yes," said Florian. "In the fifties. But with utter discretion. Most people didn't even know he was here. He took a seat near the door after the music began, and slipped out before the applause." He added: "People left here in a daze, you know. Olivia had bewitched them."

They roamed about the salon as they waited for their hostess. Music clearly inhabited this room. Perhaps it was the silver-framed photographs of musical luminaries, made even more luminous at Olivia's side. (Among them Audrey spotted the late Reginald himself, pot-bellied and mustachioed.) Or maybe it was the wonderment that never leaves a place where it has been so earnestly felt.

Audrey approached the Bösendorfer: she'd played it on several occasions, with Florian and Jonas in full swing beside her. She remembered all her concerts, and could say without hesitation that the performances she'd given in this room had been among her best.

One photograph on the piano arrested her. She drew closer: a man seated at a keyboard was turned toward the photographer with irritation, as if he'd been disturbed at an important task—or perhaps caught with a secret. His eyes were as black as his hair, and there was a wild aspect about him, enhanced by the blousy white shirt a peasant might have worn galloping his pony across the steppe; and by a most extraordinary set of features, soaring and angular.

"Is it the first time you've set eyes on Konstantine, Audrey?"

The voice was clear; playful. The voice of a young woman.

Olivia Taverner advanced across the parquet, heels lightly clicking. She wore a tailored cashmere suit of the palest mint green, and a gold chain at her neck so fine, it would have been invisible had it not glinted occasionally as she turned her head.

Soft, snowy, scented...she hasn't changed! Audrey thought, except that as with many older people, Olivia's physical volume had diminished since they'd last seen each other, and like an essential oil, had achieved its purest, most potent self.

Olivia kissed Florian on both cheeks, ruffled his curls, and clicked her way over to the piano to embrace Audrey.

"Konstantine?" Audrey echoed. Olivia's cheek was as plush as chamois, and had left a trace of jasmine on her own.

"Konstantine Zar," Olivia said. With exquisite subtlety, her gaze swept over Audrey's long gray skirt and black cardigan, lingering on the sturdy walking shoes. She repositioned the photograph on the piano so that it stood apart from the others.

"You've heard of philosopher-kings," Olivia said. "Well, Zar was a philosopher-musician. A seer. A prophet. Oh, but where are my manners?" She grasped Audrey's hands in both of hers with admirable strength. "How have you been, dear Audrey?" A lapse followed, like a breath before singing. "Oh, I know what happened," Olivia continued in her low, amber voice. "We needn't speak of it."

Audrey smiled to herself. *Of course she knows!* The Kepler Players' disaster had been broadcasted on international television, for heaven's sake. Only a true lady could have navigated around this behemoth in the room.

Their hostess picked up a little silver bell and gave it a vigorous shake. Within seconds, the maid reappeared with a decanter of rosé and three crystal glasses. The wine had a flare of summer to it, even in the February light.

Olivia perched on the edge of a damask love seat and indicated two embroidered chairs to her visitors.

"You don't feel too lonely in this great big house, Auntie?" Florian asked, moving his chair closer to the love seat.

Olivia smiled indulgently. "Ah, dear Florian. You know well enough that in the presence of Music, one is never alone."

"Tell us how you met Konstantine Zar," he prompted her.

Olivia's smile faded; her attention wandered. It was as Florian had predicted: memory seemed to have joined the gathering so tangibly that it might as well have pulled up another chair. Their hostess sighed, poured wine, and sighed again. Audrey observed the inclined head, as white and elegant as an egret's, and the tiny hands without a single blemish. And there was something else, too...something that made this otherworldly creature seem to flutter unevenly, as if uncertain how to traverse this final stretch before paradise.

"Zar...oh, Zar," Olivia whispered, handing two brimming glasses to her guests. "I met him in 1939—the year before the German army invaded Belgium. I was so very young. So idealistic. Imagine: I was convinced that music held all of life's secrets...that harmony and beauty would keep war away!"

"Did you influence Florian's philosophy, by any chance?" Audrey interrupted.

"Maybe," Olivia said, but kept to her story. "Zar came to Brussels in 1939 from Prague. But he wasn't Czech by origin. His roots were deeper eastward, in Austro-Hungary. His name was originally 'Zarándok'—or 'pilgrim'. He spoke quite good French, but with an odd cadence. He was full of paradox: aristocratic in bearing, yet rough around the edges; a consummate musician, but he never seemed to practice.

"His grandparents migrated from the Hungarian hinterland to Prague," Olivia went on, a pink flush infusing her cheeks. "They set up a small music shop, which his parents took over eventually." She shook her head. "Zar was obviously poor. I felt so sorry for him in the beginning. He only had a few shirts to his name—the kind that peasants wear." She glanced over at the piano. "Like the one in that photograph."

"But you say he was aristocratic," Florian said.

"A beggar can be aristocratic, Florian," Olivia chided him. "It's a question of bearing...of innate nobility." She sipped her wine and gazed out at the pond. "It's hard to say what Zar was, exactly. Violinist, pianist, teacher, philosopher. All of those things, in fact."

"What brought him to Brussels?" Audrey asked.

"He came to study at the Royal Conservatory, with the great violinist Emile Hendrickx."

"Emile Hendrickx?" cried Florian. "He was a legend...world-famous." He paused. "But infamous, too, wasn't he? A Nazi collaborator, if I'm not mistaken."

Olivia waved an impatient hand. "Just because he performed for the occupiers doesn't mean he was a collaborator. We all performed for them, my dear. We all played the music they wanted to hear. We couldn't perform Mendelssohn, for instance—he was a Jew, of course. Or any Russians, for that matter: no Borodin; no Mussorgsky, Rimsky-Korsakov, or Tchaikovsky. You young people don't understand what it was like to live in shackles, as it were—to be denied your freedom. We did what we had to do to keep the wolf from the door, and we weren't always proud of it, believe me. Not everyone was a hero."

Olivia put her glass on the table and turned to her guests. "It was the fear, you see," she said, barely audibly. "Every day. Day and night." She twisted her hands in her lap. "Such deep, debilitating fear."

Audrey shivered. An eddy of cool air had crept in along with the maid, who tip-toed across the parquet with a bowl of nuts. The air seemed to stir elsewhere in the room, too. Somewhere in the vicinity of the piano.

"I don't think that Zar ever knew fear," Olivia said. "He had the calm of a mystic." She glanced down at her hands. "But people were afraid of him. Because you see, he could look into your very soul."

CHAPTER 14

Olivia Courtois was a sweet-eyed dairyman's daughter of seventeen when she enrolled at the Royal Conservatory of Brussels in the autumn of 1939. Up to that point, she'd known only her ancestral village near Namur, and sung only to the cows. But even so, her talent had been apparent. Villagers lingered at the farm gates, drawn as much by the girl's voice as by her goodness, which attracted humans and bovines alike. She'd told her parents that she wanted to perfect her singing at the *conservatoire* in order to bring some beauty into the world.

And so, swallowing their emotion, the dairyman and his wife bid good-bye to their only child at the village station. They knew that her talent belonged to the wider world—that even though war was leering once again at the borders of their little country, the young should not be held back.

Olivia left home with only the few clothes and music scores she could carry in her cardboard suitcase...and of course, the voice that had incited such rapture in the cow byre.

She arrived alone at the door of Madame Hazard's rooming house in Avenue de la Couronne. The great bourgeois metropolis daunted her at first. Regiments of stately townhouses stretched in both directions, each a fortress unto itself, though they all concealed their bulk with ornamental iron, stone, brick, and tile of such delicacy, one might have ventured into a colossal boudoir.

The young girl balanced on her toes to reach the bell-pull. She was studying the iron boot-scrape set into the side of the house, wondering what it was for, when the massive door rasped open. There stood a woman who dispelled any notions of grandeur that the *maison de maître* might still have been harboring—as well as a good deal of the country girl's fears.

"Madame Hazard?"

The woman nodded. She wore a house dress of brown floral and a soiled apron. She had a high, frank forehead and cheeks flushed most probably from the kitchen, given the smell of roast chicken wafting out into the street.

"You're a singer, then," said the landlady, waving Olivia inside. Her voice was reedy and cool. "I only house music students, you know," she added with a pinch of pride. "There are only two rooms with pianos, so piano students must have those. But there's an old Bechstein in the parlor if you need it." She led the girl up several flights of stairs to a room at the front of the house.

Olivia exclaimed at the spare, high-ceilinged space, so much airier than her tiny room under the eaves at the farm. Net curtains hung at windows so tall, a ladder would have been necessary to take them down and wash them. (Although clearly no one had done this for some time.) Olivia parted the curtains and looked across the avenue at a similar townhouse, with a splendid iron railing on which laundry had been hung to dry.

"Madame Meunier always hangs her washing from her front balcony," Madame Hazard sniffed, wiping the windowsill with her apron. "It's so indelicate. She has a perfectly good balcony behind the house, after all." She turned to Olivia. "I hope that you'll be happy here, chérie," she said, and left the room.

Olivia flopped down on the narrow bed. A little miasma of dust rose from the mattress and hung on the air. She studied the ceiling, high enough, she imagined, to collect its own atmosphere. She surveyed the furnishings: a washbasin, armoire, and kitchen chair were the only items, although Madame Hazard had included one conceit: a carved wooden music stand on which Olivia would rest her precious volumes of Schubert and Schumann. Her gaze shifted back to the ceiling, where she pictured fleecy clouds drifting on a summer's day. Or were they songs, waiting to be sung?

In October 1939, just a month after Germany invaded Poland, a young man from Prague came to stay at Madame Hazard's rooming house. It seemed a singular time to traverse Europe for music lessons. But Konstantine Zar was a singular young man. His face resembled a distant rampart, while his eyes reflected an inner preoccupation, as if he were listening for messages from a deep, echoing well. He'd taken the room above Olivia's, but she rarely saw him, or heard him practice, though it was rumored that he played the violin and piano equally well. His footsteps passed her door early in the morning, and she noticed that he often appeared at the dinner table still wearing his overcoat.

"He walks," Madame Hazard told her, with a pinch of deference.

"He *walks?*" Olivia said.

"Oh, yes! Don't you know? All the best philosophers are walkers." Madame Hazard savored every scrap of information she could glean from her mysterious lodger.

Konstantine Zar was only nineteen, but he already had the air of a master—of an older person who'd retained his youth through some mysterious nourishment. He studied music in unusual company: with Pythagoras, Plato, and Kepler. Music was a living, sentient thing, he said. A force that could heal, as the ancients had understood so well. Zar would walk for hours in the Bois de la Cambre—the park at the top of Avenue Louise—and in the deeper forest beyond. When he'd worn holes in his shoes, Madame Hazard bought him a new pair with her own ration tickets. The shoes had wooden soles (leather soles being almost impossible to find), and they soon turned his feet into raw flesh, but he wrapped his blisters in old scraps of linen and still he continued to walk. Even during the Occupation, when young men were routinely stopped for their papers, and the Germans closed the forest to unauthorized activity—even then, Zar never stopped walking.

♦ ♦ ♦

Madame Hazard did her best to brighten the existence of her lodgers. Her antennae, of military accuracy, led her unerringly to the most economical butcher, or a *poisonnerie* with a fresh catch that day; or to a bakery where she could save a few francs on brioches. She didn't seem to mind the challenges, believing as she did that she was serving a greater cause by giving Music's disciples shelter.

After their lessons and rehearsals, the boarders gathered in the dining room, where a pattern of dark-green vines twisted up the wallpaper and made them feel as if they'd stumbled into Orpheus's glen. Madame Hazard kept an empty chair at the table every evening and lit a candle in front of it. The musicians seemed to understand this oddity, though Olivia, who had not yet been apprised of the ritual, dared not ask about it. Anyway, she was far too distracted by the dour fellow sitting next to her.

He'd come in late again that evening and his dinner had gone tepid. Inevitably, the conversation turned to the gathering war.

"Should we keep studying at the *conservatoire* and brave the consequences?" asked the skittish Dutch flutist.

"Maybe we should go home to our families," said the clarinetist from Liège. "It will be safer in the provinces."

"*Ah, non!*" exclaimed Madame Hazard, passing around a bowl of steamed potatoes. "You remember what Monsieur le Directeur said."

And indeed, they remembered. The director of the conservatory was determined to keep the establishment open...to continue playing music in the face of whatever bombardment or privation they might have to endure.

"Will we have to play for the enemy?" asked the composer from Toulouse, though no one could offer an answer.

"Poor Belgium," the dour young man said to his hostess. "Surely your country has provided enough killing grounds already with the War of Wars. Ypres...Passchendaele..."

"*Eh, oui,*" Madame Hazard sighed. She sawed through the gristle on her meat. "Blood, mud, poison gas...and the worst thing of all: the fear. And that was only twenty years ago, dear Konstantine." She smiled indulgently at him, and then at Oliva. "Some of you weren't even born yet!"

Olivia stared at her plate.

"Belgium can't stay neutral for much longer," Zar said. "Or soon she'll become a doormat again. Such a tragic little wedge of land." There was not a trace of condescension in his remarks, but rather a startling, heartfelt empathy.

The boarders bent over their cheap cuts of pork, and the potatoes that always tasted of celery root, and said nothing.

Olivia finally summoned her courage and asked, "Madame, why do you always leave an empty chair at the table?"

There followed the bemused tittering of cognoscenti.

"Ah, *chère* Olivia," said Madame Hazard. "I forgot that you don't know. It's to make Music feel welcome, of course!"

This time it was the dairyman's daughter who giggled. She'd missed the fact that the previous laughter had been at her expense.

She shot a flirtatious glance at Zar for good measure.

His soaring face darkened. Daylight had slipped entirely from the ramparts.

He turned to Olivia with a glower. "If you don't think that Music should be welcomed as an honored guest," he said, "then maybe you've chosen the wrong profession."

Zar turned back to his dinner and acknowledged her no more.

His words would change her life—perhaps even more so than the day that would change everything.

CHAPTER 15

May 10, 1940

The morning dawned impossibly bright and clear. It was a day so vibrant that the blue of the sky, and all the colors spread out beneath it, seemed to tremble, as if these glories had reached their zenith and were about to begin the slide toward their own destruction.

Olivia drew aside the net curtains and thrilled at the prospect of singing Schumann that day. She smiled at Madame Meunier's washing on the balcony opposite, and thought how quickly it would dry in the crisp sun. The opening measures of *Du Ring an meinem Finger*—"Thou Ring on my Finger"—played on her lips as she tidied the bedclothes, and filled the basin with cold water to splash her face. The sky had been just too blue not to glance at it again, which she did. But this time, something made her heart grow cold. She remained at the window, uncertain. The Schumann vanished from her lips. A shirt on Madame Meunier's balcony flipped in the breeze and caught a flash of sun, as if in warning.

A deafening shudder rocked the house.

Olivia slumped from the force of the blast. As she straightened, she noticed a blotch on the peerless sky. The stain ran in various directions, like ink on paper, until it resembled calligraphy. There was a terrible sort of beauty in it—in that anti-aircraft shell tearing a wound in the sky.

The spectacle had only begun. Soon a plane appeared over the rooftops and spawned ten parachutists. Olivia counted them as they were jettisoned, one by one, and floated so serenely, so gracefully, they reminded her of milkweeds.

The next boom seemed to dislodge her teeth.

At first she didn't hear the banging.

"Mademoiselle! *Mademoiselle!*"

She flung open the door: it was Zar.

He said nothing. His face was closed even to her terror. He grabbed her arm so firmly it would leave a bruise.

Another explosion.

Plaster cracked over the stairs and broke away. Debris rained down.

"We must get to the cellar!" Zar shouted, and pulled her along the hallway.

The gracious proportions of the house had been drawn by peacetime architects, for residents to take their time and rest on the landings. No one had planned for the demented pace of war.

The stairs seemed never to end. Olivia cried in pain as Zar yanked her around each turn, while all along the avenue the shells screamed and boomed.

They reached the ground floor and Olivia collapsed in tears. Her face was a plaster-dust ghost.

"Come," Zar said, more gently now. He helped her up. "We're almost there."

We're going to die here, Olivia thought, with sudden equanimity. Calm enveloped her. So this was it: the apocalypse that the village priest was always droning on about. There was something disappointing about it, all things considered. No spitting devils. No judgment of souls. Just Madame Hazard's hallway, smelling of roast chicken.

"Thank God that's everyone!" cried the landlady. She wept with relief when she saw them. "*Venez vite!*" She ushered them down a steep, dank flight of stairs to a cellar lit only by two small oil lamps. A recent delivery of potatoes lay piled in one corner.

The other six students were already there, huddling on benches, mute. Their shoulders flinched at each detonation in the street.

Olivia gaped: not at the grimness of the setting, or at her miserable colleagues, but at an untoward presence in the potato cellar.

A piano.

The ancient upright had somehow been muscled down the narrow stairs to furnish this bunker. It looked as if it had already gone through a war, and there was no doubt that it would make it through this one. Music could be summoned even on the darkest of days, it seemed.

Not that anyone felt much like playing.

They cowered on the benches, sick with terror. Madame Hazard had prepared a stash of honey cake and bottled pears, and these were eaten without a word, while upstairs, in the real world, chaos raged. The bombs were muffled at this depth, as if war were hammering on the hull of a submarine. Plaster dust occasionally filtered down the stairs along with the smell of the chicken Madame had been roasting for their lunch and was now starting to burn.

Zar and Olivia sat shoulder to shoulder, thigh to thigh. The young philosopher from Prague stared straight ahead without speaking. Olivia, looking askance at him from time to time, realized that those black, gleaming eyes were fixed not on the cellar wall, but on a point far beyond it. During one glance, she took in the loose, homespun shirt and baggy trousers; during another, his hands, splayed over his thighs with ready strength. They were the most beautiful hands she'd ever seen, and it didn't surprise her that they had mastered both the violin and piano.

Zar refused to eat, or acknowledge anyone in any way. Olivia assumed this was out of fear. The whole cellar reeked of it, after all. But when he finally turned to her—just once—she could see that his eyes, which had hitherto seemed opaque, actually glistened with light; with resolve. There wasn't a hint of fear in them.

♦ ♦ ♦

Night came. At least, they assumed it must have come by now. Overhead, unabated, the monster stalked and roared.

After another round of Madame Hazard's honey cake, Zar got up abruptly and went over to the piano. He began playing very slowly—single tones, letting each one animate the bunker before he played the next. He seemed to be coaxing them not from the piano, but from the air itself, and indeed, the other musicians glanced up as he played, as if the tones were visible in the yellowish glow of the oil lamps.

Olivia knew very little about music at that point in her life. But one thing she did know for certain: it was not a living thing. Now, however, Zar's music was casting doubt even on that basic truth. Each note he played seemed alive, buoyant. It rebounded from the walls as would any creature trapped in a cramped space. The other musicians were definitely looking at something. *But at what?* Maybe Music is like a ghost, Olivia thought, remembering Madame's honorary dinner guest. Ghosts can seem alive, too. After all, one Christmas Day in the village, their neighbor claimed she saw her dead husband pass through the kitchen into the garden and slam the door on his way out. Maybe Music is invisible to us, but not to God. (Though where God was on that dreadful day, no one would dare speculate.) Olivia concluded that if Music *is* alive, but you can't see her, then she must be divine.

Zar continued to play: intimate phrases…gentle, impressionistic caresses, all strangely audible over the bombardment. Gradually, the din outside seemed to lessen, though of course no one would ever have been able to prove any cause and effect. How ludicrous the thought! It would be like trying to stop a hurricane with a feather. But in that potato cellar, caught in Zar's aura, Olivia found herself thinking about the empty chair that Madame Hazard pulled up to the dinner table every evening, and regretted having ridiculed it.

♦ ♦ ♦

They didn't venture outside until early the next morning.

Dust hung over the avenue in a choking shroud. Citizens crept from their hiding places, haltingly, a shadow-play in the dense air. Madame Hazard's house had been spared any major damage. But as the dust settled, it became clear that the house opposite had taken a direct hit. The railing lay on a pile of rubble, grotesquely twisted, with a clean, dry shirt still attached to it. It took the *pompiers* three days to dig Madame Meunier from the wreckage.

Only Olivia noticed Zar turn his back on the scene and stride away into the smoking ruins of their world.

CHAPTER 16

No one at the *conservatoire* knew what to make of him at first: the oddly angular musician who didn't seem to come from Prague at all, but from a sweeping landscape farther east where his ancestors must have wandered the steppe.

Konstantine Zar still craved that windy plain, it seemed, for his spirit longed for light and space. He was incapable of smallness in any way; of taking fearful, shallow breaths. Instead he stared down the depravity of war, as if daring it to stifle the creativity everyone was trying so earnestly to keep alive.

Zar's fellow students shunned him, even as the strange foreigner intrigued them. They took to repeating his ideas among themselves, and like the best sorcery, they hardly noticed when he'd begun to enchant them.

"Didn't you know that beauty is the only antidote to war?" Zar asked rhetorically while they were waiting in the frigid corridor outside Emile Hendrickx's studio.

The others shuffled their feet and averted their eyes. Most of them were blowing on their hands, or tucking them into their armpits in a fruitless effort to warm them up before playing for the master.

"What if we were to take our instruments into the street and play the most heartfelt, the most truthful melodies for our occupiers?" Zar demanded. "What would happen then?" He was not warming his hands, they noticed; he didn't even seem to practice, though he played better than anyone else, which in itself was a form of sorcery.

"Only Music can move the soul toward its noblest intentions." And with that, Hendrickx opened the studio door and Zar filed in behind his colleagues, bowing to the master as they did.

Until then, the Occupation hadn't changed their habits much. They practiced their violins for hours, long enough to bruise their necks with the hard, cold wood of their chin rests; they smoked cheap cigarettes before their lessons to steady their nerves; they trolled the black market on the Rue des Radis, and made sure to make it home before the curfew. With whispered insults they ceded tables at their favorite cafés to German officers, who amused themselves as if they were still in Berlin.

The stranger from the steppe changed everything. He made them realize that their vocation was important...vital. Maybe even a matter of life or death. Zar convinced them that musicians handled the rarest, most powerful substance on Earth.

They clamored to know more.

"Music is alive," Zar told them. "It breathes. It moves. Remember what Plato said: 'Music is a more potent instrument than any other, because rhythm and harmony find their way into the inward places of the soul.' The soul of the universe is made of musical concord, too."

Soon students were stopping Zar in the corridor, asking him questions about things that would have seemed utterly irrelevant just a short time ago. What was it, exactly, that these lifeless objects they played for hours a day were producing? Why expend so much time and energy perfecting these sounds?

"They are not just lifeless objects," Zar said. "You are producing *musica instrumentalis* with them: the earthly version of the greatest form of music: *musica mundana*—the Music of the Spheres." After lessons, he gathered a group together in the café across from the *conservatoire*, where an iron stove ticked and hissed with whatever ersatz fuel the proprietor could get his hands on, and lively discussions ensued about Plato's notion of a World Soul...about what Pythagoras had actually meant when he'd said that music *is* number, and the cosmos *is* music. There was indignation, too. For how could the cosmos ring with harmony reflected in every human being when humans were creating such mayhem on Earth? And Zar answered: "Europe is descending into barbarism and darkness, it's true. But we are musicians. Our weapon is beauty. We have the power to coax Music down from the heavens and give people hope. We have the power to inspire forgiveness. To encourage peace."

They called him simply "The Greek". A loose le band of followers took shape, among them the dairyman's daughter, who drifted along behind the others, too shy to speak with Zar directly but drawn, as was everyone, to his mystique. He was irresistible, in the way that an approaching storm cannot be avoided.

Olivia took to following Zar home to Madame Hazard's. She always kept a discreet distance behind him, hoping he wouldn't detect her. In any case, his stride was too vigorous for her to keep up. She would lose sight of him as he crossed the Parc de Bruxelles, and in the damp tangle of streets around Chaussée de Wavre she would simply give up, arriving at the dinner table even later than he.

As it happened, she was not far behind him on the day he was forced to put his philosophy to the test.

♦ ♦ ♦

It was late January 1941. Twilight. Clouds hung low and full-bellied. Olivia hummed with delight as she trailed behind Zar toward the Parc de

Bruxelles. She'd always been able to smell snow in the air, even as a child, and she could smell it now.

Zar didn't seem to notice them at first: the two soldiers standing just inside the entrance to the park, as straight and alert as the surrounding trees.

But they'd seen him.

Olivia hesitated. She'd spotted the long greatcoats from across the cobbled parade ground: the telltale set of the soldiers' right arms, indicating a machine gun slung over the shoulder. *Why was Zar ignoring them?* Aghast, she watched him march heedlessly toward them, eyes to the ground, swinging his violin at his side.

Olivia slipped across the parade ground and hid behind one of the pillars at the park entrance. She anguished, remembering the imminent curfew. The soldiers were probably rounding up stragglers at that hour.

She peered around the column, holding the collar of her coat against her mouth lest her exhale expose her presence.

Zar came to a stop before the soldiers. He stood very still in his thin gray coat, hatless, without gloves. He seemed taller, somehow...though not as tall as the men he was facing.

"*Halten Sie! Papiers!*" they barked in a mix of German and French.

Zar said nothing; he made no move.

A ghostly light filtered into the park from above, and despite the gravity of the circumstances, Olivia smiled up at the sky. That was the other thing she remembered about snow: it lit up the landscape even before it started to fall.

The soldiers took two steps toward Zar. They raised the barrels of their weapons half-way.

"*Papiers!*"

How the men gleamed in the twilight! Helmets, boots, leather belts, guns. Olivia noticed details she never had before whenever the occupiers passed her on the street: the silver buttons on their coats, and silver eagles on the sides of their helmets. She noticed, also, how pale they looked—how young.

Slowly, as if in a dream, Zar bent over and set the violin on the ground.

The gun barrels lifted a few centimeters.

Zar's details, too, would stay with Olivia forever: the glossy black hair; the strong hands; the preternatural calm that seemed to envelop him always, even now, standing just a few meters from tyranny.

He began opening the clasps of the violin case.

The soldiers bristled. They took aim. "*Hände hoch!*" one of them bellowed. *Hands in the air!*

But with exquisite ease, Zar continued. Olivia watched, spellbound, as the beautiful hands lifted the violin from its worn velvet bed.

"*Hände hoch!*" the soldier yelled again. Olivia held her breath. She looked into the youthful faces, shocked to see that fear lurked in them. No doubt the young soldiers thought that Zar was concealing a weapon in his case.

Which in a way, he was.

He lifted the violin as if it were a baby emerging from the womb, unaware of the hate and violence that would soon taint its innocence. One soldier was still aiming at Zar. But the other, uncertain, lowered his gun, and began searching the pocket of his greatcoat for a cigarette.

Olivia drew back against the column and stared up at the sky. The clouds swelled and darkened overhead. She closed her eyes, waiting for what was sure to come. But no shot was fired. She peered around again at the drama in the park—this quivering brew of war and peace: Zar, cheek pressed against the violin, drawing a melody from it that Olivia had never heard before; and the two soldiers, one idling, his mouth slack, and the other some distance away under the trees, his back turned, smoking.

It began to snow. The flakes seemed in no hurry to reach Earth, however, mingling as they must have been with the rising notes of Zar's melody.

♦ ♦ ♦

At dinner that evening, as they were finishing Madame Hazard's potato pie, Zar turned to the young girl next to him and without preamble said:

"Your voice sounds like dark cherries and honey."

Olivia put down her knife and fork and stared at him. "But I've never sung for you."

"I heard you practice your recital program in the hall the other day."

"Oh..." Her cheeks flamed.

Zar mentioned nothing about the incident in the park, even though Olivia was sure he'd detected her there, and knew she'd seen the soldiers let him walk away.

At once his strong, supple hand reached for hers on the table and enclosed it. "If you don't mind," he said, "I would like to accompany your recital."

♦ ♦ ♦

There was no heat in the hall on the day of their concert. March 1941 was a cruel month. Cold as death. Zar played in gloves with the fingertips cut off. Olive wore the coat her mother had made for her onstage. The hall was full despite the cold, with students and professors, and many German officers in the crowd, their wives chic in their furs.

All of them wept when Olivia sang.

CHAPTER 17

Olivia set down her wine glass, rang the little silver bell, and folded her hands in her lap. At length she looked up at her visitors. Astonishment suffused her face, as if she'd just crossed the last few meters on the journey back from 1941 and had happened upon Audrey and Florian in her salon.

The maid padded in and gathered the wine glasses and decanter. "Lunch is ready, Madame," she announced.

Olivia stood up, followed immediately by her guests.

"I sang Schubert," she said dreamily. "Including *An die Musik*. 'To Music'. Such difficult, profound simplicity. It was far beyond my abilities at that point in my life. But Zar insisted."

Olivia drifted to the door of the salon door and said, as if to herself:

You lovely art, in how many bleak hours
When life's savage circle ensnares me,
Have you inflamed my heart to the warmth of love,
Have you carried me away to a better world!

"Ah," Olivia sighed. "It is a splendid song, is it not?"

She ushered them toward the dining room. "I had the recklessness of youth on my side," she said. "And absolutely no fear—least of all of the

Germans in the audience. Anyway, they seemed to be drinking in that moment of beauty. It was as if they'd already felt themselves slipping inevitably toward depravity, and couldn't do a thing to stop it." She paused, "Zar was the one who should have been afraid."

Florian glanced at her quizzically. "Why is that, Auntie?"

"Oh, he had the stupid idea of playing one of Mendelssohn's *Songs without Words* while I was trying to warm up backstage. A banned composer, of course. A Jew. Three officers walked out in protest. The director nearly throttled Zar afterward. You see, people were sent to the front for far lesser offenses than playing Mendelssohn. But Zar retorted: 'Tyrants are impotent in the face of Music, for nothing can restrain her.'"

♦ ♦ ♦

Olivia motioned them into a room square in shape and intimate in size, where a round mahogany table had been set to perfection. Hand-painted scenes of orchids and exotic birds unfolded around the walls without a single repetition. Olivia's jasmine scent, overripe and heavy, seemed to be immured there.

Audrey savored every step of the luncheon ritual. It contrasted so drastically with the meager pastas and sandwiches she made in her garret, after all. She was no stranger to luxury, however. In that paradox of the artistic life, she and her bohemian colleagues had spent enough time giving lessons to rich students, and playing concerts in salons like Olivia's, that they knew how to behave in the presence of foie gras and caviar. (With the exception of Jonas, who plundered buffet tables like a beast at a waterhole.) *Thank God his cello playing made up for it!* Audrey mused. She stumbled over these thoughts and suddenly, viscerally, missed him.

They spoke sparingly as they ate. Like most European females of a certain class, Olivia had mastered the illusion of eating. She picked through her buttery wedge of salmon, and lifted a sprig of fresh dill with her fork as if she'd made a rare botanical discovery, but otherwise ingested little. Audrey observed how their hostess dismissed the maid—how she cast a falcon eye over the proceedings, and perfectly timed the interval between the salmon and the chocolate mousse—and it was difficult to imagine that this was the same naïve girl from the dairy farm, who'd given her first recital in her mother's homemade coat, and stared up in wonder at the snow.

That girl from the farm had gone on to marry Reginald Taverner, the world's preeminent conductor at the time; she'd become the most beloved lieder singer of her generation. All this could easily have explained the transformation from farmer's daughter to aristocrat.

But what about Zar?

Audrey studied the grande dame across the table. She could see now that Olivia's pauses between mouthfuls were not due to any kind of decorum. Rather, the lady seemed to be slipping back down the time-corridor she'd so artfully constructed with her memories, just to snatch a few more moments with Konstantine Zar.

♦ ♦ ♦

They adjourned to the salon for coffee.

Audrey paid another visit to the Bösendorfer to look at Zar's photo. It was as if she knew him now: she could perceive the depths behind those charcoal eyes, and detect the light in them.

"I can't believe I didn't notice that photograph before," she said. "I've played this piano several times. I even removed all the photographs myself so I could open the lid, and put them all back again."

Olivia slipped up behind her so lightly that her shoes made no sound on the parquet. "I put Zar's picture there only recently," she said. "I decided to bring it down from my bedroom and display it here for a while." She hesitated. "After I heard the awful news."

Florian joined them at the piano. "What news?"

"Oh, that terrible business in Rue Nova."

Audrey moved to the keyboard, which was closed. She ran her fingertips along the shimmery walnut cover. "What business?" she asked.

"You didn't hear about it?" Olivia hesitated again. "A woman I knew. About my age. A friend, actually. She'd been living in the same house since the war."

Olivia suddenly went waxy pale.

Florian helped her to a *chaise longue*. "Auntie!"

"She was murdered last week," Olivia managed to say. The words had exhausted her, and she leaned back against the chair.

"Murdered..." Florian and Audrey repeated in unison.

Olivia took a sip of the coffee Florian offered her. "It was a burglar, apparently," she said. "My friend must have confronted him, because he pushed her down a flight of steps. At least, that's what the police said. Her maid found her on the floor of the hall. There was a huge pool of blood around her head. Imagine that...imagine living for as long as I have, and then dying for such a stupid reason."

"Did she have many valuables?" Florian asked.

"No, not that I know of," Olivia said. "Just a rather nice piano..." Her voice caught. "But you can't walk off with that, can you?"

Florian glanced at Audrey.

"They say that she might have known the intruder," Olivia went on. "There was no sign of forced entry." She shook her head. "I hadn't gone to see her for years. Oh, how I regret that now! Poor, dear Klara…"

"Klara?" Florian said, sotto voce.

"Yes. Klara Náhoda."

"K. Náhoda," Audrey mouthed.

Olivia struggled to her feet and looked around for the silver bell. Florian fetched it for her and she summoned the maid. "That's why I put that photograph of Zar on the piano," she said. "To honor Klara, as I don't have any pictures of her."

The salon door opened and the maid appeared with their coats.

"You see," said Olivia. "Klara Náhoda was Konstantine Zar's sister."

CHAPTER 18

They walked beside the ponds after lunch, Audrey and Florian, wrapped in thought. Not even the delights of Olivia's salon could lift the general gloom out here. The clouds had clamped Brussels under their great iron lid. Willows drooped over the water in leafless mourning. The paths were deserted except for a man in a long overcoat, walking a small white dog at the water's edge.

"Do you think that your watcher from last night had anything to do with Klara's death?" Florian asked.

Audrey gaped at him. It was the first time she'd considered that she might have locked stares with a murderer.

"Maybe," she said. "But why do you think he was so obsessed with the piano?"

"I don't know. And a Náhoda piano, no less. Belonging to Konstantine Zar's sister."

"Why is that relevant?"

"Audrey!" Florian stopped abruptly and turned to her. He had the light of a disciple in his eyes. "It all makes sense: the tetractys...the other symbols...*Zar*. He was a great admirer of Pythagoras. Olivia said they even called him 'The Greek.'"

"So you think the piano actually belonged to Zar?" Audrey said.

Florian took off his glasses and wiped the condensation on the sleeve of his coat. "Yes. Zar—or perhaps Klara—must have carved those symbols into it."

"But why?"

"I don't know. As a clue? A covert sign to Zar's followers? He was stirring up some controversy at the conservatory, it seemed. I wonder what happened to his followers after the war. Maybe they were afraid to be associated with him. I don't think that Zar's teachings survived—except through Olivia."

"And through you," Audrey teased. "The others must have scattered into anonymity."

"Like Pythagoras's followers," mused Florian.

Audrey observed the man with the dog disappear behind a stand of yew trees. She said, "Olivia's still in love with Zar, isn't she?"

Florian bristled. "She married Reginald Taverner, Audrey! In 1948. It was the match of the year. He accompanied all her concerts after that."

"A musical match, perhaps," Audrey said.

"What are you implying? Zar was her mentor, clearly. She was so young, after all. Just a girl from the provinces."

"Not much younger than he was. There's quite a story there, I sense." Audrey could suddenly feel Zar behind history's curtain, daring her to pull it aside.

They entered the grounds of the Abbaye de la Cambre, a medieval jewel nestled in its own deep crease in time.

"Why would Klara come to Brussels in the first place?" Audrey asked. "And how did the piano get here?"

Neither knew the answers, so they walked on in silence.

"Klara must have married into the Náhoda piano family in Prague," Audrey speculated.

"Yes."

"Do you think she came to Brussels when Zar did, in 1939? Maybe with her husband?"

"Maybe." Florian put his glasses back on and wandered off, pitched forward with his hands behind his back as Schubert might have done after lunch.

Audrey hurried to catch up. "We should have told Olivia about the piano," she said. "She mentioned 'a rather nice piano'. It must be the same one."

"It's gone, Audrey," Florian said, alarming her with his bluntness. "It would only upset Olivia to learn what happened to it."

Audrey gave him a sharp look. "But I thought we were on our way to Schaerbeek to find it...to find Zar's piano," she clarified.

Florian sighed. "We are. But Schaerbeek's a labyrinth. You know that, Audrey. I'd be very surprised if we turned up anything."

Audrey pulled at his arm to stop him. "Olivia's over ninety now," she said. Her voice quavered. She recalled the otherworldly creature in her salon, caught between worlds. "We must do this for her."

Florian halted, and gave her a long, frank look. "Yes, you're right," he said. "We must do this for her."

They walked up through the terraced gardens of the abbey toward Avenue Louise, where they could catch a tram to Schaerbeek.

"Florian, what happened to Zar? Do you know?"

He pushed open the iron gate to exit the gardens. "He was arrested by the Gestapo in 1942," he said. "And executed."

♦ ♦ ♦

They took seats near the back of the 93 tram. They'd decided to pay a visit to the Casablanca General Store to see if Rami might know where Nero took his merchandise.

Though she didn't mention it to Florian, Audrey also planned to ask Rami about Jonas. She'd dropped by the shop only twice since the Europa debacle: to take Jonas's cello home as she'd promised; and to check in with Rami a year after that for any news of her friend. She'd been shocked to learn that Jonas had never returned to his flat. He hadn't even come back for his cello—an unprecedented dereliction for a musician. So Rami had had no choice but to collect his tenant's few possessions in a cardboard box and rent the flat out to someone else. He kept the cello with him in the shop, where the case stood in a place of honor next to the plastic garden chairs he set out for friends who stopped by for tea. He wanted to keep an eye on it, he said. But he also considered it a sort of beacon. *So Jonas will find his way back someday.*

"Audrey, look!" Florian hissed in her ear.

A man with a Jack Russell terrier was boarding at the front of the tram.

"It's the man from the abbey gardens!" Audrey whispered.

She ogled the long, black overcoat, arresting on a broad-shouldered individual, and the dark glasses, which she hadn't noticed before. The dog minced over the rocking floor of the tram, unable to settle. The man grasped a pole near the exit with a black leather glove, and with the other hand snapped the leash until the animal stood still, haunches quivering. Even as the tram filled up, and crowds jostled around him, the man with the dog commanded a space that no one dared infringe upon. He never removed his dark glasses, leaving in doubt the exact target of his observations.

Audrey found herself staring openly at the man. He had a whiff of the past about him—the old-world elegance that Avenue Louise was once famous for. Skilled hands had cut the classic lines of his coat. His white ponytail, tied with a piece of black velvet, hardly contrasted with the pallid skin.

The tram turned onto Chaussée de Haecht and stopped across from the Casablanca General Store. Audrey and Florian exited through the rear door.

The man with the dog got off at the front and walked away.

CHAPTER 19

Rami Chadli was a slight, dreamy-eyed widower in his sixties utterly unsuited to the commercial life. Indeed, he didn't even seem to care if he sold anything. He had no taste for haggling, as it pained him to take advantage of people. And anyway, he reasoned, why would someone waste their time debating the price of bananas or onions when such a discussion illuminated nothing? His shop was a neglected jumble, therefore. Occasionally, when the grocer was idling in the doorway next to his produce, contemplating higher things, friends like Jonas Liebling would discreetly remove items that had long since passed their expiration date and leave the appropriate change in the till.

"Oh, this is wonderful, indeed!" Rami opened his arms to the two musicians and ushered them into the shop. "Mint tea?" he asked. "But of course!" he answered for them, and indicated the plastic garden chairs.

Audrey noticed it at once: the empty space where the cello had been.

"Rami!" she exclaimed. "But...?"

A smile lifted the grocer's melancholy moustache. "Yes, it's true," he said. "He came back!" Rami turned on the kettle and began stuffing fresh mint leaves into a silver pot.

"But when?" Audrey said, sinking onto a chair. She was light-headed with joy...and consternation. She removed the cloche hat and ran a hand over her hair.

"Three days ago."

"*What?*"

Florian said nothing. He wandered about the shop, repositioning a can of tomato soup, and wiping the dust from a jar of mayonnaise.

"Did Jonas say anything about where he's been all this time?" Audrey pressed. "Was he in Germany? Where is he now?"

"He didn't stay long," Rami said. "He rang the bell late on Tuesday evening. He grabbed a few things from the box I've been storing them in. And his cello, of course. Then he left."

Rami's eyes filled with tenderness. Audrey knew well that along with the gathering of his possessions, Jonas had stopped long enough to wrap his landlord in one of his operatic embraces to assure him that all would be well.

"Do you know where he's staying in Brussels?" Audrey asked.

"With the baroness lady, I think," Rami said, avoiding their eyes.

Florian let out a cynical laugh. "Baroness Van Overberg, no doubt. The baron's probably away again. Christ! Will he never learn?"

"I fear not," Rami conceded, handing them glasses of tea in carved metal holders. His visitors breathed in the steaming, fragrant mint and closed their eyes with pleasure.

Rami had no children of his own, so he'd happily welcomed Jonas as a son. Some years back, after his wife had deserted him, gone back to Morocco, and unexpectedly died there, he finally decided to rent out the flat over the shop and didn't hesitate when the bumbling, amiable German answered his advertisement. Friends had had their doubts, though. *How can you trust a European who drinks too much beer and hauls around such an ungainly instrument?* they'd cautioned him. They would gather every afternoon on the plastic chairs, sipping tea and shaking their heads.

Rami duly pondered their concerns. But if anyone could banish doubt, it was Jonas himself. It was impossible to ignore the heart that he wore perpetually inside-out, and that brimmed with kindness. Nor could anyone resist the gorgeous music, such an unexpected balm for the immigrant neighborhood's own, bruised heart.

"How did Jonas seem, Rami?" Audrey said at length.

The grocer stroked his lips in thought. His hair had retreated far enough to expose a broad and contemplative forehead. "He seemed different," he said. "Quieter. Like..." He searched for an image. "Like he went through a tempest and came out changed."

"I can imagine," Florian said, unmoved. "All three of us went through the same tempest."

"Bitterness does not become you, Florian," Rami said softly. "You are better than that. It's not good to harbor anger, you know. Your soul will become ill."

Audrey nodded, clasping her hands around the glass of hot tea. "Whatever happened to your *musica humana*, Florian?" she asked, without humor.

"Perhaps you'd understand, Rami," said Florian, ignoring Audrey's comment, "if someone had ruined your career."

Rami chuckled, and pulled a piece of mint leaf from his moustache. "Not if one doesn't have much of a career to ruin!"

Florian reddened, and looked away. "Rami, I'm sorry. I didn't mean to imply..."

"*Tiens, tiens,*" murmured the grocer, his eyes widening at Florian's softening. "Now, that's the Florian I used to know." For a moment he reveled in his little entrapment. He gave the musicians a compassionate look. "I really am very sorry." he said, his kind face grave. "I saw what happened on television. It was…"

"A catastrophe," Florian helped him.

"But the concert itself was marvelous," Rami exclaimed. "You played like gods."

"Maybe," said Florian. "But it's not what people will remember."

Rami got up to pour them more tea. He lingered with his back to them. Then he slowly turned.

"The police came by the day after the concert," he said. "Asking about Jonas."

Audrey blanched. She knew what could happen when police paid a visit to an immigrant neighborhood: harassment…identity checks…surveillance. Even if the actual suspect was an EU citizen.

"I hope they weren't too unpleasant," she said. The words sounded hollow.

"They searched the flat."

"Oh, Rami," Florian muttered, solicitous now. "You shouldn't have had to go through that. Were they looking for the money Jonas embezzled?"

"Allegedly embezzled," Audrey corrected him.

"I assumed so," said Rami. "But the police weren't the only ones who came by."

The others stared at him.

"That crazy man from the concert turned up." Rami's tone was full of trepidation. "You know: the one who made such a spectacle of himself. He was worse than the police."

"Van Overberg," Florian whispered. "How was he worse?"

"I'll never forget him," Rami said. "He seemed to take over the shop." He stretched his arms out wide to indicate the man's scope.

"What did he want?" Audrey asked.

"He threatened to kill Jonas."

The comment was like a detonation. They all waited for the fragments to settle.

Rami continued: "He also threatened me. He said that if Jonas came by and I didn't tell him about it, then he would..." He couldn't go on.

Audrey's eyes filled with tears. She couldn't bear the thought of any harm coming to Rami. "But that can't mean now. Three years later." She wavered. "*Can it?*"

"Oh, I think so," said Rami. "There's madness in that man. The whole world saw it." He paused. "And I saw it myself in his eyes."

CHAPTER 20

Jonas could never have done such a thing," Rami said as he took their tea glasses. "Mistakes with women, yes. Stealing money, no."

"I have a possible theory," Florian said. "Van Overberg invented the embezzlement charge, so he wouldn't have to parade his wife's infidelity in public, but could still ruin Jonas. Embezzlement is a perfectly legitimate reason to expose someone publicly."

Audrey regarded Florian with surprise. It was an unusually conciliatory theory for him to put forward.

Rami patted Florian's knee as if he were a child. "You should forgive Jonas," he said.

"He seduced the wife of the richest, most vengeful man in Europe," Florian reminded him.

"Yes, yes. I know. He can't say no to attractive ladies. But theft?" Rami paused. "Maybe Van Overberg's wife is the one behind it—maybe Jonas wanted to leave her, realizing the huge mistake he was making, and she convinced her husband to punish him in this way. Women can be formidable." He got up to rearrange the display of dish soap.

"So why did Jonas go to see her now, when he came back?" Audrey asked.

"To be chivalrous," said Rami. "To bring the affair to an end properly."

Audrey reflected on this. Jonas had told her before going on stage that he wasn't in love with the baroness. So perhaps it was true...perhaps he'd been trying to leave her.

"Rami," she said. "There's something else we wanted to ask you." She wandered around the shop as she spoke. "It's that...well...I've lost a friend."

"Lost a friend!?" Rami abandoned the dish soap and clasped his hands together. "Oh, Audrey, I'm so very sorry. An old friend?"

She hesitated. "Very old," she said. "And very new."

"Oh...?"

Florian smiled. "It's a piano, Rami!"

"Ah, of course!" Rami sighed. "But how is it possible to lose such a friend?'

Audrey tried to describe what happened not only over the past twenty-four hours, but also more than seventy years ago, when a piano had somehow made its way across Europe from Prague to occupied Brussels. It was as convoluted as any explanation would have been that included a discarded piano, a World War II mystic, a murdered woman, and a Pythagorean symbol.

"Well, well," murmured Rami, shaking his head.

"Rami, do you know who Nero is?" Florian asked.

The merchant gave him a dubious look. "Yes, I do."

"Apparently he takes his wares to a Ukrainian *brocanteur* somewhere around here. Do you know who that might be?"

Rami stroked his moustache, troubled now. "You must mean Bébé," he said.

♦ ♦ ♦

There was no point in taking the van, Rami told them as he locked up the shop. There were too many cramped, one-way streets where they were going. He gestured across the road at a vehicle parked in front of the laundromat, dusty-red like a Moroccan sunset, and with faded lettering that read: *Chez Rami. Fruits et Légumes avec un Sourire.* Fruits and vegetables with a smile...

They followed the pulsing *chaussée* for a block or two, where veiled women pushed strollers, and shopkeepers slouched in doorways; where young men smoked, or talked on cell phones, and older men lingered in all-male cafés. Fried meat and cumin overpowered the stench of car exhaust.

Soon they turned into a tangle of wastrel streets—clichés of Schaerbeeks all over Europe. Shops were few. Rubbish lay in gutters and alleyways. Bourgeois houses seemed haunted not by the ghosts of their long-vanished white tenants—proud subjects of the colonizing Leopold—but by the sun-filled nostalgia of those who lived there now.

Rami walked with a spritely clip. He deftly maneuvered the uneven cobblestones, divining which ones were loose and liable to spray stagnant water when stepped on. The busy Maghreb and Turkish emporia on the high street gave way to an unhealed wound of a place. Foul-smelling inertia clung to everything. It was easy to forget that the power center of the European Union was an easy walk from here.

Audrey glanced up from the treacherous footing to spot one of the Commission buildings, rising above all this decay like an alien ship. It occurred to her that at the very moment she'd been sitting at the piano under the Europa lantern, entertaining the most privileged and powerful individuals on the continent, out here, in this shabby warren, the underprivileged had been dragging to the end of another unremarkable day. She wondered if the notion of European harmony ever crossed their minds, given the doleful dissonance between their own neighborhood and posh world up the street.

◆ ◆ ◆

"Here we are," Rami said. He was out of breath and anxious. "You mentioned something about a murder, so perhaps we should be prudent."

They entered a cobbled tributary with a curious bend in it, flanked by houses with filthy windows and cracked steps. Everything was bereft of upkeep...of any vital sign.

Rami pulled his friends into a recessed doorway. The house was boarded up and seemed deserted.

He motioned across the alley to a perfectly ordinary garage door.

"That's it?" Audrey whispered, though she knew well that behind such commonplace doors, Brussels frequently concealed her greatest marvels: a topiary garden...a restaurant...a sculpture court.

All of which seemed unlikely in this street.

"Let's wait here," Rami said, his voice low.

"How do you know this place?" Florian lowered his voice in tandem.

Rami grinned. "I found my vacuum cleaner here. You wouldn't believe what's behind that door."

They waited.

"Rami, who's Bébé?" Audrey asked.

"Bébé is a...*salopard*," Rami said. He clearly would have chosen a ruder word than "bastard" had a lady not been present. "Let's just say that he's not someone you'd want to make an enemy of."

Rami told them that Bébé (his real name was Voloshyn) had met Nero while they were both serving time in a Marseille jail. After Nero escaped, and Bébé bribed his way out, they met up again in Brussels, where they'd formed an underworld pact: Nero would keep an eye out for houses that were being emptied—even poring over obituaries for a head start, and lurking like a hyena for discarded objects. Bébé would give him cash (saving a little extra for the police to keep them from Nero's door) and trawl his nefarious network for buyers.

"He operates through threats and coercion," Rami added.

"Coercion…" said Florian. "Nero sounds like the perfect business partner for him, then."

"There's something else about Nero," Rami said. "A curious thing: they say that he was abandoned as an infant on a wharf in Marseille and raised by a madam. *Attention!*" he gasped, and pulled the others deeper into the entryway.

A car had turned into the lane.

CHAPTER 21

The car crept along the cobbles and stopped in front of Bébé's garage. A man got out and rang an unmarked bell. The garage door began opening at once, revealing a cave-like tunnel beyond which, in the cave itself, an occasional sheen could be discerned.

"*Mon Dieu!*" Florian muttered, adjusting his glasses.

"Indeed," said Rami. "And those aren't just discarded items. Many are stolen."

Something moved in the dimness. A shape coalesced from the shadow, as wide as it was tall. The man wore a pure-white track suit and had pure black hair, and from a distance, there was an almost ecclesiastical air about him.

"That's Bébé," Rami intoned.

The vision advanced with a rolling motion. Bébé nodded to the newcomer, and swept the beam of his flashlight over the goods. As any feast, the first bites impressed the most: a mirror with gilded frame; a fire screen, flushing bronze. But even from across the street it was obvious that this was a junk meal: a plastic Venus de Milo, propped against a washing machine; a linoleum table with three legs. An immense armoire darkened one wall and seemed more suitable for stashing bodies than for storing crockery.

"I don't see a piano," said Audrey.

"Maybe the valuable items are in the back somewhere," Florian offered.

The visitor left empty-handed and the garage door closed.

"Nero may not have delivered it yet," said Rami. "Hang on…"

A tall man was advancing down the sidewalk with a loose-limbed gait, slowing at each house as if to check the number.

He stopped at Bébé's and rang the bell.

Audrey's blood rushed. She squeezed Florian's arm. She would have recognized the man even if he hadn't been wearing his fedora.

The garage opened again.

Bébé and the tall man stood face to face.

A few words were exchanged. Then Bébé shrugged, and shuffled into the far reaches of his cave.

There was the grating roll of something heavy.

Bébé reappeared, pulled the cover off what he'd produced, and shone his flashlight on it.

"That's it!" Audrey cried.

The piano exuded the same intrepid air she remembered. Once again, it had been compromised; and once again, it was holding fast.

The visitor brushed a spidery hand over the keys, as Audrey had; he ran a finger along the rosewood coffering, where her finger had been. Then he lifted the lid and spent quite a while examining the piano's innards.

"Do you think he's studying the tetractys?" Florian asked.

"He's a very strange man," Rami whispered, ignoring the very strange question. "And you say that he might have murdered that woman in Rue Nova?"

Florian hesitated. "He's been behaving very suspiciously."

The two men in the garage began to argue. Words boiled over. Hands sliced the air. The piano stood between them, an indifferent arbiter. The fedora man reached into his suit and waved cash at Bébé, who ignored him, and commenced a leisurely tour of the instrument, pointing out its qualities as if it were a cow at a fair.

"He's driving up the price!" Rami said with admiration, unable to do such a thing even for a kilo of bananas. "Is it very valuable?"

Audrey balked. Until then, she hadn't considered the piano in those terms.

She settled on: "It's of historical value."

"Maybe there's something of value *inside* it," Rami suggested.

Audrey stared at him. She hadn't considered that possibility, either.

The fedora man pulled more cash from his suit pocket. Finally, Bébé took it. A discussion followed. Then the visitor turned briskly and left.

Bébé threw the cover back on the piano and prepared to wheel it away.

"That's that, I'm afraid," Florian said, putting a hand on Audrey's shoulder. "It's been sold."

The words crashed over her. They would have drowned her, too, had something not welled from within and buoyed her.

She stepped from the doorway.

"Audrey!" Rami cried.

But she'd already crossed the street.

♦ ♦ ♦

Bébé watched the advance of this resolute little figure and left the garage open. He ogled the baggy coat and solid shoes, and like many men, seemed befuddled that beauty could be found in such a disguise.

Audrey rushed to the piano.

"Madame! *S'il vous plaît.*" The Ukrainian heaved his bulk toward her. "What can I do for you?" It was a warning, not an offer. His French had the finesse of a Soviet truck.

Audrey ignored him. In the flush of reunion, she lay her hands on the piano's cover and prepared to pull it back.

"Oh, no, *ma petite,*" Bébé said, crowding up to her. His sweet after-shave caught in her throat. "It's sold, I'm afraid." The ecclesiastical air had more in common with a deviant choir boy. He yanked the cover from Audrey's grasp and draped it over the piano. She was momentarily trans-fixed by his hands: soft and doughy, with several huge gold rings that crimped the flesh.

"May I ask who bought it?" she said. The mix of motor oil and cologne made her head turn. She put a hand on the piano to steady herself.

Bébé passed the beam of his flashlight up and down his customer as if she were merchandise. Then he rolled back his massive head and laughed, revealing a row of gold teeth that (Audrey could only speculate) might have replaced the ones lost in a fight. "No, you may not ask, *ma belle.*"

"Audrey!" Florian called. He'd been lingering with Rami at the en-trance.

"Your minders, I see," Bébé said, with a curl to his lip.

Audrey straightened her shoulders and lifted her chin. Her luminous eyes caught the man off-guard and erased his smile. *You're like one of those figures on the prow of a ship,* Jonas used to say, just before they went on stage.

"I have no minders, Monsieur," she said. "I have reason to believe that this piano is stolen...that it's part of an inheritance." She wavered. "Of a woman who was murdered recently."

She took in the gold chain draped around Bébé's neck, and the black hair, extravagantly dyed, falling to his shoulders.

"Can you prove it's stolen?" Bébé asked. Then, dismissively: "Is it *your* inheritance?" He pulled a packet of cigarettes and a lighter from the pocket of his warm-up pants.

"Well...no." Audrey glanced over at her friends, who signaled frantically for her to leave. She went on, "The murdered woman was called Náhoda." She lifted the heavy cloth from the piano, undeterred this time, and indicated the name inlaid on the fallboard. "This instrument was made by her ancestors in Prague."

Audrey thought of Zar and Olivia. She could feel their stories being sucked away into the undertow of time. *Was anything of their lives preserved in this rosewood box?* Her spirit soared at the thought. "That man has no right to this piano," she blurted.

Bébé flicked the lighter and took a long draw on the cigarette. "Well then, *ma petite*, it seems that you have nothing to worry about. The piano is on its way to Prague, in fact."

Audrey gaped at him. "You mean the man who was here just now is taking this piano to *Prague?* How do you know that?"

Bébé slipped up toward her—a gesture uncannily deft for such a corpulent man. Audrey could smell the bog of stale breath now.

"You ask too many questions for such a little lady," he said. He smoothed a moist finger along her cheek and his flesh left its sweet odor on hers.

Audrey pressed against the piano, her stomach heaving.

"Maybe these gentlemen would like to discuss a price for *you.*" Bébé said.

Florian and Rami advanced a few steps, then reconsidered. Hardly saviors on white horses.

Power affirmed, the Ukrainian returned to the recesses of his lair.

"Please…" Audrey could no longer steady her voice. "How can I get in touch with the buyer?"

But Bébé had vanished.

Florian and Rami hurried in and bustled her from the premises.

CHAPTER 22

I'll walk home," Audrey announced. "*Alone,*" she added, and the men knew her well enough not to dissuade her.

She headed off into the early darkness. Her route home seemed long, and the illumination in short supply—not only of the tangible kind (the streetlamps had trouble penetrating a February night), but also the inner light that usually accompanied her nocturnal rambles. She tried to keep her mind on the great visionaries of the night sky: the temple priests of Egypt; Pythagoras; Kepler. It would have cheered her greatly to have had a fellow wanderer at her side: Konstantine Zar, perhaps. How sad, she thought, to have been born too late to have known him. She imagined what a conversation with him might have been like. He must have walked these same streets...observed the same sky. *Would she even know what to say to him?*

Alas, she was plagued by other company: the spidery man who'd taken possession of the piano—*Zar's piano;* the man in the long overcoat and dark glasses. *Had he really followed them to Schaerbeek?* Her thoughts churned with the sordid fate of Zar's sister, Klara. *Have I become so fragile that a man with a dog can unnerve me so?*

Audrey hurried toward the lights of Pascal's place, as if it were a barque taking on the last orphans and stragglers before setting sail.

◆ ◆ ◆

"Maestra!" Pascal gushed. He stepped over the snoring Hermes to greet her. "No Florian tonight?" He seized her shoulders and kissed her on both cheeks.

"No, just me." Audrey headed to her usual table by the window. She glanced around, happy that all the candles had been lit so early in the evening.

"You're pale," Pascal said, padding after her.

"I'm tired, that's all," she said.

Pascal shook his head. "No. It's not that." He laid her shapeless coat over a chair as he would a fine fur, then took a step back to assess her. "Ah, *voila!* That's it: you are worried about something. I will make your coffee, and you will tell me all about it."

Audrey took her seat and stared out at the church. There was a lull in customers, so Pascal brewed her Irish coffee at once, using a loose wrist with the whiskey and whipped cream and joining her at the table.

"*Alors,*" He said, waiting for her to speak.

Pascal always wore a white shirt and black cardigan—standard colors for any confessor, although the shade of his bowtie changed every day, perhaps indicating a confessional style more adventurous than could be found across the road.

"Pascal," Audrey began, plunging her spoon into the cream. "Do you know anything about that murder in Rue Nova?"

"Ah," he said. "Now I see what's up. You live just around the corner from there, don't you? And they haven't caught the killer yet." His eyes, damp by nature, grew even moister. "Klara Náhoda...*la pauvre.*"

"You knew her?" Audrey exclaimed.

"Everyone knew *of* her," he said. "But she never went out, you see. She was an enigma, that lady. And one of the few people left in the *quartier* who'd actually witnessed the Occupation." Pascal shook his head. "Another link to the past broken, I'm afraid."

Audrey swiveled the candle on the table and watched the flame dance.

"Klara had a very distinguished brother," she said. "Konstantine Zar. He died at the hands of the Gestapo in 1942. I just spoke to a lady today who remembers them both...who knows their story. The past is far from dead, Pascal."

Audrey smoothed her hand over the table. She recalled Florian's open palm—how convinced she'd been that the thread of Music, stretching unbroken across millennia, had been lying there.

"Has anyone...*unusual*...come to the café lately?" she asked.

Pascal's round face darkened like a full moon heading into clouds. "Well, now that you mention it, there was a man who came in about ten days ago." He toyed with his bowtie. "A few days before Klara was murdered. He stuck in my mind, because..."

"...because he was emaciated and wore a fedora?" The words tumbled from Audrey.

"No. Not at all."

Hermes let out a long, juddering sigh. His paws twitched with some youthful exploit and Pascal went over to calm him. "You remember the man's dog, don't you, old boy?" he murmured.

Audrey laced her fingers around her coffee. "His dog?"

"Yes. A Jack Russell.

Her fingers tightened. There were many such dogs in Brussels, she thought. You couldn't walk down the street without seeing one.

"The man wasn't emaciated," Pascal continued. "*Au contraire.* He was big...rather intimidating, I must say. His long coat made him seem even bigger. He had a white ponytail. The oddest thing about him was that he never took off his dark glasses. And his skin looked like chalk...or plaster. Like he was ill."

Audrey took a sip of coffee that burned her tongue. "I think I know who you mean," she said.

"Oh, Audrey," Pascal moaned. He came back to the table and covered his face in his hands.

"Pascal...?"

"It's my fault," he said. "I never should have told him about Klara. What an idiot I am!"

"How do you mean?" Audrey reached over and squeezed his arm.

She had no trouble imagining the scene Pascal went on to describe: the dark-coated hulk entering the café, alert, searching; the brief spat between Hermes and the Jack Russell, which had exhausted the old mongrel for the rest of the day; the man sitting in his overcoat and dark glasses, removing only his gloves. His hands had been like porcelain, Pascal said. Dead-white. He'd ordered an espresso, and asked all about the neighborhood during the war: where Gestapo headquarters had been located; what the Germans were doing in the forest nearby; whether there had been much resistance in this neighborhood; if any witnesses remained. All sorts of things. Specific things.

"Why was he interested in all that?" Audrey asked.

"He didn't say."

"Did he speak French?"

"Yes. But with a heavy German accent. He was refined...courtly, even. But a great block of a man. I didn't think his questions were so odd at the time. Other people have come in asking about local history. So I talked too much. I told him there was a woman in Rue Nova who'd lived through the Occupation." Pascal stared out at the church. "I told him about Klara, Audrey. I even gave him her address, for God's sake."

She grasped his arm again. "That doesn't mean he did her any harm. What motive could he have had? You can't jump to such a conclusion."

"Maybe. But they say that she hardly ever had any visitors. Who else could it have been?" Pascal got up and wandered behind the counter, re-lighting a candle that had gone out. "Oh, Audrey. I might have been responsible for Klara's death."

CHAPTER 23

The garret felt cold and lifeless when she returned. The radiator was as old as the house, so whatever warmth it could still muster disappeared into the uninsulated rafters.

Audrey rustled up a couple of eggs to scramble, and a glass of wine, slightly fermented. After this refreshment, which only a working musician would call dinner, she was unable to relax, or even to sit down, so instead she paced the attic from one eave to the other, back and forth over the old pine boards, pondering as she went. There was plenty of room for this activity. Apart from the upright piano in one corner, there was only a sofa, her bed, and a kitchen table and chairs. After a few tours of the room, she'd warmed up enough to take off her coat.

There was nothing much to do in these lodgings except sleep. And practice the piano, of course, which she finally settled down to do.

She sat for some time at the keyboard without playing. The three pigeons that roosted in the gutter overhead sensed her there, and scrabbled in their sleep. Beyond them, the winter sky seemed to stretch to infinity, and one had no trouble imagining that the northern hemisphere would be tilting away from the sun for some weeks yet. The thought filled Audrey with melancholy. But it was comforting to remember that all her fellow northern inhabitants—rich and poor, oppressor and oppressed—

were also tilting toward the darker part of the solar system, and were just as hungry for the return of the light as she was.

Johannes Kepler had thought long and hard about the plight of his fellow humans traveling through space on this Earth, Audrey knew. In creating musical intervals from planetary ratios, he'd come up with a semi-tone for the Earth (the smallest distance between two keys on a piano). It was a restless interval. A thorny, sighing one. Audrey also remembered Kepler's interpretation of this (via Florian, of course): "The Earth sings Mi, Fa, Mi [E, F, E]: you may infer even from the syllables that in this our home, misery and famine hold sway," he wrote in Latin in his *Harmonices Mundi*, or *Harmony of the World*.

How apt those syllables still are today! Audrey thought. In Kepler's time, the Europe of 1600 was already lurching toward the Thirty Years' War: Catholics and Protestants locked in most unholy carnage. But it was just another cataclysm, as it happened. Humanity had a peculiar talent for them. Cataclysms would abound over the centuries after 1600 as they had over the millennia beforehand, maybe with different actors and different motives, but always with the same wrenching inevitability.

Audrey put her broad, stubby hands on the keys and played E-F-E. The single notes sounded brittle in the cold space. Comfortless. *Misery and famine, indeed.*

But might there be another interpretation?

She played the tones again, and this time laced them together with harmonies both major and minor, strumming them softly. At once the tiny theme sprang to life and beauty warmed it a little.

Concord and discord. The world was constructed around opposites. Pythagoras had lectured on this subject to his secret band of followers. Audrey rubbed a finger over the piano's two missing ivories—a rough sensation that always transported her back to the school gymnasium. What a contrast to the exquisite creaminess of the Náhoda! *Rough and smooth...*

Opposites.

*Finite and infinite...great and small...hatred and love...*Each half of a duality depended on the other for its existence. Without dusk, there would be no dawn.

Audrey stared up through the skylight. She could see how Kepler would have craved the serenity of the night sky. How peaceful it would have been calculating the universe from a quiet knoll, far from the squabbling of his family in their cramped village house—from the senseless squabbling of religions. She smiled. He'd probably never encountered the lady with the lantern, though.

She played another note. This time her hand trembled, not with cold, but at the thought of the man in the overcoat ringing the bell on Rue Nova, and the elderly Klara opening the door...

She struck a chord: the man in the fedora sprang into view. What did he want with the Náhoda piano, anyway? Was Rami right? Was there something valuable inside it? She played away these thoughts and her hands grew warm. The pigeons clicked along the old lead gutter, awake now.

The Greeks believed that music and the human soul were both aspects of the eternal, Florian used to say. *Remember Orpheus, Audrey? He embodied the healing power of music and renewal of life. What more do we need in this world?*

A melody appeared, and Audrey's hands went where it led them. Kepler's dour little interval blossomed into a lilting little waltz—a sort of plea in three-quarter time. She looked up as she played. The notion that Music could be called down to Earth by a humble musician such as herself surely meant that hope and comfort were only as far away as her piano.

She realized now where Florian had first found his inspiration: in the teachings of Konstantine Zar, filtered through his great-aunt and her obvious love for the man.

♦ ♦ ♦

She played for over an hour. Madame Mertens's piano responded with its usual agony of taps and twangs, and the occasional, ominous knock. But true friend that it was, it limped along beside Audrey to the high, empty crossroads to which her life had taken her.

I'm not alone at those crossroads, she thought, weary now. She stopped playing and leaned against the piano, her head on her arms, remembering what Olivia had said: "In the presence of Music, one is never alone."

She fell asleep.

The taps that woke her could not have issued from the piano, therefore.

Audrey lifted her head: the kitchen clock read nearly midnight.

The taps were coming from the stairwell, it seemed. *Footsteps.* They approached rapidly, past the abbé's apartment and up the next staircase. Louder now.

Madame Mertens must have let someone in. The thought brought a bit of comfort, as whoever it was would have been vetted by the badger herself.

Audrey stood up from the piano and went to the door. Her hands were as icy as when she'd begun playing.

Oh, why didn't I ask Madame to fix my lock?

The footsteps rounded the last bend.

They arrived at her landing.

She could hear labored breathing through the door.

There was a hollow *bong*. An expletive.

Audrey opened the door to the smell of roast chicken and a bruised and bleeding Jonas.

CHAPTER 24

Oh, my God!" Audrey took the plastic bag with the chicken, and the cello, and led Jonas from the dim hallway into the comparative glare of the garret's single bulb.

She let out a cry of shock: his face had been demolished.

"Who did this to you?" she stammered.

He said nothing.

She helped him over to the sofa. Her stomach churned at the sight of his lips, swollen like blood sausages, and the lurid cheeks. A cut above one eyebrow, precise as a butcher's, was bleeding steadily into his eye.

Jonas sank onto the sofa and immediately vomited.

Audrey busied herself in the manner of an automaton. She brought a wet dish towel and a glass of sparkling water, taking a sip herself to steady her nerves before helping her friend to drink. Elation soon overcame her chagrin. She could hardly berate Jonas for his disappearance, and all the distress it had caused her for three years, when here he was on her sofa—diminished though he might be.

"Audrey..." He said her name as if drawing his bow over a string with a whole sonata left to play.

She helped him out of his leather jacket and mopped up the vomit. Then she examined his face: aside from the scrappy beard and kind, mournful eyes, Jonas was unrecognizable. Anyone would have known enough to say: "You need stitches," which she did.

"No!" he snapped. He struggled up, only to sink back with a groan. "I can't go to the hospital."

"Why ever not?" Audrey balked. *Good God. He must still be on the run.*

She brought a bowl of warm water and a fresh towel and began dabbing at Jonas's wounds. The big German whimpered like a puppy. Blood had matted his beard and crusted on his forehead. He could barely open his eyes. .

Audrey rummaged in her tiny kitchen for the bottle of Amaretto Pascal had given her for her birthday, and poured a large glass of it. "Here," she said, giving Jonas a straw for easier drinking. "This will help."

More rummaging turned up some painkillers, expired the year before, and a roll of duct tape. From a drawer under her bed, Audrey produced the lace-trimmed handkerchief she used for concerts.

She watched her friend slurp the liqueur. Superficially, he was the same, unkempt charmer. But Rami was right: something had changed in Jonas. Aside from the obvious tempest he'd just weathered, there had been others, clearly—a whole ocean of them.

In lieu of proper medical attention, Audrey set to work. She cut the lace trim off the handkerchief and made strips of the fine linen. These she placed over Jonas's wounds, and then, gingerly, attempted to pull the broken skin together under the linen, fixing everything in place with duct tape. "You might not be able to get these off very easily," she said.

Jonas forced one eye open long enough to say: "Isn't that the handkerchief you used for the Europa concert?"

Audrey went on mutely with her ministrations. It amused her that Jonas, who painted life with large, careless brushstrokes, would have noticed such a detail. "Maybe it's appropriate that your blood should be on it, then," she said.

She brought the pillow from her bed and settled him against it, then stepped back to admire her handiwork.

"Are you hungry?" she asked, rhetorically, as she'd never known Jonas not to be.

She cut the roast chicken into bite-sized pieces and put the plate between them on the couch, along with a towel for the grease. It was a testament to Jonas's kindness (or perhaps to his constant hunger) that in his desperate state he'd still dropped by the grill on the corner.

He swept his arm woozily to indicate his surroundings. "You've found some sort of secret to life in this place, haven't you, Süsslein?" he said. "I bet that if some prince offered you a palace, you'd prefer it up here, with the pigeons."

Audrey laughed. "Well, that would depend on the prince, wouldn't it?"

"And on the pigeons."

They lapsed into silence, eating with their fingers and staring up at the rafters. The only sounds were Jonas's pitiful little cries as he ate, and the occasional gust of wind rattling a skylight. It was already after one o'clock—a time of night that Audrey knew well, and cherished, because only then could one begin to understand the wisdom of the sky.

"Maybe Florian was right about celestial music," Jonas said, as if reading her thoughts.

Audrey gaped at him. Florian had never been right about anything in Jonas's eyes.

"Maybe we should look more to the sky," he elaborated. "Because things here on Earth are pretty shitty."

"Jonas," she said softly. "What happened?"

CHAPTER 25

The cocktail of painkillers and Amaretto allowed for few embellishments.

"I went back to Germany," Jonas said.

"To Stuttgart?"

"Hamburg. My sister lives there."

"But...weren't the authorities looking for you?"

"Yes. They still are. So I gave up performing."

"But not the cello!"

Jonas sighed and put his head back against the pillow. "Yes, Süsslein," he said. "The cello. I haven't touched it since...well, since we last saw each other onstage. Rami's had it all this time."

"Yes, I know," she said. Complicity stirred in her at the news that Jonas, too, had been estranged from his instrument.

"What happened to your telephone?" she asked. "I tried to reach you countless times."

"I threw it away. I didn't want anyone to track me."

Audrey shook her head. *Trust Jonas to throw away his phone!*

"What have you been doing all this time?"

He said, "Working at McDonald's."

Audrey stared at him. Her spirit crumpled. How could he have sunk so low? If Beethoven had given up before he'd had a chance to compose his piano trios, the world would have known a similar loss.

"And Van Overberg?" she asked.

Jonas took a sip of Amaretto. He regarded her through the swollen slits of his eyes. Then, without warning, he began to weep in wrenching, guttural sobs.

Audrey let him cry. She took the plates of chicken bones to the kitchen and set about washing up. Heartsick, she listened to the misery unfolding on her sofa.

At last it abated.

"I never meant to take the money," Jonas said, his voice thick.

Audrey crept back beside him. She handed him a tissue and he dabbed his bruised nose. "So Van Overberg was right," she said.

"The baroness promised to support my career," Jonas went on. "She also said that she loved me."

"And you believed her," Audrey said. Irritation vied with her pity.

To her surprise, the new, deeper Jonas manifested himself. "Stupidly, yes, I did believe her," he said. "Oh, Audrey! What a fool I was...and have been. She was so nice to me. So...well...*affectionate.* I should have smelled a rat when she gave me the foundation bank card one day. She said she was ill, and could I take some money out for her. She said she'd give me most of it. I could book concert halls. Travel around the world. Make recordings..."

"Solo, you mean," Audrey said, trying to conceal her bitterness. "Without the trio."

"Yes."

"And you didn't stop to consider that she might have had another agenda?"

"No."

"How much did you take out?"

"Eighty thousand euros."

"*What?!* When?"

"The morning of our EU concert."

Audrey fell silent. She got up to walk around. *So he was ready to jump ship,* she thought, resuming her usual route along the pine boards. *Even as we were preparing the most important performance of our lives, he was ready to ditch the Kepler Players for his own career.*

"Then what happened?" she asked.

"The baroness wasn't there when I went to her place with the money. It was after our afternoon rehearsal. It's like she just vanished or something."

"What did you do with it?"

"I put it in my cello case."

Audrey had no words for this.

"Well, I couldn't go back to the bank, could I?" he protested, He seemed feverish now. Audrey brought a fresh damp towel for his forehead. Worry stabbed at her that the wounds might become infected.

"Why couldn't you take it back?" she ventured.

Jonas managed a sheepish look. "The bank was closed. We had the concert that night. I was going to return it the next day anyway."

"But instead..."

"Yes. Instead we all know what happened." He pressed the towel against his forehead. "The whole world knows what happened."

"But what *really* happened, Jonas?"

"The baroness told Van Overberg that I'd stolen her bank card, and found the code in her papers somewhere. Total bullshit, of course."

"So it was entrapment," Audrey said. *And how easy to accomplish with the gullible Jonas!* "She never intended to give you any money, did she? She told Van Overberg you'd stolen it. But why?"

Jonas sipped the last of the Amaretto. "Revenge," he said. "I told her I was leaving her."

"Ah. Hell hath no fury..."

"Yes, well. There was something else, too."

Audrey braced herself.

"I got her pregnant," he said.

The bell of Trinity Church struck the hour three times, as if to indicate that the universe outside the garret was ever-present, and ready to intervene harmonically if need be.

An immense sadness engulfed Audrey. She mourned for her friend: for the loss of his naiveté...for the brutal reckoning that life had visited upon him.

"So the entrapment was for abandoning her," she said, adding, "and her baby. Rami was right, then."

Jonas looked at her quizzically. "Rami?"

"Yes." Audrey returned to the couch. "He intuited all of this. He loves you like a son, Jonas. You know that. He knows your character—that you were over your head with this affair. And that you would never steal money from anyone. Rami guessed that you wanted to leave the baroness—that she would seek revenge, through her husband if necessary. It probably wasn't all that difficult for a cunning madman like Van Overberg to disgrace you before the world."

In a voice graver than Audrey had ever heard from him, Jonas said, "He didn't just disgrace me. He ended up disgracing all three of us." He turned his sorry face toward her. "Can you ever forgive me?"

She squeezed his hand. Hers was cool; his, burning. "There's nothing to forgive," she said.

"What about my arrogance? I was willing to put my own career ahead of the trio's."

"Yes, I know." Audrey smiled, "Perhaps I can't forgive you just yet."

"Do you think Florian will?"

She paused. "I don't know. But before you pass out on my couch, I have three questions for you."

"OK."

"Who did this to you?"

"Van Overberg himself. I came back to Brussels a couple of days ago, thinking it was about time I talked to the baroness and made things right. She said he wouldn't be there. But she lied. He was. He came downstairs and saw me, and...Oh, Audrey. He really is a lunatic."

Audrey tightened. She had no trouble imagining the iron-souled Aymeric Van Overberg reducing Jonas to this state.

Jonas attempted a grin. "There's some prestige in being beaten up by the richest man in Europe, *n'est-ce pas?*"

She ignored him, and asked her second question: "What happened to the child?"

He looked away. "She never had it."

"Oh."

Jonas stretched out fully on the sofa and groaned. Audrey brought the blanket from her bed and draped it over him.

"Ah, Audrey," he said in a drugged voice as she fussed over him. "You have that look in your eyes."

"Which look?"

"The one you used to have right before starting the Mendelssohn scherzo. That..." He could only summon a single word. "*Life.*"

She smiled. "That piece is brimming with life."

"Yes. And so are you."

She went over to the piano to tidy up her scores.

"Audrey..." Jonas murmured, half-unconscious. "Have the past three years been difficult?"

"Yes," she said, her back to him.

She turned, and asked her third question: "Jonas, where's the money?"

"I never touched it."

"So you returned it."

But he could speak no more. Instead he waved a hand in the direction of the door where the cello was standing.

Audrey gasped. "Christ...you mean it's still in the cello case? So Rami has been babysitting eighty thousand euros these past three years—along with a valuable cello?"

But Jonas had fallen into oblivion.

Audrey put on her coat and curled up on her bed. She considered opening the cello case and having a peek at such an enormous sum of money. But then she remembered what misery the money had caused. And anyway, exhaustion carried her off to sleep before she could indulge her curiosity.

CHAPTER 26

The next day brought an angry wind and scudding sky. Fissures opened in the clouds, gleaming inside with pearl and quick-silver, only to close again as if they'd never been. There was passion in such a day. Immediacy. Audrey had decided what to do even before getting out of bed: she would return to Olivia's that very afternoon to learn more about Zar and the piano—and about Klara.

First, though, there was Jonas.

She let him sleep for most of the day. He barely stirred as she went about her routine, showering and dressing in the cubicle behind the curtain, and making her toast and coffee. She clambered up on the piano stool to leave some crusts of bread for the pigeons, studying Jonas's face as she went by to check that it hadn't gotten any worse. It looked as if an army had raged across it, but his forehead was cool to the touch and the swellings had gone down a little.

The landlady accosted her as she went out to teach her lessons.

"What happened to him?" Madame Mertens chittered from her doorway.

"An accident," Audrey said. She'd been expecting this.

The badger face emerged into the light. "*Tiens, tiens.* It didn't look like an accident to me. It looked more like a fight. I hope there won't be any trouble."

"No, Madame," Audrey said, swinging open the heavy front door. "No trouble."

"Poor soul," said the landlady, shaking her head, for in spite of everything, she, too, was in Jonas Liebling's thrall.

Audrey gave four piano lessons in the neighborhood, and afterward bustled up and down Rue du Bailli, filling her shopping bag with food that Jonas might be able to eat in his condition: soup; custard; tea; soft rolls and jam. On her return, Madame Mertens appeared from her lair again.

"I forgot to tell you," Madame Mertens said as Audrey started up the stairs. "You were asking about Nero. Well, I saw his van just yesterday evening. Near Place du Châtelain. That's not so strange, of course. He lives around there somewhere. But I wanted to tell you because..."

"Because...?" Audrey set her shopping down on the landing and descended a few steps.

"Well, the door of the van was open, and there was a piano inside. Imagine that!"

"A piano?"

"Well. I assumed it was. It was all covered up. But it certainly had the shape of a piano."

Was Zar's piano leaving for Prague already? The thought filled Audrey with anguish. *Why would Nero be taking it?*

"Did you see Nero himself?" Audrey asked.

Madame waved away the notion with a scrawny hand. "Oh, no! I didn't linger. I avoid him at all costs." She lowered her voice, and glanced around the hall as if a third person might be lurking. "You know what he did, don't you?" she said.

Audrey ignored her. "You're sure it was a piano, Madame?"

The lady hesitated. "Well, perhaps it was an armoire. They look the same when they're covered up, after all."

♦ ♦ ♦

The cello was already audible on the abbé's landing. The sound was so sweet, so heartfelt, it could pass through walls without difficulty, and even *pianissimo*, make its way across vast arenas. Just the memory of it could make Audrey stop everything she was doing.

Now here it was: the real thing.

She opened the garret door and waited on the landing. Jonas was sitting on a kitchen chair with his back to her, playing scales. He drew his bow over the strings slowly, deliberately, his head bent close to the fingerboard. It made her think of a review he'd received once: *Jonas Liebling could play scales and still enchant his listeners.*

"Oh, Jonas," she said, tip-toeing in.

He turned around and she recoiled: she'd momentarily forgotten about the blood-soaked bandages.

"It sounds like crap!" he grinned.

"That would be impossible for you," said Audrey, taking the groceries to the kitchen. She lingered at the open cello case.

He read her thoughts. "Oh, I took the money back while you were out," he said.

"*What?*"

"It's OK. His mailbox is near some bushes. You can't see it from the house."

"You stuffed eighty thousand euros into a mailbox?"

"The envelope just fit."

"You shouldn't have gone out at all, Jonas!" Audrey cried. "It's not safe. Van Overberg could be anywhere. Anyway, you should have sent the money registered mail, at least." She gave him a harsh look. "That's not the end of it, is it?"

"No." Jonas put the cello away and went to rest on the couch. "He won't stop. Not until he sends me to jail. Or worse…"

"Worse than this, you mean?" Audrey indicated his wounds.

Jonas said nothing. They both knew how much worse Van Overberg's violence could have been; they also knew that he wasn't the type to give up on a vendetta.

"I need a lawyer," Jonas said, defeated.

"And you think you can afford a lawyer who could take on the legal team of Europe's richest man? Jonas, think! You need to get out of Brussels."

"Again?"

"Yes. But this time…" She paused, "With us."

"*Us?*"

Audrey made Jonas a mug of ginger tea and brought it over to the sofa along with a soft, sugary roll. Then, to guarantee his undivided attention, she took up position at the center of the garret, lifted her chin, and said:

"Jonas."

He stared at her gravely over the mug: "You look like one of those figures on the prow of a ship," he said.

Audrey smiled. She was fairly certain that among all the women Jonas had become entangled with, none of them had received that particular compliment.

"You've come up with a plan," he said.

"Yes."

Their eyes locked.

"Don't tell me you want to resuscitate the trio. Is that what you meant by 'us'?"

They continued staring at each other.

Audrey said, "We used to have this kind of synergy when we played together, didn't we?"

"I guessed it, then?"

"Well, maybe. I saw Florian yesterday."

"Florian?" Jonas repeated the name as if she'd raised a ghost. "I'd have to mend fences with him," he added, glumly.

"It's not so much about the trio," Audrey said. "At least, not yet."

"What do you mean?"

"I need help." She kept Jonas in her sights. "For...*something*."

"For *what?*"

Audrey stood as tall as a petite person could manage. Figurehead that she was, she set her eyes on an invisible horizon and said, "To follow a piano to Prague."

No sound came from Jonas.

Audrey went to her upright and sat down—her best place for thinking. She recounted her discovery of the Náhoda, bringing Olivia and Zar into the story, their mystical love, Klara's murder, and anything else that might lure Jonas to her scheme.

"Is the piano valuable?" he asked.

"Historically, yes," Audrey said. "Konstantine Zar was an extraordinary figure during the Second World War—albeit a clandestine one." She regarded Jonas. "There might be something valuable *inside* it," she said, taking Rami's lead.

Jonas sat up with interest.

She went on: "It has some strange symbols carved inside it. Considering who once owned it, it might even contain secrets of the universe."

This was a stretch, she knew. But she'd hit her mark.

"Wow!" Jonas said, his mouth full of sweet roll. "That's funny: on my way here I passed some people loading a piano into a van."

Audrey got up from the stool. "Where?" she said. "What people?" *So Madame Mertens had been as sharp-eyed as always!*

"Near Place du Châtelain. A beaten-up white van. A loud guy who sounded drunk."

Audrey's heart jumped. "With long gray hair?"

"Maybe. A tall, thin guy was helping him."

"With a fedora?"

"How the hell did you know that? He's stronger than he looks."

"Is that all you saw?" Audrey pressed him.

Jonas washed the roll down with a gulp of ginger tea. "Besides the dog?" he said.

"What dog?" Audrey asked faintly.

"A nasty little Jack Russell. Dogs usually love me. But not that one."

"Who was with the dog?"

"A big guy with white hair. There were other people, too. Piano-moving is a spectator sport, as you know."

Audrey left Jonas to his practicing and slipped behind the curtain to change into a dressier version of her gray and white ensemble.

"I'm off to see Olivia Taverner," she said, collecting her coat and hat. "Keep thinking about my plan."

Jonas beamed at her appreciatively. "All the allure of a nun without actually having to be one!" he said.

"You could do with a dose of monasticism yourself," Audrey snapped.

He smiled. "I'd lay down my life for you, Süsslein. You know that. But I'm not sure if I'd do it for a piano."

"Well, please consider it," she said, opening the door. "And whatever you do, don't leave the house!"

CHAPTER 27

Audrey had decided not to ask Florian along for this visit. She reckoned that Olivia might open up more if the two women were alone; she didn't even call beforehand, which was rash, and perhaps more than a little rude given Olivia's age and social standing.

It took two rings this time, and several minutes in between, before the lustrous door opened to reveal Olivia herself.

"*Xairetízo ti melodía mésa sou!*" said the vision, resplendent in a sweeping floral robe. She smiled at Audrey. "It means 'I salute the melody within you'. In Greek, of course."

Olivia beckoned her guest inside. "It was how Konstantine always greeted his initiates," she said.

It's as if she was expecting me, Audrey thought. She followed Olivia down the familiar corridor to the salon, past the frondy plants on their Grecian columns, and the portrait of Olivia and Reginald Taverner at the Bösendorfer—a wayside shrine where visitors could linger. The floral robe wafted in a mysterious breeze as Olivia walked along.

The protocol was the same as before: the little silver bell; the maid taking Audrey's coat with a curtsey; Olivia settling herself on the damask love seat, which took a bit more maneuvering in a long robe than it had in a cashmere suit.

The atmosphere, however, had changed utterly.

Intimacy burgeoned. The vast salon reduced itself to the cozy sphere occupied by the two women, sitting close to each other, face to face. Outside, glancing off the ponds, the wind roamed in fits and sighs.

"I thought it was suitable to begin with Zar's greeting," Olivia said. "That's why you're here, Audrey, isn't it? To know more about him. I sensed it when you came with Florian: your fascination with Zar."

"Yes," Audrey said, relieved not to have to explain herself. "And to know more about Klara...and her piano."

"Her piano?"

"Yes. You mentioned when Florian and I were here that Klara had a rather nice one."

♦ ♦ ♦

It was the hour for early cocktails. The maid slipped in bearing a tray with two glasses of rosé and a crystal bowl of pretzels.

Audrey sipped the peach-scented wine, waiting for the right moment to tell Olivia that Klara's piano had fallen prey to the Brussels underworld, and that she'd taken it upon herself to recover it.

But Olivia seemed even more eager to talk.

"You know," she said, "Pythagoras was tall, and graceful in speech and gesture. This was Zar, Audrey. Utterly. And there was such an air of mystery about him. He was a cipher with infinite interpretations. Oh, I could never speak with Reginald about him, of course," she went on conspiratorially, as if her husband had just left the room for a moment. "By the time we married in 1948, six years had gone by since Zar was executed. In fact, I never talked to anyone about Zar. Florian and I mainly discuss his teachings. I rarely visited Klara. When I did, it was very formal, and we didn't talk about her brother. She was eaten alive by guilt, you see. It seemed better not to talk about Konstantine."

"Guilt?" said Audrey. She lifted her glass, and watched the wine flush in the light from the pond.

Olivia plumped the bun at the nape of her neck. She looked away and said, "Yes. Klara felt responsible for what happened...for the Nazis taking Zar."

"In 1942," Audrey said quietly.

"Yes."

"What happened, Olivia?" Audrey regretted at once using her hostess's given name.

"It wasn't Klara's fault, that much I can tell you," Olivia said, unfazed by Audrey's intimacy. "She'd just gone off to find a doctor. But it was late...there was a curfew. She'd forgotten her papers."

The women fell silent. The older one, wrapped in scented floral, and the younger one in simple dove-gray and walking shoes, didn't look like equals. But they were regarding one another as if they were—in the way that members of a guild are bound by a code more important than social status.

Olivia resettled herself on the love seat. "Klara Náhoda came to Brussels from Prague in the autumn of 1941," she said. "She'd married into the family of piano-makers. Far too young, in my opinion: at eighteen.

"The marriage soon fell apart. As her parents were both dead, Klara had no one left but her brother, who was in Brussels at that point. They were inseparable as children, you know. It must have been terrible for Klara when Zar went away to study. So of course she didn't hesitate when he asked her to join him, even with a war gripping Europe." Olivia played with the belt of her robe. "And even when he asked her to bring a piano with her."

So that's how it got here! Audrey thought.

Olivia continued: "But not just any piano. Zar wanted Klara's father-in-law, Petr Náhoda, to build one according to his specifications."

"His specifications?"

"I never quite understood it, either. It was only many years after the war that I asked Klara about this, and she answered only vaguely. She said that Zar wanted the piano's action made in a certain way; that the rosewood case should be especially sturdy for the long journey. That sort of thing. She said that Zar fell in love with it the moment it arrived."

It was the obvious moment for Audrey to tell Olivia that she'd encountered that very instrument on the street just two days before. But instead she said, "How on earth did Klara travel with a piano from Prague to Brussels? And in wartime?"

"With the help of Emile Hendrickx."

"The collaborator at the conservatory!"

"He was Zar's violin teacher," Olivia said, with the same impatient tone she'd used with Florian. "He was high up in the conservatory administration, it's true. If that's what you mean by 'collaborator'. Anyway, there were many of them, in all walks of life, mainly just trying to survive the war.

"Hendrickx prepared the order on Zar's behalf," Olivia went on. "He made a formal request from the Brussels Conservatory for a piano to be made in the Náhoda workshop in Prague. No questions would be raised. Klara could then travel with the piano to Brussels legitimately, in a German transport truck. Zar wrote his specific design requests in a private letter to Klara in Prague."

"Hendrickx did Zar a huge favor, it seems," said Audrey. "Who paid for it? I mean, Zar was so young...and poor."

"That remains a mystery," Olivia answered. "Zar could be extraordinarily persuasive, though. I've long believed that Náhoda made the piano for Zar for free, and paid for the transport himself." She stopped to register Audrey's surprise. "Such was the devotion Zar inspired in people."

"Did Klara move into the rooming house?" Audrey asked.

"Oh, no. Zar left Madame Hazard's as soon as Klara arrived. He was lucky: the librarian at the conservatory let them occupy two floors in her house across from the forest on Chaussée de Waterloo. Rent-free. He moved the piano into the parlor on the ground floor."

Olivia paused. In accordance with females of her standing, she nibbled on a tiny twig of pretzel and no more. Audrey, in accordance with the ever-hungry members of her own class, helped herself to a handful while Olivia was retrieving a crumb from the carpet.

"I was devastated when Zar left the rooming house, of course," Olivia said. "He'd begun letting me accompany him on some of his walks, you see. I no longer had to follow him incognito. It was a huge gesture on his part. And such an honor. I was terrified to speak to him at first. There I was, suddenly alone with this great thinker. We often just walked in silence. But it was a full, meaningful silence. Like the best silences in music."

"Didn't he come back to see you at Madame Hazard's?" Audrey asked, trying to gauge her hostess's feelings for Zar. Was she already in love with him when Klara arrived? And what about him? He admired Olivia's singing, clearly. She was charming and lovely. But was there something more?

"Not often," Olivia said. "Gestapo headquarters were on Avenue Louise, after all: the infamous no. 453, where the cellar was used for interrogations. Not so very far from Zar's new lodgings, in fact. The forest was just across the road. So he went there directly and walked alone. Or he lost himself in his studies."

"Did you go to visit Zar and Klara?"

Olivia stiffened. "No. Klara was such a stern woman. So very loyal to her brother. And protective. I don't think she liked me very much, to be honest. She never said it, of course, but I don't think she thought I was good enough for Konstantine."

Olivia took a sip of her wine and said, "Actually, Zar came to the rooming house to ask me to walk with him on the day he was arrested."

Audrey's eyes widened.

Olivia gave her a sad smile. "Let me tell you more about Zar, Audrey. You might understand all this a little better."

"Yes, please do," Audrey said. But in truth, she felt that she'd already met this man, though in which dream, or on what phantom walk, she couldn't say.

CHAPTER 28

The faculty at the *conservatoire* knew that the students were hungry—not only for food (rationed, of course), but for beauty: for something nobler than the sight of the world they knew being devoured by cruelty and ugliness. They'd already been gathering for some time in cafes and corridors to listen to the young foreigner. So during the winter of 1941-42, an unused teaching studio was offered to Zar—an unheard-of privilege for a student—where he would lean against the battered Pleyel grand and talk about the nature of music.

It was a winter that would live on in infamy. Temperatures hovered below minus twenty for weeks at a time. Existence, already constrained, reduced itself even further to the obsessive quest for warmth. The cold had become a stalking, animate thing. It never slept. It made each task a penance, and controlled every moment of the day. The fug of crowded trams and cafes, unbearable before, was sought after now. People wore their coats and hats to bed; they slept with bricks they'd warmed up on the kitchen stove. That such a winter should have accompanied the shackles of occupation seemed a cruel joke on Nature's part.

None of this seemed to matter to Zar or his followers. His unheated studio became an oasis on their dreary, monochrome search for food. For fuel. *For hope.* They thronged to listen to the pariah with oddly-accented

French and a smoldering trove of ideas. Zar's starkness—his unfathomable, coal-black eyes—put off some. But his admirers sensed that he was not an arrogant young man, or condescending in any way. They'd already divined one of his great paradoxes: that although he was by nature taciturn and moody, some inner compass guided him toward what was compassionate and true.

♦ ♦ ♦

January 1942

The conservatory's central heating had been cut off entirely. Cast iron stoves in the classrooms had only enough fuel for a few hours a day. In Zar's studio, there was no stove at all.

It was a doleful place. Jagged sheets of plaster had broken off the walls. The windows, lofty and church-like, were so filthy that little light could penetrate them. Indeed, the room had been abandoned for so long that it had the mustiness of a lost tomb, where the Pleyel piano, encased in dust, was the sarcophagus, and the scattering of school chairs facing this relic had once been occupied by a long-departed faithful.

And yet somehow, Music had found her way here.

A large group was crowding in through the door one afternoon. There were barely enough chairs for half their number, so people perched on dirty windowsills, or jostled for a place on the floor, happy for the warmth of their fellows. A large space around the piano was left free for Zar to do his pacing and play his violin. Klara Náhoda, who took notes at every lecture her brother gave, sat near the door.

As for Olivia, she'd pressed herself into a cluster of friends sitting on the floor, half hoping that Zar would notice her, and praying that he wouldn't. For it was his habit to occasionally gesture to someone in the audience to ask their opinion, or begin a debate, and it terrified her that she might appear naïve or shallow in his eyes.

No one noticed the military police at first.

They'd slipped into the crush at the last minute, three of them, and kept to the back of the room. Their presence was soon detected, however. At once three students rushed up to offer their chairs. It wasn't the Germans' first visit: Zar had already caught the attention of the authorities. They'd sent their spies to shadow this renegade foreigner; to observe the extraordinary effect he had on his colleagues. They knew that he'd dared to play that Jew, Mendelssohn, in public—and in front of high-ranking officers, no less.

The studio settled, and went still.

"Music is a living thing," Zar began, his gaze fixed on that imagined horizon. His breath floated off into the frigid room. "She lives in the air over our heads. You must play with joy. Reverence. Only then will you tempt her to Earth."

Everyone glanced away, wary that at any moment Zar might tear his gaze from his horizon and fix it on them. The charcoal stare was hotter than anything a stove could have produced in that miserable, shivering city.

"We must try to live as Music does," he went on. "Guilelessly. With grace. At the perfect tempo. And in harmony with our fellows—no matter how far those fellows have strayed into discord and immorality."

Zar's searing eyes rested briefly on the policemen. The three Germans, who must have been comfortable on their chairs, and in their thick woolen greatcoats, shifted uneasily.

"Because you see," Zar said. "Music is a moral force. She has the power to guide us toward our finer natures." He paused. "Even a single note can carry the truth."

He began pacing in front of the piano. "Consider, please," he continued, "that the invisible substance we spend hours with every day moves in waves, and has energy. It vibrates, and resonates. We can feel these waves in our own bodies. Think of sitting in the middle of a symphony orchestra while it's playing." Zar warmed up as he paced and unbuttoned his tattered, unlined coat. Underneath, the spotless peasant shirt flashed white in the general gloom.

"We've talked before about the great thinkers—Pythagoras; Plato; Kepler. How they believed that the music we play on Earth reflects a Great Theme in the heavens. Let's think about Music as the manifestation of a greater force. After all, Christians believe the same thing, don't they? That is to say, Christ is the manifestation of an inchoate God. For millennia, Music was also considered divine in nature."

Zar stopped abruptly. A ripple of anticipation passed over the room.

"I'd like to show you just how alive Music is," he said.

Without further preamble, he opened the lid of the old Pleyel. The wooden wing creaked on its hinges. Zar propped it open with a stick that had been gnawed by some unknown creature. A miasma of dust escaped from the belly of the instrument, along with the smell of mildew, and of something less tangible. Relief, perhaps. As if Zar had cracked open the casket of something that had been buried alive and that was still, miraculously, breathing.

He sat at the keyboard and played a few arpeggios. A woeful clang filled the room, followed by a few nervous giggles.

"Now, please," Zar said. "Be very quiet and listen carefully."

He played the A below middle C, letting the note vibrate. "This is the note I'll sing. I'll depress the pedal, so that all the strings will be free to vibrate."

He leaned into the piano near the strings and sang the A he'd indicated. The piano's corresponding note sprang to life with a ghostly twang, accompanied by a wash of overtones.

Gasps filled the studio. The policemen sat up straighter for a better view.

Zar repeated the exercise. Then he demonstrated the same principle by singing other notes, which in turn set their own counterparts in the piano vibrating.

"The A string in the piano resonated sympathetically with my voice," he explained. "Because the A that I sang has the same resonant frequency as the one in the piano." Zar opened his violin case, quickly tuned, and leaned into the piano, drawing his bow over the violin's A string. The piano let out another unearthly, A-centered *whoosh* in response. "Come and try it for yourselves," he said, beckoning his audience to the piano.

Everyone crowded around, eager to share Zar's space. One by one, they depressed the sustaining pedal on the piano and sang a note into the strings, listening with delight to the answering resonance.

One of the Germans drifted up to Zar.

"Fascinating," the man said in French.

"Yes, it certainly is," Zar replied in German.

The policeman recoiled in surprise. "*Sie sprechen Deutsch! Woher kommen Sie?*" *You speak German! Where do you come from?* The question was not a casual one.

"Near Prague," Zar answered vaguely. He turned back to his colleagues, who had all tried their hand at sympathetic resonance.

"Everything on Earth has its own resonant frequency," he said, ignoring the German. "A chair. A window. A bridge. Even the human body." He paused. "Maybe those of you who sing feel it the most." The dark eyes fixed on Olivia. "Sometimes a singer produces a note that turns her whole body into a sounding board. Then you know that you've found your natural tone."

Olivia froze, caught in his snare.

"I believe that this can also happen between two people," Zar went on, enfolding Olivia in his aura. "I believe that sympathetic resonance exists between two like-minded souls. Which proves, I think, Plato's point." Zar finally released Olivia from his gaze and addressed the room at large: "That is, that Music and the human soul are both aspects of the eternal."

CHAPTER 29

Emile Hendrickx issued the first warning.

"You must be careful, dear Konstantine," he said the next day after Zar had finished his lesson. He'd grown quite attached to this precocious twenty-year-old. "The Gestapo has taken an interest in you, you know. I spoke to the director this morning, and in principle, he's still willing for you to continue giving your talks. But still, the police are everywhere. I don't know..." Hendrickx hesitated, and watched as Zar put his violin back into its case. "I wonder if perhaps you should stop for a while."

Zar laughed. "How is the notion of celestial harmony threatening in any way?"

Hendrickx could not answer this question.

Zar elaborated: "We musicians are the only keepers of harmony in this whole wretched war. As Kepler said: 'Let us despise the barbaric neighings which echo through these noble lands, and awaken our understanding and longing for the harmonies.'"

Hendrickx looked at his student wryly. "Is it really possible, do you think, to awaken harmony in our neighing occupiers?"

♦ ♦ ♦

Zar continued despite the danger. Soon rumors tainted his lectures. The insinuations caught fire, and couldn't be stamped out: *Is he a priest incognito? A fugitive in disguise? Maybe he's delivering encrypted messages for the Belgian Resistance. Zar spoke so enigmatically, after all.*

When he said things such as: *Everyone must go on a journey to discover their own truth*, surely it could be a code for something else—a journey somewhere specific, perhaps. Antwerp, maybe. To relay some sort of instruction to the Underground.

"You don't know who is an ally, Konstantine," Klara whispered, catching him alone in the studio after a lecture. "And who is a spy."

They pulled up two chairs close to the Pleyel, as if the piano might offer them some warmth.

"Please, find another venue," Klara pleaded. "Somewhere less visible." She reminded him that the public was seeking spiritual nourishment wherever they could—in clubs, cinemas; and also in clandestine locales.

"You could find a private salon for your talks," she suggested. "It would be safer."

"Now, Klara..." Zar spoke to her indulgently, as always. "You mustn't fret so." He got up and wandered about the studio, as Klara watched him and bit her lip.

Whatever dazzling raw material had gone into the creation of Konstantine Zar had been in short supply when it had come to his sister. But he realized this, and in some ways even rued it. For Klara Náhoda could pass anonymously through life without a second glance from anyone. As loyal as this plain, dogged woman was to Zar, so Zar was to her.

"I have good reason to fret," Klara said. She explained how just the day before, she'd observed two officials in German uniforms mingling in the courtyard of the conservatory before Zar's talk. She'd slipped through the crowd and eavesdropped.

"Konstantine, you're in danger," she said. "The officials were striking up conversations, trying to seem casual about it. Laughing, even. They were asking things like: 'Why is he so popular, this strange young man?

Can you say?' And: 'Where does he get his ideas from?' But Konstantine, their tone was not casual."

Klara knew that tone—and their laugh. She'd seen them laugh that way loading prisoners into a lorry bound for St. Gilles prison. From there, she knew, they would be taken to the Tir National and shot.

And so the lectures were moved to the parlor of the house across from the forest that Zar shared with his sister. He spoke to small groups from the keyboard of the Náhoda piano. The instrument had become his beloved muse; his confidante. Sometimes, it seemed to Klara that the piano was her brother's only earthly link to the cosmic harmony he so revered— that if something happened to it, and that link were to be broken, he would simply vanish into the ether and never be seen again.

They gathered in the evening, when blackouts were in force. Windows had to be draped with thick covers, or painted with dark paint, as the occupier didn't think twice before firing his rifle at the slimmest ray of light. All this furtiveness fed on itself, and grew, and spawned even more secrecy. *Keep these ideas to yourself,* Zar told his followers. *Even when you think no one is around. Even after they come for me.*

CHAPTER 30

March 1942

It was late in the afternoon...too late, really, to be heading off into the forest. And during a war, too. But neither weather nor human affairs ever altered Zar's plans much.

He stopped by Madame Hazard's to ask Olivia to accompany him. It was the first time he'd gone back to the rooming house since the arrival of his sister. That he'd gone there expressly for Olivia instilled in the girl a sort of stage fright. There were things to discuss, he told her, with his usual air of detachment.

"But it will be dark soon," she protested. "And it's so cold and damp. Let's just work on some Schumann, Konstantine." But even as she said this she trembled with joy, as she always did at the prospect of his company.

They squeezed into a packed tram heading up Avenue Louise, indistinguishable from the other travelers in their coarse overcoats and cheap boots.

Zar bustled Olivia from the tram at the top of the avenue. "Come, we mustn't linger here," he said, and they hurried toward the park.

No one ever lingered there. Number 453 was only a few blocks away, after all. As it was, the austere young man striding like a herdsman, and the pretty, petite girl struggling to keep up with him, attracted notice.

It was soon obvious where he was going.

They'd crossed the landscaped paths and valleys of the Bois de la Cambre and were heading into the Forêt de Soignes: a deep, isolated remnant of the ancient charcoal forests that once stretched from the Rhine River to the North Sea.

"Please, Konstantine," Olivia begged. "Let's turn back."

He said nothing, and instead increased his tempo. Twilight was already seeping into the grandiose nave of beeches, and with it, a cathedral stillness.

Olivia pulled at Zar's elbow. "What about the depots?"

Everyone knew it was a foolhardy place to walk. The Forêt de Soignes concealed a vast network of German munition supplies, ringed by defensive trenches into which a walker could easily stumble, even by day. By night, Olivia and Zar might as well have been two blind people traversing a minefield.

Zar ignored her. He marched down the somber beech avenues until they'd reached a wide grove opening onto pastureland.

Here they finally rested.

Zar leaned his back against the rough trunk of an oak. "I wanted you to see this place," he said. "It's where I do my best thinking." As was his habit, he studied the sky. "We might see Mars tonight, if it clears up."

Olivia stood a few meters away, shivering and miserable.

"Do you know what a Great Conjunction is, my angel?" he asked.

She shook her head. His endearment befuddled her far more than his question.

"It's when Jupiter and Saturn come close to each other in their orbits. It happens about every twenty years. Kepler was fascinated by this. And every eight hundred years, the Great Conjunction occurs in roughly the same part of the sky."

"Oh." Olivia felt herself crumpling under the force of his presence.

There was never a single way to get to this enigma of a man. Sometimes there was no way in at all. One ended up in a sort of breezy antechamber, where Olivia herself often found herself, waiting for the door to open onto Zar's inner chamber. Even when they'd lain side by side on old coal sacks in the Parc de Bruxelles, studying the night sky during a blackout, and when they'd stayed late at Madame Hazard's dinner table drinking tea...even then, the door had not opened. Only much later would Olivia realize that she had, in fact, already visited that chamber: that Zar had invited her in to consummate their spiritual union through music. Any devoted chamber player knew what that meant: the intimacies passed back and forth between partners in blissful waves of suspension and release.

"Konstantine," Olivia said softly, drawing his attention back to Earth. "What are we doing here?"

He suddenly focused every atom of his being on her.

"I'll never forget the way you sang *An die Musik,*" he said. It was not the evasion of a calculating man, but of a struggling one. "It's true, isn't it, what the lyrics say?" he went on. "That Music warms us to love, and carries us away to a better place." The angles of his face had softened in the forest light.

"Yes," said Olivia, trying to keep her teeth from clacking. Spring had not yet set foot in the forest, and torpor gripped the scene. The ferment of last year's leaves hung heavy, smelling more of death than of the new life they harbored underneath them. Across the nearby field, a farmhouse cut a low silhouette against the twilight, its windows unlit.

Zar stepped closer and reached for her hands. His eyes held a light that she'd never seen in them before.

"*Musica mundana. Musica instrumentalis. Musica humana,*" he said, sotto voce. "You felt it during our concert, didn't you, darling? I'm certain that together, in that frigid hall, we found the link between cosmic music, our instruments, and our souls."

"Please, Konstantine," she said. "It's too cold to discuss these things."

"You're the only one in the world I want to talk about them with, Olivia."

"Oh," she said, struck by his solemnity. He didn't often address her by her name. She ignored the water seeping from the boggy ground into her cheap boots.

"If we could just stay out here," he said, "I'm sure we would feel the same harmony that we experienced in our concert."

Olivia stared at him. "But Konstantine, we can't stay out here!" She pulled her hands from his. "Is that what you were intending? That we wouldn't be going back?"

"No, of course not." He smiled. "Although you remember what I said about musicians going on a journey to find their own truth."

Olivia gave a short, nervous laugh. "Of course I remember! But a lot of people thought it was some kind of coded message."

"Oh, no," said Zar earnestly. "I meant a real journey—a real quest." He grasped her hands again and lifted them to his lips. "Perhaps we're beginning our journey now, here in this forest." He stroked her cheeks and drank in her devastating sweetness.

He began to kiss her, starting with her forehead and temples, and then the delicate hollow between her jawbone and her neck; the tip of her nose, and then, finally, her lips, which had been waiting so impatiently.

"Our coming together is like a Great Conjunction, isn't it?" Zar whispered in her ear.

"I suppose so," she said, drawing back. "But I hope we don't have to wait another twenty years for it to happen again...or eight hundred, for that matter."

He laughed. "No, we don't have to wait a moment longer. I brought you here because I have something to ask you."

"Apart from whether or not I know what a Great Conjunction is?" she quipped.

"Olivia," he said, with the gravity of a poet. "I love you."

She stood motionless. She could no longer feel her toes in her boots. But she would have happily spent another twenty years enduring this, and much more, for the sake of what she assumed he intended to ask her.

But at that moment the Greek...the orator...the man who had mesmerized the entire conservatory with his eloquence, faltered.

"Olivia..." Zar looked up into the trees, as if for counsel. He veered. "Can't you feel how our tiny souls reflect celestial harmony?" It was not the question he'd been aiming for, obviously. But it was more than many men would have found to say under such circumstances.

He folded her in his arms where, despite the unuttered question, she reveled in the rough wool of his coat and his clean, soapy smell, and in the pulse of cosmic music that did, indeed, lay trapped between them.

CHAPTER 31

They stood entwined in the cold under the old oak tree long enough for the stars to wander to their next positions.

If we keep standing here, Olivia thought, *maybe he'll find the courage to ask me.* She let herself believe that Zar, too, was thinking the same thing.

Nothing moved in the grove apart from the drifting exhales of the two lovers.

Olivia lifted her head from Zar's chest.

And of someone else.

♦ ♦ ♦

She'd spotted it first: a tiny patch of gauze on the air, just meters away.

She hissed a warning.

Too late.

A twig snapped like bone.

A pistol clicked.

Zar grabbed her arm. "*Dépêche-toi!*" he breathed. "Hurry. *Run!*"

A man stepped into the grove from behind a tangle of brush, blocking their escape. He wore a leather helmet and jacket, and a parachute vest.

How long had he been hiding there?

He raised his pistol.

Olivia grasped Zar's hand and closed her eyes. *Konstantine will never ask me now,* she thought. *We'll die even before we've had a chance to talk about marrying.* At least they'd created music together. It was a form of marriage, after all.

At once the man let out a cry and collapsed to the leaves.

Zar and Olivia gaped at him. Their terror dissolved at the sight of his trouser leg, dark with blood, and his singed leather jacket. Anguish had gouged deep furrows in the young face.

Zar bent over him.

"Are you Belgian?" the man gasped in English, half-conscious.

"A British soldier!" Zar exclaimed under his breath, also in English.

"Pilot," whispered the man.

"Are there others?"

"No. Plane...crashed." He swooned.

A crossroads had arrived, it seemed.

A great, echoing conjunction.

For had they left the man to die, and hurried home through the twilight, Olivia and Zar might have weathered the rest of the war unscathed; they might have nourished their love, and married, and made music together for the rest of their lives.

But that didn't happen. Of course not. Whatever higher power roamed the heavens and played with the lives of humans, he or she liked nothing better than a deceptively easy choice. For the genius of life, Zar once told his followers, lay in what followed that choice. His wisdom tasted bitter now, for he and Olivia couldn't very well leave the man there to die—and certainly not an Englishman. That much was easy. It was afterward, in all the messy, unexpected twists and turns, glorious and perilous, that sprang from that simple decision, where the divine architect found true inspiration. Not, alas, in the perfect geometrical schemes of earthly thinkers.

"We can support him between us," Zar said. "Can you manage it?"

"Of course I can!" Olivia exclaimed, thought she knew full well that she couldn't.

She wanted more than anything to impress Zar. But this was not the Zar who just a few moments ago had declared his love for her, and kissed her so tenderly. Now the angles of his face soared higher than ever. His eyes, misted from romance, had sharpened with the task at hand. The pilot's blood had already stained his coarse wool coat.

"He must have water," Zar said, searching the tangle of equipment still hanging on the man's chest. He found a canteen in a canvas carrier and unbuckled it from its strap: it was empty. He gave it to Olivia. "Go across that field and fetch some water from the trough," he demanded,

She went without thinking; she would have gone anywhere Zar asked her to go without thinking, though she could barely make out the trough through the thickening air. By the time she was half-way across the meadow, her cardboard boots had filled with water. Matted hillocks of grass rose like islands from the bog, but they had no substance, and collapsed underfoot. Once Olivia had made it to the trough and slogged her way back to the men with the full canteen, she felt she could walk no farther.

Her trek had only just begun.

♦ ♦ ♦

No doubt more strenuous rescues had been performed over the course of the Second World War. More dramatic ones, certainly. But few had been as bizarre as this: two young musicians keen on Pythagoras and Kepler dragging a bleeding British pilot through the Forêt de Soignes in darkness.

It took them half the night to traverse the woods. Zar had bound the man's wounds as best he could with strips of a ground cloth he'd found in his haversack, but the bleeding could not be stopped. Even so, in his purgatory, the pilot let out scarcely a moan.

The sound of two people dragging someone through last year's leaves and twigs could have filled a concert hall, it seemed. Olivia and Zar spoke only in whispers. The forest housed a thousand eyes—hostile eyes guarding trenches and munitions that could be anywhere...perhaps only a cough's-length away. They dared not use the flashlight in the haversack, or the matches. They navigated solely by the stars, therefore.

Starlight...

Olivia peered up through the crowns of the beeches. Her arms had gone numb from supporting the man's weight for so long. Light-headed, she imagined that overhead, in the starry vapors, a lady with a lantern was roaming. You could see the hem of her robe glimmer where it had caught on a branch. Was she called Music, this lady? Olivia mused, for she remembered how Zar had said that Music lived in the air over our heads. He'd neglected to say what she looked like, though.

Olivia considered how notes of music always rise; how light they must be, like smoke. Was death like that? she wondered. A floating toward a light-bearing lady? These thoughts uncoupled her mind from her aching body, and for a short time she could lift the wounded man without pain.

During their many stops to rest, the pilot managed a few words: his name was Tim Morrison, and he'd been bound for Essen when his plane was shot down a few kilometers from where they'd found him; he came from Plymouth; and he had a baby boy.

CHAPTER 32

They exited the woods across from the house where Zar and Klara lived. It was well past midnight. The blackout was absolute. A phantom city lay before them, without shape or substance. Intersections glowed bluish, as if from a submerged ruin. Only one car passed at a creep, its lamps obscured under special hoods.

Klara met them at the door, white-faced. "Oh, dear God!" she cried. "Where have you been?" She hesitated when she saw Olivia: the girl never came to this house.

Klara clasped a hand to her mouth at the sight of the stricken pilot. "Who is this?" she muttered, but at once helped drag him over the threshold. Tears shone on her cheeks. "Oh, *le pauvre!* Where did you find him?"

Tim acknowledged Klara, then went slack between Zar and Olivia. "He's lost a lot of blood," Zar said. "Too much blood," he added.

They carried him up six flights of steps to a storage room under the eaves, and covered him with blankets. Klara tried in vain to trickle water between his parched lips.

"If he recovers well enough to travel, we can arrange for him to be smuggled over the Pyrenees into Spain, along one of the escape routes," Zar said. But even as he spoke, they all realized how hopeless this was.

"I'll fetch a doctor," said Klara. "We must do something."

"At this hour?" Zar exclaimed. "But chérie, the curfew! You shouldn't go out. Please…"

Klara glared at him. "Well, you certainly can't go out," she retorted. "You've attracted too much attention as it is. We can't very well leave him to die, can we?"

Olivia lingered in the stairwell, unsure. She wondered how the night would proceed from this point, afraid to say anything that might snuff out forever the last remaining embers of her evening with Zar. Madame Hazard was probably sick with worry by now after she hadn't turned up for the evening meal.

"Margriet's husband is a doctor," Klara said, referring to the grocer on Avenue Legrand. "He'll come, I'm sure." She'd already slipped down the stairs and out the front door before Zar could stop her.

Unable to say another word, or even to lift her arms, Olivia lay down next to the pilot and fell into oblivion. She was too exhausted to notice that Zar had lain down beside her and gathered her close.

♦ ♦ ♦

The pounding started while Klara was still out.

Zar shook awake and crept downstairs, Olivia close behind him. He waited before opening the door: Klara would never hammer on it like that. He turned to Olivia instead. Roughly, desperately, he snatched her against him, as if he knew what was about to happen—as if for those few moments only, there was still hope for their union.

"*Aufmachen!*"

Zar opened the door.

Olivia's blood congealed at the sound of German. She peered around Zar: sandwiched between the two uniformed men stood Klara, even paler than before.

"I forgot my papers," she stammered to her brother. For this offense—and for breaking the curfew— she faced a stiff fine...or worse.

There was no doctor with them.

The men pushed Klara inside. Zar flattened himself against the wall of the entry next to Olivia. It was a futile gesture, of course. They were in full view of the police. But perhaps they would be dismissed as irrelevant.

Klara flung open the parlor door and dashed to the sofa. She'd left her handbag there, and in a panic began tearing through it.

The policemen pushed past Zar and Olivia in the narrow passageway and followed Klara into the parlor. Olivia recalled the gleaming details of the men who'd detained Zar in the park, and they gleamed now beneath the hall light: silver buckles and buttons, and silver eagles on the sides of their helmets. The rifles slung over their shoulders gleamed, too. But dully. Ominously.

The men looked around the simple, tasteful room with appreciation. They removed their helmets, not out of respect, but in the manner of those who feel entitled to make themselves at home. As Klara rummaged in her bag, one of the Germans sank into an armchair and put his boots up on the small table.

"*Schönes Klavier*," said the other, drifting over to the piano. The Náhoda stood in a place of prominence, as proud and inscrutable as its owner. The policeman lit an unfiltered Gauloise and sat down on the piano stool. He launched into *Für Elise* with some skill, the cigarette wedged between his fingers as he played.

This proved too much for Zar.

He strode through the parlor door toward the piano. His black stare zeroed in on the cigarette ash sprinkled over the creamy keys. Then it clamped on the police officer himself, as if the man were a wayward student and not the deadly foe that he was.

The officer stopped playing.

"Your tempo is too fast," Zar said, his stare unchanged. He placed a hand on the piano in a proprietary way.

The man stood up and blew smoke in Zar's face. He ran his gaze over the white peasant shirt, now wrinkled and soiled. "And you have blood on your shirt," he said.

"Konstantine," Olivia called softly from the doorway.

How she would rue saying that word! Her mind would repeat the sound of it, endlessly, numbingly, until she'd worn the name of the man she loved to a collection of letters. She would analyze the tone of her voice—how loudly she'd spoken; how Zar's name had felt on her lips on that occasion, so different from all the other times she'd spoken it. *Oh, why did I say anything? Why didn't I go back upstairs to check on Tim, instead of giving Konstantine away like that?*

Most of all, she would remember the effect the name had had on the two imposters.

The man with his boots on the table got to his feet at once.

Klara hardly breathed. Her bag trembled in one hand, her papers in the other.

And Zar...Already he seemed to have squared his shoulders to his fate. For they'd known at once who he was, just from his given name. It was too unusual to miss. And he'd been sought by the Gestapo for some time now.

"Konstantine Zar," said the piano-playing one, bemused. "Konstantine Zar," he repeated with derision. "*Unglaublich*...unbelievable! We've been looking for you for ages. *Fräulein!* he barked at Klara. "Bring us some wine! We must celebrate this discovery."

Klara stared at her brother through the cigarette smoke. He nodded slightly, and she left the room. She returned with two glasses, and the coveted bottle of wine that Zar bought for her once a month on the black market.

"Now, what I'd like to know," said the one in the armchair, draining his glass in one gulp, "is why the young lady was looking for a doctor." He turned to Zar. "And why you have blood on your shirt that obviously isn't yours."

After a leisurely interval, the policemen pushed by Olivia in the doorway and began to search the house.

Perhaps it was fortunate for the British pilot that he'd already bled to death in the room under the eaves, watched over only by the stars blinking through the skylight, and by the gentle keeper who had carried him home.

♦ ♦ ♦

"They took Zar away that night," said Olivia, resurfacing from her tale.

She got up and wandered over to the window, standing straight and motionless with her back to Audrey as she looked out at the ponds. Having delivered the final note of such a wrenching opera, one would have expected a legendary singer like Olivia Taverner to face her public.

After a different opera, perhaps. A make-believe one.

"We barely had a chance to say good-bye," she said, her back still turned. "I remember that he stayed at the piano for as long as he possibly could before they escorted him from the house. I don't know how Klara and I escaped their clutches. When we heard they'd imprisoned him at St.

Gilles, we knew what would happen—we knew he'd be taken from there to the Tir National. The only question was, when?"

"But what did they charge him with?" Audrey asked.

"Sedition," said Olivia.

"His lectures...his teachings..."

"Yes. They were convinced that Zar had another agenda; that he was slowly but surely gathering a following that would turn into a particularly powerful resistance."

Olivia finally left the window and returned to the love seat.

"No one can explain the randomness of human events, Audrey," she said. "I mean, why wasn't I taken away that night? Or Klara? Those of us who have had the luxury of growing old after a horror like war wonder why we did—and why those we loved didn't. The old have learned that good cannot always vanquish evil; that the reasons why some people live and others die are often so banal, no god would ever own up to them. I mean, I had a friend who was forced out of the tram by the Gestapo on a winter's evening, and made to lie face-down on the icy ground. She escaped arrest simply because the person lying next to her had forgotten his papers, and the tentacles of evil had stopped with him. People spend their whole lives asking themselves why."

Neither woman spoke again for some time. Audrey welcomed the silence. She'd immersed herself so completely in Olivia's story that part of her had become lost there, and was still roaming the Forêt de Soignes with that elusive, sky-gazing man.

Audrey regarded her hostess, and with a frisson realized that this white-haired lady—this snowbird who was happiest when she was singing—was the only actor left from the drama she'd just reenacted.

Until Audrey remembered the other remaining participant.

"Olivia?" she said.

"Yes?"

"I have something to tell you."

"Oh?"

"About Zar's piano."

CHAPTER 33

Darkness had fallen by the time Audrey emerged from the Taverner mansion. Her whole being quivered and hummed as if she had, indeed, spent the past three hours in an opera, and was entering nocturnal Brussels not as Audrey Nightingale, but as a young farm girl prone to wonderment.

She took the back streets home. The ancient city had set her past free to roam as it wished, and on this particular occasion, Audrey found herself walking beside the ghosts of 1942. Her own recent phantoms—gaunt, cadaverous or deadly—had all made way for the characters from Olivia's youth.

Find the piano, Olivia had told her as they'd parted, *and you'll uncover many truths. Don't be afraid of this journey, Audrey.* She'd been quoting Zar, and now, as Audrey strode home through the shadowy streets, his words placed him so firmly at her side that she smiled at the empty air by her shoulder.

"I've found my journey, Konstantine," she whispered.

She studied the sky as Zar would have, but clouds had inked out even the brightest stars. Dawn was at least twelve hours away. *Another twelve hours on a planet adrift in lightless space,* Audrey mused, considering how Zar, Kepler, and Pythagoras would have made profitable use of such a long night. (Florian, too, if he hadn't had to play in the opera pit.) How extraordinary that Olivia, traversing that deadly forest with only a dying man and a doomed one for company, had still summoned the lightness of spirit to imagine a lady with a lantern overhead.

Maybe there really is a grand design to the universe, Audrey thought, her step buoyant. Maybe there was still time for her to find her resonant tone.

She almost walked right past the battered white van with a buffalo head stenciled on the door.

♦ ♦ ♦

She stopped just meters away.

Nero's van was parked close to Place du Châtelain where Jonas said he'd seen it. It was a particularly lugubrious corner. Rubbish lay scattered over the cobbles, and the townhouses, chic debutantes a century ago, had aged into ill-kempt dowagers.

Audrey approached the van from behind. *The Náhoda must be inside!* Jonas and Madame Mertens had both attested to certain piano goings-on in the area.

She spotted the face in the rear-view mirror too late.

Nero was looking straight at her. He'd been on guard, apparently.

He struggled down from the driver's seat.

"Piss off!" he yelled. There was an operatic resonance to his voice, blurred by drink.

Audrey stood her ground. She lifted her chin, though her lower lip quivered. She'd known of this man for years. She'd feared the violence in him...the cruel caprice. But she'd never been this close.

He weaved toward her.

Nero gave off a cheap sheen: a lurid crimson warm-up jacket, and greasy hair gleaming under the street lamp. But there was also preternatural energy in the man, coiled and at the ready. It was like discovering stealth in a broken-down circus animal.

"What are you doing here?" he growled, drawing nearer.

Audrey balked. *I hardly know*, she was tempted to answer, when defiance sparked and she said: "I'm interested in the piano you have in your van."

Nero's eyes glistened. "Why?"

"The piano belonged to a friend," Audrey said. Her voice sounded distant, as if it were someone else's. "Well, a friend of a friend: Klara Náhoda." She watched the man closely as she added, "The woman who was murdered in Rue Nova recently."

Nero went quiet. He swayed slightly.

"It's sold," he said. He took another step toward Audrey. She could smell him now: a gamey brew of the unwashed and the underworld.

He killed a man, you know...with his bare hands... The gossiping matrons clamored in Audrey's head.

"Where can I find the person who bought the piano?" she ventured. She tried to imagine what she would do with this information. Confront the fedora man? Blackmail him by threatening to expose Klara's murder if he didn't hand over the piano? And what about the man in the overcoat? Was *he* the one to confront? Her heart withered. Pianists lacked the skills for such espionage.

Nero said, "He hired me..." A sudden confusion overcame him.

Pity stabbed at Audrey. She remembered what Rami had said: that the infant Nero had been left on a wharf in Marseille. No story of an abandoned child could leave another abandoned child unmoved. She'd never considered Nero worthy of her attention before. But at that moment, standing just a few blocks away from the church in which she herself had been discarded, the only obvious thing that distinguished Audrey from this outcast was the fact that she could play the piano, and (as far as she knew) he could not.

"Who hired you?" she demanded "The man with the hat?"

"*Oui! Le chapeau,*" said Nero. "He was obsessed." Fear laced his words as he added, "I saw him leave the house in Rue Nova. In the night..."

"What did he hire you to do?" Audrey asked. It was obvious now that the fedora man must have murdered Klara. To think that she'd actually felt some warmth for this individual, who'd tracked down a piano so intently, and gone about in the middle of winter without a coat!

"To drive," said Nero.

"He hired you to drive? *Tonight?*"

"*Zut!* Why the questions?"

"Because...oh, please!" Audrey's voice broke. "You're going to Prague, aren't you? *When?*" She reached out and touched the van. Somewhere inside it, Zar's precious instrument—the only remaining link to his legacy—was stowed like a crate of vegetables. It seemed ridiculous that she couldn't somehow claim the piano now, instead of trailing across Europe after it.

Unless this was part of her journey.

Audrey drew a sharp breath. The words had come out of nowhere. So did the image of Klara Náhoda, loyal keeper of her brother's legacy, lying at the bottom of the stairs with blood draining from her head. It would be madness to confront the author of that deed.

"Leaving on Friday," Nero said. He swayed back to the van and rummaged about the front seat, producing a folded scrap of paper which he handed to Audrey. Then he climbed into the vehicle and slammed the door in her face.

She hurried away: past Pascal's, and past the church where her life had begun so precariously, and only when she'd reached her door did she unfold the paper:

Náhoda Pianos
Kampa Island, Malá Strana
Prague

CHAPTER 34

It wasn't the sound of the cello that greeted her this time, but of men arguing.

Audrey leaned against the banister on the abbé's landing. *So the baron found Jonas in the end.* Her fingertips went cold at the thought of Van Overberg passing up these stairs. Had he followed Jonas here? Watched the house from inside a car—no doubt one of those sleek sedans with smoked windows that could be seen all over Brussels—waiting until Audrey had left?

Madame Mertens hadn't been at her post just now: an unheard-of lapse in surveillance. Perhaps she'd let Van Overberg in as she was going out, enthralled by the expensive suit (or more likely, by the title of the man who was wearing it).

Audrey slumped down on a step. Her resolve evaporated. What was it that Jonas had said about the baron? *He won't stop. Not until he sends me to jail. Or worse...*It was obvious, of course: that someone as rich as Van Overberg wouldn't have the slightest interest in whether or not Jonas returned the eighty thousand euros. No. He was after bigger game: character; reputation; *soul.*

She flinched at a sharp escalation from upstairs.

Despite the general roughness of Jonas's character, his soul was probably the tenderest that Audrey had ever encountered, and would make light work for the baron.

She crept up the stairs.

"Haven't you ever made a mistake in your entire, goddamned, perfect life?" Jonas was saying.

Audrey perched on the top step outside her door. She was so terrified to go in that she didn't consider how strange this comment seemed.

"You don't give a shit about anyone else," Jonas went on. His voice echoed out to the landing. "All you care about is people fawning over you. Arrogant prick!"

What a reckless thing to say to Van Overberg!

"We had such a precious resource, too: Audrey Nightingale." Jonas's voice suddenly sounded more like his cello.

What do I have to do with it?

"I don't think you ever really appreciated her," continued the cello-voice. "Maybe to have someone to spout your irrelevant ideas to. There isn't another woman in the universe who would listen to your bullshit about Pythagoras—and all those other dead guys."

He can't be talking to Van Overberg...

The garret went quiet. Then finally the other one spoke:

"Are you quite finished?"

Florian.

Audrey sagged with relief.

"You are selfish," Florian began. "Ill-disciplined, unreliable, and shallow. And you have the basest appetites of anyone I know.

"I can play the cello, though," Jonas riposted.

"It's just like you to make light of it all!" Florian snapped. "You've ruined two lives—mine and Audrey's—well, three, if you count your own. And probably numerous others, as well. Female ones, of course. Because you just can't help yourself."

Audrey opened the door.

♦ ♦ ♦

The men were standing at opposite ends of the garret, rooted at their positions. Their faces burned: Florian's, with self-righteous affront; Jonas's, with the heat of his wounds, which looked worse than they had earlier.

"Audrey!"

"Süsslein!"

She threw her coat and hat on the sofa and went over to feel Jonas's forehead. "You have a fever," she said. "I'll get you more aspirin. And lie down, for heaven's sake!"

Jonas did as he was told.

Florian wandered over to the piano and played a few random notes. He was still wearing his coat, his violin slung over his shoulder.

"Olivia said that you'd been to see her," he said. "I thought I'd drop by to ask how it went." He glanced over at the form sprawled on the sofa. "I didn't know he was here."

Audrey brought a cool wet cloth for Jonas's forehead, two aspirins, and a glass of water. "You'll have to go to the doctor if your fever doesn't go down," she said. "Your face is more swollen than before."

Jonas groaned and said nothing.

Audrey gave each man a long, frank stare.

"We are better than this," she said.

An eerie calm filled the room.

"Just now," she went on, "the two of you broke your vows as musicians."

The calm took on a questioning edge.

Audrey joined Florian at the piano, clambered onto the stool and opened the skylight. "You've frightened away my pigeons with all your discord," she said. She climbed down, fetched some stale bread from the kitchen and clambered up again to leave it the gutter. "They'll be back in the morning."

The men still said nothing. Florian took his violin case from his shoulder and drifted to the kitchen.

Audrey sat on the piano stool and folded her hands in her lap. "We must set an example," she said. "As musicians we are obliged to live as Music does. With integrity. In harmony with our fellows. In tune with our finer natures."

"Konstantine Zar..." Florian murmured.

"Who?" Jonas asked, struggling up on the sofa. "Anyway, he has a point."

"*Had*," Florian corrected him. "He was executed during the war."

Audrey leafed through a pile of scores on the piano and pulled out Mendelssohn's Trio No. 1 in D Minor.

"I'm glad you brought your violin, Florian," she said. She fetched two music stands from the corner and set the string parts on them.

The men gaped at her.

"But Süsslein..." Jonas began.

Audrey ignored them. Standing there at her piano with her eyes trained far beyond the men, she could, indeed, have graced the prow of any ship.

"You may have forgotten." she said. "But when we became musicians, we gained special powers. To heal. Comfort. Unite. Dear friends. Let us pick up where we left off three years ago."

This was a gamble, she knew. She was treading on invidious ground. Neither man seemed in the mood for healing or uniting. Regardless, Audrey opened the scores to the slow movement. Then she sat down at the piano and waited.

Without comment, Jonas took out his instrument and tuned. Florian, still hesitant despite Audrey's astonishing foray into ancient philosophy, did the same. The men fetched kitchen chairs and took their places. Neither acknowledged the other. It was the most fragile sort of truce: a mere lowering of weapons.

Audrey played an A for them to tune. *This was a stupid idea*, she thought. She glanced up at the skylight, surprised to see the pigeons there—all three of them, hours before sunrise, not eating the crumbs she'd set out for them but looking in, like muses.

She began.

It was one of those long, suspended melodies given wings not by the composer himself, but by the force that had guided him: a melody that would span the entire arc of sky if given the chance.

The strings were supposed to pick up the tune in tight harmony. Instead, a ragged wailing filled the garret. Audrey tried not to react. Her own solo had been substandard, after all. Obviously no one had touched the piece in three years. And then there was the lingering rancor: one of the most corrosive substances in existence, that eats away at compassion and civility as handily as acid on flesh.

They were more like a pick-up ensemble than the celebrated Kepler Players.

Faltering, they soldiered on to the end of the movement.

Audrey glanced up: the pigeons had disappeared.

Jonas said, "That was the worst thing we've ever done."

"Yes. But at least we did it," Audrey countered.

Florian stood up, stretched, and astonished even himself by giving Jonas a quick pat on the shoulder.

The three of them tarried in silence, as if not to awaken this infant concord.

Audrey turned from the keyboard. "I almost forgot to tell you," she said. "The rosewood piano is going to Prague. And you two are going with me to recover it."

PART II

CHAPTER 35

Johannes Kepler did much wandering along Europe's rutted byways before arriving in Prague in 1600. Weil-der-Stadt. Leonberg. Tübingen. Linz. Graz. Ancient towns that once fashioned the great patchwork quilt of the Holy Roman Empire and that now, in prettified modern Germany and Austria, still offered peeks at their turbulent histories. It was in this part of the world that Kepler was born, grew up, studied a wide array of subjects including music and astronomy, taught mathematics, and made astrological charts for the rich and powerful to help pay the bills.

Kepler wandered much greater distances in his mind, as it turned out. Perhaps this was normal for a man constrained by poor health and tragic family circumstances; for a deep thinker who lived at a time of ignorance and suspicion. Witches were still burnt at the stake in Kepler's neighborhood—a fate narrowly avoided by his own mother. Books were destroyed; ideas stamped out. The Thirty Years' War loomed on the horizon, pitting Protestants against Catholics and ultimately costing Europe eight million souls.

And yet passion blazed in Kepler: for learning; for the night sky; and for that most glorious, mathematical harmony that he claimed ordered the cosmos, and might even eclipse humanity's barbaric neighings one day if people only stopped to listen to it.

Perhaps it was no coincidence that Kepler completed his epic work, *Harmonices Mundi*, just as religious violence was once again spilling its poison over the land—just days, in fact, after the Defenestration of Prague on May 23, 1618, when Bohemian Protestants threw three Hapsburg Catholics from a window of Prague Castle, sparking the Thirty Years' War. (The men survived, as it happened, having fallen onto a large pile of dung.)

♦ ♦ ♦

"Interesting stuff, Florian," Audrey said, watching the verdant hills and farms of southern Germany slip by the train window. "Music was as important as science back then, wasn't it?"

Her friend had been enlightening her about Kepler on their journey from Brussels to Prague via Weil-der-Stadt, the great scientist's birthplace.

"But let's return to this century for a moment," she added wryly. "Do you really think that Jonas is all right?"

"If he avoids talking, moving, eating, and generally being Jonas, yes," Florian said.

Everyone had agreed that the cellist should travel separately. Van Overberg wouldn't give up until he'd fulfilled his vendetta. Traveling as a trio, complete with musical instruments, wouldn't have afforded them much cover. Florian and Audrey took the cello with them on their train, therefore, and Jonas would meet them late that afternoon on the town square of Weil-der-Stadt, where one of Olivia's contacts would pick them up.

Money. Car. Rehearsals. Concerts to pay their way... The first item had turned out to be the most meager pooling of resources. The second hadn't materialized at all. And the last two...well, most professional ensembles could pull their repertoire together within a few days. But after three years? And with only the faintest thaw between the string players? They'd planned to rehearse at Olivia's, on the Bösendorfer. But the grande dame had had a sudden a change of heart. She'd claimed she was unwell; and she hadn't offered them any money as they'd hoped she might.

"Do you think Olivia's sick?" Audrey asked. "Or just hiding herself away?" She broke off a piece of the cheese sandwich she'd bought at the Brussels Midi station and offered it to Florian.

"It was probably all that talk about Zar," he said.

Audrey set her sandwich down. Stricken, she stared out the window. It was she, after all, who'd gone back to the Taverner house and coaxed Olivia's tragic love story from her.

"She never got over him, did she?" Audrey said.

"No." There was so much implied by that tiny word that Audrey marveled at how coolly Florian had uttered it. Of course, he hadn't made the journey that she had, trailing after Zar and Olivia on their fateful walk through the forest.

"It was kind of her to make that contact for us," Florian said. "Friedrich Graf hails from the days of the Taverner salon, apparently. He's supposed to meet us this afternoon. Olivia said he might arrange a concert for us." He turned to Audrey. "We can't play as the Kepler Players anymore, of course. We'll have to find a name that isn't so badly sullied."

To everyone's surprise, Madame Mertens had stepped in to facilitate their departure. It turned out that the old badger had hidden talents. She'd shown admirable nursing abilities, somehow managing to pry Audrey's duct tape from Jonas's face and dress his wounds properly. She'd also revealed a gift for subterfuge—perhaps not surprising given her profession. The tiny eyes shone when she'd learned that someone of Van Overberg's stature might bring his villainy to her house and she'd be required to intervene.

The landlady borrowed one of the old abbé's clerical outfits and draped this over Jonas when he'd left for the station. The disguise came with a wide-brimmed black hat that could be pulled low over an injured face, which might have been more conspicuous than Jonas himself had the abbé, in a show of priestly fraternity, not consented to accompany the cellist to the taxi in his own clerical robes. Jonas had played the part with gusto. He'd patted the abbé on the back, as if they were old drinking pals, and even crossed himself a few times for good measure. As for the real priest, he'd been happy to help. He'd spent too many hours listening to the cello upstairs not to realize that saintliness came in many vessels—even in a flawed one like Jonas—and therefore, technically, the ruse was not a sin.

CHAPTER 36

Jonas was waiting for them by the fountain on the market square. Audrey and Florian approached wheeling two suitcases and carrying two instruments. The wheels clattered so loudly over the cobbles that surely a ghost must have been jolted awake somewhere on the dormant square, and was even then peering out at them from under a Renaissance eave.

Florian handed Jonas the cello, who embraced his instrument as he might a lost lover. "Süsslein!" he gushed, and greeted Audrey in the same way.

"No sign of our contact yet?" she asked.

Jonas shook his head. "Damn, it's cold!" He had no hat, and the leather jacket afforded little warmth. His scrappy beard was festooned with frozen droplets. Madame Mertens's bandages flashed white in the gloom.

"Where's your disguise?" Florian asked him.

"In my suitcase."

"It might make you warmer...and holier."

Jonas ignored him. "OK, let me get this straight: we're jeopardizing our careers to track down the piano of some long-dead mystic all the way to Prague, using an address scribbled by a drunken convict, and trying to avoid a dangerous character along the way who might have murdered the mystic's sister."

"What careers?" said Florian "Anyway, isn't it time we take some risks again?"

Jonas patted his bandages. "I've already taken them, thank you very much."

"Are you sure we're supposed to meet Graf here?" Audrey asked

"That's what Olivia told me," Florian said.

Jonas added: "Are we invited to dinner?"

They sat close together on the edge of the empty fountain. A dusting of snow lay in little half-moons on each of the myriad cobblestones and capped the undulating roof tiles all around the square. Hibernation enveloped every gable and shopfront. The last car had driven away some time ago, and were it not for the green LED pharmacy sign, it would have been difficult to know which century it was, exactly.

Things wouldn't have looked much different on December 27, 1571, when Katharina Kepler had gone into labor in the narrow, timbered house just behind the fountain: a troublesome, seven-month birth for a quarrelsome, hard-headed woman. Ironically, one of the few things that would not have been on the square at the time was the statue of Kepler himself, a handsome, pensive rendition from 1870.

Florian could barely contain his excitement. "You know," he bubbled. "Believing in the Music of the Spheres was not the extraordinary lapse it might seem for such a brilliant scientist. After all, Kepler understood gravity, and introduced the science of optics. What made him great was his openness to other dimensions of his subject. Remember that music was one of the pillars of Kepler's rigorous liberal arts education, along with grammar, logic, rhetoric, arithmetic, geometry, and astronomy."

"You should have been a professor," Jonas moaned, his lips deathly in the cold.

Florian said, "Did you know that thirty-eight witches were executed on this spot between 1615 and 1629?"

The comment hit its mark.

"How?" Jonas sat up straighter and blew on his hands.

"Burnt alive."

The three musicians pressed closer together on the edge of the fountain, Audrey providing a buffer between the other two. No one dared to admit that a blazing bonfire would have been very welcome at that juncture.

"Who is this Friedrich Graf, Florian?" Audrey asked.

"Olivia didn't say much about him. Only that they met in Brussels when he was a student. He's an unusual man, she said. He lives alone in the forest like some kind of gnome."

"Hmm. How much does he know about our real mission?"

"Recovering Zar's piano, you mean?" Florian asked.

"Yes...and the fact that Klara's murderer is probably involved in this whole thing."

"Olivia said she told him only that we're going to Prague for a concert."

Jonas guffawed. "He must be the only person on Earth who didn't hear about the demise of the Kepler Players!"

A frisson passed over Audrey as she considered that they might face a peril as grave as Klara's if they weren't discreet about their plans.

Florian read her thoughts. "I'm not sure how well Olivia knows Graf," he said. "And there's something fishy about the business with Zar's piano, after all."

Headlights swept the bottom of the square and a vehicle came into view.

"That must be him," said Audrey.

An antique VW van spluttered up to the Kepler monument and stalled.

CHAPTER 37

In person-years, the vehicle was probably about the same age as its owner—eighty, more or less—although Friedrich Graf seemed to have a much healthier engine. He bustled with the earnestness of someone who has much to do, and increasingly little time to do it in.

"Ah, my friends!" Graf exclaimed, getting out of the van. "Here you are! Hello! Welcome!" Graf's French was lilting; Bavarian. "My goodness...the Kepler Players in person!"

"We're no longer the Kepler Players," Florian said under his breath.

"Welcome to the birthplace of your namesake!" Graf enthused, oblivious. "But you must be exhausted. Come, let me help you." He grabbed two of the suitcases. "You didn't drop your bags at the *Gasthaus* yet?" He gestured to one of the old buildings on the square. "Never mind, you can do that after dinner. How is lovely Olivia, by the way?"

Graf was rotund, florid, balding. His eyes, of the most inquiring blue, held their brilliance in the twilight like mountain tarns. He wore a woodsman's coat and tall, dark-green boots, as if he'd been out shooting pheasants.

Audrey answered the bag question: "The lady at the guest house said we have until 10 p.m. to check in"; while Florian obfuscated about Olivia: "She's rather tired—maybe a bit depressed. She's just lost a friend. But you must know that, of course..." Jonas simply beamed at this individual who still seemed to be clutching life by two horns, even at his age.

"What on earth have you done to your face, for God's sake?" Graf said to him in German. Then, with a wink, "Don't worry, there's plenty of anesthetic at my place—of the drinkable variety, *natürlich!* And I'll get you back to the *Gasthaus* early enough for a good night's sleep."

There ensued the usual confusion of unacquainted people getting into a vehicle, complicated by luggage and musical instruments, and in this case, by the vehicle itself.

"Oh, come now, Pamina dear," Graf said to the van. "We have visitors." He coaxed the diesel into a sort of death rattle. Audrey, in the passenger seat, watched him wield the stick shift as a sort of divining rod to find the right gear. In the absence of seatbelts, Florian and Jonas bounced with abandon on the back seat. Each clutched his instrument for ballast. There was a sickly smell of rotting plastic, into which Graf's brisk cologne had thankfully made some inroads.

"Professor Graf," Audrey began.

"Friedrich, please!"

"Friedrich...We're so grateful that Olivia spoke to you on our behalf."

"Oh, I'm very fond of musicians." Graf's glance took in Audrey's fine profile and rested with even more admiration on the stubby hands in her lap. "The best pianists have hands like yours," he said.

Florian leaned forward to catch the conversation. "Did you study music, Friedrich?"

"My subjects are philosophy and history," Graf said. "I'm professor emeritus at the University of Tübingen. But I contemplated becoming a musician. I studied a bit of conducting in my youth." He puffed slightly. "In Brussels. With Reginald Taverner, in fact."

"Olivia's husband!" Florian cried over the roar of the engine.

"Olivia's superb, of course," said Graf, then chuckled. "But goodness me, Taverner was a colossal ass...may he rest in peace."

Camaraderie burgeoned as they jounced through the outskirts of Weil-der-Stadt.

"Olivia told me you're on your way to Prague for a concert," Graf said. "Tomorrow I'll drive you to a mutual friend of ours who lives near the Czech border: Countess Gloria von Helden. Maybe you've heard of her. She's a great patron of the arts. She used to frequent the Taverner salon in its heyday. She organizes a chamber festival every summer, as you might know. She's generally off skiing at this time of year, but agreed to invite some of her friends to hear you tomorrow.

The musicians gave a collective gasp. "*Tomorrow?!*"

Never had they performed at such short notice. They'd counted on another week at least to resuscitate the trio.

There'd been time for only a few rehearsals before leaving Brussels—and in Audrey's garret, alas. Her piano was no Bösendorfer. Three strings had snapped in quick succession during an allegro, like a corset ripping. Wrong notes swarmed. Florian and Jonas were out of tune with each other most of the time—musically, and in every other way. Relief had come in the form of Madame Mertens, who'd struggled up the six flights of stairs bearing tureens of carbonnade and fish soup, and numerous bottles of wine and beer. These she'd left outside Audrey's door so as not to disturb the artists. But sometimes she would linger there, a mysterious youthfulness lighting her face.

"A single listener is all you need to close the magic circle," Audrey said as she carried the food to the kitchen.

"The magic circle..." Florian echoed.

"Yes: between the player and audience. Your great-aunt taught us that, Florian."

♦ ♦ ♦

"Gloria usually asks for donations at the door for her private concerts," Graf said. "She has a large castle, you know. And some very rich friends. You may well earn enough tomorrow night for your whole trip. It's not unusual for people to drop one hundred euro bills in the urn she leaves at the door. She said she still remembers coming to a concert of the Kepler Players in Stuttgart years ago."

"Really?" said Jonas, who'd perked up at the mention of his hometown.

"Is that so?" Florian said, perking up at the mention of one hundred euro bills.

"We can no longer play as the Kepler Players, Friedrich," Audrey added. "It's too...well...dangerous for Jonas." She instantly regretted bringing attention to Jonas's plight.

"Nonsense!" Graf chortled. "I saw what happened. Everyone did. But everyone knows Van Overberg is deranged. And people have such short memories. Gloria's crowd will adore you, whatever name you play under."

"So you met Olivia through Reginald Taverner, then?" Jonas asked, eager to change the subject.

"Yes," Graf replied. "I had the great privilege to be invited to one of their salon concerts, in the late 1950s." Suddenly his demeanor changed. A heavy mantle descended on him as he said, "I met Klara Náhoda at that concert."

The van fell silent.

"What a terrible, terrible business," Graf said at length, shaking his head. "Olivia told me what happened."

"Yes," said Audrey.

"A robbery gone wrong—that's what the police said, according to Olivia. Though there was no sign of a break-in, apparently. Klara seemed to have let her aggressor in. I'm surprised that Roland wasn't with her.

"Roland?" Florian said.

"Yes. Roland Wilmots. A sort of general factotum Klara's had for ages. I met him about fifteen years ago when I visited her in Brussels. He did her grocery shopping, paperwork, house repairs. That kind of thing. He was incredibly loyal."

More silence. Although this time it carried an odd resonance, as if a low, mournful bell-tone had been struck in honor of Klara Náhoda

CHAPTER 38

Soon the town of Weil-der-Stadt lay behind them. Winter fields slept, while distant, forested knolls stood vigilant in the gloaming. The van's grinding progress intruded upon the landscape like a chainsaw in a church. Graf made his way along the sinuous river, crossing it a few times over bridges hundreds of years old. No doubt the river was a refreshing delight on a summer's day, shaded by oaks and linden as thick-set as the bridges. But now the water beckoned to no one. The trees were naked and skeletal, and the river itself, a remote, steely thread, guarded memories too bleak to reveal.

They rode along without speaking until Audrey said, "Was Klara a pianist, Friedrich?"

"Oh, I don't think she played—despite her connection with the Náhoda piano maker. She existed entirely in her brother's shadow."

"What courage she must have had!" Audrey went on. "Coming to Brussels on her own like that to join her brother. In wartime. And so young." She made no mention of the piano Klara had accompanied to Brussels in a German transport truck. Olivia had not apprised Graf of the trio's real mission, it seemed, and Audrey worried that in light of what had happened to Klara, their quest for her piano might seem crass and selfish—just an excuse for three soon-to-be-middle-aged musicians to get out of Brussels and escape their own obscurity.

Graf muscled the van into low gear. "Here we are," he said.

Audrey caught her breath: the forest had appeared without warning. With the twisted logic of a fairytale, Graf accelerated toward the impenetrable green-black wall and drove directly into it. *What lay on the other side? Would they ever make it out again?*

The lurching and rattling that commenced seemed never to end. They plunged into craters and roared their way back out again. Even Graf's high beams could penetrate only a few meters ahead. Trees crowded in, their branches fringed like great wings: conifers soaring darkly in the manner that the Black Forest was famous for. Beyond the van's lights, the route had no earthly dimension. Whatever had tied the four travelers to the outside world seemed to have been well and truly severed.

In a show of solidarity, Florian put a hand on Audrey's right shoulder, and Jonas squeezed her left one. This bolstered her spirits considerably. Chamber playing, after all, had as much to do with the human ensemble as the musical one—especially when the ensemble in question had landed in an ensorcelled forest with only this singular guide to bring them out again.

Graf braked suddenly and cut the engine.

"Is that your house?" Audrey exclaimed.

♦ ♦ ♦

The headlights illuminated a boisterous stream tumbling around boulders, and on the other side of it, what appeared to be an old millhouse: a defunct waterwheel stood near the front door. The house itself was a fantastical jumble of gothic gables, chimneys and cupolas, all sprouting from an earth-centered core. The seat of a woodland enchanter, perhaps?

He lives alone in the forest like some kind of gnome.

Their host took a flashlight from the glove compartment and led them over the stream via a narrow wooden walkway.

"You can see why I get so excited about visitors," he chuckled.

Audrey paused on the bridge mid-way. She breathed in the zest of damp pine, and lost herself in the din of the torrent. Did the universe make such a sound? *Did the womb?* Upstream, the forest towered ever-higher and eventually crested on a ridge. Light suffused the sky here, and Audrey realized that behind the clouds, the moon was full. Its glow was enough to stage-light a boulder here, a rotting trunk there, all covered in the most luxurious moss. Winter seemed to have been shut out on the other side of the green-black wall.

"I hope he doesn't plan to cook us up for supper," Jonas muttered, shouldering his cello through the front door.

"I bought the place years ago, intending to renovate it," Graf said, taking their coats in the dim, mildewed entry. He beckoned them into what surely was an enchanter's drawing-room. The space was the size of a great hall, with a distant, shadowy ceiling.

"Alas, I couldn't find a contractor willing to come all the way out here," their host explained. "So I did some things myself—the shelves, for instance." He swept his arm to indicate the wall of books, a graceful gesture not surprising, perhaps, for a student of Reginald Taverner. "With the rest, I decided just to let the forest do what it will."

In one corner of the room, a staircase spiraled up to what one could only imagine was a labyrinth of hallways and dead-ends. Large skylights opened the main room to the crowns of the trees and presumably, on a starry night, to a generous sweep of sky. Oak and pine had been used for every detail, so the house was quite literally at one with the forest. The stream passed under one side of the structure on its way to the millwheel.

Its rushing filled the air like a distant surf, though the sound was in itself a kind of silence.

Graf set about coaxing a blaze in the stone fireplace.

"You must get lonely out here," Audrey said, rubbing her hands in front of the fire.

Graf turned to her. His eyes sparkled. He was wielding the fire iron more like a magician than a conducting student.

"One can never truly be lonely in the presence of the sky," he said. "Especially at night."

They helped Graf draw four mismatched armchairs closer to the fire.

"But where are my manners?" he said. "You must be in dire need of refreshment!" He bustled away to a kitchen area separated from the huge space by a low wooden partition.

Jonas followed in his wake. Soon there was the commotion of drawers and pans, a hammering of schnitzels, and great merriment as the two men fell into their native language.

◆ ◆ ◆

Florian and Audrey drifted along the wooden divider. Arrayed on top of it was an astonishing collection of crystals, carved figurines, Roman coins, fossils, and pottery shards. The musicians stopped at a small wooden box with a glass top, in which a slim piece of bone lay on a bed of velvet.

Graf brought over a tray crowded with various beers and wines, as Jonas followed with bowls of nuts and chips. They set these things on the divider near the glass-topped box. Graf served the drinks, and motioned for them to help themselves to snacks.

"I'm not really supposed to have that," he said sheepishly, indicating the item in the box. "It's on loan from the university. I have a close friend who was on the archaeological team that found it. I'm writing an article about it, in fact."

"A flute?" Audrey asked, peering through the glass.

"Ah, but not just any flute!" Graf sparkled.

"Prehistoric?" said Florian.

"It's 40,000 years old."

To their astonishment, Graf opened the glass lid and picked up the flute with his bare hands.

"It's made from a hollow bone of the griffon vulture," he said. "It was found in a cave not far from here."

He handed the flute to his visitors, who passed it from one to the other without lingering, as if the object might spring to life at any moment. The bone was skinny, only eight inches long or so, and crude. Had it not been for the five evenly-spaced holes carved along it, anyone would have confused it with dinner scraps.

Audrey held the flute longer than the others. It seemed weightless, lying there across her palms. She tried to comprehend something so old that even the ghost of its creator had aged and died.

Graf gave her a knowing look. "I think that a woman carved it," he said.

Audrey closed her eyes and imagined that woman: dark-haired, restless, fiddling with the cold piece of bone just for something to do on a winter's night. Outside the cave was an ice-world that seemed so empty— so in need of a kind of warmth that fire couldn't provide. An errant wind sighed through the hollow bone as the woman held it. She closed her eyes as Audrey had, for she, too, had felt her soul stir.

"Yes, I think you're right," Audrey said dreamily. "I think that a woman did fashion this."

She handed the flute back to Graf. Everyone watched with amazement as he put the notched end to his lips and blew. Suddenly forty millennia collapsed into a dense, alchemized substance. The sound he made glinted, like a shard of light left over from some cosmic event.

Graf produced more breath than tone at first. But gradually, lilting and spare, a melody emerged from the relic. The three friends stared at each other, wide-eyed.

"Schubert!" Audrey gasped. "*An die Musik*, isn't it? *Oh lovely art, in how many bleak hours have you carried me away to a better world…*It was one of the lieder that Olivia sang in her first recital, during the Occupation."

Graf winked at her as he played.

*Schubert…*That dark-haired woman could have played the same melody on this very flute forty thousand years ago, had Schubert not been destined to discover it first.

Graf ended his prehistoric recital with a mournful, beseeching wail. Audrey swallowed hard. She realized that that single note—that most fragile plea—had traveled tirelessly across the breadth of time to be with them that evening, only to have to make the exhausting journey back again.

Graf wiped the bone with a cloth and put it back in its box. He turned to Audrey, as if he'd read her thoughts:

"Even a single note can carry the truth," he said.

"Yes," she murmured. She glanced up through a skylight, where branches splayed against the soft glow of a moon that was, she mused, more or less as bright as a lantern.

CHAPTER 39

What I've always wanted to know," said Jonas, his mouth full of schnitzel, "is why nobody can actually hear cosmic music."

They were seated at the kitchen table near the stove, for which Graf apologized, but that much to Jonas's delight allowed for an efficient restocking of food and drink. Graf turned out to be an exemplary cook for a forest bachelor: the schnitzels were light and crispy, and the fries could have seduced the most discerning Belgian.

Graf topped up everyone's wine and smiled at Jonas. "Can you hear the stream?" he asked.

Jonas reddened. "The stream?"

"Of course!"

Forks in mid-air, they all stopped chewing to listen.

Jonas said, "You mean that whooshing sound in the background?"

Graf smiled again. "Exactly. The whooshing, as you call it. Someone once said that the soul carries with it the memory of the music it knew in the sky, and like those born next to a rushing stream, people no longer notice the sound."

Graf cleared the table, leaving the wine glasses, and put on a pot of coffee.

"The notion of celestial music goes back to Pythagoras, as you know," he said, scraping the schnitzel pan into the rubbish bin.

"Yes!" exclaimed Florian. His cheeks flushed with this union of physical and intellectual nourishment. "The fact that the movements of the heavenly bodies were regular meant that they were subject to a certain order—as musical intervals have a mathematical order. Heavenly motions must create harmonious music, it was reasoned."

"Precisely," said Graf, "As far as we know, Pythagoras understood the Music of the Spheres as single tones. Each planet sounded its own note. It seemed logical that such enormous objects must make some kind of noise when they moved. Kepler, on the other hand, claimed that the music of the planets was polyphonous—several tones in harmony with each other. He came up with detailed ratios of planetary movements that corresponded with actual musical intervals. They were astonishingly close to the intervals used in music today."

Graf turned from the counter, where he'd been setting dessert plates out on a tray. "Kepler never lost sight of the beauty of it all, though," he said, his eyes momentarily misty. "He was a devout man: he believed that a divine creator was responsible for the phenomena he was studying as a scientist—even though the Church and science were on a collision course." Graf regarded the musicians one after the other. "Beauty and harmony hold the secrets of life...of our place in the universe."

Jonas said, "What happened to all that? To the Music of the Spheres, I mean?"

Audrey regarded her friend with surprise. Such a comment would have been unthinkable from Jonas three years ago.

"Well," said Graf. "Consider the world back then. Our ancestors lived at a time when humans still regarded the sky with wonder."

His guests all glanced up at the skylights.

"Wonder..." echoed Audrey, sipping her Riesling.

"Yes," Graf said quietly. "But such a time will probably never come again, I'm afraid. Scientists have made sure of that: there must be a rational explanation for everything these days." He sighed, and added, "Our age is too cynical and utilitarian to go back to revering the sky. Primitive, too. We haven't even figured out how to stop killing each other yet."

Audrey considered the sky above Graf's house—the same one that Kepler had studied over four hundred years ago, just a few miles from here. Maybe on a late-February night such as this, with the hush of the fields all around him, and awe brightening his weak, astigmatic eyes. Could four hundred years really stamp out such reverence? Scientists considered Kepler one of their own. And yet he'd spent his whole life considering the heavens with equal measures of logic and mysticism.

Audrey nodded to Graf, who was holding the bottle of Riesling over her glass. *Exploring the marvelous*, she thought. *That's what our trio used to do.* Kepler probably never lost his sense of wonder. Not even on his deathbed with fever (he'd suffered from so many). As he'd slipped into delirium on November 15, 1630, Audrey imagined that he'd found comfort not so much in the priest who'd been summoned to his side, but in the knowledge that he would soon find himself in those splendid skies he'd spent his whole life studying, where Music herself would see to his comfortable and airy accommodation.

"There's one thing that Pythagoras, Kepler, and all the religions agreed on," Graf said, his natural effervescence returning. "That is, that our better natures exist over our heads somewhere. Hopefully, not as far away as the heavenly bodies," he laughed. "Musicians agree on this, too—the good ones, I mean." He acknowledged his guests with deference.

"Did some kind of god create this heavenly music?" Jonas asked, distracted by the baking pan with a cloth draped over it that he'd spotted on the counter. "*Apfelstrudel?*" he whispered to Graf, who nodded.

"The Demiurge," said Florian. "That's what Plato called his idea of god. It means 'craftsman'. Not a bad name, is it? It was the first deity we know of who supposedly crafted humans with an immortal soul distinct from their bodies. And this soul possessed pre-existing knowledge—that is, knowledge known to the creator."

"Kepler..." Graf muttered.

"Pardon?" Florian said.

"Kepler believed that the human mind, because it reflected the mind of God, was inherently capable of understanding cosmic harmony."

"It's funny," said Jonas. "You'd think that musicians could hear it all the time. But we can't."

"I heard it once," Florian said, as if speaking in a church. "Onstage. At the Europa concert, of all places."

The revelation stunned his colleagues. How could the Europa concert, which had been an unmitigated catastrophe in Florian's eyes, have left him with this epiphany?

No one spoke for a while.

"I felt it too," Jonas offered timidly.

Everyone gaped at him.

"So did I," Audrey whispered.

Graf busied himself with the dessert tray, then said, "How lucky you all are, spending your lives with the last great mystery."

He poured coffee and put the cups on the tray, indicating to Jonas to bring the apple strudel over to the fireplace.

♦ ♦ ♦

They settled into the mismatched armchairs, munching strudel and watching the flames nip at the chimney's void. Night deepened outside; the forest pressed against the house. It wasn't difficult to imagine this place without walls at all—to believe that they were actually sitting on the mossy rocks next to the stream, as embers rose up from the fire and returned to their inchoate source.

"Your philosophy is very much in line with Konstantine Zar's, Friedrich," said Florian, and complimented Graf on his strudel. "Surely Olivia must have mentioned him."

That name again, thought Audrey. *The name that altered every space it was uttered in.*

Graf responded, "Actually, it was Klara who told me all about her brother,"

"Olivia mentioned that Klara attended all of Zar's lectures," Audrey said. "But that her notes didn't survive. Does that mean his legacy vanished? How tragic!"

"Yes, that's true," said Graf, sipping his coffee. "It was, indeed, tragic." He got up to take a photograph from a shelf and handed it to Audrey. "This is Klara. You can see that she was the sort of person who would die with her secrets intact."

Audrey met the stare of the woman in the picture. Klara Náhoda was a closed door, no doubt about it: chin, forehead, regard—all tightly shut. The soaring angles that had distinguished her brother's face were flat and low on hers. Small, suspicious eyes were shaded by brows that were masculine; forbidding. It was impossible to imagine a smile on that face—or even the emotions that might lead to one. And though the photo was only a portrait, one could well imagine the body beneath it: square and solid.

A peasant's frame. The only nod to femininity was the brooch Klara wore on her plain frock: a spray of jewels in the shape of a flower.

"I see what you mean," Audrey said.

"You can probably understand that she was fiercely jealous of Olivia. Not just of her beauty, but of her hold over Zar."

"It's a lovely brooch," said Audrey, and passed the photograph to her friends.

"It was her grandmother's," said Graf. "She never wore it, of course. Only for photographs. And there weren't many of those."

"Hmm. I wouldn't mess with her," Jonas said. He rued his misstep at once.

Graf put the photograph back on the shelf and began to pace the room. "Well, someone did mess with her," he said. "And regretted it."

Their silence was an invitation.

Without hesitating, Graf accepted.

CHAPTER 40

It was 1955, I believe," Graf began, still wandering about the room. "I first met Klara Náhoda at one of Olivia's salon concerts. After that, she would invite me for tea occasionally. She'd already been living at the house in Rue Nova since a few years after the war. I was intimidated at first by her severity. You'd think she'd dismiss one of Taverner's hapless students. But we'd formed a connection. She trusted me.

"We would talk in her kitchen, where she served me tea. I was amazed by the lack of furniture around the place. Except a piano, naturally. Her brother's: a gorgeous rosewood instrument. Simple. Classy."

Audrey glanced at her companions. Collectively, without a word, they agreed not to mention the piano and see where Graf was taking them.

"Klara told me about her brother's deep attachment to the instrument," he went on. "He was worried that something might happen to it. After they arrested him, she considered herself its keeper. She treated it as if it were flesh and blood...as if it were a manifestation of Zar himself."

Graf paused. "I know what you're wondering," he said. "Yes, I suppose I did fall for Klara. Well, not for her, exactly. I was fifteen years her junior, after all. But for the extraordinary enigma that was her brother. Maybe I felt I could get closer to him through her. The more she told me about Zar, the more mesmerized I became. He might have been young, but his ideas were those of a great sage."

"Friedrich, you said that someone...um...*messed* with Klara," Jonas said. "What did you mean?"

Graf stoked the fire and returned to his chair. "As you may know, the Gestapo took Zar away after he and Olivia rescued an English pilot in the Forêt de Soignes. It was early in 1942."

"According to Olivia, Zar was executed for sedition," said Audrey.

Graf stared into the fire. "Indeed. Well, what she didn't tell you—because she never knew—is that Zar was already being sought by the Gestapo. For murder."

The word paralyzed the room.

Graf waited, then continued: "You must know by now that Zar was a great walker. But I'm not sure even Olivia knew that Klara was, too. Restless Hungarian roots, I suppose. Anyway, she had guts, that girl. She walked by herself, in all weather. Like her brother did. She told me her story in 1957 because she'd been guarding the truth for long enough, she said—almost fifteen years.

"About a month before Olivia and Zar came across the pilot, Klara was assaulted by a German officer on one of her walks, near a munition depot in the Forêt de Soignes. He talked her up. Then he molested her..."

Graf faltered. "Then he raped her."

Audrey set down her cup. She clasped her hands in her lap. It seemed she'd only recently paid a visit to that part of the forest herself, through Olivia's story.

"Klara didn't arrive home until well after dark," said Graf. "Naturally, Zar was beside himself with worry. The curfew was in place. It was the period of the war when Allied planes were bombing strategic zones around Brussels—train stations, factories, munitions. Bomb shelters were dotted all around the city. People were asked to leave their front doors unlocked during air raids so that passersby could take shelter.

"This was the mood of the time, my friends," said Graf, regarding his guests. "This was the fear that poisoned everyone's life. Klara told me she would have made up a story—any story—so that Zar wouldn't discover the truth. But she had bruises on her face; her clothes were ripped. She was in shock. It was obvious what had happened.

"Zar changed after that. He barely communicated with anyone. He stopped going to the conservatory; he even stopped giving lectures. I think he already knew what he was going to do and didn't want his followers implicated in any way. He'd made his decision out of loyalty—out of love."

Graf paused. He got up again to dust a fossil on the mantelpiece.

"Zar took to leaving the house at night," he said. "Klara pressed him about it, and finally gleaned that he'd been meeting with the Resistance. It was ironic, she told me, that Zar's benign philosophizing had made him suspicious to the authorities. But when he'd stopped, and become involved in things that actually *were* suspect, they seemed to leave him alone...at least for a while."

"So Zar joined the Resistance?" Florian asked, incredulous. "It's not the image one has of him."

"He wasn't a member, exactly," Graf said, leaning on the mantelpiece. "But he hung around with local sympathizers. Just until he could get his hands on a revolver."

A log tumbled with a shower of sparks.

Audrey could observe Graf freely now, for he'd entered the realm of his story, as Olivia had entered hers. He looked every one of his eighty years just then. The man who just minutes ago had been set alight by the idea of cosmic harmony, and who possessed the whimsy to talk to his van, had vanished. It occurred to her that perhaps this was common in old people, as if such vanishing and reappearing were some sort of gentle preparation for the glorious, definitive vanishing to come. In any case, it did seem that whatever immaterial thing animated the body could come and go at will, and as Friedrich was demonstrating, one didn't necessarily have to die for this to happen.

"When Klara felt stronger," Graf said, "she described her attacker to Zar. He walked with a limp, apparently—maybe an injury from the first war. He was very tall, with thinning hair. He had the palest blue eyes she'd ever seen. Strangest of all, he'd had a violin case slung over his shoulder."

"A *violin?*" exclaimed Florian. "Unbelievable!"

"*Unglaublich!*" Jonas repeated.

"Yes," Graf said. He returned to his chair. "An extraordinary detail. But I find that life's brimming with them, don't you? So much so that they're really not that extraordinary, if one stops to think about it. Anyway, Klara said she would never have told Zar about the man if she'd known what he was planning to do."

They all stared into the fire.

Graf said softly: "Zar took to loitering near Gestapo headquarters on Avenue Louise. He would wait for Klara's officer to appear, and make note of his movements. He'd become obsessed, she said. It was as if something had given way deep inside him. She didn't recognize him anymore. She feared what he was thinking...what he might do. It was like living with a wild animal.

"Afterwards, Zar told her everything: He'd paid a lorry driver to give him a lift and follow the officer's car as far as Boitsfort, near the munition depots. Then he tracked the man into the forest. It was late January.

There wasn't much cover. But if anyone knew where to hide in the woods, it was Zar."

"Did he confront him?" asked Jonas.

"Yes." Graf hesitated. "He hadn't planned it that way…to look the man in the eye, that is. But the German had heard someone behind him. He turned around. Astonishingly, he didn't seem to be armed. At least, he didn't reach for his own weapon. Maybe Zar looked so deranged pointing the revolver at him that it was obvious he'd fire at the least provocation."

"Did they speak?" Audrey asked.

Said Graf, "They looked at each other for a while. Imagine the force of their eyes: glacial blue staring down obsidian black. The man begged. *Bitte, bitte. Ich habe ein Kind!*"

"'I have a child…'" Jonas murmured.

"Yes." Graf struggled from his chair. "That's what he said." He began arranging the dessert try.

The fire hissed and smoldered. A chill filtered into the room.

Graf picked up the tray, turned slowly, and said:

"Then Zar shot him through the heart."

CHAPTER 41

Graf's tale haunted the drive back to Weil-der-Stadt. The Black Forest made sure of that. Each tree loomed in its fringed shroud as if presiding over a death that had occurred not decades ago, in a forest hundreds of kilometers away, but here, that very evening, when a brilliant musician and thinker betrayed his soul.

They were the most beautiful hands I'd ever seen. How lucky, thought Audrey, that Olivia had experienced the beauty those hands could conjure—Schubert, and love—and had never known the evil they'd done. *I wish I didn't know. I wish I could erase everything that Friedrich just told us.* Audrey glanced at their host as he drove, and wondered if he, too, wished he'd never known.

No one spoke during the drive back. Audrey said only, "It's good that Olivia never knew." To which Graf added, "Yes. Thank God. She was in love with him, as you must know by now. Imagine what such knowledge would have done to her. I gave Klara my word that I'd never tell Olivia."

♦ ♦ ♦

They exited through the green-black forest wall the way they'd come. Pamina growled across the dozing fields, where frost lay pearly beneath the moon. Graf, obviously tired, still managed to point out the timelessness of the landscape. The fields and forested knolls in old engravings of Weil-der-Stadt were still recognizable today, he told them. Indeed, it was easy to imagine Kepler and his family on the road just ahead of them, rattling along in a horse-drawn wagon.

"Kepler's parents were not exemplary individuals," Graf said. "His father was a reckless mercenary, absent most of the time at foreign wars. And by all accounts, his mother was thoroughly unpleasant. Home life was cramped and chaotic."

A relaxed air filled the van once more. Everyone seemed eager to move away from the subject of Zar and Klara.

"Despite all that," Graf said, "Katharina and Heinrich Kepler changed their son's life forever—and science, too." He gestured toward an invisible horizon. "Just over there is the little village of Leonberg. Kepler moved there when he was four. One night, when he was not yet six years old, his mother took him to a high knoll where he witnessed the comet of 1577."

The musicians pressed their noses against the windows. There was no comet, of course. They couldn't even discern any hills in the obscurity. But their imaginations could easily picture the sickly youngster, weakened by smallpox, clasping his mother's hand and staring up at the sky, as yet unaware that he was already drinking in the order and harmony that would be so sorely missing in his earthly life.

"Three years later," Graf said, "on a bitter January night, Kepler's father called young Johannes outside to see a total lunar eclipse: a reddish blood-moon. How could any boy forget that? Indeed, Kepler would be the first to offer a largely correct explanation: that light at the red end of the spectrum is refracted by the Earth's atmosphere and shed on the moon."

Graf guided Pamina into the slumbering town. He said, "We all have moments that define our lives, don't we? Historians tend to skip over them. They shouldn't, though. Maybe the most important thing that ever happened to Kepler was that his mother took him up that hill. Who knows? Maybe that was all it took for a little boy to become a great man."

Graf parked on the deserted square in front of the *Gasthaus*. The silence in the wake of the grinding gears felt tired; depleted. It seemed only natural to sit for a few moments in the van and contemplate the evening.

They'd all had plenty of wine and beer, and confidences had already been spilled, so no one thought it at all inappropriate when Florian asked, "What was your defining moment, Friedrich?"

Graf didn't hesitate. "Meeting Klara Náhoda," he said. "Because through her, I discovered the legacy of her brother. *In the presence of Music, there is no old or young, rich or poor, good or evil.* Those are Zar's words." Graf paused. "Think what power you wield, my friends."

They all disembarked and unloaded the instruments and suitcases. "Good nights" were exchanged, and everyone embraced.

"I'll pick you up at nine-thirty tomorrow morning, if that suits," Graf said. "Gloria's castle, Schloss Helden, is about a three-hour drive."

♦ ♦ ♦

Audrey kissed her friends on the cheek and headed off for a stroll. The evening had been far too stimulating for her to sleep.

What was your defining moment?

Florian had meant his question for Graf. But it dogged her as she wandered under the arches of Weil's medieval town hall and past the miniature door and windows of the Kepler residence.

What was your defining moment?

She followed the lane near the Keplers' house and went up some stairs. Timbered façades leaned over the narrow way in their sleep. No one seemed to notice the little figure in baggy coat and cloche hat passing by.

Audrey turned up the hill and stopped by the bell tower of the Church of Saints Peter and Paul.

It was when I was nine years old…when I first touched that piano in the school gymnasium.

She rounded another corner. A dog barked behind a garden fence and another answered. A man yelled at them, and the barking ceased.

Yes, that was it: when I discovered that something lived inside that broken-down box of strings.

Old-world lamps lit Audrey's way along Weil's ancient wall, where winter parkland crisped underfoot, unmarked by any other prints. She was walking a singular byway, it seemed—a moonlit corridor between the medieval town on her right, and the river on her left, a route that Kepler himself might have taken on such a serene evening.

What if the janitor hadn't let me in?

She stumbled over the memory of Bo, leaning on his mop, listening. Her heart still ached for the soul that had been trapped inside that dying piano. How could someone have painted it with graffiti? Who would strip off the ivory and leave the keys so naked and scarred? The young Audrey had tried to imagine the pain—the tearing of a nail from a finger. That other pain—abandonment—she could understand without having to imagine it. *Don't worry, I'll take care of you,* she'd whispered to the wretched object. They were words she'd so longed to hear herself.

CHAPTER 42

She halted, dumbstruck. *What was Pamina doing there?*

The van was parked on the other side of the river near one of the town's oldest bridges. At this time of night, with history roaming at large, the vehicle was a far stranger apparition than Kepler would have been, searching for a place to set up his telescope.

Audrey drew closer to the bridge. The riverbank was slick underfoot, and pitched sharply. She slipped to the water's edge, where a huge oak saved her from tumbling into the gleaming black torrent.

She peered around the tree:

Two men were standing at the railing of the bridge, facing each other.

One of them was Friedrich Graf. And the other...

Audrey put a hand to her mouth.

The other man was spidery. He wore no overcoat. And a fedora perched high on his head.

Spellbound, Audrey inched toward the bridge. She found refuge behind the next oak on the bank and watched. She was close enough to hear what the men were saying, but even so, the river drowned out their voices and the scene unfolded in pantomime.

Graf, the shorter one, lifted his arms from his sides as he spoke, as if egging on an orchestra. The fedora man listened in his stark, reticulated way. There was none of the desperation he'd exhibited in front of Klara's house the night the rosewood piano had been hauled away. But there was something else.

Complicity.

Audrey sucked in her breath.

Graf's companion reached into his suit and produced a piece of paper. This he handed to Graf, who unfolded it and studied it for some time under a street lamp. In the lull, the moon unveiled herself fully for a few seconds, revealing a pencil-sharp watchtower beyond the bridge...a fragment of ancient wall...branches stenciling the sky farther down the river.

At length Graf handed the paper back to his interlocutor and turned to watch the river. Neither spoke. Then both of them moved off the bridge. They shook hands when they'd reached Pamina, at which point the spidery man strode away, and Graf drove off.

♦ ♦ ♦

Audrey leaned back against the tree. *Klara's presumed murderer, here in Weil-der-Stadt! And with Friedrich Graf...who just served us schnitzel and apple strudel, and played Schubert on a prehistoric flute.* The thoughts tumbled freely and made no sense. *The two men had shaken hands, for God's sake!* Audrey braced her palms against the trunk of the oak as the world shifted around her. What was it that Nero had said? *Oui...le chapeau. The hat. I saw him leave the house in Rue Nova.* His fear was even easier to remember. Audrey also recalled that according to Bébé, the fedora man had engaged Nero to drive the piano to Prague. *Was the white van nearby?*

She gazed up at the medieval walls flooded with moonlight.

Her heart seized: A silhouette loomed against the ramparts.

A trick of illumination, surely.

But no.

She squared her shoulders. "Who is it?" she stammered.

And then she saw them: the white patches on the man's face, glowing eerily.

Bandages.

"Audrey?" Jonas only used her name in a crisis.

He skittered down the steep bank to her side.

"Are you all right? What are you doing here?"

Audrey sagged with relief. "How did you find me?" she said, ignoring his question.

Jonas managed a grin through the bandages. "I followed your footprints in the frost." His gaze grew somber. "Süsslein? What is it?"

"Jonas..." Audrey wavered at the river's edge.

He caught her up and pressed her against him. His grip was as tight as it had been outside the Europa building, just seconds before the police had arrived...before he'd disappeared from her life.

"Your jacket smells different," she murmured.

"I stopped smoking," he said, and gently steered her up the bank.

She smiled against the worn leather. Something else was different, too—something that usually stirred only when they were playing music together, but that was stirring now, without any music at all (at least, not of the earthly kind).

"How are your injuries?" she asked, pulling away to examine Madame Mertens's handiwork.

"Fine. But what the hell are you doing out here?" he pressed her.

Audrey set off across the parkland. "It's freezing," she said. "Let's get back to the *Gasthaus* and have some hot chocolate. Then I'll tell you everything." She glanced around at Jonas, and wondered if he would believe her when she told him that Klara's killer was in town. And that the charming Friedrich Graf was not the man they thought he was.

213

CHAPTER 43

I t was a waking dream she had that night in her spotless *Gasthaus* bed:
the kind that drifted along reality's blurry edge just at dawn, when the
brightening of the curtains made it so difficult to know what was truth,
and what was fancy.

♦ ♦ ♦

Bo had possessed more initiative than anyone had given him credit for.
One afternoon at the school, when everyone assumed the janitor was leaning on his mop somewhere, daydreaming, he'd in fact slipped out to the
communal music academy. After mustering his woeful French with the
secretary, he found himself in the studio of a Professor Claessens. This
gentleman initially took offense at the imposter in custodial clothes. But
his interest grew in what the man had to say—and with so few words, too.

There was a very unusual girl at the neighborhood school. (Bo managed a deranged look on his soulful face.) This girl coaxed such beauty
from a piano. (He clasped his hand against his heart and swooned.) But
the piano she played was not at all like this one. (Bo gestured to the re-
spectable grand in Claessens's studio, shook his finger, and mimicked slit-
ting his throat.)

It was enough. Claessens locked up his studio that evening and made
his way over to the school gymnasium. The janitor held a finger to his
lips. "*Silence,*" he whispered, although he could hardly be heard over the
cacophony issuing from within.

Claessens slipped inside.

He recoiled at first at the stench of countless unwashed students. But the sound soon entranced him: full of anguish, as if the girl sitting at the wreck in the corner were forcing an invalid to walk. Claessens tip-toed closer: he deduced that she'd developed a system of navigating the piano's clang and rattle by using a special touch for specific keys. She'd clearly discovered how to thread a melodic line through the chaos. There was no score in front of her, but nevertheless she was playing recognizable music: bits of *Für Elise*, and a Clementi sonata. She'd obviously heard them somewhere and was reproducing them by ear.

Without warning, Bo switched off the lights. Claessens turned to him, annoyed. But the girl at the piano seemed to have been waiting for this signal. She lifted her resolute gaze to the rafters, where anyone else would have seen only dreariness, and seemed to have spotted something of interest there. What emerged from under her hands at that moment convinced Professor Claessens that he'd heard enough.

He left the gym without a word. The following week, a letter arrived at the principal's office with the instruction that Audrey Nightingale was to present herself at the communal music academy for piano lessons, and that no fee would be charged.

Three years later, she was ready for her first recital.

Professor Claessens had chosen her repertoire carefully: the *Allegro* from Haydn's Sonata in C; Mendelssohn's *Venetian Boat Song No. 2*; and Chopin's Nocturne in E-flat. A courageous program for a girl of twelve. But then, Claessens was a courageous teacher. He'd been warned about this singular pupil. *She's very bright. But her head is in the clouds somewhere. She's an orphan, you know...*

"Yes," he said. "I know." And he also knew that because of those things, she was hungry for tenderness and beauty and would work very hard for Music to reveal them to her.

The recital took place in Claessens's studio at the academy. Audrey was one of eight pupils who would be performing.

"Perhaps you should play for your gym class, Audrey," Claessens said in his avuncular way, two weeks before the recital. "To practice playing in front of an audience."

She looked at him gravely. "But I play for an audience every evening," she said. "For Bo."

"Yes, yes. But he's..." Claessens cut off this thought, befuddled by those probing eyes. "Yes, Audrey, you're right," he pivoted. "Even a single listener is an audience."

The recital was set for five o'clock in the afternoon.

Pupils crowded into the studio along with their parents, siblings, grandparents, aunts and uncles. If this had disturbed Audrey in any way, no one would have guessed it. (Bo had come to hear her, after all, though he'd stood at the door the whole time, not having had a chance to change from his coveralls.) Nor could anyone have known that Audrey already possessed the firmness of heart that would accompany her throughout her life and help insulate her from situations such as these, where love was bestowed on others nearby, but not actually on her.

That she herself could bestow love, however...well, that had been a discovery she hadn't expected. One didn't have to rely on anyone else's participation in love, it seemed. In fact, the object of affection didn't even technically have to be animate. The gym piano had taught her that. People were seduced by inappropriate targets all the time, and surely Audrey wasn't the first to lose her heart to a relic with cracked teeth and ailing innards.

It was a strange thing about orphans. Unlike most people, they could never count on solid ground under their feet; they'd never received the ur-love that provided this unshakeable foundation. It was perhaps better to be born without an arm or a kidney: you could get through life quite well without those things—prosper, even. Lost maternal love, however, left a phantom ache that came and went without warning.

Audrey's pain always vanished in the company of the piano.

♦ ♦ ♦

"Everyone, please welcome Audrey Nightingale," Professor Claessens announced. He read out the pieces she would play as if delivering a sentence.

Applause smattered, then died.

The petite girl in gray skirt and dark-green sweater stepped around the students sitting on the floor and approached the piano.

She remembered curious details from that day: the smell of nerves; the shriek of the piano stool against the wooden floor; and the eager eyes of her audience, anticipating calamity.

Terror seized her.

She'd played this piano many times in her lessons. But suddenly the keys looked unfamiliar. Audrey smoothed a hand over them, expecting something else: the raw wood of her beloved friend. The system she'd so painstakingly devised on the gym piano—*the remnant of glue is on D; the sharp edge marks the G above it; a splash of red graffiti is where the Haydn begins*—had no meaning here. Tears scalded her eyes. She glanced overhead, but surely Music could not be anywhere near this apocalypse.

Sniggering. Whispering. Gasps. Even before the strange girl had played a note.

Claessens bustled up to the piano. "Audrey, chérie," he said gently. "Thank you for your courage. Perhaps this is not the best day for you to play for us."

His words seemed to have the immediate effect of plunging the studio into gloom.

For someone had turned off the lights.

Audrey straightened at the keyboard.

Come, this way.

The voice was at once impossibly distant, and as close as her heartbeat.

She glanced overhead again: something glimmered in the shadows.

You are not alone.

She began.

Her hands stopped shaking. Lightness was suddenly everywhere: in her shoulders, and wrists, and in the sound she was so unexpectedly producing. Her passion spilled into the music as if she'd composed the pieces herself—as if everyone in the room was hearing them for the first time.

When she finally finished, no one dared to move or speak. It was some time before the first hands clapped together, followed by two more, and then a tsunami of others. No one dared to reprimand the man at the door who'd been guilty of flipping the switch, as emotion had overcome him.

CHAPTER 44

They were back at the fountain on the Weil marketplace, waiting for Graf. Nothing—and everything—had changed.

"I just can't believe that Graf might be tied up with all this," Florian said. He'd been agitated since breakfast, when Audrey had told him about the meeting on the bridge. "And after everything that Klara meant to him."

"Everything that he *said* she meant," Jonas corrected him. "He was lying, clearly. He's mixed up in her fate somehow." He'd removed his bandages: Van Overberg's savagery was still purplish, but healing.

"Thank heavens we didn't reveal anything about our true mission," said Audrey. "He still thinks we're on a concert tour to Prague."

"Maybe we should reconsider," said Jonas. "Let's forget all this...let's call a taxi and go directly to the station." He paused. "Friedrich's schnitzel wasn't that good."

"We don't have a choice at the moment," Florian said. "You can't very well go back to Brussels, can you? Van Overberg has the police on your trail. Anyway, our immediate goal should be to find somewhere to rehearse, and play well enough for Gloria von Helden's people that they'll leave plenty of hundred euro bills." He turned to Audrey: "Did you see Nero's van parked anywhere last night?"

She shook her head. Then, with melancholy: "Maybe we misread Graf's emotions when he spoke about Klara."

"But he said that his defining moment was meeting her," Florian said. "Because she taught him about Zar. He couldn't have been so drunk that he didn't mean it—or *we* so drunk that we misunderstood it."

"I don't know," said Jonas. "I might have been."

"At least this von Helden countess seems to be a friend of Olivia's," said Florian. "Otherwise, who knows where Graf might be taking us?"

"Oh, it's all my fault," moaned Audrey. "I should never have dragged you both on this escapade." She paused. "All for a stupid piano."

Florian smiled. "You of all people know that there are no stupid pianos in this world, Audrey...least of all this one."

They heard Pamina even before she hove into view. Like yesterday, the van sputtered up to the statue of Kepler; and like yesterday, Graf bounced from the driver's seat and greeted them heartily. But now everything seemed tinged with omen.

"We've decided to go directly to Prague...by train..." Jonas blurted, to the stupefaction of his friends.

"Whatever do you mean?" Graf said. His eyes clouded. He was already loading their suitcases into the van.

Audrey gripped Jonas's elbow. She glared at him and turned to Graf: "Everything's fine, Friedrich. Jonas just meant that we've taken up enough of your time already."

"No I didn't!" Jonas exclaimed, though Graf's head was in the van at that moment and he hadn't heard him. Jonas bent toward Audrey. "Süsslein!" he hissed. "We shouldn't go with him."

"But you haven't taken up my time at all!" Graf enthused. "Gloria von Helden is an old friend."

◆ ◆ ◆

Soon they were jolting along as before, only this time they faced three hours of misery instead of only twenty minutes.

Audrey had ceded the front seat to Florian. She and Jonas were gripping the edges of the back seat, their hands occasionally touching. A small carry bag bounced on the seat beside them containing the box with the prehistoric flute. "I'm returning it to the university on my way home," Graf said.

This is exactly what it feels like when a concert starts to go wrong, thought Audrey. What one did in such circumstances depended on how good a musician you were. The first rule of thumb, of course, was to continue playing, and so the three of them tried to keep up the congeniality they'd enjoyed with Graf the evening before. This included some of the same subjects, although when pressed by Florian about where Konstantine Zar might be buried, Graf remained vague. "There's a burial ground in Brussels—*L'Enclos des fusillés*—where the old Tir National used to be; where the Nazis shot their prisoners. It's behind the modern radio building. Zar might be there." When Audrey asked about Klara living in that enormous house by herself, Graf responded, "She was very frugal. Olivia and Reginald helped her out."

Pamina forged on toward the Czech border. They were crossing what had once been, in Kepler's time, an assemblage of independent states and cities, either Lutheran or Catholic, under the aegis of the Holy Roman Empire. (The Keplers were Lutheran.) Peace during this ambiguous arrangement would last only sixty years. Stuttgart, Augsburg, Munich—modern Germany had triumphed completely now. But ancient nuclei still pulsed in the land: hearth; wall; church; village—many were contracting, like dying stars, but still had a gravitational pull. Fields plowed under for winter hid the secret of sustenance in their folds, as they had for millennia. Today's hooves clattered over the same stones trodden for centuries, for they marked the best way home.

Audrey watched the vestiges of Old Europe slip by, and found herself wishing that they were jolting along in a horse and cart with Kepler and his family instead of in this cursed VW van, with a man whose motives were increasingly suspect. *Don't be afraid of this journey, Audrey.* Olivia's words made her sit up taller, and in a rash moment she squeezed Jonas's hand against the vinyl seat. He woke up briefly, smiled, and fell asleep again.

♦ ♦ ♦

They passed a sign to Regensburg.

"Kepler died there," Graf said softly, so as not to wake Jonas. "In 1630."

"Yes, I know," said Florian. From behind, Audrey could tell how rigid his shoulders had become. Exceptionally, he seemed to have no interest in discussing Kepler.

Graf seemed oblivious to the pall of mistrust. He went on to describe Kepler's final journey. The great man had traveled to Regensburg in desperation, to collect money that was owed to him. He'd served as an official adviser to Wallenstein, one of the Holy Roman Emperor's generals, providing him with astronomical calculations and occasionally, horoscopes. It had been quite some time since Kepler had been paid. Exhausted and ill, he rode a skinny mare to Regensburg and sold her for two *gulden* as soon as he got there. He never made it back home. He was buried in a Lutheran cemetery outside the city walls, as the Catholics were in charge of the cathedral in Regensburg and Lutherans were forbidden burial there.

Kepler's grave was eventually destroyed by the religious wars that had blighted his final years.

I measured the skies, now the shadows of the earth I measure.

Sky-bound was the mind, the shadow of the body lies here.

"It's a lovely sentiment, isn't it?" Graf said. "Kepler wrote it himself, and asked that it be placed on his tombstone."

Talk of tombstones dampened spirits even further.

Audrey caught Graf's gaze in the rearview mirror. How many people his age still hummed with the life force as he did? In a weak moment, she wondered if indeed sorcery had been at work the night before, and the person she'd witnessed on the bridge with the spidery man had been someone else altogether.

CHAPTER 45

I haven't been entirely straight with you," Graf said after coffee at a wayside inn.

They'd crossed the Danube and were entering a landscape of greater sweep and isolation. Spring snow powdered the meadows and swelled the quilted clouds.

Audrey stared out at the bleak countryside. *At last,* she thought. *He's going to confess to us what he's been up to.*

"It's about Gloria von Helden," Graf went on, "You see, her father, Count Ernst von Helden, was stationed in Brussels during the war. He was a high-ranking official in the cultural ministry during the Occupation."

The three musicians digested the news that Gloria's father was a Nazi.

"So he knew about Zar, then," Audrey said.

"You mean to say that we're heading to the family seat of one of Zar's enemies?" Jonas demanded.

"Listen, all of you, please," Graf said, lifting a hand from the steering wheel in a conciliatory gesture. "It's far from what you think." He locked stares with Audrey again in the mirror.

Graf maneuvered Pamina back onto the road from the shoulder, where the wake of a lorry had blown her, and explained: "Among his other duties, von Helden was asked to attend some of Zar's lectures. To observe him, they said—make sure he wasn't speaking in some sort of code. According to Gloria, Zar's ideas haunted her father. He couldn't stay away from the lectures, even when he didn't have to go. He'd turn up incognito, without a uniform, and speak to no one. Zar's philosophy made him ask himself some very tough questions about why his countrymen were doing what they were doing. When Jean de Sélys flew his Typhoon down Avenue Louise and machine-gunned Gestapo headquarters, von Helden confided in a colleague how much he admired such bravery. Well, he'd chosen the wrong colleague. He was sanctioned, and almost relieved of his post."

"A man of some conscience, it seems," said Audrey, queasy at the thought of von Helden's connection with Zar. Then she recalled what Zar himself had done—murdered one of von Helden's compatriots in cold blood— and not for the first time did it strike her how inextricable good and evil were, sometimes so tightly woven that it seemed impossible for one to exist without the other, or even to distinguish them in the weave.

"Conscience, indeed," Graf said. "Audrey, you seemed shocked to learn that Zar had killed a man in cold blood. As indeed was I."

"A man who raped his sister," Jonas added.

"Yes, yes," Graf said brusquely. "It goes without saying that Zar had a motive—that he sought revenge. But I also wanted to make the point that people—inherently good people—sometimes find themselves tangled up in events that they want no part of. I believe that's what happened to Zar. And it's what happened to Gloria's father when he was posted in Brussels."

"You mean he was a 'good' Nazi?" said Jonas.

"What I mean is, Count von Helden took a page from Zar's lectures: he stood up to the barbarity around him. Not with music, of course. But he helped wherever he could. Although after the de Sélys episode, he was far more careful how he went about this. Sometimes he simply engaged in passive disobedience: looking the other way when someone was out during curfew; ignoring illegal sales on the black market. That sort of thing." Graf paused. "Then he grew bolder. Through his contacts in the SS, he arranged for a release of prisoners from the notorious St. Gilles prison. He even aided in their escape over the Pyrenees."

"The Pyrenees route was perilous," Florian said. "Von Helden would have had to have made contact with the Belgian Resistance. And behind the backs of his commanding officers."

"He was essentially a traitor to Germany, then," Audrey said.

Graf let a few moments go by. "Yes. He was arrested as a traitor."

Graf turned off the main road. They passed through the hamlet of Blutmond, where a statue of a medieval saint raised his staff forlornly on the tiny marketplace.

"Von Helden was tried for treason by a Nazi court," Graf said. "He was given the death penalty, but this was commuted to many months of hard labor. He died relatively young."

Graf lightened his tone. "His daughter inherited that mettle," he said. "You'll see. Gloria's not like anyone's idea of a countess."

♦ ♦ ♦

"That must be it!" Jonas cried. He pointed to what, from a distance, looked like a chunk of rock rising from a forested ridge.

An arrow indicated the turn-off for Schloss Helden.

"That's it, all right," said Graf, chuckling. "Gloria's little pile of mortar."

The road spiraled upward through misty and forbidding woodland. Pamina wheezed her way up the steep ridge until they arrived at a small park dotted with oaks. The chunk of rock had morphed into a soaring keep, with pitched roofs and small, suspicious windows set high in the walls.

"Gloria must have one hell of a dungeon," Jonas said. Under his breath he added, "Does she ever lock up her guests?"

Graf ignored him. "The black-and-yellow striped shutters warn visitors that the building has a moat," he said. Pamina stopped of her own accord at the narrow bridge spanning this chasm.

"I don't think the old girl can go another centimeter," Graf said.

They got out and breathed in the pure, keen air. A rook lifted from an elderly chestnut tree and wheeled down over the ridge, leaving behind a faint hiss of wind, constant but soothing.

"Parts of the castle go back to the 1400s," Graf said, helping Florian unload the van.

Jonas slipped up to Audrey and drew her aside. "At least if we get stuck here, I'll be trapped with my muse," he said, laughing.

"And who might that be?" Audrey teased him. "The countess? She's probably a little old for you, don't you think?" She was studying the high windows on the keep. Her cheeks blushed in the cool wind, and like most of her admirers, Jonas took a moment to savor her delicate profile.

"No, not the countess, Süsslein," he said softly, suddenly earnest. "I meant *you.*"

The only entrance to the keep was an arched wooden door on the other side of the drawbridge. It was set in a tower that obviously had never been intended to be welcoming. The bastion was relieved only by an arrow slit,

a coat of arms weathered into unrecognizable shapes, and a meager lantern, which blinked on now as the door swung open.

"Friedrich!"

CHAPTER 46

A woman emerged onto the bridge, although she was only obviously female through her voice. She was very tall and thin and had no discernable feminine contours. In her dark-green oilskin and high rubber boots, she resembled a malnourished gamekeeper. Her graying hair seemed to have been shorn with a blunt knife. A pair of diamond stud earrings caught the failing light and hinted at her gender.

Gloria von Helden loped across the drawbridge.

"*Xairetízo ti melodía mésa sou!*" she exclaimed, and embraced Graf, whom she dwarfed. Her cheekbones had been sculpted by generations of pedigree.

I salute the melody within you. Audrey glanced at Florian in shock. He knew Zar's greeting, too. She whispered it to Jonas, all the while steadying her nerves. *Where were they, exactly? And with whom?*

"You haven't grown much, Friedrich, my dear," Gloria laughed tunefully. The corners of her eyes fanned with tiny lines. "I'll have to feed you tonight!" She'd been speaking in German, but switched effortlessly to French and said, "It's always an honor to meet friends of Olivia Taverner. Welcome!"

The countess embraced the musicians as if they were returning relatives. To Florian she said, "I understand Olivia is your great aunt. Ah, yes..." She sized him up as she might a favorite horse, and ruffled his curls. "You really do look like Schubert!"

Gloria turned to Graf. "It looks as if you've finally killed off that ridiculous vehicle. Never mind. There's an old Škoda you can drive to Prague. It's the dark-blue one in the stables. The gardener usually uses it, but he's off on his annual holiday. The keys are in it, I believe."

She led them over the drawbridge, through the square tower and into a courtyard where several centuries appeared to have been walled in, alive. Torches flanked the main entrance to the castle, and in their lilt, frescoes of Bavarian scenes trembled and flitted around the courtyard walls: village fetes and dances; hunters and wild animals; musicians playing lutes and fiddles...everything in ochre, peach, forest green, misty blue.

The visitors gaped and marveled. Graf broke away to share pleasantries with the countess.

"Are we hostages?" Jonas said under his breath.

"Don't be an idiot!" Florian snapped, although each of them had detected the foreboding in the others.

"We must not forget that these are Olivia's friends," Audrey said, though this reassurance was wearing thin. Olivia Taverner was many hundreds of kilometers away. And in any case, what sort of friend was Gloria von Helden? Even Florian had never heard his great-aunt mention her.

The door between the two torches swung mysteriously open and four fox terriers bounded out.

"*Hunde!*" cried Jonas. He lay his cello case on the cobblestones and fell to his knees. "Yes, yes, I know," he murmured into the crush of fur. The dogs yipped and whined and ignored the other newcomers entirely.

"A fellow dog lover, I see," said Gloria. "They sense it immediately."

The dogs wandered off to do a round of the courtyard, glancing back at Jonas as if he might join them. He probably would have. But the afternoon was coming to a close. A rehearsal awaited. "*Auf Wiedersehen*, my dears," he called, and picked up his cello.

"I hope your audience will make it tonight," Gloria said, glancing at the heavy sky before going into the castle. "Snow is brewing."

CHAPTER 47

They stepped into a cavernous entry. Twin staircases of lustrous wood arced gracefully to the upper floor. A maid darted from behind the front door, where she'd obviously been gauging her mistress's every move.

"You'll find your concert fee in there," said Gloria. She indicated a silver urn in a wrought iron holder next to the door. It looked as if it usually contained ice and a bottle of champagne. "People leave money coming *and* going," she added with a wink.

They processed after the maid up one of the staircases.

The great hall of Schloss Helden was an odd hybrid of hunting lodge and cathedral nave. Antlers on the walls, and a stone fireplace vast enough to roast an entire stag, attested to the former. As to the latter, gothic vaulting spanned the length of the room with delicate, vertiginous tracery. The same lustrous wood was in evidence everywhere: in coffered paneling, and pediments over doorways; in the railing leading up to the minstrels' gallery; in fluted columns decorating the windows over the courtyard. At the opposite end of the room, so distant from the fireplace that no warmth could have reached there, a stage of sorts had been set up, with a Bechstein grand of some pretension, two plush chairs, and two antique music stands with candle holders. Between fireplace and piano lay an acreage of pale-pink carpet, where guests in their dozens could sink into sofas and wing-backed chairs, or lounge on padded window seats.

"Well, here's your office, as it were," Gloria said, threading her way across the expanse. The tuneful laugh seemed to be a habit of hers. "There are electric heaters on this side of the room, so don't worry about the cold. And by the way," she added. "I never put chairs out in rows. It discourages complicity with the performers. Musicians play better this way—more truthfully."

"It almost sounds like Konstantine Zar's lectures," Audrey said. She regretted the remark at once. Gloria's father had been a Nazi official, after all, charged with attending Zar's lectures in Brussels as a spy—even if he did turn against his own country in the end.

"Yes, indeed!" Gloria exclaimed without reservation. "Tragically, Zar's teachings have largely been lost. My father recounted some of them to me when I was young, and I remembered everything he told me. In fact, after the war, my father tried to recreate Zar's approach, here, in this room." Gloria laughed. "Of course, most of my friends are too decrepit now to sit on the floor—which would be truly in the spirit of a Zar gathering. Egalitarian." Gloria grew suddenly solemn. "In the presence of Music, there is no old or young, rich or poor, good or evil."

"Zar," Audrey said. The sentiment seemed to be following them across Europe.

"Yes," said Gloria. "And remember: a musician can close the magic circle with just one listener."

They all took a moment to consider this comment, coming as it had from a woman who regularly entertained dozens.

*The magic circle...*The Kepler Players had closed it many times over the years, before countless listeners. But no circle had been as pure as the one they'd forged only recently, with a rejuvenated Madame Mertens listening outside Audrey's door with a pot of mussels.

Gloria removed her oilskin to reveal a scrawny frame exaggerated by black trousers and turtleneck. As with many women of her class, she could have been anywhere between fifty and seventy.

"You're as lovely as ever, Gloria," Graf said, beaming up at her.

"And you, as ever, are a liar," she riposted. She patted him on the cheek. "I look like an old crow, Friedrich, and you know it."

She headed to a side door, waving an arm as she went to indicate that she'd be back immediately.

"It's incredible," Graf said in a stage whisper as their hostess shut the door. "Even out here, in the middle of nowhere, Gloria attracts the very best musicians, writers and painters for her salon. And I can assure you that her concert audiences...well, let's just say that they're a veritable Who's Who of European VIPs. Belgians turn up regularly, by the way. Her salon is often featured in Paris Match and Point de Vue."

Panic flickered between the musicians.

"Oh, don't worry," Graf assured them. "Tonight's concert will be a totally private affair. You'll be disguised as the 'Brussels Players.'"

"How original," Jonas muttered to Audrey. "Until they recognize us."

None of them felt chummy enough with Graf just then to mention what they were clearly thinking: that Aymeric Van Overberg was precisely the sort of luminary who could be found on Gloria's guest list.

Graf had arranged for the trio to rehearse after tea and spend the night in the castle. "Concerts at Schloss Helden begin promptly at 19:30," he said. "I'll drive you to Prague tomorrow. The gardener's Škoda is no Mercedes, mind you." He giggled. "But it's no Pamina, either...thank God."

♦ ♦ ♦

The maid reappeared bearing a large silver tray with tea things and tiny sandwiches. Gloria strode up behind her. "Just set it there, Imelda," she said, pointing with an imperial finger.

The countess poured the tea herself and handed cups to her guests.

"There'll be a buffet dinner after the concert, in this room," she said. "To build on what your music will no doubt have forged between people." She grabbed three tiny sandwiches in a single pass at the tray, which impressed Jonas mightily. "By the way, everyone claps between movements here. It's so silly not to express one's appreciation, I find."

Gloria returned to the subject of the late count. "I'll never forget Father's description of Olivia's debut concert at the Brussels Conservatory in 1941, with Konstantine Zar at the piano."

"Your father was there?!" cried Audrey.

Gloria smiled. "Yes. Shivering in his coat like everyone else." She went on to describe what her father had never been able to forget: the intensity between singer and accompanist, so taut that their link seemed in danger of breaking. And the love...Oh, it was there for all to see! It was as if on that stage, protected by Music, no one could come between the tall, glowering man with unlit depths, and the girl from the dairy farm who spilled joy with every note she sang.

Audrey sipped her tea and stared up at the distant vaulting. She could only imagine that a love born in the weightless realm of Music would return there one day, and echo long after all material traces had gone. With heaviness she realized that any earthly love between Olivia and Zar had lasted only as long as a moth could emerge from its cocoon, spread its wings, and char them against a flame.

Gloria regarded her visitors. "It was more than love," she said. "My father told me that something even more powerful had been present at that concert—an urgent plea that more than ever, in the midst of a war, harmony and beauty were the keys to our very survival."

She paused. "I think that was the moment when my father realized he could no longer support what his country was doing."

CHAPTER 48

When are we going to confront Graf?" Jonas asked, after Gloria and Friedrich had left them to rehearse. He unpacked his cello and began to tune.

Florian wandered over to survey the courtyard. "It's starting to snow," he said. He fingered his violin softly.

"Confront him about what?" said Audrey, warming up. The old Bechstein had a thin, shallow tone which it made up for in looks: superbly tooled legs, and a music desk carved in a lacy sunburst. Bechstein's bronze crest announced that it was the royal provider to His Majesty, Kaiser and King.

"We can't very well mention the rendezvous on the bridge in Weil," Audrey said, halting in mid-arpeggio, "without him thinking that I was spying on him. We can't risk it."

"Not while we're trapped in this fortress," said Jonas. "I wish we could get to Prague without Graf's help." He played the most exquisite scale, then said, "For my part, I feel a little better knowing that her father was a traitor to the Third Reich."

Florian drifted from the window. A suggestion of light filtered in from the courtyard, increasing with the snow. "We must complete our journey, wherever it takes us," he said, tuning a stubborn E string.

His pompous tendencies usually elicited groans from the others. But this time, they kept quiet. He'd spoken the truth, after all.

A footman slipped in as they were playing and began lighting candles in wall sconces and lanterns, on tabletops and windowsills, and in the splendid silver candelabras on the buffet table. Gloria's great hall began to resemble the redoubt of a fairy queen.

Imelda reappeared as soon as the music had stopped to show them to their rooms.

"You go," Audrey said. "I'm going out."

♦ ♦ ♦

The courtyard was ablaze. Torches had proliferated since their arrival, and now lined the drawbridge as well as the drive crossing the park. Tradesmen scurried back and forth carrying catering and flowers. They had to dance around the four fox terriers, who, as the castle's welcoming party, had to give everything a sniff of approval.

Audrey crossed the moat and turned her face up to the whirling snow. The flakes sizzled on the torches, and as she traversed the park and started down the access road, there seemed to be something missing from this elemental scene: a prehistoric flute, perhaps, sending its cry into the beyond. The thought reminded Audrey of something that Kepler himself had said: *The occasions by which people come to understand celestial things seem to me not much less marvelous than the celestial things themselves.*

He hadn't been speaking of love, she thought, making her way through the muffled landscape. But he could have been.

She skittered through the snow as she was sure she would skitter through the Mendelssohn that night. She was ill-prepared for this concert. Worse, her thoughts were far from it. Surely a love like the one that had united Zar and Olivia was celestial in origin—a Great Conjunction of hearts. Audrey sighed. *I'll probably never know such a thing.* And then: *Does great love by definition have to be doomed?* She sighed again.

She took off her mitten to tuck her hair under her hat. The snow caressed her bare wrist, and she remembered that other fleeting touch—Jonas's—as his hand had brushed against hers in the van.

The memory brought her to a halt. What had he meant about her being his muse?

Never play chamber music with a lover. It was well-known advice in the trade. Good ensemble-playing was as mysterious as the best carbonnade: certain ingredients essential to the overall taste didn't mingle very well when separated from the whole. Brown sugar and parsnips, for example.

Or Jonas and Florian.

She strode on down the winding road.

Olivia had fallen in love with her musical partner, after all. But it hadn't ended very well, had it? There'd been a war, of course—an impossible aligning of circumstances that had trumped their own Great Conjunction.

Why was Jonas flirting with her? Surely the two of them would be just as unworkable outside of the trio as brown sugar and parsnip. *Was he trying to make up for derailing her career?* Audrey considered her dear friend...his incorrigible magnetism. Women of all ages flocked to him. For his charm, of course. And his height. (There were so few tall men these days.) But also for that rare mix of childlike candor and masculinity.

Audrey tried to imagine Jonas in this new light. His affection for her—which she'd always considered more brotherly than anything else—had never wavered over the years, even through all his affairs and misadventures. Nor had hers for him. But she realized sadly that she'd taken him for granted. Now, it was as if a piece of music she'd grown tired of and put away had begun playing in her head again with new, intriguing sonorities.

♦ ♦ ♦

She reached the bottom of the ridge road and emerged from the forest. Anyone could have missed it at first: the white van parked in the snowy field. Although the buffalo head stenciled on the driver's door was clearly visible.

CHAPTER 49

There was nowhere to hide. Nor could she run. She tried, but as in dreams, her sodden shoes slid backward with each step.

A door scraped open behind her.

It cracked shut again.

A hurried crunch of steps.

"Audrey!"

Her heart shrank.

"Audrey Nightingale!"

She caught her breath. The nasal voice was familiar: a clarinet, poorly played.

"It's Roland Wilmots," the man called. "Wait, please!"

Audrey slowly turned.

The figure was a hieroglyph against the snow: a black suit sketched by a skinny pen. He held the fedora in his hands, as if out of respect.

"Roland Wilmots..." Audrey repeated, her voice dreamlike.

"Yes. I am—that is, I was—Klara Náhoda's assistant. Please..." Wilmots approached obliquely, as if reassuring a stray animal.

Audrey backed away. Her thoughts tumbled into mayhem and she grasped at any passing familiarity. What was it that Graf had said about Roland Wilmots? *Klara seemed to have let her aggressor in. I'm surprised that Roland wasn't with her. He was incredibly loyal.*

Wilmots pointed to the van and said, "It's too heavy to make it up to the castle in this weather."

Audrey gaped. "You're going to Schloss Helden?" She glanced at the van and her blood warmed. The rosewood piano must have been inside! *That's why it was too heavy.* An ache flared as if for a lost lover. Even hidden, the piano cast a beneficence over the scene into which malice would have had trouble making inroads.

"You're on your way to Prague, aren't you?" Audrey said, feeling bolder. "With Klara's piano."

The hieroglyph sagged. He played with the brim of his hat.

Audrey tried to remember how the two men had interacted on the bridge in Weil-der-Stadt. She said, "Klara was murdered, as no doubt you know." She took a deep breath. *Yes, the man with the hat.* Nero had confirmed the perpetrator—a lifetime ago, it seemed. Could she trust a belligerent drunk? Her heart hammered. "And the piano in that van belonged to Klara's brother, Konstantine Zar," she added.

She watched Wilmots closely for the slightest irregularity—an impossible task, as the man was irregular in every way.

Wilmots reached into his jacket pocket.

Audrey jerked backward. .

"Please," he beseeched her. "Don't be afraid."

He pulled out a piece of paper and extended it to Audrey without stepping any closer. It was the same gesture he'd performed with Graf on the bridge. His hands were not only spidery, but hairy, and in one of those irrelevancies that bedevil tense moments, Audrey recalled that Paganini had had hands like that.

She removed a mitten and took the paper from Wilmots.

It was the first time she'd looked him in the eye. She'd expected the cadaverous face to disorient her. But not like this—not through pity. His lips trembled. The sunken, searching eyes didn't seem capable of harm. He was still holding the fedora in his hand, which she noticed now was also trembling, even as the snow began to circle his bald crown like an eggshell.

"It's Klara's will," he said as Audrey unfolded the paper. "That is, her final wish. The notary sent it to me after she died." He hesitated. "After the landlord disposed of the piano."

Audrey turned her back to the angling snow so the paper wouldn't get wet. A pale shroud of light lingered over the fields, enough to read the few handwritten lines:

To whom it may concern:

I, Klara Náhoda, of Rue Nova, Brussels, Belgium, hereby instruct my personal assistant, Roland Wilmots, to duly enact the following task in the event of my death:

To take responsibility for the upright piano in my possession, manufactured by A. Náhoda in Prague in 1941, serial number unknown, but with the symbol of a tetractys engraved next to the sounding board, and accompany it to Prague, where it should be returned to the Náhoda family atelier at its original address: Klavíry Náhoda, Kampa Island, Malá Strana, Prague, or to wherever the aforementioned atelier is currently located. The contents should then be removed, and distributed by Roland Wilmots to the closest family member, along with the piano itself. In the event that there are no family members extant, I hereby bequeath the piano and its contents to Olivia Taverner, widow of Reginald Taverner, Ixelles, Brussels.

The simple testament was signed by Klara and dated from eight years ago, witnessed by Roland Wilmots, and stamped by a Brussels notary with a fashionable Avenue Louise address.

"The contents…" Audrey whispered, folding the paper and handing it back to Wilmots. "Whatever did she mean by that?"

"I don't know," Wilmots said. "But now you understand why I was there on the night you found the piano. Klara's landlord threw it out on the street like rubbish. I didn't know what to do."

"Monsieur Wilmots…"

"Roland, please." Wilmots brushed the snow off his head and finally donned the fedora.

"What happened to Klara?" Audrey asked. She sensed—she dearly hoped—that Wilmots couldn't have had anything to do with her death. But as she was learning by the hour on this journey, nothing was as it seemed.

"Her maid found her at the bottom of the stairs," Wilmots said. "I was out of town, visiting my aunt. Oh…" he moaned. The sound seared through Audrey, "How could I not have been there? I never go away. *Never.* The maid called me immediately. Apparently Klara had had a visitor that afternoon."

"A visitor?"

"Yes. The maid said she'd never seen the man before. But she let him in, as he seemed quite a gentleman. He went upstairs to the sitting room, where Klara was. Oh…" Wilmots moaned again. He hung his head and shivered. "I should have been there for her. I should have…"

"Did the man murder Klara?" Audrey blurted.

Wilmots looked at her in agony. "The maid left for the day after she'd let him in. She didn't find Klara until the next morning."

Audrey rearranged her jumbled mind. "He could have pushed her, then."

Wilmots said nothing.

"Who was this man, Roland?"

"The maid described him as commanding. Though not young—late-sixties or more. His hair was pure white, she said, and he wore it in a ponytail. His glasses had dark lenses, as if he had an aversion to light." Wilmots hesitated. "Klara was elderly. She would have been no match for such a man."

"But why? What do you think he wanted?"

Wilmots hugged himself, bereft. His exhale hung on the gathering damp.

"Some sort of information, I think," he said. "I'd been seeing a man of that description for a few days. On Klara's corner. On Place de la Trinité. Near Pascal's. Everywhere, it seemed. Then he turned up on the night the piano was loaded into the van."

Audrey's head spun with Pascal's words: *He asked all about the neighborhood during the war. I never should have told him about Klara.* She watched two rooks lift off from a pine tree, trailing wingfuls of snow. She felt cold as stone. It would be a miracle if her fingers warmed up enough to be able to play later.

The door of the van scraped open again.

"*Merde!* Are you finished out there? My balls are frozen solid!"

After the events of the evening, Audrey was less shocked than she otherwise might have been to encounter this particular resident of her Brussels neighborhood in a Bavarian field.

Nero stumbled through the snow toward them. His lurid aspect had intensified somewhat since Brussels. Or perhaps it was simply the shock of crimson polyester against the snow. He took a long pull of a cigarette, followed by a sip from a can of Jupiler beer, and acknowledged Audrey with a grunt.

Wilmots said to her: "He's the only person I know with a van. And who would be willing to transport a piano such a long distance. Friedrich extended an invitation for tonight on behalf of the countess."

Audrey balked. "For both of you? After all…" She made sure that the Marseillais was out of earshot, but lowered her voice anyway: "I mean, that man was convicted of…" They were uncharitable words. But then, people like Nero were not the sort of demographic one would expect to turn up at Gloria von Helden's salon. Audrey rued these remarks at once. Hadn't the countess herself cited Konstantine Zar just that afternoon? *In the presence of music, there is no rich or poor.* Surely he'd also meant: *There is no chic or disreputable.* Did Gloria really believe that? Or was it simply for show? After all, Graf had gushed about all the glitterati who turned up for these events. He certainly hadn't gushed about all the vagabonds and criminals. Audrey regarded Nero and her stomach heaved at his general foulness. Still…How could she deny anyone—especially him— the healing powers of her art?

"You're both frozen to the bone," she said. "Let's get you warmed up in the castle."

And so this singular trio headed up through the snow to Schloss Helden.

CHAPTER 50

It was an arduous climb to the castle. The access road had been plowed, and it had stopped snowing. But the footing was still slick. Wilmots could barely stand up in his city shoes. Nero, cursing, began to wheeze after a few meters.

"You're not just on a concert tour, are you, Audrey?" Wilmots asked, struggling behind her.

"No." she said. "But clearly my journey has to do with yours." She turned to him and managed a smile. "With the same piano, that is. I'm following it to Prague for Olivia's sake. It's her last remaining link to Konstantine Zar. And now it seems she's mentioned in Klara's will, after all." Audrey lifted her chin with resolve. "I shall see the piano to its destination...wherever that may be."

She checked her watch: there was still an hour and a half before the performance. All she had to do was swap her habitual gray ensemble for the black one she performed in, and somehow thaw out her hands and feet. The ritual would not be so simple this evening. Her two companions would need a radiator to help them dry out—if Gloria would even let them in. In any case, it was heartening that a piano trio wasn't much good without a pianist, so even if Audrey got stuck on this hill somewhere, the concert couldn't begin without her.

Glossy sedans were making their way up the access road, one after the other, all with the same, entitled purr. No doubt their drivers assumed that the three stragglers on the road were simply locals, walking up from the village to serve at Gloria's buffet. The cars skidded around the tight turns, splattering snow as they went. Audrey noticed a Belgian license plate among them.

"Asshole!" yelled Nero. The Belgian car had forced him into a ditch.

A Jaguar glided up beside them and stopped. The passenger window drifted down. "*Möchten Sie mitfahren?*" a woman trilled from inside. A wave of perfumed heat escaped the car. No translation was necessary: they climbed gratefully into the back seat.

Gloria's guests endured the presence of what were obviously serving people with forbearance. French was established as the common language, though no one used it beyond the barest niceties. The man and woman, their hair lacquered silver and squirrel-red respectively, stared straight ahead, clueless that one of their hitchhikers was, in fact, the pianist of the evening. Distaste crept in as the smell of exquisite leather mingled with wet clothes. And no perfume, no matter how expensive, could have masked the stench of Nero.

"Well, well!" The driver perked up as they entered the courtyard. "*Schau mal!*" he exclaimed to his wife, and parked next to the car with the Belgian plate. "Aymeric has made it from Brussels after all."

Audrey gripped her seat. *Van Overberg!*

This meant nothing to her companions.

But for Jonas...

She sprang from the car with a hurried thanks.

Gloria was greeting her guests at the door in full-length furs.

"Audrey!" she heralded. "Whatever happened to you?" The countess's confusion deepened at the sight of the person with no coat, mincing behind the pianist; and the...Well, women like Gloria didn't possess the vocabulary for men like Nero. However, even if she'd known that an escaped convict was about to enter her home, she probably would have performed the same maneuver she did now, and to perfection: she simultaneously dismissed him, and invited him in.

"Sorry...so sorry..." Audrey brushed by her hostess and made a dash for the main staircase. She turned back just once, to signal to the maid that her two companions would need resuscitating.

◆ ◆ ◆

Audrey found herself in a dim, vaulted corridor running parallel to the great hall. She dashed down it without thinking, assuming that she'd end up at the anteroom near the stage, where she'd left her suitcase. She'd have to change into her concert clothes there, as there was no time to go to her room.

She also hoped to God she'd be able to warn Jonas.

Wood paneling and a floor of dark tiles made the hallway feel narrower than it was, and subterranean, as if it were leading her to the castle's deep, secretive heart. She passed double doorways with carved pediments, and sconces no brighter than candles. An astonishing collection of hunting trophies decorated the walls—hundreds of skulls and horns that had once been beautiful creatures, but that now tracked Audrey's progress through eyeless sockets. It was difficult to imagine Gloria von Helden ever pulling a trigger, what with her far greater arsenal of breeding and influence, It seemed unlikely that the pacifist, Ernst von Helden, had been the executioner, either. So that left some earlier ancestor who, aided by gamekeepers, shooting blinds, fine horses and even finer cognac, had had the stomach for this slaughter.

Audrey's dash ended abruptly:

Someone was standing in her way.

In the dimness, he could only be defined by the power of his stance. Most petite women would have balked. This one, however, had already faced this particular predator and survived the encounter, even if here, in the half-light of an ancient keep, he seemed to have gone rogue.

"The pianist of the Kepler Players, I see," said Aymeric Van Overberg. It was the voice of a robot. His gray suit had an expensive sheen, even in the weak light of the sconces. Something much denser gleamed from behind the black-framed glasses.

Audrey summoned all her resolve. "The trio that you destroyed, you mean," she said.

At one time, before she'd embarked on this journey, she might have cared what a patron of the arts like Van Overberg would have thought, confronting her in her present state: shoes that were soaked and misshapen; a coat of the same description; hands too ruddy and stiff to make music.

But she *had* embarked.

"Surely you can't be ignorant of Mr. Liebling's crime," said the baron. "Embezzling foundation money. A large sum of it."

"The crime that you and your wife framed him for, you mean?" Audrey stared at him without flinching. "Anyway, he returned the money. In your mailbox."

This confused Van Overberg. Or perhaps it was Audrey herself who had confused him: not her egregious assault on feminine style, but those eyes...the eyes that no man could ignore.

"In my mailbox?" Van Overberg said, incredulous. "I never received it. At any rate, he can't prove that he didn't keep the money. I'd be surprised, in view of his character, if there was any left by now."

Audrey blanched. Jonas had no proof, of course. What a foolish thing he'd done! Someone must have taken it from the box; or the baron himself had received it, but was exploiting the lack of proof. In any case, he'd never believe her if she told him that for the last three years, the eighty thousand euros from the Kepler Foundation had been safely tucked away in Jonas's cello case and watched over by the unsuspecting proprietor of the Casablanca General Store.

"Jonas Liebling has more character in his little finger than ten of you, Mr. Van Overberg," Audrey said, without taking her eyes off him. Her legs had turned to water.

He glided several steps forward.

Faintness engulfed Audrey. "What about all your tax havens?" she blundered, to keep him at bay. "All your luxury villas..." She hardly recognized her own voice.

Van Overberg stiffened. "What do you know about those things?" he asked. He seemed suddenly unsure.

What the hell am I talking about? Audrey could not answer this question, although she was fairly certain that the richest man in Europe must have been able to.

Van Overberg advanced one more step. Audrey flinched, waiting for the inevitable blows of the sort he'd dealt Jonas. There was only one thing left to wonder about: *What will become of the concert?*

But the predator had already eaten, it seemed.

"I look forward to your performance, Miss Nightingale," he said.

Audrey could see it clearly now: the complete control the man had over his deranged nature.

"You see," the baron went on. "I've summoned the police to the castle. They'll arrest Mr. Liebling after the concert. So you needn't worry about me interrupting you this time."

♦ ♦ ♦

"Aymeric?"

Gloria materialized behind Audrey still wearing her furs. "What a surprise to find you here!" Displeasure laced her tone. Van Overberg had clearly not been invited to this soirée. And although news of the event would have spread to the farthest reaches of Gloria's circle, few would have been rude enough to turn up without an invitation.

"Ah, Gloria, my dear," said the baron. His words oiled their way through the corridor. "I was just greeting your admirable pianist."

"And I suppose you're expecting to hear her tonight?" Gloria baited him.

Audrey glanced at her hostess and suddenly realized that in the creaking hierarchy of European nobles, Countess van Helden outranked the baron (even if her coffers might have been, relatively speaking, meagerer).

"Hadn't you better get yourself ready, Audrey?" Gloria asked, frowning at her dishevelment.

Audrey nodded, and the baron stood aside to let her pass.

CHAPTER 51

The *police?*" Florian lowered his violin. He'd paled several shades at Audrey's account of the baron, although there'd been no time to fill him in on what had happened in the snowy field. She'd found him in the anteroom, already dressed in suit and tie and softly warming up. Jonas was nowhere to be found. Through the paneled door, their audience could be heard assembling in the great hall.

"It looks like you hit close to home with that luxury villa comment," Florian said. "Maybe Van Overberg has embezzled foundation money himself, judging from his reaction."

"Maybe," Audrey said. "Turn around!" she snapped. "I have to change." Florian resumed his warm-up facing the wall.

Audrey peeled off her waterlogged shoes and stockings and opened her suitcase. Then she stripped off her gray skirt and sweater and replaced them with their black counterparts. With considerable difficulty, she inched dry stockings up her damp skin and wedged on her concert shoes. To complete her toilette, she ran a hand over her hair and applied some lipstick.

"I've never felt more unprepared in my life," she said. "How do I look?"

Florian turned around and smiled. "Well, even though it pains me, I have to agree with Jonas: you look like one of those figures on the prow of a ship."

Audrey snubbed the compliment (for it had been one, she knew). She leafed through her scores, then attempted to thaw out her hands on the tepid radiator. Furtively, they discussed whether or not they should tell Jonas about Van Overberg. For once, it was a blessing that the cellist was always late.

"Do you think he really called the police?" Florian asked.

"Anything's possible with that man," said Audrey. "I think we have to tell Jonas. Can you imagine how he'd react if he looked out and saw Van Overberg in the audience? He wouldn't be able to keep playing."

"On the other hand," said Florian, "he probably wouldn't go on stage at all if we told him beforehand. Either way, it looks like we'll miss out on all those hundred euro bills."

Audrey glared at him. "Jonas could go to jail!" she exclaimed. "How can you think about money at a time like this?" She breathed deeply to restore some sense of calm. "Maybe this concert will be the last moment of freedom for all of us," she said. "After all, we've been harboring a fugitive."

As if on cue, the fugitive himself bumped through the door with his cello.

"Sorry," Jonas mumbled. "I couldn't find my tie." His shirttail was protruding from underneath his jacket, and he'd not touched his beard, what with all the cuts and bruises. Jonas's carelessness never extended to the cello, however, which he removed from its case as if it were an article of feminine clothing.

"Jonas..." Audrey began.

"How ravishing you are, Süsslein!" he said, taking one of her hands and planting a kiss on it.

"Jonas, please be serious." Audrey reached up to touch his cheek. "Apropos of these wounds..." But she couldn't go on. There was something in his eyes that hadn't been there before. Affection welled in her, and with it the epiphany she'd had in the snow: the vision of an altered Jonas—or rather, of the contrite man he'd been struggling to become.

Audrey sighed. The new Jonas notwithstanding, she realized that if she told him about Van Overberg now, he might disappear again. This time, forever.

The paneled door opened to reveal Gloria herself.

It was a bold countess indeed who didn't bother to dress for her own soirée, but there she was, still wearing the black trousers and turtleneck from the afternoon. Through the doorway behind her, they could see guests making their way to the chairs placed randomly about the vast pink carpet. There was a dazzle of candlelight. Anticipation hummed. Steadily, it grew louder.

"Ten minutes to go!" Gloria announced, patting their shoulders. "Good luck!" She hurried back to her guests.

"Oh, my God!" Florian cried, peering around the door sat the crowd. "Audrey, isn't that the guy we saw outside Klara's? The man Graf was speaking to on the bridge?"

Audrey picked up her scores. "Yes," she said. "I'll explain later,"

"And the bum next to him in the red warm-up jacket...?"

"That's Nero."

Ladies and gentlemen, the Brussels Players!

"Damn!" Jonas whispered. "Here we go. Sorry guys. No tie this time."

Audrey mouthed to Florian: *Let's hope he doesn't see Van Overberg.*

"To the universe and back!" Florian said.

Solemnly, the other two repeated the oath.

♦ ♦ ♦

Audrey approached the Bechstein to warm bursts of applause.

Where is he?

Her eyes darted about the room while the strings tuned. Wilmots and Nero were directly in her line of sight through the open piano. They'd taken seats against the wall, as far from the rest of the audience as possible. Audrey cast them a vague smile, and nodded her thanks to the room at large.

From the crowd near the stage, many expectant faces beamed back at her. She went limp with relief that the baron wasn't among them. She rubbed her moist palms against her skirt. *At least he wasn't obviously present.*

The trio shared long, charged looks.

Audrey glanced up at the distant vaulting. The candlelight couldn't penetrate that stratosphere. *But hadn't something gleamed there?*

She bent over the keys and began the turbulent opening of the Saint-Saëns E minor trio.

Their tempos were too fast...headlong, even. Such recklessness usually horrified the cognoscenti. But with this rush of passion came something far more meaningful than convention. The audience had sensed it at once: raw honesty. And although most of Gloria's guests had already visited the buffet table as she'd instructed, and even taken off their shoes, they'd settled down at once when the music began and put their plates to the side, for it was clearly spiritual nourishment that they'd been after.

Where is he?

The question plagued Audrey at every pause...at each tuning of the strings.

He's here somewhere.

She fought this poison. She commanded the old Bechstein until it shook...until her face flushed with music's extraordinary power to lift the body from its moorings.

Were the police waiting in the courtyard? The poison returned.

Florian shook his head at her before the last movement of the Mendelssohn.

He's not here, he indicated.

They tuned for the finale.

There was a hush; a collective holding of breath.

Audrey glanced through the piano at the two outcasts. Wilmots, immobile, held his hat on his knees; Nero attempted invisibility (as much as this was possible while wearing crimson polyester in a room full of gentry). But they'd been altered, somehow. One could have mistaken them for two parched travelers at an oasis.

Audrey returned her attention to the vaulting as Jonas tuned to her final A. There was no doubt about it: there was a lumen there, like a planet through mist.

CHAPTER 52

Jonas spotted the baron during his last big solo.

It was one of those melodic lines he excelled at. Typically, he would linger on the sumptuous D longer than most cellists, as his bow had unlocked the secret of how to turn any string into its infinite playground. He would lean his head back in a moment of surrender, making women swoon. Generally, he also shut his eyes.

Tonight, though, he kept them open. And when he leaned back, he saw not a swooning female, but a gray suit at the back of the room near the door.

Jonas lingered too long on the D. Audrey, who was adept at threading her accompaniment around his excesses, had to delay more than usual, which meant that Florian, who joined the cello a few measures later, had to wait with his bow in the air.

They were seconds away from the greatest sin in classical music: full stoppage.

An ugly ruddiness infused Jonas's injuries.

The trio recovered. Professionals that they were, they'd spun a moment of beauty from imminent disaster.

Audrey launched into the final barrage of octaves as if chased by demons.

Everyone made a perfect landing on the last chord.

Applause thundered through the hall.

The musicians bowed, and retreated at once to the paneled room.

"What the hell happened?" Florian hissed. He knew, of course.

So did Audrey. "Where was he?" she grilled Jonas.

He stared at her, stricken. "You knew he was here?"

Applause continued unabated. Protocol demanded another bow.

"No curtain calls," Jonas snapped, packing his cello into its case with far less tenderness than he'd taken it out. "We have to leave. *Now.*"

"*What?*" Florian cried. "You have to face him sometime, you know."

Jonas pointed to his face. "I did. Maybe you forgot."

Audrey grasped his arm. "Please, Jonas. I'm sorry I didn't tell you he was here. There didn't seem to be a good moment." She swallowed hard. "Van Overberg said that the police would be waiting for you after the concert." She looked hard at Florian. "We have to get him out of here."

Florian ignored her. He took off his glasses and rubbed his forehead. He stared at Jonas, walleyed, "So you kept the money in the end," he intoned.

"I gave it back!" Jonas retorted, like a hurt child.

"Well, after it sat with your cello in Rami's store for three years," Audrey added, regretting the comment at once. Jonas hardly needed more salt in his wounds. "Anyway," she said to Florian, "the money disappeared after Jonas tried to return it. It wasn't his fault."

"Damn. We're stuck." Jonas indicated the bevy of guests Gloria was shepherding their way. The time for curtain calls had passed.

Florian threw a brittle smile at their admirers. "It's finished, Jonas," he said between his teeth. "You have to give yourself up. And God help you. Because between the richest men in Europe, and a fly-by-night, philandering cello-player, who do you think will win?"

Jonas scowled. His scars had swollen like earthworms.

"Maybe you should apologize to Van Overberg," Florian persisted.

"Florian, you're being unfair!" Audrey said.

"Apologize for what?" said Jonas. "I was framed."

"For screwing the baroness," Florian suggested.

"Ah, the artists!" Gloria trilled. "Come, friends, let us say hello." She touched a velvet shoulder here, a cashmere forearm there, ever so lightly, as if her visitors were spinning tops. They duly jostled into formation around the musicians. A quartet of women closed ranks around Jonas.

The Dvořák was so soulful!

Your ensemble playing is impeccable!

That pause at the end of the Mendelssohn was so dramatic. However did you do it?

"The cellist caught sight of his lover's husband, that's how!" Florian whispered to Audrey.

The comment soured her. She turned to Jonas.

He was gone.

"Jonas!" Audrey called. She plunged through the crowd and out the other side: there was no sign of him.

"Oh, he's probably just gone upstairs for a moment," Gloria said.

The guests wandered off in the direction of the buffet.

Audrey pulled Florian aside. "He's taken his cello!"

"So?"

"He knows about the Škoda, doesn't he? That the keys are in it."

Florian stared at her. "Christ. Do you really think he'd...?"

"Bolt?" Audrey grabbed her coat and kicked off her concert pumps. Her feet immediately swelled from this bondage and she had to jam them into her sodden walking shoes. "We have to stop him!" she cried. "He's a terrible driver. And in this weather…"

"You don't think he's intending to drive to Prague, do you?" Florian asked, incredulous.

"Knowing Jonas, he probably doesn't have a clue where he's going. Away from here, that's all. He probably doesn't even have his coat. Let alone a phone."

"He definitely has no money."

They stared at each other. *The urn.*

Audrey and Florian pushed their way through the mingling guests. They rushed across the great hall, bestowing a few thanks and waving to the company in a sort of royal farewell. Then they flew down the main staircase, disapproval floating down after them.

Imelda was just closing the front door.

"Wait!" Audrey called. "Did a man with a cello just go out?"

Imelda's eyes widened. "Yes, Madame."

Florian peered into the urn. "It's empty."

"The gentleman emptied it," the maid said, with evident discomfort.

"People must have left money on their way in, then," Florian muttered.

"Are the police outside?" Audrey asked Imelda.

The maid recoiled. "The *police?* No, Madame." Comprehension brightened her face. "Ah, I see. The tall gentleman is in trouble? Perhaps I should have stopped him?" She hesitated, and added, "I didn't think. He was such a kind gentleman."

"Women never think when it comes to Jonas," Audrey said under her breath, counting herself among them.

"There he is!" Florian cried. He launched himself across the courtyard, skating over the cobblestones in his concert shoes. "Jonas!"

But Gloria's Škoda had already revved to life.

"*Arrêtez-le!*"

Audrey spun around: Van Overberg was emerging from the castle with his coat half on. "Stop him!" he yelled again, shaking his fist at Florian and Audrey. "The police are on their way." The baron sprang across the courtyard to his own car.

Jonas pulled toward the drawbridge. The two musicians jogged after him as he crossed the moat. He stopped on the other side and let them catch up.

"Can you forgive me, Süsslein?" Jonas said, rolling down his window.

Audrey reached in and clasped his hand. "There's nothing to forgive," she said, adding, "Where did you get that coat?" Jonas was wearing an elegant dark-gray overcoat with black velvet lapels.

"Gloria lent it to me," he said with a grin.

Florian gawked. "Gloria helped you escape?"

"Yes. Anyway, she was pissed off at Van Overberg for crashing her party. She said she would never have invited him. He found out about our concert through the aristocratic grapevine."

A more expensive engine roared to life in the stables.

"Jonas, listen to me!" Audrey said. "Meet us in Prague." She fished her cell phone from her coat pocket. "Take this. I don't know how much battery it has left. Now repeat after me: '*Klavíry Náhoda, Malá Strana.*'"

Jonas did this easily.

"It's the atelier where Wilmots is taking Zar's piano."

"Does this car have a GPS?" Florian asked.

Jonas shook his head. "The thing's fifteen years old at least."

Van Overberg's Mercedes skidded toward the drawbridge.

"Jonas, go!" Audrey cried. She leaned in to kiss his battered cheek. Through confusion—or perhaps, intent—he moved his head at the last minute and their lips met. *It wasn't really a kiss*, Audrey would think later, when she could indulge herself and replay the scene. *It was more like a mistake.* But a serendipitous one, surely. For despite the roughness of Jonas's beard and skin, his lips had been divinely soft and gentle, and the way he'd expressed himself with them had resuscitated the vision of the new Jonas she'd experienced only briefly.

"Be careful: it's icy," she said, drawing away.

The Škoda crossed the park at a lurch and disappeared down the ridge road.

To Audrey's surprise, while she'd been occupied kissing Jonas, a hitherto unknown facet of Florian had been triumphing: he was standing in the middle of the drawbridge, feet planted, facing down Baron Aymeric Van Overberg.

CHAPTER 53

The Mercedes sedan pulled up so close to Florian that he could have touched it. Audrey hurried to his side. The drawbridge was so narrow that a car couldn't have squeezed by one person, let alone two.

The horn blared through the snowy calm.

"Don't budge!" Florian ordered Audrey. "We have to give Jonas as much time as we can to get out of here." As they blocked the ancient bridge, it wasn't lost on either of them that the only way Jonas had averted a twenty-first-century cataclysm—albeit temporarily—had been through fifteenth-century castle design.

The horn blared again and the driver's window slid down.

"Get out of the way!" Van Overberg shouted. He let his arm drop from the open window, and banged his fist against the door as if to scatter errant cows.

"Audrey, stand your ground!" demanded Florian.

She trembled. She had no difficulty imagining that same fist smashing into Jonas's face. Not for the first time did it cross her mind how precarious an artist's life was—and how often they were dependent on people like Van Overberg.

"Aymeric?"

Gloria strode toward them in her long furs, frightening a rook from the chestnut tree.

"I certainly hope you're not intending to run over the musicians after such an exquisite concert," she said to the baron. Her comment was flat and cool.

Van Overberg got out of the car, leaving the engine to idle.

"Gloria, my dear," he oozed, "I'm sorry I didn't say good-bye. I'm in a bit of a hurry. By the way, you wouldn't happen to know where the cellist is headed, would you? There's a little police matter to attend to."

Gloria's gaze narrowed. "You called the police to Schloss Helden?" Then, with false levity: "Since you went to all the trouble of inviting yourself here, maybe you should stay for dinner."

The insult-cum-command seemed to be a specialty of Gloria's. Audrey marveled at how their hostess wielded her superior rank like a precision tool.

Gloria shifted her gaze to the ridge road. "The police have arrived," she said.

They all turned to watch the patrol car cross the park and pull up to the bridge. Two men in reflective vests got out.

The countess squeezed past the Mercedes and approached the officers.

"*Verzeihung*. So sorry!" she gushed tunefully. The policemen smiled, undone by her charm.

"My friend here wanted to report a burglary," she explained. "But unfortunately, he was mistaken." Gloria momentarily turned her back on the police and glared at Van Overberg. "Isn't that right, Aymeric?"

The baron said nothing. His face was a mask.

"There, you see?" Gloria turned back to the police. "You've made a trip for nothing. *Leider*. Would you like to come in for some hot wine?"

The officers politely declined, bowed to the countess (she was, after all, the most prominent resident for miles around), and left.

The baron got back into his car and slammed the door. He obviously had no intention of staying for dinner.

Florian and Audrey made way for him to pass.

"Lovely to see you again, Aymeric, dear," Gloria said, patting his arm through the driver's window. "Bon voyage!" She gave the musicians a knowing smile, as if to say that Jonas would be well on his way by now. Hopefully, to Prague.

"Come," said Gloria after the Mercedes had sped away. She put her hands on the musicians' shoulders. "You deserve a good dinner."

She steered them into the courtyard, where the welcoming torches still burned. The last of the concert guests were heading for their cars.

"They probably think I've deserted them," Gloria said, nodding regally their way.

Audrey leaned in to Florian. "We might as well be the kitchen help," she said.

Florian leaned back to her. "Artists outrank the wealthy in every way," he whispered. "Except in wealth."

"Konstantine Zar?" Audrey laughed.

"No. Florian Lafève. By the way: you never told me why that strange skinny man and Nero are here."

While Gloria was engaged in her imperial duties, Audrey condensed what had happened in the snowy field into a few short minutes.

They entered the castle to a piercing wail issuing from the great hall.

"God help us," said Gloria. "It's Friedrich's prehistoric flute." She led her two guests back upstairs, adding, "I believe he's playing Schubert."

♦ ♦ ♦

The great hall seemed vaster; inchoate. Candlelight could not pierce its deepest recesses. Friedrich stopped playing when the little party entered. Nevertheless, an overtone of the flute remained. Not from Friedrich's efforts, it seemed, but from another player's long ago.

"Thank heavens you're taking that bloody bone back to Tübingen," said Gloria.

"I wanted to hear what it sounded like in such a large space," Graf said, casting a sheepish look at his hostess. "Anyway, you must be more reverent, Gloria, my dear. This is not just any old bone. What I was playing was pure, raw music...music from the time of its creation."

"*An die Musik*...isn't that what you were playing?" Gloria said. "Prehistoric Schubert?"

"Yes." Graf returned the flute to its box and tucked it into his rucksack.

Gloria laughed and went off to make a few adjustments to the buffet. A huge fire had been lit, and at her command, Gloria's serving staff moved the table closer to the hearth.

"So it wasn't Schubert's melody after all," she quipped.

Audrey's skin tingled. She'd perceived it again: that gap in time through which she could glimpse the dark-haired woman who had first played that piece of bone.

There was a movement in the shadows, and Wilmots and Nero crept into the light.

"Do help yourself," Gloria said to the strays, indicating the food and drink. She was not unwelcoming.

They thanked her. But out of politeness, they joined the others at the fireplace. Thus two musicians, the general factotum for a murdered woman, a forest intellectual, and an escaped convict-turned-junk dealer found themselves shoulder-to-shoulder before flames that could have roasted an ox.

Florian craned his neck to study a large portrait hanging high over the mantelpiece.

"Is that Count von Helden?" he asked, as everyone took in the nobleman looking down at them from his gilded frame. The handsome young man had a timid smile and receding, sandy hair, and dreamy depths eclipsed by the formal regalia he was wearing. .

"Yes," said Gloria. "That's my father. The kindest man I ever knew."

Audrey began to pace back and forth. "I'm sorry, Gloria, but we really must leave at once," she said. "Jonas will be exhausted. We can catch up to him somewhere en route." She caught herself at once: for Jonas had gone off with their only means of transportation.

She outlined this snag to her fellows.

To Nero's disgruntlement, Wilmots immediately offered them space in his van.

"But you can't leave now!" Gloria protested. "More snow is expected." She added, encouragingly: "But there's no snow predicted farther east, near the Czech border. Or in Prague. It's March already, after all. Jonas will be all right. And I'm fairly certain that Van Overberg has gone back to Brussels. It's best to wait until morning."

Florian took out his phone. "I'll try to reach Jonas on the phone you gave him, Audrey," he said.

They all waited for Jonas to answer: he did not.

"Oh, the battery's probably dead already," Audrey moaned. "I wonder how far he's gotten."

A lull ensued, during which Gloria beckoned her visitors to the buffet table. "You must all eat and drink," she said. "It's the only way to think things through properly."

They dutifully filled their glasses and plates and dragged chairs close to the fire.

At length a pact was forged. They all agreed that they shared the same goal: to honor Klara Náhoda's wishes and take Zar's piano back to its birthplace, come what may. And that they should leave at dawn, in Nero's van.

"That poor piano, stranded in that field," Audrey said.

"It will be all right," Graf assured her, pouring himself a second glass of the late count's 1941 Courvoisier. "The piano is well protected. And it's best not to warm it up quickly, as you know. The sounding board's liable to crack."

"Klara Náhoda..." Gloria murmured, settling into a large wingback chair. "Poor, poor woman."

"Audrey?" Florian joined his friend at the hearth. "What is it?"

"That man..." she said, staring at the smoldering logs

"Van Overberg?"

Wilmots sidled up beside them. "I think that Audrey meant the man who visited Klara before she died."

"The white-haired man," Florian murmured. "With the dog."

"Yes," said Audrey.

"He's been turning up everywhere, it seems," Florian noted.

"He was the last person to see Klara alive," said Wilmots.

Silence.

"He's after something to do with the piano," Audrey said.

"And you think that he..." Florian was unable to go on.

"Pushed her down the stairs," Gloria helped him, as if in a trance.

"Yes," Wilmots said softly.

No one ventured any further down that road.

Gloria perked up. "Friedrich, do you remember that trip we made to Brussels together to see Klara? About ten years ago?" Her tone was both brisk and compassionate, as if Klara herself would have appreciated the diversion.

"Yes," he said

"And the story she told us...about Zar and the strange business with his piano?" She lifted her glass to the portrait above the mantelpiece. "Father figured in it, too."

CHAPTER 54

Late February 1942

Two weeks had passed since the murder of the German officer in the Forêt de Soignes. A manhunt was underway. Konstantine Zar had given up his musical activities entirely and gone into hiding in the house on Chaussée de Waterloo.

He couldn't have known what would befall him. No one knows these things during a war...if ever. Tomorrow could bring death; or perhaps, a miracle. Life was a striding edge from which one could plunge in either direction at any time. The air was bracing on that edge, though. If you stood tall and square-shouldered, as Zar did, and kept your eyes on the horizon, you could navigate without falling. For a while, at least.

Klara and her brother continued their secretive habits as best they could. They never spoke about what happened in the forest. They'd told no one—not even Olivia. But their hours were measured by this omission. Stifled by it. And day by day, it became increasingly difficult for sister and brother to look each other in the eye. *When would they come for Zar? When would he fall off the edge to his doom?*

As Zar could not leave the house, Klara spent hours on the streets scouring the city for anything that might lift her brother's mood: decent meat; butter; black market wine; chocolate. Generally, she came home with a cabbage and a few potatoes instead.

It was fortunate that Klara Náhoda was the sort of woman no one noticed. Still, she took no chances. She went out of her way to avoid Gestapo headquarters on Avenue Louise, and the cafes and squares where the occupier lingered. Once she spotted Zar's teacher, Emile Hendrickx, drinking beer with two Germans on the Sablon, and it turned her stomach to see how the great violinist's loyalties had been poisoned. It sickened her, too, knowing that Hendrickx had pulled strings to arrange the transport of the Náhoda piano from Prague, and that even Konstantine's beloved instrument carried a stain. But none of that mattered now. What mattered was the promise she'd made to her brother regarding that piano.

She remembered the exact day. Because that afternoon, she'd come home with her first bucket of herrings.

♦ ♦ ♦

No one could stop talking about it: the miraculous catch of 1942. Beginning in January, the remnants of the Belgian fishing fleet that hadn't made the exodus to England pulled in over ten million kilos of herring. The little silvery fish had been known to pass near the coast in profusion, but always some distance away. This time, they'd come close enough to shore so the fishermen didn't have to venture past the floating mines the enemy had strung all up and down the coast.

The population exulted. Overflowing trucks delivered herring to all corners of the country and Belgians set their creativity to work: they preserved the fish in brine; in vinegar; in wine. They ate it fried; with pseudo-mayonnaise; as pâté. Morning, noon, teatime, supper. Blessed, infernal herring. Trams, buses, trains, cafes—everything, and everyone, reeked of it.

Klara waited in line with her bucket at the *poisonnerie* near the South Station. The stalwart woman stood uncomplaining for three hours.

Darkness had fallen by the time she'd boarded the tram and hauled six kilos of herring into the cramped, already-fishy space. She was scarcely aware of the metal handle digging into her glove. She kept lifting the piece of paper the fishmonger had laid over the top of the bucket, amazed at the silvery gleam within. It had been an exceptional day, all things considered. Just that morning, she'd come across one of the little sachets of Congolese coffee that the R.A.F. was dropping onto the streets of Belgian towns and villages.

They would have a feast that evening.

◆ ◆ ◆

Klara roasted the coffee beans in a skillet and pounded them with a mortar and pestle. She fried enough herring for a chamber orchestra and laid it out on the kitchen table along with boiled cabbage and potatoes. Zar appeared in a worn but clean peasant shirt. His expression lightened at the sight of this bounty. He kissed his sister on the cheek, and opened the bottle of Merlot an admirer had given him months ago after a lecture.

They ate in silence. Afterward, they adjourned to the parlor with their coffee. It was a ritual they clung to, absurd though it seemed so near the tyrant's jaws, but they knew that it was these frail human pleasures that would save them from hopelessness.

Zar sat at the rosewood piano, rested his head on his arm and played a series of simple melodies, probing and tender. *Like your thoughts, cheri,* his sister liked to say. The sounds also helped stifle the dread that set in of an evening: of Zar's imminent arrest. But also of that sleeping beast, the air raid siren, that could awaken at any moment.

Zar stopped playing and turned to his sister. "Klara."

She knew the tone. Her nerves contracted: he had a pronouncement of some sort.

She looked up from her mending. "Yes?"

"I want you to promise me something," he said.

"Oh?"

"You know how much I love this piano."

"Yes, of course."

"Enough to have had a tetractys carved in it, for heaven's sake!"

"Yes."

"And you know what it contains."

"It contains every note that was ever played on it!" Klara teased. Then, soberly: "You used to say that, didn't you? And we all believed it. Because it means that music never dies."

"I'm not talking about the music, Klara."

She hesitated. "Konstantine..." Klara stared at the bare floorboards, and at a wafting ball of dust that had escaped her mop.

"You must promise me," Zar pressed her, "that when they come for me, you'll do everything in your power to protect the piano...to keep the contents safe."

"But you know I'll do that, no matter what!"

"Good. Because you know that when I'm gone, it's all you'll have left of our family."

A flush spread over Klara's doughy cheeks. "Please stop talking about when you're gone!" she exclaimed.

Zar came over to her chair, and in a dramatic gesture knelt before her. Klara let out a nervous giggle as he set her mending aside and took her hands in his.

"Klara Náhoda," he intoned. "I hereby hand over to you possession of this Náhoda piano, which you will maintain and watch over as you would a member of the family." He paused. "No matter what happens to me."

Klara laughed again. "Yes, yes, all right."

Zar's brow darkened. "Swear it," he said.

"Oh..."

"Swear it!"

Klara shifted in the chair and finally looked at him. "I swear it."

Zar kissed her hands. "Thank you. You smell like herring, by the way." And with that he wandered back to the piano.

Somewhere across the city a siren began its demented wail. Zar, oblivious, continued playing. Klara got up to adjust the two dark-blue blankets draped over the parlor windows and turned to her brother. "Go back to Madame Hazard's, Konstantine," she implored him. "*Please.* She'll take you in. We're too close to headquarters here. It's not safe. She needn't know about what happened in the forest."

Zar got up and paced the room.

"Olivia's still living there, after all," Klara ventured. It was a magnanimous comment on her part. Klara had no fondness for the girl from the countryside who was exerting such a pull on her brother.

"My place is here with you," he said, though his voice was lifeless. Klara could tell from the professorial way he was crossing his arms that he'd made up his mind, even if he obviously hadn't convinced himself.

Zar stopped pacing and turned to his sister. "I think we should organize a concert here," he said. "As soon as possible." He paused, then added, "Hopefully with Olivia," though he hadn't seen her since he'd gone into hiding.

"A *concert?*" cried Klara. "Are you mad? The police are looking for you!"

Zar smiled sadly. "Mad compared to what? To all this insane violence? Come, dear Klara. Music is one of the only sane things we have left in this world."

CHAPTER 55

Before dawn the next day, Zar left the house on Chaussée de Waterloo for the first time since the murder. He slipped down obscure side streets and sprinted across intersections, sheltering in doorways as he went to make sure he wasn't being followed. In this manner he made his way to Madame Hazard's boarding house on Avenue de la Couronne.

The proprietress of the faded *maison de maître* had fallen on hard times. With the exception of Olivia Courtois, and a reclusive Polish horn player who never left his room, all the other boarders had gone home to their families. Her income dwindling, Madame Hazard had decided to raise food to sell. And so this kindly woman, who'd always prided herself on housing musicians, had found herself housing something else entirely: rabbits.

As she had no outdoor hutch, Madame Hazard spread hay in some of the students' empty rooms and set her energies to a task about which she knew nothing. She soon found that she had no stomach for the specifics. The few times she'd taken one of the poor, kicking creatures into the courtyard behind the kitchen and wrung its neck, she'd lost her appetite for days—an uncommon affliction in a besieged city. She'd also grown far too attached to her prospective food. Consequently, the landlady sold a few rabbits every week to a plug of a man in a beret, who was happy to deliver them to their fate elsewhere (Madame didn't want to know where), and bring one or two back to the boarding house in a more edible form.

Madame Hazard finally gave up on the whole enterprise. She let the remaining rabbits roam about the house in a state of grace, clean as cats, with the odd habit of scratching on closed doors, and bounding off as soon as someone opened them.

Zar rang the bell.

Several minutes passed before the door opened.

Madame Hazard stepped back in surprise. "Konstantine! Oh...*Dieu merci.* You're all right!" She had the rheumy eyes and blotched skin of someone who wept often.

"Madame..." Zar embraced her.

"Where have you been?" she asked, motioning him inside. "Are you still living with your sister?"

He glanced up and down the street before entering.

The landlady searched his face. "Are you in any trouble?" she said, hesitating.

"No, Madame," he lied. "Don't worry."

He followed her over the smooth tiles of the entryway. It didn't escape his notice that they were immaculately clean, something that required daily devotion in a city coated with destruction. Zar sniffed the air: the usual smell of roast chicken had given way to an earthier odor.

Madame Hazard smiled. "I've been keeping rabbits," she said. "Olivia adores them." She pointed to the staircase. "You know where to find her."

♦ ♦ ♦

They regarded each other across the threshold for a long time without speaking.

"Konstantine," Olivia whispered, as if unsure it was he. "What happened to you?"

More than a month had passed since they'd last seen each other—since unbeknownst to Olivia, the attack on Klara had set Zar's fate in motion.

Zar stepped into the room and closed the door.

"I went by your house to see if you were all right," Olivia said. She avoided him and went to the window. The light through the *voile* curtain fashioned a perfect porcelain cameo of her face.

Zar caught his breath. The dairyman's daughter had disappeared. In her place was this queenly, aloof being. Already one could detect the woman she would become: the artist who would seduce the world with her voice, and hold her listeners in her lovely white hands.

"Darling," Zar said, approaching her.

Olivia stiffened. "Didn't Klara tell you that I came by? I thought that something happened to you, Konstantine." She spoke his name as if she didn't know him. "Klara said you were unwell. Feverish. And couldn't see anyone."

Zar sighed, and turned away. "No, Klara didn't tell me. She's always been rather jealous of you. Of..." He faltered. "Of my esteem for you."

The porcelain face flushed. "Esteem?" Olivia said, incredulous. "You're obviously all right. Klara is feeding you well. You were too busy, perhaps, with all your endless philosophizing." She regretted her pique at once. She hung her head and clasped her hands, as if pausing between lieder in a recital.

"Olivia," Zar said, with a tone that made her look up. "Something has happened...something I can't tell you about. But I fear that I'll have to go away soon."

Olivia bit her lip. "Where?" she asked. "For how long?" She smoothed her pinafore and looked up at the farthest reaches of the room, where the farm girl had once imagined clouds and air-borne fancies, but the young woman saw only cobwebs and dirt.

Zar knew he wouldn't be able to answer her. *How could he?* How could he tell her about the crime he'd committed? How would he ever be able to deliver such a blow to the palace of harmony they'd constructed together?

So instead he said: "I've arranged for us to give a concert at my house. Next Friday."

She blanched. "A *concert?* Next Friday? But…"

"We'll perform *Frauenliebe und Leben.*"

Olivia backed away a step. *A Woman's Love and Life.* It was Robert Schumann's tenderest, most intimate song cycle. Olivia had sung it before, always with Zar at the piano, but in shabby classrooms, or in the musicians' café across the street from the conservatory. Never in a concert. Zar, as inexperienced in love as Olivia, hadn't been able to coach her on the depths of the woman's devotion in those songs; nor had it occurred to him that the girl from the farm was almost twenty now, and battered by war, and might have an inkling about the depths Schumann had set to music:

O let me die in this dream,
cradled on his breast,
let blessed death drink me up
in tears of infinite bliss.

Abandoned, I see myself stare straight ahead,

the world is empty.
I have loved and lived,
I am no longer living.

The sweetness drained from Olivia's face.

"Oh, my darling!" She flung herself at Zar. "You won't be coming back, will you?" Her voice caught. "Are you and Klara going home to Prague?" She began to weep on his white peasant shirt until it lay damp and crumpled against his breast.

He held her fast. Then, gently, he pried her away.

"No, I'm not going back to Prague, my treasure," he said. The words fell with deliberation—with longing, like the opening chords of Schumann's masterpiece...chords that sounded again at the end of the cycle, but with renunciation.

Zar tried to read what was playing over the bloodless oval of her face.

He pulled her close again. "You know that no music is ever lost, don't you?" he murmured.

She nodded.

"It waits in the air until we call it down."

"Yes," she whispered. "I know."

"And you know that harmony underpins all that is noble and right in the universe. It's reflected in our souls, and resides there forever."

"You taught me that, Konstantine."

"Well, then. Next Friday, let us drown out all this brutality and ugliness before it swallows us whole."

They stood entwined until their consonance returned.

And until a scratching sounded from the hallway.

Zar opened the door.

At first it seemed there was no one there. The visitor was so very close to the ground, after all.

"That's Johannes." Olivia laughed. She picked up a pale-gray rabbit and buried her cheek in its fur. Her eyes were dry and bright once more.

"Johannes Brahms?" Zar asked.

"Johannes Kepler," she said.

CHAPTER 56

Thank God you're home!" Klara scolded, taking Zar's coat. She'd rushed to the door as soon as he'd come in. Coolly, she added, "I hope you told her that a concert would be just too much of a gamble at the moment." (Klara never used Olivia's name if she could help it.) She urged her brother to the kitchen, where she'd laid tea for him, with some of those spicy *speculoos* biscuits from the corner bakery he loved.

"I told her she's to sing here next Friday," Zar countered.

And that, Klara knew, was the end of it.

He offered to compromise, however: he suggested that they invite only ten guests; and he would write a different time on each invitation so everyone wouldn't arrive all at once and raise suspicions in the neighborhood. This would inevitably result in some people coming too early, and others at the last minute, but Klara had saved a store of delicacies from the black market on Rue des Radis after Zar had gone into hiding, including wine and whiskey, and she agreed, albeit reluctantly, to share these things with the audience.

There was to be an eleventh guest, as fate would have it: a promising young English conductor and friend of one of the invitees, who'd come to Brussels for master classes at the height of the Occupation and found himself stranded on the wrong side of the Channel.

Perhaps, had he possessed a crystal ball, Zar would have followed Klara's advice and canceled the concert. For the young conductor on whom Olivia would make such a lasting impression was Reginald Taverner.

♦ ♦ ♦

The air raid siren went off just before Olivia began singing her favorite stanza of the Schumann:

Just as yonder in the blue depths,
bright and glorious as that star,
so he is in my firmament,
bright and glorious, lofty and distant.

She turned to Zar, who'd stopped playing. He turned to Klara: she was standing against the wall, as there were no more seats in the crowded parlor. "Is the front door unlocked, chérie?" he asked, to which she nodded. One never knew when a passerby might need shelter.

"Perhaps we should go to the cellar," suggested one of the guests. The others glanced at each other nervously and stood up.

Klara threaded her way through the group to tweak the black-out curtains.

"The irony of it all," someone said, "is that these bombs are being dropped by our allies, *nom de Dieu.* To free us from tyranny! By the way, what's happened to Taverner? He's awfully late."

No one knew.

The siren moaned to its apex, spilled its bottled fear, and slid down to gather more. Again it did this. And again.

The guests looked wistfully at the table Klara had provisioned—pâté, salami, bread, crevettes, herring (of course), and bottles of Bordeaux and whiskey—then headed for the cellar.

"This way, please." Klara shepherded the group into the hallway. She threw a look of triumph at Olivia, as if to say: *You see? I was right all along about this foolish concert!*

"No!" Olivia cried.

The exodus halted.

It was the same, burnished voice with which she'd been singing, and for a moment her audience thought the outburst was part of the performance.

Zar gazed at Olivia, entranced. He'd grown wan and febrile over the past month, in spite of Klara's ministrations, but now, as if summoned, vitality surged through him.

"Olivia's right," Zar cried over the din of the siren. "We must not abandon Music in our darkest hour."

The group shuffled, uncertain. With a grim set to her mouth Klara motioned them back into the parlor. She never was able to contradict her brother.

Everyone returned to their seat.

"That's the front door," Klara said. "Maybe it's Mr. Taverner." She slipped back into the hall.

Indeed, it was the Englishman, pale with fright. His round young face already carried the weariness of middle-age.

"Please, come in," Klara said, shutting the door behind him.

Taverner hesitated. "Did you know there's a German official standing in front of your house?"

Klara froze. "Pardon?"

"Yes. He said that he'd been listening to the beautiful music."

Klara gaped at him.

At once a blast shuddered in the street. It seemed to have come from the nearby forest.

The front door opened again to reveal a tall young man. He was wearing a handsome woolen greatcoat with a double row of silver buttons and eagle insignia on the arm.

"May I take shelter here?" he asked timidly. He put a polished boot on the threshold as if, had they said no, he would have taken it off again and gone away.

Klara and Taverner nodded at him without comment.

The German came in and shut the door. He listed slightly, in the manner of people uncomfortable with their height. His blond hair was already receding. He had an earnest, apologetic look, and seemed mortified by this imposition.

"Please," he said, as another blast sounded from across the city. He hadn't moved from the door. "Continue with your wonderful concert."

Just then Zar emerged from the parlor. "Taverner!" he cried. His voice went dead at the sight of the other visitor.

"Konstantine Zar!" exclaimed the German, dumbstruck. "*Mein Gott!* I'm a great admirer." He extended his hand, which Zar ignored.

No one moved or spoke.

"Please," said the German again. "I don't want to disturb you. I just wanted to get off the street."

The twisted logic of the situation was lost on no one: a German official, seeking safety with the enemy, while bombs friendly to that enemy threatened that very sheltering house.

"Konstantine!" Olivia called from within. "*Viens!*"

Zar locked his black gaze on the German's gentle blue one until the imposter wriggled with discomfort. Then he spun around and went back into the parlor.

Klara pushed in behind him, followed by Taverner. "Is he here to arrest you?" she hissed in Zar's ear. "Maybe we should stop the concert."

"Nonsense!" snapped Zar. "We shall continue, no matter what."

To Olivia's dismay, Zar stood before the gathering, and as solemnly as one could in a room redolent with herring and unwashed bodies, said: "We shall conclude our concert with Schubert's *An die Musik*."

Olivia stared at him. She hadn't prepared this work.

"It will be fine, my darling," Zar whispered to her as he opened the score and put it on the piano. "You know this song by heart. Just remember: Look to the skies! Music comes from above."

Olivia did as he said and looked up, as bombs continued to fall from the skies where Music was supposed to live.

Another explosion juddered the walls.

There were gasps. A sharp cry.

A little cascade of plaster sprinkled the piano lid.

The guests crowded as close to the instrument as they could, as if Music would protect them from the tumult outside, and if they were lucky, carry them away to her paradise.

Zar seemed unaware of the chaos. The presence of the man in the hallway had only heightened his resolve. He glanced up at Olivia beseechingly, inviting her into the innermost reaches of his heart.

Oh, beloved art,

In how many a bleak hour

have you borne me away to a better world!

The bombing stopped when the Schubert began.

Some of those present might have considered this a coincidence. But as far as the artists were concerned, there was no doubt in their minds that they'd mounted their own campaign armed only with Music, who, herself trembling in terror at this obscenity of noise, nevertheless had had the courage to venture down Chaussée de Waterloo that evening.

Klara collected the empty glasses on a tray and stepped into the hallway.

The German hadn't moved from his place by the door.

She stopped in surprise: he'd been weeping. She couldn't have known then how different he was from the officers who would take Zar away just a week later.

He thanked her, and smiled sadly. "I will not report Zar," he said.

Then he opened the door onto a bruised and violated city.

PART III

CHAPTER 57

I have spent my whole life with something not of this world. Music is just a trick of the air. A phantasm. Isn't it?

Nero changed gears and Audrey opened her eyes. The interior of the van was a dim jumble—no different from the interior of her mind.

She leaned her head back against the cold metal wall.

I've fallen in love with a wraith, she thought. *Who slips through my fingers when I try to touch her.* Audrey closed her eyes again. *But she's lifted me up countless times, to that place where she lives.*

The van braked suddenly.

"*Merde!*" yelled Nero. He pulled into the slow lane and made a rude gesture at the passing traffic. Graf straightened up in the passenger seat and yawned loudly.

What if was true what Plato said? Audrey wondered. That everything the eye can see is illusory—that reality is everything we *cannot* see. That would prove that musicians are more in touch with reality than people give us credit for. Priests must appreciate Plato, too. Although *their* invisible substance is vastly different from ours—authoritarian, and not nearly as melodious. And Music would never impose obedience on those who seek solace in her.

♦ ♦ ♦

They'd left Schloss Helden at dawn. A spring thaw had already set in, leaving a mist hovering where the snow used to be. A few birds had formed an advance party of sorts in the woods and fields of the von Helden estate and were warming up, two-toned and brave.

"It shouldn't take more than five hours to get to Prague," Graf had said with his usual élan, although everyone knew that this was optimistic on such roads.

Graf was sitting next to the driver partly in deference to his age, but also because of his experience with vans, which meant he could spell Nero from time to time as well as offer advice should there be any engine trouble. The others—Audrey, Florian and Wilmots—huddled side by side on the floor in a purgatory of roaring and jerking. Nero had furnished his digs with a mattress on which he could sleep off his binges—a convenient item, but one that probably should have been burned. Now, however, along with the blankets reeking of petrol, it seemed a luxury.

There was one other passenger:

Audrey regarded the rectangular object, swaddled in its quilt and strapped to the side of the van. The cover was stained, and stuffing spilled from numerous rips and open seams. How unassuming it was! Anyone would have thought it was just a piece of second-hand furniture. An orphan.

And yet...

This orphan was lucky enough to have a pedigree.

And it was going home.

It contains every note that was ever played on it.

The thought electrified Audrey. She sat up straight against the metal wall and stared at the piano, as if her gaze could penetrate the soiled cover and probe even deeper, through all the rosewood and bronze to the place where Music came and went. It was Zar's hands that had played the last notes caught inside this instrument: the concert he'd performed with Olivia during the air raid.

Audrey shivered. No, not Zar's hands. But those of the military policeman. It was he who'd played *Für Elise*—badly—as the English pilot lay dying upstairs...the evening that Zar had tried so gallantly to propose to Olivia in the forest, but failed.

The evening they'd taken him away.

Audrey's heart swelled. She clasped her hands around her knees. *But how could I have forgotten? I was the last one to play this piano, under the night sky. And Roland was my witness.*

The man sitting next to her seemed to have heard her.

"Hungry?" Wilmots asked. He opened a foil packet of Gloria's tea sandwiches from the day before.

Audrey shook her head. "No, thank you."

Nero reached around as he was driving and Wilmots stuffed three sandwiches into his hand.

Audrey glanced down at Florian. He was curled up on the mattress, fetal and limp: Schubert the infant, as yet unmarked by the rigors of genius.

"I don't suppose there's been any sign of Jonas anywhere," Audrey said.

"No," said Graf. "He'll be all right, Audrey. Don't worry."

Her thoughts strayed to the horrors of what might be lying on the side of the road: a wreck they would never have spotted in such weather—an accident they'd find out about only later, when the police had gotten in touch with the owner of the Škoda and Gloria had made a frantic call to Friedrich.

Don't be afraid of this journey.

Olivia's egret elegance filtered in with her words, but was soon gone.

♦ ♦ ♦

"Friedrich?" Audrey said softly. She couldn't tell if he was sleeping.

"Yes?"

"Did Gloria's father betray Zar in the end—after the concert?"

"No," Graf said. "Gloria's certain that the count kept his word."

The van forged on through the dull March morning. They were on the Czech side of the border now. It would be the type of day that never truly shakes off the night...that has no dawn, noon or sunset. Only perpetual dusk.

"What did Klara mean in her testament by the piano's contents?" Audrey asked.

Graf said nothing for a few moments. "Roland told you," he said at length.

"He let me read it." Audrey glanced at the man beside her. His hands were draped over jutting knees. He had a moist, sickly turn to his lips. A reluctant executor, it would seem. And yet here he was, carrying out Klara Náhoda's final wishes. Regret gripped Audrey that she'd ever thought Roland Wilmots capable of harming anyone.

"I only found out about the testament myself two days ago, in Weil," Graf said.

"Would the man who visited Klara have been interested in the contents of the piano?" Audrey pressed him.

Graf said nothing.

Wilmots picked up his fedora and idly examined the brim.

Audrey stayed the course: "I mean, would he have insisted in a way that might have led to her death?"

"Possibly," Graf said.

Audrey looked over at the piano. "So perhaps there's some kind of treasure inside," she teased. Then, in earnest: "I mean, don't you think it odd that someone from a humble background like Klara's would be able to afford such a large house on Rue Nova?"

"The Taverners rented it for her from a Belgian family that still owns it." Graf said. "Before then, Klara lived on in the house she'd shared with her brother."

"Yes, but still..."

Graf unfastened his seatbelt and turned around to face Audrey. He looked far more tired and anxious than his voice had let on.

"I sense what you're getting at, Audrey," he said. "About the contents of the piano. About the Zar family. In fact, Klara confided in me with the utmost confidence." He paused. "But I suppose now that she's gone, there's no reason you shouldn't know."

Florian stirred and sat up. "Confided what?" he asked.

Graf turned around to face the road again, and with his back to the others, he explained:

"Klara didn't want to go back to Prague after Zar was arrested. In any case, it was in Communist hands by that time. How I pitied her! Like you, Audrey, I thought she was poor; I just assumed that the Taverners had been supporting her. No one could have ever guessed the truth. I certainly didn't."

"The truth?" Audrey echoed.

"Yes. As you might know, Klara and Konstantine's grandparents came to Prague at the end of the nineteenth century from farther east, and changed their name to Zar—from Zarándok. They were unassuming people." Graf took a deep, slow breath. "They'd come to join other members of the Zar family who'd been in Prague since the eighteenth century."

"So they were poor musicians," Audrey said

Graf swiveled once more to face her. "Oh, no. They were far from poor. You see, the Zarándoks were one of the oldest and wealthiest families in Austro-Hungary. They owned a palace on Maltese Square in Prague until 1945, when it was taken over by the state."

CHAPTER 58

Kepler's coachman had probably found the streets of Prague as tortuous as Nero did, even if the astronomer's journey from Graz, in January 1600, would have encountered far greater calamities along the way: broken wheels; choking mud; rat-gnawed inns; bandits. Perhaps most disagreeable of all was the effect that such interminable jolting would have had on a delicate constitution like Kepler's. Even the sumptuous carriage of Baron Johann Friedrich Hoffmann, councilor to the Holy Roman Emperor Rudolf II, had not mitigated the woe. It was Hoffmann who'd offered Kepler this journey to Prague to meet the flamboyant Dane, Tycho Brahe, Rudolf's court mathematician and astronomer. Brahe would die just a year later, as it happened, leaving Kepler to take over his research on the planets, as well as the court appointment. As for the royal patron himself, the mournful Rudolf wandered the acreage of Prague castle alone, dressed in black, with only his madness padding after him for company.

The travelers from Brussels reached Prague by mid-morning.

"Where the hell are we?" muttered Nero.

Audrey and Florian leaned around the front seats for a view. In the windowless van, addled by the ceaseless lurching, they could well have imagined they were in a horse-drawn conveyance. In any case, Nero's van seemed to be picking up where those phantom carriages had left off, joining the continuum of journeys that had traversed these same worn stones: *Kepler...Brahe...and Klara Náhoda, with this very piano.* Even Mozart's carriage might have passed this way in 1787, when he'd arrived in Prague and been feted like nowhere else at that point in his career.

♦ ♦ ♦

The van skidded around a narrow corner behind Prague Castle and clipped a lamppost.

Someone yelled in Czech.

"Kiss my ass!" Nero yelled back. He rolled down his window and brandished his middle finger.

Graf chuckled. "Or in the words of Kepler's coachman: *Leck mich im Arsch!* Look! There it is: No. 76. *U Zlateho Gryfa*—At the Golden Griffin. Tycho Brahe's lodgings. Kepler would have visited him there."

The inn was thick-walled and squat. It had been clinging to its neighbors on this steep lane for four centuries. On such a vaporous morning, it wouldn't have been surprising to see Tycho Brahe himself on his way home from a soirée, the lamplight glancing off his silver nose. (He'd lost the real one in a duel with another Danish nobleman, apparently over a mathematical formula.)

"This is the wrong way," Graf said. He refolded his map and peered at it through the blurred light. "We have to turn left somewhere. Then descend to the river. The Náhoda piano atelier is on Kampa Island."

Nero made the turn and inched the van down the slick byways of Hradčany.

The powerful shoulder of rock above the Vltava River had been harboring human settlement for over a millennium. One after another, the ages had staked their claim, each stratum fusing to the one before so that an untold weight of towers, battlements, churches and monasteries was pressing down on that rock until it was probably beginning to metamorphose. High on the hill, the gothic tracery of St. Vitus cathedral stood dour in the mist. Ever vigilant. Whisper-still.

"There's the Wallenstein Palace!" said Florian, pointing to a coffee-and-cream façade. "We played there, Audrey. Remember?"

"Yes," she laughed. "I remember the ballroom. The crystal and gilding almost blinded us. We played Mozart, didn't we? In the city he so loved."

"You see?" Graf said. "History has no beginning and no end. We can change its course. But we can never, ever escape the flow."

Audrey drank in the city that had bewitched her. Spires and cupolas in their dozens lifted the gaze. From the hill of Malá Strana—or Lesser Quarter—the old roofs spilled in a frenzy of tiled geometry. There was restlessness in them, too, as if they might shake loose at any moment, like wings.

"Finally!" Graf rolled down his window. "Malá Strana Square. We're not far now."

They all stared out at the sculpted mass of St. Nicholas cathedral. The original tracing of medieval lanes, alleys and squares lay entombed underneath this Baroque layer, though on musty days such as this, a reek filtered up through cracks in the paving as ghosts exhaled.

A whiff of cinnamon wafted into the van, chased by something plummy.

"Hot wine!" Florian cried.

"Stop here, please," Graf asked. "We need sustenance."

"I never drink this early in the day," said Wilmots, unfolding his legs on the mattress.

"Well, now's a good time to start!" Graf chortled, heading across the square with Florian. They returned with six wines and *trdelník*: dough rolled in cinnamon sugar and turned on a cylinder over an open flame.

"There's enough for Jonas as well," Graf said, handing Audrey a plastic cup of mulled wine.

"Do you think he made it all right?" she asked with a tremor.

"We'll soon find out," he said.

♦ ♦ ♦

The van crept through the crooked lanes and dead ends of Kampa. The tiny island hugged the bank of the Vltava in the shadow of Charles Bridge and was home to the river's wraiths and specters.

Graf looked up from the map. "Maltese Square is over there somewhere," he gestured. "Where the Zar family had their palace."

Audrey squinted through the windshield. She was still digesting Graf's revelation about Konstantine Zar: that his family had not been poor wanderers at all, but people of great wealth. She could imagine the photograph on Olivia's piano so clearly that the charcoal gaze seemed still to be locked on hers. *He was obviously poor...he only had a few shirts to his name.* Wasn't that how Olivia had described Zar? Had she known about his wealth—or why he'd concealed it?

A beggar can be aristocratic, Olivia had also said. *It's a question of bearing...of innate nobility.*

They turned into a deserted, dog-leg lane. The ancient housefronts leaned in close. Through Nero's open window drifted a stagnant, earthy smell.

"Stop!" Graf cried.

Nero stamped on the brake

"There it is!"

They all stared at a three-story house with simple pediments, and double doors above which a dusty fresco depicted three fanned keyboards. Underneath this decoration, gold lettering had faded almost to nothing, and would have been illegible to anyone who hadn't been on the lookout for it:

Klavíry Náhoda.

CHAPTER 59

It was a lane cast off from all things modern. Except one: a car, powdered with snow.

"Is it...?" Florian began.

"Gloria's Škoda!" Audrey cried.

Nero pulled up behind it and they all got out.

Two shapes dozed inside the car: Jonas, asleep at the wheel. And next to him, somewhat more alert, his cello.

Graf tapped on the window.

Jonas shook awake. "Jesus, Mary and Joseph!" he cried out at the five pairs of eyes peering in.

Graf opened the driver's door. "You could add Johannes Kepler and Emperor Rudolf to that list," he laughed, "considering the location."

Everyone helped pry the frozen cellist from the car.

Jonas pulled Audrey from the group and held her close. "Oh, Süsslein, you can't imagine how glad I am to see you," he said with a sob, and pressed his face into her cloche hat.

Florian handed him a cinnamon pastry and cup of mulled wine, to which Jonas said, "I hereby add St. Florian to the list."

"Did you see any trace of Van Overberg?" Graf asked.

Jonas shook his head.

"Why didn't you ring Náhoda's bell?"

"I did! No one answered. The place seems empty."

They all turned toward the house, which indeed looked moribund.

"We need to get Jonas inside," Graf said. "The Van Overbergs of this world can track anyone anywhere. Did you speak to someone at the atelier?" he asked Wilmots.

"Yes," Wilmots said. "Karel Náhoda: a distant cousin. I told him about Klara's final wishes."

"Then where is he?"

"I'll call him again." Wilmots took out his phone and wandered to the turn in the lane to stretch his legs. His dark suit was just another rune in a city brimming with them.

Nero took out a cigarette.

"Can I have one of those?" Jonas asked, and the two smoked in silence.

A few snowflakes pirouetted down on the gathering. From a dormer overhead, a woman shook out a duvet, glared suspiciously, and slammed the window shut.

"He's there!" Wilmots said, and hurried back to them.

At once a bolt sounded from the door of Klavíry Náhoda. A key clinked, rattled in the lock, then turned twice.

One of the double doors drifted open.

A gnome of a man appeared: balding, with downy tufts of hair sprouting from his ears, and a dark-blue work coat that reached almost to his ankles.

"Welcome, Klara's people!" he said. His dreamy, mottled-green eyes tended upward and exuded kindness. "I am Karel Náhoda. I've been waiting for you for years." He unbolted the second door. "Quickly, please. You can park in here." He indicated a cobbled carriageway leading to an inner courtyard.

♦ ♦ ♦

Jonas and Nero inched their two vehicles through the passage.

"It's safer in here," Náhoda said. He gave a furtive look up and down the lane before shutting the doors and bolting them again. He seemed further dwarfed by the lid of a grand piano undulating against the wall beside him.

Introductions were made in the dim passageway. There was a hint of mildew in the air...of yesterday's cooking.

"I'm sorry I didn't answer the bell earlier," Náhoda said to Jonas. "Forgive me. I saw you there in the car." He looked at his feet. "You see, I just couldn't be sure you weren't associated with the man who came by last night."

They all froze.

"Which man?" Graf asked. His blue eyes flashed in alarm.

"I don't know who he was. He seemed agitated; upset. Imagine: he pushed his way into the shop!" They'd agreed on English as their common language, and Náhoda's rose and fell with a sad cadence.

"But *who?*" Graf asked again.

Audrey drifted to the piano lid and ran her glove over the bell-curve. "Did he have white hair, by any chance?" she ventured. "Dark glasses?"

"Yes. *Yes!*" Náhoda exclaimed. "And a dog...not a very friendly one."

"What did he want?" Florian asked.

"He wanted to know if I had a war-time piano in the workshop—if I knew anything about an instrument from that era. From 1941, specifically. Of course, I told him I knew nothing."

Wilmots turned angrily on Nero. "It's the man who watched the piano being loaded into your van in Brussels. Did he ask you where it was going, by any chance?" He grabbed Nero's arm. "*Did you tell him?*"

"Calm down, please," Graf said.

Nero shook Wilmots off. "I may have," he drawled.

"And how much did he pay you for that piece of information?" Wilmots demanded.

Nero grunted, and sidled to the door. "I'm going out," he said.

Karel unlocked the door and Nero disappeared.

"Let's hope he's not followed," said Graf. "You can probably see that red jacket from the top of Hradčany."

*I never should have told him about Klara...*Pascal's words spun again in Audrey's mind. "Do you know what happened to Klara, Monsieur Náhoda?" she asked softly.

Náhoda's eyes filled and soon overflowed. He looked down at his feet again and shook his head. "Yes. It's unimaginable." He wiped his eyes with his sleeve and said to Wilmots, "Thank heavens you were able to bring the piano back home."

Wilmots reached into his suit and mutely handed Klara's testament to their host. Overcome, Náhoda put the document in the pocket of his work coat without reading it.

"That man, Monsieur Náhoda," Audrey said, hesitating.

"Please, call me Karel."

She began again: "Karel, the man with the dog is extremely dangerous. You must be careful."

The air in the passage grew heavy. A crow rasped in the courtyard. On a balcony nearby, someone began beating a carpet.

At last Karel said, "Oh, but where is my hospitality? You must be exhausted. Come in, come in!" He seemed relieved to forget about his nocturnal visitor. "My assistant will come around later to help unload the piano. It must be acclimated carefully."

He opened a door off the carriageway and beckoned them into a chilly space vast enough to house an army of pianos, although only a few intact ones were in evidence: one grand, obviously old enough to have witnessed the break-up of Austro-Hungary; and three massive uprights, dotting the landscape as if they'd been beached. Otherwise, the piano as a viable musical instrument was only implied here: by the lids leaning against a wall in a single, breaking wave; and by the detritus scattered across the cement floor in all directions: key mechanisms, pedal housings, blocks of wood, brass fittings, iron frames. The entire enterprise was illuminated by a wall of uninsulated windows overlooking the courtyard, although the light filtering in appeared to have more of a beatific function than a practical one. The workshop exuded the air of a shrine, where nothing has been moved or altered in an effort to preserve its sanctity...where its patron saint, Music, eked out an existence through the ministrations of a humble repairman.

CHAPTER 60

Like most private enterprises in Prague after the war, Klavíry Náhoda was shut down by the Communists in 1948 and the building confiscated. Petr Náhoda and his son, Antonin, found work at the Petrof piano factory during the Communist years, grinding out soulless clones. But in 1991, under restitution laws, Karel Náhoda got the building back. He tried to resuscitate the workshop: He engaged an assistant, and scoured the city for used tools and equipment. But life was hard for small craftsmen. Cheap Asian pianos were flooding the market. Karel eventually resigned himself to being a technician instead of a builder, and the Náhoda brand of piano went extinct.

Karel offered his visitors this brief history as he brewed coffee on an electric ring at the center of the workshop. He dragged a motley collection of piano stools and benches around a pot-bellied wood stove that emitted a modicum of heat.

"I'm the last remaining Náhoda," Karel said. "Just a distant cousin." He handed cracked mugs of coffee to his guests, and upended a crate on which he set a plate of stale gingerbread. They all drew their seats even closer to the tepid stove. Certainly no one felt the need to take off their coat.

"Antonin died years ago and left no heirs," Náhoda went on. "Klara married Antonin's cousin, Jan, in 1939, but the marriage lasted hardly a year. As you know, she went to Brussels in 1941 to join her brother."

"Was Klara ever in touch with you directly, Karel?" Graf asked.

"No. Never. I was contacted only recently, by this gentleman." Karel nodded to Wilmots.

"The rosewood piano was an unusual order, wasn't it?" Audrey said. "Konstantine Zar wanted it built to his specifications, apparently."

"His specifications?" Jonas echoed, grabbing another piece of gingerbread.

"I don't know anything about the details of that order," Karel said. "Anyway, it wasn't the first order we had from the Zar family. They lived just a few streets away from here, on Maltese Square. The family owned a huge residence for over two hundred years—right up until 1945. Their salon concerts were famous across Europe."

Audrey shared a look with Graf at this confirmation of the Zar wealth.

Karel wandered to the windows and regarded the courtyard, where scraps of wood and metal protruded from dirty remnants of snow: a pedal lyre...a row of stripped keys...a music desk. It was a piano graveyard where the corpses had been buried too hastily.

"It was 1937, I believe," Karel continued, returning to the stove. "Konstantine's father was looking for a new grand for their salon. I was born just after the war, so I never experienced their legendary soirées—I never even met any of the Zars personally. The house has been empty for decades now." Karel's gaze drifted. "They say that on a windy day, you can still hear piano music coming from the salon window."

All eyes were on him.

Karel hesitated. "I've heard it myself. Kampa Island is full of ghosts, you know."

"Really?" Jonas breathed.

"No soul of an executed person can ever rest easily," Karel added, obviously meaning Zar.

Audrey studied Karel Náhoda. He looked frail in the gauzy light—a gnome in his seventies who might have wielded a magic wand in his prime, and made all the broken piano limbs whole again, but who no longer had the strength to do so. He was still able to conjure the Zar aura, however, and Audrey stepped eagerly into the scene that Antonin Náhoda had described to the young Karel:

The reigning Zar patriarch had passed under Klavíry Náhoda's fanned keyboards to discuss a new instrument worthy of for the luminaries who performed in his salon. He hadn't come alone: his teenage children, Klara and Konstantine, had tagged along from nearby Maltese Square.

Audrey closed her eyes, and at once Karel's phantom drama played out before her. Spellbound, she watched the Zar children trail behind their father as he examined the display of pianos in this very room. Konstantine, the moody one, wandered off on his own; Klara, the awkward, adoring sister, lagged in his wake. At sixteen, Konstantine was already an enigma—a musical genius whose talent could not be pigeon-holed. He'd shown great promise on both the violin and piano, but didn't seem to have a preference for one or the other. Instead, his passion seemed to lie in deep mysteries...in musical knowledge with roots in remote antiquity.

Saying nothing to anyone, the young Zar sat down at one of the showroom pianos and played a succession of haunting sounds—strange intervals, and melodies that seemed more celestial than earthbound. The boy's singular music riveted Antonin. He left the elder Zar to his browsing and slipped up to his son. *Come and play whenever you want, young man. Perhaps you might be interested in knowing more about music's ancient origins. My study is just over there...*

Karel's story came to life in the piano wasteland. Audrey had no doubt that the young Zar's hand had brushed the air near hers; that it had rested on a bright new set of keys close by, and caressed them. His playing had set the molecules in the room quivering.

Something remained of that energy, it seemed. For the molecules were quivering still.

♦ ♦ ♦

"It all came to an end during the war, of course," Karel said, wrenching Audrey back to the present. "The Zar soirées. The glittering dinners. You see, Konstantine's mother was Catholic. But his father was a Jew, and was arrested in 1939."

This piece of the puzzle dropped without warning.

"It all makes sense now," Florian exclaimed. "The secrecy around him. The flight from Prague. Not that Brussels was a safe haven, with the Germans invading Belgium in 1940."

Karel turned on the electric ring to brew more coffee. He lingered there, his mind clearly roving. "One could make such a conclusion, of course," he said, "in view of Zar's Jewish ancestry." He heaped coffee grounds directly into the pot. "But only if one had little knowledge of the beliefs Zar was trying to revive. Antonin liked to say that Konstantine Zar was an old soul—so very young, but with uncanny wisdom."

Karel turned to Graf. "You know much about ancient history, Professor Graf," he said. "I am so honored to have such a distinguished historian present."

"Call me Friedrich, please!" Graf gushed. "These days, I seem to know more about vulture-bone flutes than anything else," he added self-deprecatingly.

Karel refilled their mugs. "Oh, but not long ago you published a brilliant article on mystery cults," he said. "Orpheus in his grotto; Egyptian priests in their temples; Pythagoras the Master, dressed in white, and his followers dispersing into the arid Greek landscape. You made it so riveting! As you see, I remember every detail. I think that your topic was secrecy, if I remember rightly."

"Yes, it was," Graf said, sipping his coffee.

"You also mentioned Freemasons—of whom Mozart was one—and other groups in history that dealt in sublime principles: coded knowledge; the musical universe..." Karel glanced playfully at the members of the Kepler Players. "Every musician should know that *The Magic Flute* is absolutely brimming with this sort of symbolism."

"You're setting the stage for Zar's teachings, aren't you, Karel?" Florian asked.

"Exactly," Karel said. "He'd written to Emile Hendrickx at the Brussels Conservatory even before the arrest of his father. Maybe he naïvely thought that Belgium would remain neutral during the war. Anyway, Zar was already looking for a safe harbor for his ideas—a place where he could teach his own musical philosophy, but deeply inspired by the ancients."

"Olivia said that people flocked to Zar's talks in Brussels during the war," said Audrey.

"Yes. But I doubt he liked taking such a risk."

"Especially if he was part Jewish," Audrey said. *And after he killed a German officer,* she would have added, had a gleam of Zar himself, pulsing faintly, not prevented her.

"He wasn't interested in promoting himself," said Karel. "Far from it. He wanted to teach other musicians to spread his message: to give people wings in the darkest of times.

"Like a sort of religion," Jonas offered.

"Maybe," Karel said.

"And why not?" Graf chimed in, picking up the thread. "Think about it," he said, with a wink at Karel: "A powerful, invisible force that lives overhead somewhere. That heals and comforts. That promotes unity and love and knows every human emotion. Why would something like that be any less plausible as a moral guide than a man born of a virgin, who cheated death and rose up to sit next to his father in the sky...along with a holy ghost, for heaven's sake?"

"Zar must have had the Nazis *and* the Catholic Church after him," said Jonas.

Karel beamed at Graf. "I've found a kindred spirit, I see. We shall open the plum brandy tonight, my friend, and discuss all this further."

"So, we musicians venerate a substance, rather than a man?" Florian asked.

Audrey looked up at the girders and pulleys near the workshop's ceiling. "Well, I don't know," she said. "I've often thought of music as a lady, carrying a lantern." She laughed at their befuddlement. "It's an image from my childhood. It's strange, but I think that Olivia Taverner used to think the same thing."

All five men stared at her. The admission had surprised not only Audrey herself, who'd never revealed it to anyone before now, but also her colleagues, who evidently had never been aware that during all those countless hours spent perfecting their art, they'd in fact been courting the company of a light-bearing female.

"Please," Karel said, wandering away from the stove. "I'd like to show you something that I think will interest you. Come, everyone."

CHAPTER 61

They followed their host to the windows overlooking the courtyard. "This was Antonin's private study," Karel said. He indicated an area separated from the rest of the workshop by tall bookcases. "This was where the young Zar spent many hours, reading the subjects that would fire his intellect. Antonin was a lover of mysticism; the Music of the Spheres; old mysteries that still resonate."

"When did he have time to build pianos?" Jonas asked.

Karel laughed. "He built very few of them, in fact! But he built them well."

Audrey glanced at the bookshelves: Plato, Cicero, Shakespeare; biographies of Da Vinci, Kepler, Newton, Emperor Rudolf II; and much more besides, in several languages.

The space was large enough to accommodate an antique desk and workbench; a globe; a telescope; and a stretch of wall on which hung a smorgasbord of photographs, engravings, pages ripped from scientific journals, fragments of musical scores. It was the workplace of a hungry mind.

"There he is." Karel pointed to a black-and-white photograph: an old-fashioned studio rendition of a middle-aged man with Karel's misty focus, as if he'd just put down a volume of Greek philosophy and had settled in for a good think. Anyone could see they were a family of dreamers, more suited to dallying with the secrets of music than to fabricating machines that could produce it.

"Emperor Rudolf II…" Florian mused, joining Audrey at the bookshelf. "Wasn't he Kepler's royal patron?"

"Yes," said Karel. He gave a nod in the general direction of Prague Castle: a steep climb from the Náhoda workshop. "Rudolf was more interested in the mysteries of the universe than in governing. He was unfit for state business, in fact. Magic stones, alchemists, astrologers—that's what he loved. He was devoured by melancholy and despair. He went into wild rages. (He was the great-grandson of Joanna the Mad, after all!) He dined alone, and avoided windows." Karel idly moved a few things around on Antonin's desk.

"He gathered the greatest minds of the age at his court, didn't he?" Florian said. "Tycho Brahe…Kepler."

"Oh, yes! The greatest, and the strangest. His court was like a giant alembic—the vessel they used for alchemy. You heated it up, and never knew what you'd find afterward. Rudolf was very fond of Kepler, by the way, and treated him well."

"Good heavens!" cried Graf. He rushed over to Antonin's workbench. "Isn't that Kepler's model of the universe?"

A series of geometrical shapes, fitting one inside the other like nesting eggs, was balanced on a discarded piano leg.

"The five Pythagorean solids!" Florian exclaimed.

"Antonin built this model himself," Karel said. "Kepler considered these shapes perfect, because around each one, and inside each one, you could inscribe a sphere—the shape Plato claimed was closest to the image of God. Kepler imagined that the orbits of the planets fit neatly between such nesting geometric shapes." Karel ran his finger over the model and smiled. "The theory obsessed Kepler. He thought he'd discovered the secret of the cosmos. The irony was, he destroyed his own argument in the end. He himself was the one who discovered that the planets moved in elliptical orbits, not spherical ones, so try as he might, he couldn't get these beautiful Pythagorean shapes to fit his scheme."

"Most people don't know how important music was to Pythagoras and his followers," Florian said. "Forget all that geometry! Basically, he considered himself a healer through music."

"Yes," Graf agreed. "He soothed the passions of the soul and the body through rhythms, songs, incantations."

Karel went over to one of the upright pianos on the workshop floor. He sat down on a low stool, his work coat brushing the floor, and began to play simple tones. "Kepler calculated that the ratio between a planet's minimum and maximum angular speeds—that is, when it's farthest from the Sun and closest to it—corresponds (more or less) to our musical intervals here on Earth."

He played pairs of notes. "So, for instance, Kepler argued that the difference between Saturn's maximum and minimum angular speeds fit a 4:5 ratio, corresponding to a major third; while Jupiter produces a 5:6 ratio, or a minor third."

After each set of notes Karel whispered: "Saturn, a major third; Jupiter, a minor third; Mars, a perfect fifth..."

The sounds drew Audrey's gaze upward, as sound always did. One couldn't have called what Karel was playing music, exactly.

But still.

Still...

Her attention drifted to the window and the rooftops beyond, and to the sky beyond that, which was the same sky Kepler would have studied in 1600.

Karel stopped playing.

"Modern astronomers are embarrassed by all this, of course," Graf said. He leaned on the piano to address Karel. "They don't understand why a great scientist like Kepler would waste his time with such ridiculous notions."

"I don't think that scientists were prepared for the beauty they discovered along the way," said Karel, getting up from the piano. "They ignore it. Or downplay it. They have to, of course, or they'd face universal derision and condemnation from their peers." He smiled at the assembled company. "Not everything in the world has to be explained and proven. Certainly music cannot be. But that doesn't mean that the raw material musicians work with every day—clearly of divine origin—is a less legitimate path to the truth than a scientist's."

To everyone's surprise, Roland Wilmots had the last word.

He'd been listening all along from a chair near the wall, his head cocked to one side, his fedora on his lap.

He stood up suddenly and said, "Isn't everyone looking for the same thing? Pythagoras. Kepler. Jesus..."

No one spoke or moved.

"That is to say," (he indicated his own spidery frame) "a means to liberate the soul from its physical constraints."

♦ ♦ ♦

Everyone drifted to the door.

"My assistant will be coming by soon to help move the piano," said Karel. "It needs to warm up gradually. This room is cool enough: I'll leave it wrapped up here until tomorrow." He added: "There's a little hotel just around the corner: At the Night Sun, near Charles Bridge. Not too expensive. I suggest you find rooms there."

He escorted them through the carriageway.

"Tomorrow," he said, "we'll open Zar's piano."

CHAPTER 62

So, it looks like we're broke." Jonas set a cardboard beer coaster spinning on the table and watched glumly until it came to rest.

The trio was finishing a frugal lunch in the hotel cafe—omelets, and a few pieces of dark bread with butter. It was all they could afford. Their table overlooked the sleepy, cobbled expanse of Kampa Square, just a short stroll from the stone staircase that led up to the promenade on Charles Bridge.

"The journey's over," Florian said. "I'm sure everyone wants to see what Karel finds in the piano tomorrow. But then we have to find a way home."

"I can't go home," Jonas blurted. "The police are looking for me."

Florian grew irritated. "Yes, I remember. You could always try walking around Brussels in that priest's outfit. That might work. And anyway, how do you know Van Overberg didn't follow you to Prague?"

They all considered this as they studied the river vapors over the square. The afternoon was already heading into an early twilight."

"Graf can drive us back to Schloss Helden in Gloria's Škoda," Florian said. "We can find our way home from there. I'm not driving another kilometer with Nero, thank you very much. But we need money. Audrey, do you have enough cash to get you back to Brussels?"

She shook her head.

Florian turned to Jonas. "How much did you grab from Gloria's urn on your way out the door?" he asked.

"About four hundred euros," Jonas said. Despite his scars and burgeoning beard, he looked remarkably functional for a man who'd spent the night in a Škoda. "But I had to buy gas and stuff. There's about two hundred and fifty left."

"I have about the same," Florian said.

The hotel had offered them their cheapest option: a triple room, with Florian and Jonas in the double bed and Audrey in a cot. Graf, apparently as strapped as they were, had gone off to stay with a university friend in Old Town. Wilmots, less strapped, had booked a single room in the same hotel. As for Nero, no one knew his whereabouts.

"Süsslein?" Jonas said softly.

Audrey had said little during lunch. She was making her delicious Moravian wine last, turning the glass between sips to watch the thick garnet liquid catch a few shards of light.

She set the glass down and regarded her friends.

"Our journey is not over yet," she said. Her expression was frail; otherworldly.

The men stared at her.

"What makes you think that?" Florian asked.

"Intuition," she said simply.

Jonas stroked his beard and smiled. "Ah, of course. I've always trusted Audrey's intuition above all else."

"There's more to the piano's story," she said. "I'm sure of it."

"Like treasure, you mean?" Jonas laughed.

"Like something we can't possibly imagine," Audrey persisted. " Not treasure. I can't explain it. We've accompanied the piano this far, to its origins. Maybe we still need to act as its guardians." She hesitated. "Maybe Prague isn't its final destination."

"What on earth does that mean?" Florian demanded. "Are you sure you're not just trying to avoid going back to our sorry lives in Brussels?"

She didn't answer.

"She's obsessed with Zar, that's what it is," Jonas said with a twinkle. "In love with him, even," he goaded.

"In love with a ghost, you mean," Audrey said, her voice drifting. "Yes, perhaps you're right. Fitting, don't you think, in this city of ghosts?"

Florian took a pen from his violin case and scribbled a few calculations on his napkin.

"There's no doubt about it," he said. "If our journey is not over yet, as Audrey has intuited, we'll have to do some busking."

Everyone looked out at the bleak square.

"Out there, you mean?" Jonas moaned. "We'll freeze to death!"

"No, not there," Florian said. "On Charles Bridge."

♦ ♦ ♦

They set up on the south side of the bridge near the statue of St. Ludmila. The hotel had lent them two folding chairs, and they had their own music stands. In the absence of a piano—or Florian's electronic keyboard, which they powered with a car battery whenever they played on the streets of Brussels—the Kepler Players were reduced to a duo. Audrey's task was to stand next to her colleagues and encourage passersby to leave donations in the violin case lying open on the ground.

It was an afternoon of chicanery...of misty sleights of hand. Church spires sketched the sky with their dark tips, then vanished into the blur. The swans that normally drifted up and down the river along the Kampa embankment now seemed to float in place, as if entranced.

Florian and Jonas tuned with difficulty. They began a duo by Pleyel and stopped at once.

"This is crazy," Jonas said. "The humidity's terrible."

They blew on their hands, tuned, and started again.

The acoustics on the bridge were hollow, diffuse, like in a museum. The promenade with its stone saints usually seethed with visitors, but not today. Only a handful of vendors huddled behind their stands. A group of Japanese tourists gathered around the musicians, but they had to crane to hear the notes that the wind didn't snatch away, and quickly moved off.

Audrey stood by her friends as a sort of mascot. Below them, the river hissed and wrinkled, black with currents. The *vodník* had his home in that darkness, Audrey knew: the water goblin of Czech lore. She shivered, and drew her coat around her. No one could say where this little man with green hair lurked. It wasn't safe to swim at noon...or at midnight. Or on Fridays, for that matter. Sometimes, he turned himself into a drowning child and drowned his rescuer.

"Süsslein," Jonas called out between movements. He poked Audrey in the leg with his bow. "Hot wine, please!"

She headed toward the Old Town side of the bridge. It was an excuse to walk down the alley of saints. They had the best view of the city from here, posturing high on their pedestals, but not one of them had the peace of mind to enjoy it. After all, they'd ended their lives as martyrs, having been stoned, burned, or thrown into the river...axed, beheaded, or stabbed. Sainthood was not casually bestowed.

The Japanese tourists closed in around Audrey. She pushed through them to the mulled wine stall and ordered the drinks. The group parted, giggling, as she headed back across the bridge—not for her, clutching three cups of hot liquid, but for something at ground level.

She looked down.

A small white dog darted through the gap in the crowd: a Jack Russell terrier.

♦ ♦ ♦

Audrey handed the steaming wine to her comrades without a word. A knot twisted in her stomach. She put her nose close to the spicy drink and breathed deeply. *I won't tell them about the dog. It could have been anybody's.* She glanced up at St. Ludmila, who met her gaze with lowered lids. She hadn't had an easy time of it either, that saint. According to Florian's guidebook, Ludmila, a fervent early Christian, had been strangled by pagans in 921 AD with the veil she was holding in her left hand. With her right hand, she was pointing out a Bible passage to her grandson, Wenceslas I, the future Good King.

Daylight faltered; the lamps on the bridge blinked on.

It was then that Jonas noticed it: the purple bill lying in the violin case. It was not a color of money with which the musicians were acquainted:

Five hundred euros.

The *Allegro* of the Hoffmeister duet petered out.

All three crowded around the case.

"Holy crap!" cried Jonas.

Florian retrieved the bill. "Is it real?" he whispered.

"Who could have left this?" said Audrey.

They peered up and down the bridge through the dusk.

"One of the Japanese tourists, probably," said Florian.

"Or maybe someone who won big at the casino and feels sorry for musicians," Jonas offered.

"I'm not so sure," murmured Audrey.

The Japanese sightseers were still lingering near the Old Town Bridge Tower, staring up at its dour, sorcerer's regard. From a distance, in the failing light, one could perceive only a mass of modestly-sized individuals. But at the edge of the mass, one figure towered briefly before disappearing. Audrey couldn't have sworn to it—and she didn't tell her companions—but against all the dark heads in the group, the head of the tall person had seemed very white indeed.

CHAPTER 63

Audrey added a thick sweater and extra pair of socks to her gray ensemble and left her companions sleeping in the hotel room.

The night had cleared; the full moon rode high. Shadows splayed over the cobblestones in humanoid forms. The air was raw, and burned in the lungs, and Audrey held a mitten against her mouth as she strode along.

She took a detour to Maltese Square, listening for the phantom piano music Karel had heard on the wind. But she wasn't sure which mansion had belonged to the Zar family, and anyway, a café was blaring music through its open door, drowning out ghostlier tunes.

Tonight she had exceptional company: Zar. Klara. Kepler. How easily they'd all fallen into step beside her! The paradox of Konstantine Zar unsettled the mood somewhat. *Had the young guru worn simple peasant clothes to disguise his wealth?* A car's headlights fell on a patch of snow, and Audrey imagined a white shirt lying there, its arms flung wide. *Had he worn those clothes to his execution, remaining true to his beliefs until the very end?*

She picked up her pace through Kampa Park and followed the river path. It was a place of ephemera...of unfinished business. The air seemed tainted here; impure. The *vodník* himself squelched along the bank of an evening, or slapped the water out of boredom. Streetlamps appeared to float through the bare branches, and the moon floated with them in surreal conjunction. Audrey stopped to look up. It could have been October 17, 1604, when the Prague sky had finally cleared and Johannes Kepler had witnessed Mars, Jupiter and Saturn, all strung low on the western horizon and remarkably close to another extraordinary sight that year: a supernova—*Kepler's Supernova.* It was the sort of event that signaled something immense. The overthrow of the Turks, maybe. A plague. Or the death of a monarch. It had been a personal portent for Kepler: the birth of his beloved son, Friedrich, who would live for only seven years.

Audrey crossed Charles Bridge and entered Old Town. She passed the house on Karlova Street where Kepler had lived during his stay in Prague, now a museum. (A hair salon and tobacco shop, too).

Without beauty and wonder, shallowness and greed would devour us.

Her heart ached for Kepler—for his endless struggle between the intellect and the soul...between science and the divine. He would have emerged from this very doorway for his rendezvous with Emperor Rudolf up at the castle; he would have crossed the teeming bridge, with its idlers and beggars and merchants...gathered his coat around him against the river wind to protect his frail constitution, as well as the emperor's latest astrological chart. With all the dissonance in Kepler's private life—the squabbling, and illness, and death—he would have found a kindred mind in his royal patron. In the hush of Rudolf's chambers, the two men had discussed the marvels of the planets and the secrets of cosmic music, and for a short time at least, they'd left the trials of statehood and family outside the castle walls. It was rumored that no one had ever seen Rudolf smile. But perhaps Kepler had.

♦ ♦ ♦

The medieval labyrinth of Old Town suddenly confounded her. *But I know these streets! I've walked them many times after concerts.* Audrey quickened her step. She swallowed hard. *What had changed?* Houses huddled as they always had, like common gossips. A restaurant she'd frequented shone amber and welcoming. But a hollowness was distorting sound—stretching it, so that people who were laughing on a nearby corner seemed to be laughing far away, in another dimension. Perhaps a fissure had cracked open. The Prague night was riddled with them, after all. It tempted unnameables from the bottom of these clefts: flitting things that made statues uneasy, and set into motion the most famous one amongst them.

The giant one.

The Golem.

A gargoyle leered...not at Audrey, but at something behind her. She wheeled around. "Is anyone there?" she whispered, but only to herself. She squinted through the murk.

A tall man?

Legend said that in 1580, Rabbi Loew fashioned the Golem from river clay to protect the ghetto from persecution. In order to give the creature life, the rabbi placed a strip of parchment in its mouth on which was written the name of God.

Audrey found herself in a crooked lane with no exit.

Doorways yawned, slack as mouths. Smells filtered out from gaps in walls, of urine, and beer; of pickled cucumber not from yesterday, but from a lunch a century ago.

Audrey remembered the rest of the legend:

One Sabbath eve, Rabbi Loew forgot to take the parchment from the Golem's mouth as was his habit, so that the creature could rest like everyone else. Catastrophe struck: the Golem rampaged through the ghetto, crazed and twitching. It smashed wooden housefronts, strangled cats and chickens, crushed everything underfoot until the rabbi finally managed to remove the magic Shem and return the creature to clay.

Audrey retraced her steps and arrived at the river. She wondered what would have happened had the rabbi not been able to remove the parchment. Having destroyed the ghetto, would the Golem have gone off to terrorize the city at large?

No one would have been able to contain it then.

CHAPTER 64

She was alone on the bridge.

Except for the saints, of course. It was impossible to be entirely alone, even when the bridge was empty. The statues seemed to be made of a flexible substance—river air itself—which would account for the tilting of a shoulder from time to time, or a cross thrusting higher than usual. Or, in St. Ludmila's case, the closing of her heavy eyelids at the end of the day.

Audrey peered over the stone balustrade into the void. The wind whipped up icy drops from the river's surface that grated her cheeks. She listened to the rushing beneath her and held fast to the bridge, as if it were a point of reckoning at which her life had arrived, and beyond which an obscure but bracing future was pulling her.

She straightened up.

The air had thickened in one particular place.

A shape took focus: a great, dark oblong.

Audrey's mind swarmed: *How could the Golem have approached so silently?*

The figure wavered, as if it had just risen from the mud of the Vltava and wasn't sure where to go next. It stepped from the mist and halted a few meters from Audrey.

Surely at no time in Prague's history had anyone wished they'd been followed by the Golem rather than by a human being. But at that moment, Audrey would have preferred the company of a giant clay humanoid bent on destruction to this man's.

For he was no stranger.

The only strange thing about him was that he had no dog.

♦ ♦ ♦

"I recognize you from Brussels," the man said in a bleak monotone. He stared at Audrey through dark glasses. His long black overcoat—a slab of anti-matter against the pale air—swayed in the river draft. Beyond him, the city seemed but a distant moonstone, milky and numinous.

She backed away. "Why have you been following me?" Her own voice was just as toneless.

"You're acquainted with Klara Náhoda, I think," he replied. His French was heavily accented.

For a moment Audrey couldn't breathe. *Who would speak so casually about the woman whose death he'd caused?* She recovered and said, "I've never met her." She pulled herself up and lifted her chin. "You, Monsieur, on the other hand, visited Klara on the day she died, I believe." Her pulse had lost all rhythm.

The man took two steps toward her. "What are you saying?" The two steps had transformed him instantly from human back to Golem.

Audrey shrank from him. She knew he was tall, but not like this. What was it that Pascal had said? *A great block of a man...*

He took off a glove, and with a bloodless hand removed his glasses.

Audrey sucked in her breath: the man's eyes had almost no color—just a hint of the blue a glacier held in its ice.

328

"Klara was alive when I left her," he said. He looked confused. "What happened? How did she die?"

"You don't know?" Audrey said, incredulous. Then, flailing, "You asked plenty of questions of Pascal, didn't you?"

"Who?"

"The man who runs the café on Place de la Trinité in Brussels. He regretted ever telling you about Klara—about her surviving the Occupation. That's what you were interested in, wasn't it?"

Audrey remembered something else Pascal had mentioned: the man's chalky skin, and the fateful air about him. For a moment her fear eased, and she felt as the rabbi must have done after sunset on the Sabbath, when he'd removed the parchment from the Golem's mouth and could finally get a good night's sleep.

"My name is Hans Meyer," the man said. "I am indeed interested in the Occupation of Brussels. My father died in Belgium during the war. And my mother told me about a fascinating individual from that time."

Meyer's voice moved around a single tone, and the effect was hypnotic.

"Oh?" Audrey said faintly.

"Yes. A remarkable musician who was studying in Brussels. His name was Konstantine Zar."

The rush of the river welled around them. It was capable of such violence, Audrey knew—stupendous floods that over the centuries had swept away large chunks of the bridge. What had happened to the *vodník* then? she wondered, her mind seeking refuge in trivia. Had he buried himself in the mud where the Golem was born? Or slunk off to glare out from puddles and baptismal fonts, and slip down the drain with the bathwater when you'd turned your back?

"Why are you in Prague?" she demanded, her teeth clacking in the cold.

"Klara Náhoda told me that Zar's piano had been made here. You see, my father was a musician. I suppose I'm on a sort of..." he paused, and the glacial eyes intensified. "A sort of personal quest."

Panic seized Audrey. *He's after the Zar inheritance! He found out from Klara about the fortune—that it was hidden in the piano. Dear God, he must have forced the information from her...*

"Why are you following me?" she cried.

How far was the end of the bridge from here? Could she make it to the Kampa steps at a dash?

Meyer didn't answer. He put his dark glasses back on and said: "What happened to Konstantine Zar? Do you know?"

Audrey stared at him. "He was executed by firing squad in 1942," she said. "He was buried in the Enclos des Fusillés. It's behind the modern radio building now."

She wasn't sure what sent her hurtling away across the bridge. Foreboding? Dread that the clay monster would appear where Meyer had been?

She turned around just once, at the top of the Kampa steps. The statues were nothing more than floating imprints on the fog, closer to the incarnation their sculptor would have wished for them had it been at all possible to achieve in stone. The lanterns were no stronger than phosphorescence.

Even the anti-matter of the man's overcoat couldn't penetrate such murk.

If he was still there.

If, indeed, he had been there at all.

CHAPTER 65

Well, well!" Karel Náhoda chuckled at the group gathered around the rosewood piano. "This is the rarest of planetary alignments!"

Audrey, Florian, Jonas, Graf and Wilmots had all convened at Klavíry Náhoda the next morning to witness something as rare in the realm of music as a supernova was to an astronomer. (Nero, for his part, had returned from his carousing to sleep in his van and gone off again.)

"We are living proof of Galileo's sun-centered universe," Graf declared.

Karel patted the piano's quilted wrap. "For many, a piano *is* the sun. Isn't that so, Audrey?"

She bowed her head by way of an answer.

"Süsslein, are you all right?" Jonas asked.

"I'll explain later," she said. She'd as yet told no one that the universe she'd encountered on Charles Bridge the night before had had something altogether darker at its center.

Graf laid his hands on the cover next to Karel's. "There's definitely gravitational pull here."

The two men had stayed up until the early hours, drinking plum brandy and discussing anything arcane, after which they'd drawn up piano benches around the wood stove for beds. The box with the bone flute was sitting out, proof that the evening had taken a prehistoric turn. The men shone with vigor: the oldest people in the room could well have been mistaken for the youngest.

"The instrument is probably acclimated by now," Karel said. He was still wearing his dark-blue work coat, and Audrey wondered if he'd slept in it.

Everyone inclined toward the cocooned mass.

Karel began removing the quilt. At once he stopped, and turned to Wilmots.

"Would you like to do the honors, Roland, as Klara's executor?" he asked.

Wilmots nodded. Like any true gentleman before a solemn task, he took off his hat and held it for a moment against his heart. Then he began the last stage of his mission: he pulled the cover from the piano and let it slip to the floor.

The group caught its collective breath: *the grace...the bearing.* No one could take those things away once bestowed. Not from anyone. Or from anything.

Audrey stroked the domed fallboard where the grains of rosewood formed a perfect diamond.

"Go on," Karel said. "Open it."

The wood had swelled with dampness and she had to tug hard. She'd performed this gesture already—in private, under the night sky. She was prepared for the row of creamy, uncracked keys.

"Ah, what a beauty!" Karel murmured. He ran his fingers, knotty as desert roots, over the inlaid bronze lettering: *A. Náhoda, Malá Strana, Praha.*

He opened the lid.

"There it is!" Audrey cried. "The tetractys!"

Like a blind man, Karel turned his eyes upward and studied the tiny depressions in the wood with his fingertips. "These are neatly done," he said. "Obviously someone knew how to use a gouging tool—Antonin, I would imagine. Hang on: what's this?" He shone his torch on the surface next to the tetractys.

"Yes, I noticed those, too," Audrey said. "Strange marks scratched into the wood."

Florian and Graf squeezed between the others to have a look."

"Greek letters!" Graf exclaimed. "Looks like V, and E…" He peered closer. "An R, I think. Maybe an N after that. There are two more I can't make out."

"Hmm…" Karel mused. "V-E-R-N. The letters are lightly scratched. With an improvised tool, I would say."

"It's all so mysterious," Wilmots said. He found a piano bench to sit on, crossed his legs, and folded himself over them in contemplation.

"Secrecy was Zar's modus operandi," Graf said. "Which perhaps was not such a bad habit during the Nazi occupation."

"Olivia told us that the piano was built according to his specifications," said Audrey. "But she couldn't have meant a few symbols carved into the wood."

"Indeed," said Graf. "Still, the tetractys would have meant everything to Zar: the symbol of unity…harmony…the cosmos. It was his signature—his talisman against evil, as it had been for Pythagoras and his followers."

"Now I'm beginning to see why they called Zar 'The Greek'," Audrey reflected.

"Are those markings a clue to where the contents are hidden?" Wilmots asked.

"I don't think so," Karel said.

"Maybe Klara carved them herself," offered Wilmots. "She wasn't well these past few years. She wrote her testament eight years ago already. Maybe she wanted to relay something with V-E-R-N. The Greek letters would have implied it had something to do with Zar."

"It's possible," Graf said.

Stiffly, Karel knelt down to examine the panel above the pedals. "The grains in this piece form a perfect diamond, too," he said.

He removed the panel and an eddy of must escaped...perhaps, also, a whiff of reproach at this indignity.

"The innards haven't been cleaned for decades," Karel whispered. He handed the panel to Florian, who laid it on a nearby workbench.

Karel shone a flashlight inside. Everyone leaned in to study the crossed sets of strings; the cast-iron frame, its gold paint dull and dirty; the faded length of crimson felt.

"There doesn't appear to be anything broken," Karel said. "The wooden structure's in outstanding condition, considering the piano's history. Remarkably, the sounding board is intact. Everything needs to be overhauled, of course." He laughed. "And look here: the mice have had a field day chewing the hammers!"

Karel struggled to his feet with a loud popping of knees. "There's nothing unusual here, I'm afraid," he said with resignation.

"Did Antonin ever talk to you about the construction of this piano, Karel?" Wilmots asked.

"No. He referred to it only a few times...always as the 'Brussels Náhoda.' Other than that, no one ever mentioned the Zar order."

"He must have kept records somewhere," said Graf.

"Oh, he did. Both Petr and Antonin were scrupulous about that. They took note of everything: the date of completion; materials used; remarks about construction; anything new they might have tried in terms of resonance or design. But you see, all the records were destroyed in a fire, in 1942."

"Ah, yes!" Florian exclaimed. "The fire. I remember reading about it."

Karel went on: "The fire was selective—it damaged only the office upstairs. I always suspected that Antonin had set it deliberately, to destroy evidence should the Nazis get their hands on it."

"Evidence?" Jonas said.

"Yes. Evidence of an unusual order—this very piano, in fact. An order that would have drawn attention to itself. It was a strange item to ship from Prague to Brussels in the middle of a war, you must admit."

Karel replaced the panel and began making coffee.

"Play something, Audrey," Wilmots said softly.

His tone reflected the greater mood of the room.

Without a word, Audrey took off her coat, slung it over the top of the piano and pulled up a stool. She adjusted her long gray skirt and flexed her hands. Then she rested her fingertips on the keys. How invigorating their coolness felt! Like a pitcher of cream in July.

But something wasn't right.

CHAPTER 66

Audrey spun the stool around a few times to lower it. There'd been no seat when she'd discovered the piano, so she'd played it standing up.

"The keys seem so low," she said. "I can barely get my knees under them."

"Let me take a look," said Karel. With a groan he crawled under the keyboard again. He remained there for some time, staring up at the underside of the key bed.

"There's something strange here," he whispered. "There should be three open spaces between the struts. But they've been closed in with rosewood panels." He examined the smooth finish. "You're right, Audrey: the structure underneath the keys is lower than usual."

He hammered gently with his knuckles around the underside of the keyboard. At each knock, the strings gave out a phantom *whoosh*. "The middle section sounds different, somehow," he said. "Listen."

They all gathered around and cocked their heads.

"It sounds denser in the middle, Florian said. "Not so hollow."

"Yes!" Karel exclaimed. He pushed more vigorously against the rosewood. "It seems like something's inside. But the surface is utterly smooth."

Suddenly there was a *pock*, and the middle panel dropped open. A large brown envelope slid to the floor.

Everyone stared: the thing might just as well have dropped from the sky.

Karel picked up the envelope and turned it over. It was held closed by string and had no markings on it. "But how on earth..." He handed the envelope to Audrey: the paper had been softened by many hands—or perhaps, by the same hands many times.

Karel investigated the hiding place. "Ah! There are metal pins, one on each side, allowing the compartment to seesaw open. And it was held shut by magnets. Very clever, Uncle Antonin, I must say!" he chuckled. "No one but the person who built the piano would know anything was here."

"And the person who ordered it," Jonas added.

No one mentioned Zar's name.

Karel probed further. "Well, well, what have we here?" He sucked in his breath. "It looks as if the compartment has another section."

He reached in and pulled out an exquisite beaded purse with a silken drawstring.

Gasps filled the room.

"Now I see why Antonin didn't want to talk about this order," Karel said. He worked the cord loose: inside the purse were a number of smaller velvet pouches, all of which seemed empty.

Except one.

Karel fingered the midnight-blue velvet. "There's something in here." His voice caught.

"May I?" Wilmots piped up. He pried open the pouch and produced a glinting brooch: a spray of jewels in the shape of a flower.

"That's what Klara was wearing in your photograph, Friedrich!" Audrey exclaimed.

"Yes! Her grandmother's brooch."

"There's nothing else here," said Wilmots, pulling open the other velvet pouches to make sure. "It looks as if the piano was made specifically to ship the Zar family valuables to Brussels in secret. After Zar's father was arrested in 1939, the inheritance would have been in danger of being confiscated."

Graf said, "Klara must have pawned the items over the years for living expenses. That would explain the empty pouches...not to mention the big house. I always suspected that Olivia and Reginald weren't supporting her."

"Klara pawned everything except the brooch, it seems," said Karel.

Wilmots opened his palm and held the object up to the pearly morning light. Diamonds, emeralds, sapphires, rubies all leapt to life in his hand. At the center of the flower, a pink diamond drew the most light of all, and held on to it even after Wilmots turned from the window.

"It was surely the most valuable item the family had," Graf said. "Maybe the other things were more modest in comparison: gold chains, loose diamonds...things that Klara could sell off bit by bit."

Karel felt around the pocket of his work coat for Klara's testament. He held the document out to Wilmots. "Could you please translate the part about the contents again?"

Wilmots read the passage aloud in English:

The contents should then be removed, and distributed by Roland Wilmots to the closest family member, along with the piano itself. In the event that there are no family members extant, I hereby bequeath the piano and its contents to Olivia Taverner, widow of Reginald Taverner, Ixelles, Brussels.

"Which family did she mean?" Karel addressed the room at large. "Náhoda? Or Zar?

The questions hung over the vista of broken pianos.

"I am the only remaining Náhoda that I know of," Karel went on.

"And the Zar family is extinct, it would seem," Graf chimed in.

"She meant Náhoda, then," Audrey said. "The piano is yours, Karel."

"And the brooch," Jonas added.

Audrey, who was still holding the envelope, handed it to Wilmots. "But what about this?" she said. "It's also part of the contents."

Wilmots hesitated. He took the envelope, unsure. "Maybe this is something personal," he said. "Something we're not supposed to know about."

"At any rate, it didn't fit into the compartment Antonin designed for the purse," Karel said. "Klara must have wedged it inside at a later date. That's why it fell out so easily."

Wilmots took a deep breath. His thin lips were moist. He unfastened the string and peered inside the envelope.

"Letters," he said. He pulled out several small envelopes bundled together by another string, and a larger one, separate from the others, and lay them on top of the piano.

Everyone pressed around.

Graf picked up the larger letter. "It's addressed to Madame Klara Náhoda in Chaussée de Waterloo!" he exclaimed. The handwriting was bold yet refined. There was no return address.

"But Klara moved from there after the war," Florian said.

Graf lifted the envelope to the light. "This is a French postmark," he said. "Perpignan, it looks like."

"That's near the Pyrenees, isn't it?" Florian asked.

"Yes," said Graf. He suddenly went very pale and turned to the others. "The date on the postmark is November 1944."

"1944?" Wilmots took the letter from Graf. It lay like an exhausted bird across his spidery hands.

Graf drifted over to the window. "Open it, please," he said.

Wilmots did what he was asked. He produced several yellowed sheets. They were all covered edge to edge with the same handwriting as on the envelope.

"It's in French," Wilmots said.

"Please," said Graf, his back still turned to them. "Could you read the signature?"

The sheets whispered in Wilmots's hands. He took great care not to rip them, and in the ensuing seconds, the group relaxed a bit, so that by the time he'd peeled the last sheet from the others and turned it over, no one was prepared for the answer to Graf's question.

"Here's the signature." Wilmots grasped the edge of the piano as he read:

Your loving brother,
Konstantine

CHAPTER 67

Vernet-les-Bains
Le 14 novembre 1944

My dear Klara,

Please forgive the shock of this letter. I waited to tell you I was alive until I could be sure the censors wouldn't do their dirty work. Maybe even arrest you, and interrogate you. I would rather die than know that I'd put you in danger. Honestly, I didn't think I would survive this long anyway. It seemed better for you to think I'd been executed. Otherwise, you would have gone through the distress of my death twice. When I heard that Allied troops had reached Brussels in September, I felt it might be safe to write.

If you're reading this, you've survived the Occupation, and for that I rejoice. If you are not still living at the house in Chaussée de Waterloo, then by some miracle my letter was forwarded. Either way, it's a miracle that these meager scraps of paper made their way across a warzone!

They took me to St. Gilles prison on the night they arrested me. I was told I'd be executed in three days for the murder of the German officer. I was permitted no visitors. Strangely, I felt no fear. I'd done the right thing, I thought. I'd defended your honor. Even if it meant that I would be separated from you, and from darling Olivia, forever. I was so hot-headed, wasn't I? So stubborn. I'm not sure I would have acted so rashly if I'd known the consequences.

On my second evening in prison, Emile Hendrickx came to see me. This seemed strange, particularly with the ban on visitors. I hadn't had any contact with him since I left the conservatory. His loyalties were always in doubt, weren't they? Remember when you saw him drinking with those Germans on the Sablon? But the transport of the piano was all thanks to him. Later, I wondered if he'd gotten more out of my philosophy than he let on—whether helping to bring the piano from Prague was payment of sorts for my lectures.

Hendrickx spent an hour with me. We talked superficially, about the conservatory, lessons, rationing, etc. I was nervous and unsure. Just before he left, he told me that he'd made contact with someone who might be able to help me. He walked out, and never came again.

♦ ♦ ♦

I waited in that prison for over three weeks for a sign of Hendrickx's contact. Oh, I was comfortable enough. The cell had a bed that folded into a sort of table. There was a chair, and a washbasin. I had no books, though; no contact with anyone on the outside. But I was permitted pen and paper. For a few days, I could do nothing but pace my cell and sleep, and wait for news from Hendrickx. All I could think of was trying to get word to you...and to Olivia. But it was in vain. Finally, I gave up on anyone coming to help me, and prepared for my execution.

It's hallucinatory, being suspended between life and death like that. You're no longer of this world. Nor have you left it. It's almost like having wings. There's an ocean of peace in that place, and hardly any fear. A gentle force takes charge and you don't have any control over it. It's a relief, you know, to surrender—to let go. My mind wandered down unexpected avenues. I found myself back in Prague, at Klavíry Náhoda, talking to Antonin about all those wondrous things we used to discuss: Pythagoras; Kepler; cosmic music; the way our tiny lives reflect something much greater than ourselves. I remembered Antonin telling me that the huge arc between cosmic harmony and our souls is mirrored in the arc that our lives take, and that we mustn't be too impatient to discover where the arc will eventually lead us, because it's almost always a surprise.

I revisited our parents' soirées. Remember those, chérie? Champagne, Chopin, dancing, repartee. Father would open the salon window, and people would gather on Maltese Square to listen. How unsuited we both were to such opulence! But unsuitability leads us to what is truly right, doesn't it?

You must know that Olivia is with me always, even if it's only her essence. Just the notion of her gives me great joy...but also pain. I probably never should have fallen in love with someone I was destined to abandon so soon. You warned me early on. You never really approved of her, did you? Still, of all the things that helped me through the weeks and months after my arrest, it was the memory of Olivia singing in our little parlor when the bombs were falling, and the blinding strength of her resolve.

As I prepared myself, I summoned the courage to go to the place I thought my mind had shut out forever: the place in the forest where I tracked your attacker down like an animal. I thought I'd forgotten the details. Buried them somewhere. But they all rushed back to me in that prison cell: The man's limp. The pale-blue eyes. And that violin hanging from his shoulder. Time had just made it all more acute. Oh, Klara, what had I done? _What had I done?_ Until then, I simply thought I'd been avenging your honor. But it turned out to be so much more complicated.

To see such terror in the eyes of a fellow human being—to realize that you're the cause of it. It's a terrible thing, indeed. Did you know there's a strange sort of light in a person's face when they know they're going to die?

I began writing in earnest after that. I had none of my notes with me. It took many hours just to gather the themes of my lectures, for that's what I'd intended to write about before they came for me. I still have those writings from prison, and will send them to you at some point. I hope that you'll keep them safe, and show them only to people you trust.

♦ ♦ ♦

One evening, a chaplain came to my cell. My blood froze: I knew exactly why he'd come. I wondered if he expected me to confess to my crime, and repent. But not being a practicing Catholic, how could I add hypocrisy to the terrible thing I'd done? So I told him I didn't need his services. To my surprise, he said that he hadn't come for that. He'd come to tell me to be ready to leave my cell before dawn.

At 4:30 the following morning, they bundled me into the back of a military vehicle along with six other prisoners and a guard. We sat on the cold metal floor under a canvas roof, and even though it was already April, it was like being in an ice closet. Two of the prisoners kept vomiting. One of them started to cry. The truck stopped at various intersections, as it was not yet dawn and the blackout was still in effect. So it wasn't the stop itself that shocked me, but the voice I could hear through the flimsy canvas cover: Emile Hendrickx's.

Someone dropped open the tailgate and pulled me out. Standing there was Hendrickx himself, and another man who looked familiar: a German. He was smiling at me. Then I realized where I'd seen him before. He was the man who took refuge in our hallway during our concert! Incredibly, he'd been true to his word and hadn't reported me. Quite the contrary. He was helping me escape! Once again, he said he was a great admirer of my ideas; he said that only harmony and beauty would keep humanity from falling into the abyss. Then he motioned me to a car on the other side of the street driven by a man in civilian clothes. No more was said. I got into the car. I never saw Hendrickx, or my mysterious admirer, again.

I was driven across Brussels to an unremarkable house. The driver told me to get out, and drove off at once. It started to sleet. I was chilled to the bone. I rang the bell and cowered in the doorway. I had nothing with me but the clothes on my back and my writings, which I'd tucked into the lining of my coat. I was numb, not only with cold, but with the relief of salvation. I thought of my fellow prisoners in the back of the truck, and I couldn't comprehend that they would be dead in an hour. The idea made me feel faint with guilt. Why was I standing in that doorway, free? What force had guided me there?

I lived with the proprietress of that house for a month. She was a member of the Belgian Resistance and was called simply Nazarene. A lovely name, but an absolute ox of a woman! She had eight cats that she'd rescued from the bombardment, and hid me in a closet behind a bookcase. It was a fraction of the size of my prison cell, stank of cat piss, and had no light beside! the wind-up flashlight she gave me. But it was paradise as far as I was concerned. (Which makes one wonder what paradise is really like, and if we'll recognize it when we see it.) Nazarene had a piano I wasn't permitted to play, and books there wasn't enough light to read. She did let me out of the closet from time to time to stretch my legs. And though she had a raw, obtuse way about her, she was kind. And she made the best cabbage stew I've ever tasted.

One night without warning, I was taken from Nazarene's place to another safe house in Brussels. Incredibly, it was in Avenue de la Couronne, not far from Madame Hazard's boarding house! I was to stay there for only twenty-four hours, they said. Then I would be taken out of the city and as far south as possible.

They put me in a room under the eaves. There were two skylights on the Couronne side. How could I sleep so close to where Olivia was lodging? I could feel her there. It was torture. So I did a foolish thing: I clambered out onto the roof through a skylight and lay in the gutter. I could observe the street from there. I thought I might spot Olivia coming home from the conservatory before the blackout. I planned to signal to her from the roof. Then she could ring the bell at the house where I was hiding…she could come away with me. How foolish all that seems now! It's odd, but once you've been spared from death, the most outlandish schemes seem entirely within your grasp. It was in vain, of course. All I managed to do was catch a bad chill in that gutter. Doubt even crept into my feelings for the first time, and I wondered if I'd been a fool all along, losing my heart in that way.

When dawn came, they hid me in the back of a fish van and Fate had a hearty laugh at my expense. As they were closing the door, I looked out, and incredibly, there she was. Olivia! We understand time so poorly, don't you think? A two-minute passage of Mozart can seem like an hour. And that glimpse of Olivia hurrying away down the sidewalk seemed to last an eternity. I hadn't slept for days; I'd eaten very little. I was light-headed, and shivering. I imagined all sorts of things in those eternal seconds: Bliss. Tragedy. Redemption. Then it hit me that I was standing on one of Fate's striding edges and had a choice to make. Either I could stay hidden behind the barrels of herring and continue on my journey alone. Or I could jump out of the van and ask Olivia to come with me.

Oh, why didn't I take that leap, Klara? *Why?* At the very worst, we would have died together. But think what the best could have been! Instead, I simply watched her walk out of my life forever.

I didn't care what happened to me after that. I didn't mind the pain in my legs from crouching for hours behind those fish barrels; or the smell, that stayed in my clothes for weeks. I was sweaty and cold and knew I was falling ill. I couldn't eat the food they offered me—certainly not herring. The van was detained at checkpoints, but the guards were overcome by the stench when they opened the door and waved us through.

CHAPTER 68

The route to the Pyrenees was full of the kindness of strangers. I stayed the night at a farm where they hid me with the pigs and fed me like a king. Once, a retired dentist brought me dinner in the forest, along with a shaving kit and brandy, and some money for the journey. I reached Perpignan in the back of a grocer's van. By that time, I was seriously ill.

I was taken in by a madam, of all things. Tante Betty, she was called. The brothel was in a narrow, winding street in the old town. Betty hid me away upstairs in a tiny room overlooking an air shaft. It was in the same corridor where her "nieces" worked, so I didn't get much sleep at night. I developed severe pneumonia. The doctor Betty brought in said he wasn't sure I'd survive. He came only once, and was paid in kind, as it were.

Every day a maid came with water and broth. But besides that, I was left alone to sink or swim. For weeks I lay in that dirty, sagging bed. Betty provided me with a nightshirt, which I soaked through within a couple of hours but was changed only every third day or so. One morning, the maid thought I was dead and pulled the sheet over my head!

The patterns of the day were always the same: the noise of cleaning up from the night before; the smell of lunch, and of rotting garbage from the air shaft; a period of calm in the afternoon for the siesta. Then the sounds of a soirée of sorts: laughter drifting up from below, and a tinny piano. And later, the heavy tread of men in the corridor, back and forth, back and forth, well into the night. Many German clients were among them, Betty said. I won't describe the sounds that filtered through my wall until the last customer had had his fill and lumbered away.

Oh, dear sister! How far we can wander in our mind when we can't move our body. To the stars and back, I assure you! My thoughts went to you, of course; to the life we had in Prague, with all its culture and privilege. Illness affords us a reckoning, it seems. Remember that afternoon when you and I went with Father to Klavíry Náhoda to shop for a piano? When Antonin showed us Kepler's beautiful model of the universe, and explained cosmic music to us? Well, only when I was hovering between life and death did I realize how important that event had been. It was then that I vowed to myself never to live a rich man's life. Because if the secrets of the universe reached us via music, how could any material riches compare?

Olivia tiptoed in and out all the time. Then she moved in to stay. She haunted my sleep, my delirium, my lucid twilights. Endlessly, I replayed that last glimpse I'd had of her hurrying away from me down Avenue de la Couronne. I inflicted ecstatic, debilitating pain on myself, imagining her turning around when I called to her...running into my arms. I relived every hour that we'd spent in each other's company. In the forest. In cafés. At the piano. Just before the fever broke, this obsession—this phantasm I could never have—engulfed me. I imagined marrying Olivia...fathering our children. Going on tour together and enjoying the same complicity with our audiences that we shared with each other. I could almost taste the music we made together. Her voice had so many flavors, after all.

Honey. Dark cherries. Cinnamon. Lying in that sweltering room, I gradually realized that making music with Olivia over the course of a lifetime would be like having daily knowledge of the eternal. Such a life would be beyond anyone's reach.

The fever finally broke and took Olivia away with it. She simply filtered through my fingers and was gone. I could no longer hear her voice. I couldn't see her face. The only thing she left behind was the freshness that remains in a room after you've closed the window. And a sort of phantom ache, which of course I'll never be free of.

♦ ♦ ♦

Spring was well underway by the time I left the brothel. I hadn't seen the sun in weeks—only a tiny patch of sky above the air shaft. It was surreal to find myself on a bench by a fountain in a Perpignan park, surrounded by oleander and palm trees, talking to a smuggler who said he'd help me get to the mountains. I would have to ride a bicycle to Vernet-les-Bains, he said—a distance of almost sixty kilometers. (I was still barely able to walk across a room!) From Vernet, a *passeur* would guide me over the mountains into Spain. And there was more: I was to be disguised as a priest, with false identification papers. The guide cautioned me that there was a warrant for my arrest, issued in Brussels. Even the gendarmerie in Perpignan had a description of me. Which meant that the goodwill of Hendrickx's mysterious German friend had not been enough. Someone else had been less forgiving, and reported me.

I needed another two weeks to work up my strength, during which I earned my keep helping out in the brothel kitchen before the customers arrived, and giving the ladies piano lessons. Finally, I was ready. I headed off on a bicycle on a hot May day, sweltering in clerical clothes.

Maybe you heard about the round-ups of Jews in southern France in 1942, organized by the Vichy government. The prefects sent paramilitary units all over the countryside on their sinister hunting parties. Attics, barns, cellars...inns and footpaths. Nowhere was safe. They would raid villages at three o'clock in the morning; drag Jews, resistant fighters, and smugglers and their families to holding camps. The mountains were not the sanctuary that they seemed. There were patrols in the high passes on both the Spanish and French sides of the border, even in deep snow. The countryside was electric with fear.

I stopped for the night at a little hamlet in the foothills, as I'd been instructed. It was just a collection of stone houses in a valley with massive peaks behind it. The farm had goats, and an apple orchard. I was told by my contact to go to the house with the dog. He was a nasty cur—an excellent watchdog. He kept me away from the door until the farmer's wife let me in.

There were three frightened people at the kitchen table: a Jewish couple and their small son. Our hostess said only that her husband was "out". He must have been working with the Resistance because the family was dressed for departure. They were waiting for their *passeur* to guide them into Spain.

Our hostess served up cassoulet and omelets, brandy and real coffee, and some fresh milk for the boy. It was the first real meal I'd enjoyed since my illness. I couldn't help but think of you, Klara, and darling Olivia, suffering from rationing in Brussels. No one spoke during the meal. I'll always remember the dark eyes of the child, calm and wise beyond his years. And the terror in his parents'.

After we ate, the farmer's wife took the family to the barn, where she said their contact would find them, and showed me to a little room upstairs in the main house. She forbade me to open the window or turn on the light. She told me I had to rest, as I had two full days of cycling before I met up with my own guide.

The night was warm and close. It was suffocating in that little room. I knew I should have stayed indoors, but something compelled me otherwise. I slipped out. The dog was chained up for the night and only growled once. The massif of Mt. Canigou seemed like huge shoulders squared over the valley, and gave me courage.

I headed to the pasture for some air. I stood there for a long time, taking deep breaths, listening to the goat bells and rejoicing under the spangled heaven. The silence was so vast that you could hear its echo. *Was this cosmic music?* I hadn't seen the sky for months. In fact, the only time I'd ever seen such a sky was on the night that Olivia and I found the wounded pilot in the forest, and even then, it was nothing like this. You could have walked along the Milky Way, it was so crisp and near. I saw Venus, and Mercury. I lay down on the cool, soft grass—such a luxury after that wretched bed at Tante Betty's. It was perfumed, too: apple blossom, with a sour note in it—goat droppings, I believe it was. One can't have harmony without dissonance, after all!

Oh, Klara. For the first time I understood what it meant that the Music of the Spheres was reflected in each human soul: the greater reflected in the lesser. I could grasp the existence of *musica mundana*—the music made by the cosmos itself; *musica humana*—the resonance between the human soul and human body; and *musica instrumentalis*—the music made by an instrument. (Which at that moment was the humble goat bell!) Antonin explained it all to me in Prague. I'd talked about it so many times in my lectures. But that night in the Pyrenees, I finally understood it. My whole being resonated like a stringed instrument. I could even see a path forward to redemption. At least, I thought I could.

Until the dog started barking.

There were footsteps on the drive. Men yelling. A loud pounding on the door. It was obviously a police raid. I crept into the orchard beyond the pasture and hid behind the thickest apple tree I could find. The dog was hysterical now—he would have torn the men to bits if he'd been set loose. The farmer's wife screamed. There was a single shot. The dog went silent. There were more yells from the barn. I could hear the child crying. Then footsteps, retreating—a group of people this time, with the crying child among them. From farther down the valley I heard two cars start up and drive away.

I hid behind the apple tree until the dew began to fall. How the silence had changed! There was no more echo in it...no beauty at all. Just a void. I crept over to the farmhouse. The dog was dead. I called into the barn but there was no one.

The farmer's wife had been taken away along with the Jewish family. My room had been ransacked: they'd discovered the clerical clothes and my false papers. I could no longer pose as a priest. I grabbed my haversack and the bicycle and left at once under cover of darkness. Terror nipped at my heels. There was no moon that night; I had to navigate only by the stars. How could the same sky that had just offered me revelation and solace suddenly be so full of foreboding? How could the cosmos be so indifferent to human suffering?

CHAPTER 69

Everything seemed to be happening to someone else after that. I found myself in other isolated hamlets, with other fugitives, taken in by kind, circumspect people and given generous plates of food. There's an innate intelligence in those country folk that city dwellers lack. A mix of practicality and childlike awe. This is what I found in my *passeur*.

How can I describe Valerio? A Basque smuggler: powerful; illiterate. He'd been assigned to take my small group across the Pyrenees west of Mt. Canigou. I first saw him near the village where I was hiding. It was dusk. Raining. (They said it was best to travel in the rain, as it would be more difficult for German sniffer dogs to track us.)

I thought he was just another massive rock by the stream at first. Then this piece of granite stepped from the shadows and I was speechless. Valerio had a face of true grandeur. He was like a hybrid mountain animal, part bear, part stag, with all the strength and cunning of the former, and the pride of the latter. His knowledge of the terrain was absolute.

Four of us started up the trail after Valerio: a rotund, wheezing Dutchman, his history unknown; and a pair of mysterious French sisters in their middle years, twins, with the same graying, tousled hair and luminous eyes. They seemed to understand each other telepathically. I brought up the rear wearing donated boots stuffed with newspaper, and carrying some bread and cheese in my haversack. Ahead of us, Valerio's bulk was a sort of reverse beacon: a patch of blackness to steer by. He saw movements where there seemed to be none. He heard noises we didn't. Once he gave a hand signal for us to drop to the ground and lie flat, and he was right: a patrol we hadn't detected was passing nearby. Lying there with our faces in the mud, we could hear a few words of German on the wind, and the whine of a dog. We could smell their cigarettes.

We followed the stream for a couple of hours. It had swollen to a torrent in all that rain and we had to cross it twice. The Dutchman was already exhausted. Valerio carried him across on his back like a pack animal, deliberately, feeling for each foothold in the rushing water.

We stopped to rest beneath a high pass. Valerio rummaged behind a bush and produced a bottle of brandy he'd stashed there some time ago. If any of us had had any doubts about his navigational skills, they were quelled. He passed the bottle around, took a long swig himself, and returned it to the bush. The rain had cleared, exposing a sweep of stars over the ridge.

I was sitting next to Valerio on a rock when he pointed upward, and in halting French said: "There it is. The sky. It is always there for us, *n'est-ce pas?* Even in the worst conditions." He got up to go. Then he said something astonishing: "Even when you can't see the sky, you can hear it."

His words preoccupied me, and took my mind off the pain in my legs. Were mountain people born with the ability to hear the sky? Were we just then experiencing the worst conditions? If so, perhaps I'd been too hasty in my dismissal of universal harmony at the farm.

The rain returned and became driving sleet—tiny bits of glass that shredded our faces and hands. We were inching along a sheep trail high above a ravine when one of the women slipped. She hadn't cried out at all. Everyone simply carried on until her sister yelled over the wind and summoned us back.

It was obvious at once that the woman had broken her leg. Badly. Valerio hauled her back up the ravine as if she were a kitten. She was wearing thick stockings, and I practically fainted when I saw bone protruding through the wool.

She lay there in the snow making no noise. Valerio knelt beside her and shook his great head. "*Ah, non, non. Pas bon...pas bon.*" He offered the woman some brandy from his own flask and stood up. "We cannot wait here for help," he said. "Or we shall all die." The wind screeched like a demented passage of modern music. "There's nothing we can do," Valerio shouted. He reached into his sack and produced a pistol.

"*Non!*" screamed the woman's sister. She began to sob. "Sylvie...*Sylvie!*"

The injured woman looked up at Valerio. Oh, Klara. Suddenly I was the one holding the pistol—looking into the eyes of the tall, violin-playing German. The woman's eyes were like that: along with the terror, there was light in them, too.

I tried to wrest the pistol from Valerio. But the Dutchman grabbed my arm and dragged me away. "If the Germans find her, they'll torture her," he shouted. His voice was barely a whisper in that wind. "She'll compromise not only Valerio's operations, but those of all the other *passeurs* in the area. Even *he* can't carry her into Spain."

Valerio hung his head. His vast shoulders slumped, and the pistol dangled from the hand at his side. It was obvious what was going to happen— though maybe not to the injured woman, which was a blessing. I stumbled away and was sick. The Dutchman came and put a hand on my shoulder.

All sorts of strange acoustics inhabit the mountains, it seems. So perhaps it wasn't so odd that the shot itself, when it happened, was less audible in the wind than the cry of the sister who had witnessed it all: Ariane.

She didn't utter a word after that. She'd lost a boot somewhere, and cut her hand on the scree, but none of it seemed to matter. She walked on, oblivious. Clearly she didn't care if she lived or died, and probably would have preferred the latter. Valerio strode so far ahead that we often lost sight of him.

It was mid-morning by the time we finally came upon a Spanish border post. Valerio was already on his way back from his altercation with the guards:

"They say that we must go back into France," he told us, mostly in sign language. Drops of moisture had frozen on his cheeks and I was certain they were tears.

"Go *back*?" cried the Dutchman.

Valerio shrugged, and headed back the way we'd come. "It happens sometimes," he said. "Franco's Spain, you know." He gave a rude gesture in the direction of the guard post. "We can try again another day."

♦ ♦ ♦

I didn't have the strength to attempt another flight into Spain, though I didn't give up on the idea of you coming to join me one day, dear Klara. But after what I'd been through—what Ariane had been through—well, it seemed best to go into hiding in the Pyrenees.

What if? I always wonder that, don't you? No one is immune to this self-torture, it seems. What if I hadn't gone out into the field to look at the sky that night, and instead they'd found me in the farmhouse? What if that German who'd helped me escape—who'd listened to Olivia sing as the bombs were falling—hadn't attended my lectures in Brussels and taken an interest in me? What if I'd jumped out of that fish van and run after Olivia? By such gossamer threads are our lives suspended.

I asked you to promise me something once, remember, chérie? You swore to look after the Náhoda piano, which I trust you are doing. Now I must ask you something else: you must never let Olivia know that I'm alive. I heard about her engagement to Reginald Taverner this past summer. The music world gossips even in wartime! Like you, she must have assumed I was executed in 1942. Please, let her continue thinking that. She's entitled to her happiness, and I want her to have it—even if it's not with me. I beg you to do this, dear Klara. If she finds happiness with Taverner, then I will find my own kind of peace.

I'm not sure when it will be safe for us to meet. In the meantime, could you please sell a few pieces of gold jewelry from the piano and send me some money? If you can possibly make it to Antwerp, go to Fleishmann's, if he's still alive, just around the corner from the train station. He was an acquaintance of Father's and will give you a good price.

I will leave you with that, dear sister. Please write to me at the address below. Don't put my name on the envelope. I don't think I'll ever lose my fear of being followed. Ariane will see that it gets to me.

Madame Ariane Bergman
Villa Sylvie
4, Impasse Paganini
Vernet-les-Bains

CHAPTER 70

Roland Wilmots finished his long recitation. He folded Zar's letter back into its envelope as the assembled company, awestruck, watched him.

"You knew, Friedrich, didn't you?" said Audrey sotto voce. "That Zar survived the war."

After a pause, Graf said, "No. But I suspected it. There was a strange reluctance in Klara when I visited her in Brussels and we talked about her brother." After another pause he added, "V-E-R-N: Vernet-les-Bains, obviously. A little town in the Pyrenees. That's what must have been scratched into the piano. And in Greek letters, of all things! Suitably cryptic for Zar. Maybe Klara sensed that her end was near, and that whoever was still at the Náhoda workshop would figure out where Zar was."

Wilmots untied the string from the bundle of smaller envelopes.

"They're all addressed in Zar's hand to the house in Rue Nova," he said. He examined the postmarks. "The last one seems to be from October 1996. He must have passed away after that."

"There should be a death certificate on file in Vernet-les-Bains," Florian said. His cheeks burned with the excitement of Zar's story.

"Yes," said Graf. "I suppose so." He wandered about the workshop to clear his thoughts. "Klara had obviously been pawning the family inheritance all those years and sending the money to Zar in France. No wonder the pouches are empty."

"Except for the brooch," Audrey added.

Graf finished another circuit of the room: "That would have been difficult to pawn," he said. "It also must have had enormous sentimental value."

"Shall we read the other letters?" said Florian.

"Maybe we should gather them in order first," Wilmots said.

This they did, and discovered that Zar had only written to Klara two or three times a year over the decades, always in French.

Graf turned to Wilmots. "Roland," he said solemnly. "May we have your permission to read the other letters aloud?"

Pale and tremulous, Wilmots assented. He distributed the correspondence, giving a few letters to each person along with a slight bow. "I'll begin reading the earliest ones," he said. "Then Florian, Friedrich, Jonas, and Audrey. Karel, can you read French?"

Karel shook his head and smiled. "No. But I can make coffee. Please translate when you can."

Thus they were able to construct a window onto Zar's mountain exile.

♦ ♦ ♦

Ariane never spoke again after what had happened to her sister. Her pain had solidified inside her, and no one could dislodge it. The man with the soaring face and charcoal eyes seemed to understand her, however, and Ariane gave him refuge in the villa beneath Mt. Canigou that she and her sister had inherited from their father, a professor of history who'd disappeared in one of the round-ups of Jews. Ariane became his assistant;

his friend and confidante. She was older than Zar by several years, and it was unclear if that's all she was to him. She displayed no emotion, Zar wrote. Only a frank, abiding loyalty. In many ways, she reminded him of Klara.

He wrote little about music in the early letters. The pillars of his life were Olivia, who animated his correspondence like a beating heart; and Canigou, that sacred mountain of the Catalans that he could see from his study window, and that gave his life a certain constancy. Zar had transformed from city wanderer into a creature of the mountains, as if he were native to them—as if he'd been born with all the instincts needed to subsist alone for days at a time in the high valleys and passes. When the snows set in, he contented himself with striding up and down the steep medieval lanes of Vernet, or through the forests behind the thermal spa, on paths where Kipling and Paganini once took the air.

Zar rarely mentioned Olivia by name. But whenever he indulged memories of playing Schumann, or of observing the stars in the Forêt de Soignes, it was clear that he hadn't been alone. He left other clues, too. When he'd written to Klara: *You would both love it here,* he'd used the plural *vous.* He'd obviously meant Olivia, too. It was as if Zar, against his own wishes, was hoping that Klara might mention his existence to Olivia. For as he retreated deeper into himself, he also seemed to have been furnishing a splendid accommodation for Olivia in his mind.

♦ ♦ ♦

Villa Sylvie was gabled and airy, with an old Pleyel baby grand in the parlor and bookcases in every room. There were cool, patterned tiles in the corridors and creaking shutters at the windows. The house occupied a bowl of land lush with unkempt evergreens, tall hedges, and tropical trees with huge, waxy leaves and ivory blossoms. Two cypresses towered at the front door like sentries. Ariane had renamed the villa after her sister, and indeed, it was a sylvan place.

Behind the house, a broad lawn stretched to a row of poplars, where an unruly stream bore messages from the heights. Zar owned all of Olivia's recordings, and he would play them on the gramophone in his study, open the windows, and listen to her in the garden, where the sound of her voice mingled with the gushing stream and rustling poplars, and in summer, when he stayed out late, with the less audible harmonies of a mountain night.

Ariane cooked Zar's meals and tended the house. She found him violin and piano students, kept a vegetable garden, and sold their produce at local markets. It was astonishing how well one could manage not being able to speak.

The early letters were full of detail, but revealed little about Zar himself. Sparer missives followed—sometimes just a few paragraphs, with a vignette of a mountain storm, or of eating fresh figs from the tree by the stream. He seemed lost; searching. The night sky appeared like a leitmotif: even a poet would have run dry of inspiration over the decades. But not Zar. He'd been studying city skies for such a long time, he said, that when he'd had that epiphany under a mountain sky (in the company of goats, of course, for great things are often delivered by humble messengers), his soul had been set free, like a caged bird.

Sometime during the 1980s, Zar changed. His letters burned with a mission. He filled them with talk of his academy: a group he was forming, one member at a time, from talented students, local thinkers, bold professors. He talked about restoring Music to her rightful place. With Ariane's help, he constructed a sort of gazebo out of canvas and metal supports at the back of the garden near the fig tree, facing Mt. Canigou.

Benches were arranged in a circle, and Zar's followers—as indeed they could be called—would meet from dusk until well into the night, discussing the deepest meanings of the art that had once been considered divine.

Olivia had already described to Audrey the man at the center of these gatherings. *Tall, graceful in speech, in gesture, and in everything else.* In his seventies and eighties, Konstantine Zar regained the passion of the young man who had electrified his listeners in wartime Brussels. One could imagine that the black, probing eyes had not changed, either, but still looked to a horizon beyond his audience—beyond the fig tree, and the breathless stream, to where the sky joined the mountain peaks.

CHAPTER 71

Audrey opened the last envelope that Wilmots had given her. "*Mon Dieu!*" she said, pulling two brittle sheets into the light. "These look like Zar's notes, written from prison. They must be the ones he mentioned in his letter to Klara."

Audrey stood at Zar's piano and displayed the sheets on her open palms for all to see, as if they were his very essence. Her little gray figure seemed to be dissolving into the aura of the man she'd been trailing after like a pilgrim.

◆ ◆ ◆

St. Gilles Prison
March 1942

Music is a living thing. She comes to life in air; she breathes, dies, and is reborn. Like the best among us, she is without guile, or reproach, and cannot lie or cause harm. She's happiest, and achieves her fullest potential, at the unique tempo organic to every piece—to every living thing. Surely we must try to emulate her! Think of a melody you know well, and try to sing it too slowly or too quickly. You will understand this at once. The melody was born with its own personality that must be respected. If people tried to do everything at the same speed as others, and in the same way, they would fall ill.

◆ ◆

Our age is so brutally scientific, isn't it? The need to establish empirical proof above all else is a kind of psychosis. Somehow, music lost its position as a guiding force once science started explaining the cosmos. Subsequently, our sense of musical wonderment (of wonderment in general, really) began to erode, and was no longer an essential part of living. Kepler, in the early 1600s, was one of the last great minds who still entertained the notion of music as a universal positive energy.

For early thinkers, the fact that the motions of the heavens were extremely regular meant that they must have had a certain mathematical order, as the intervals of music are mathematical. If one took this a step further, it was logical that celestial motion must produce harmonious sounds, therefore. Oh, scientists have long since proven Pythagoras and Kepler wrong—that is, the most interesting parts of their philosophy! For while it's wonderful to have the Pythagorean Theorem, and Kepler's three laws of planetary motion, I swear to you that those two men let their thoughts roam to places a modern scientist would never dare to go...to notions that by their very nature can never be proven. Who can prove the existence of God, for instance?

◆ ◆

Even with all the advances in science, no one has demonstrated how, exactly, Music achieves what she does. No one will ever understand how Music works on the heart, for example. To try to do so would be futile. One might as well walk across fragile tundra to visit a shrine: you would destroy too much along the way, and understand too little once you got there, for such a visit to be worthwhile. You'll understand better in the company of people without pretension—even without any knowledge of music. Take your art to the humblest places. There you will make the deepest connections.

♦ ♦

Even if we know the scientific nature of just about everything now—the molecules involved, how they react with each other and why, etc.—it's still the <u>aspect</u> of a phenomenon that speaks to the human spirit. Take smoke, for example. I find it very similar to music, don't you? It's weightless. It rises into the air and drifts. It takes unexpected, beautiful forms. Scientists can explain why. But they don't understand why it <u>bewitches</u>; they can't explain why something is beautiful, and why it captivates us. It's fascinating to know how a sound wave is formed; or to learn about decibels, frequency, timbre—all these things are essential to music. But understanding them does not help explain why, according to the Greeks, music and the human soul are both aspects of the eternal. Somewhere along the way, society forgot how miraculous it is that a sound wave finds answering resonance in physical matter...or in a soul.

♦ ♦

I've always imagined Pythagoras as a walker. After all, he was on one of his walks when he passed by a blacksmith's workshop one day and noticed that hammers of different sizes produced different tones. This led him to discover that a string, when stretched across a piece of wood in a monochord, played different tones depending on what length of string you marked off with your finger. Every modern string player does this hundreds of times a day.

Does Music have the power to improve us—to guide us toward our higher selves? Or is she merely a shallow diversion to pass the time? Plato abhorred the latter.

♦ ♦

I come from a family of wanderers. Our name was originally Zarándok, which means pilgrim in Hungarian, although the language of my ancestors is not known: probably a dialect from the remote steppe east of

Hungary. The family migrated gradually westward over the centuries, spent some time in Hungary, became educated, and eventually ended up in Prague. We spoke Hungarian, Czech, German, French—all rather artistically, I must say! But that's unimportant. What I want to impart to you is the importance of the journey itself. This can be a literal one, like my family's. Or a spiritual one, like the one I've embarked on with you: the kind that's most likely to reveal the state of being we all seek: the unfettering from our physical selves. A piece of music is a journey, isn't it? It begins with a single note or chord—like a first step. Music is also proof that the most profound journeys are those taken by the spirit.

♦ ♦

We cannot unlearn what we now know about the universe and the planets. But that doesn't mean we should lose our sense of awe. Forces beyond our imagining still exist, after all—musicians work with them every day. We must inspire people to live by Music's example...to embrace her honesty, grace, humility, hope. She is the earthly mirror of the heavenly kingdom.

CHAPTER 72

Audrey sighed and put the papers on the piano lid.

"We owe it to Klara and Olivia to find Zar's grave and pay our respects," she said.

Everyone murmured their assent. Exhaustion mingled with the relief that a conclusion of sorts had been reached.

Audrey headed for the door. "I don't know about you," she said, "but I need some air."

Wilmots cleared his throat. "Before you leave, Audrey," he intoned, "I have something that might be important." He reached into an inner pocket of his suit and produced another letter. "This came for Klara at Rue Nova about a week after she died."

"You didn't open it?" Graf asked.

Wilmots shook his head, sagging slightly. "I wasn't sure what to do with it," he said. "Now I see that the postmark is the same as on the other letters: from Vernet." He hesitated. "The handwriting on the envelope is different, though. It's rather crude." He held up the envelope.

"Yes, you're right," Graf said. "Maybe someone in the village wrote to Klara about Zar...about his legacy, or personal effects."

Wilmots handed him the letter. "Please, you open it."

Graf tore the seal. He glanced in turn at each person in the room before pulling out two sheets of paper covered with the childish hand on the envelope. He faltered as he read the signature.

"Whoever wrote this signed Zar's name!" he said. He went as white as the paper he was holding. "That means..." He sat down at the piano.

Audrey came to his side. She could barely form the words: "It means that Zar is still alive."

The room congealed. Everything in it, living and inert, seemed caught in amber.

They all drew around the piano.

"It can't be possible," Florian said.

Wilmots ventured: "Zar would be at least..."

"In his nineties," Graf helped him.

Karel's eyes grew moist. "Zar...*alive!*"

"Please, Friedrich," Audrey whispered. "Read it."

♦ ♦ ♦

Vernet-les-Bains

Dear Klara,

How many years has it been since we've been in touch? Far too many, at any rate. I stopped writing only because you had. I wonder, now that we're both so old, if perhaps we can't put the situation right. Time is not on our side.

I understand, of course, why you didn't want to come down to Vernet anymore. Ariane could be difficult, it's true. But you know why. Perhaps you're angry that I changed my name, and took Ariane's surname; that I've been masquerading as her cousin all this time. I've actually gotten used to being known as Alexandre Bergman! It was to help me disappear from my pursuers in the early years. But then, strangely, the name began to suit me. And I still fear those pursuers. Day and night.

Ariane's been dead for over ten years now. I would have told you before, but I sensed that the news would have made you happy, and I couldn't have borne that. You see, I did love Ariane in a way. Oh, not as I love Olivia, of course. And not as I love you, dear sister. But she was my loyal and unquestioning companion.

From the moment I awake to the moment I fall asleep, Olivia still orders my thoughts. She's part of my DNA how. At night, she has even freer rein. Her marriage to Taverner imposed a sort of code of chivalry on me. A noble silence. It was strangely comforting to obey it—otherwise, I would have had to obey my own undisciplined desires and pursue a married woman. Here, in the remote Pyrenees, I've been following a kind of courtly love for her. Abstract love. Like cosmic music, I suppose. Selfishly, I thought that if she considered me dead, I would have a stronger hold over her than I would have in life

Taverner's death in 1998 changed everything. I finally felt free to contact Olivia. I knew I could write to her care of your address, as I still don't know where she's living. Oh, Klara, what a joy it was to write to Olivia at last! At first I feared that hearing from me again would be too much of a shock, and her health might suffer. So I waited a suitable length of time after Taverner died. There was so much publicity surrounding his death, after all. Memorial concerts and the like.

My first letter to her was just an acknowledgment that I was still alive, and wanted to hear from her. I waited for weeks for her answer, but none came. Perhaps, indeed, she was processing the shock. When I wrote again, it was with more emotion. I summoned the memories of the music we made together in Brussels during the war. Again, there was no response. Then I tried something bolder: innermost reflections we'd shared, and some intimacies that we hadn't, that might have made the girl from the dairy farm blush, but not a woman of the world like Olivia Taverner.

Finally, when she didn't answer any of those efforts, I begged as any lovesick swain fifty years my junior would do.

Have you seen Olivia at all? Is she all right? I'm sure you left the letters in her mailbox as I requested. Do you think they might have gone astray? Surely there would have been some acknowledgment. I would have asked her to join me in Vernet had she expressed any interest in my fate. Oh, I would have made her my mountain bride, even at our advanced ages! But now I see that I must accept that her feelings for me are not the same as they once were. Perhaps they never were as strong as mine. It's strange, but I pitied Taverner all those years rather than hated him, I flattered myself that Olivia had reserved the most exclusive corner of her heart for me, while Taverner occupied a drafty waiting room.

Last year, I celebrated my ninetieth birthday with members of my academy. I looked in the mirror, and it seemed that the last time I'd done that, I was twenty-five years old! Funnily enough, I could still see that young person through all the white hair and weathered skin. But the years spoke to me loud and clear, and I knew it was time I found the courage to ask you this favor:

If Olivia is still alive, could you please convince her to come to see me in France? I'm still in Vernet-les-Bains, but no longer at Villa Sylvie—though I still own it. I've finally become a true man of the mountains! I have no phone. No internet. You'll never find me without assistance. Just ask in the village for Enrico. Everyone knows him. He's the handyman and gardener at the villa. He'll tell you how to find me.

I hope you will accompany Olivia. You can fly to Perpignan, and travel by taxi from there. Perhaps Roland can assist you, as it will be a long and tiring journey.

I will wait for you both. It doesn't matter when you come. Just come soon.

Your faithful

Konstantine

CHAPTER 73

Zar...*alive!*" Audrey spoke the words into the mist as she marched up the steep route to Hradčany. *The philosopher-musician...the wanderer...still on this Earth!*

Pedestrians stood aside for this little striding woman with the cloche hat and uncompromising gait.

"Audrey! *Wait!*"

Florian and Jonas lagged far behind. She'd left Karel's workshop at a dash, desperate for air.

Nerudova Street wound its way up to the castle through a leaden thaw. Tourists drifted through the miasma toward the lights of shops and taverns. Church bells, flat and muffled, sounded as if from a chasm.

Where is Konstantine Zar? Hans Meyer's question dogged her.

Had he meant Zar's grave? *Or the living Zar?*

The encounter with Meyer seemed even more of an illusion now, like so many things in this city. Audrey's mind could only summon the towering form that had been Meyer, and the statues themselves, just as unreliable, their robes frozen in the river wind.

"Audrey!"

She glanced back. *Was it really her friends calling her?* She couldn't see them through the vapors. Fear rose in her throat. *Where was Meyer?*

Surely a tall, white-haired man would be easy to spot, even in this heavy air.

She pressed ahead up the cobbled way. *I just want to be alone.* Behind all these pastel façades, and inside every seeping crack, breathed time. *Maybe I can disappear into it; maybe I can slip back to 1600, and walk up to the castle with Kepler to see Rudolf...*

The hill steepened: Kepler would have had trouble catching his breath, too. He'd been frail, unwell. As he struggled up Hradčany, he'd probably missed the arcane symbols over doorways and niches, proof of old Prague's obsession with magic and alchemy. They'd been Rudolf's obsessions, too. And no wonder. 1600 had dawned with manifestations strange and terrible: nocturnal suns and talking cats; bells that wouldn't ring; fires flaring up in St. Vitus cathedral in the dead of night. Planets were aligning. Meteorites falling. One couldn't be blamed for trying to find answers in these unearthly things.

How relieved Kepler must have been to escape into the labyrinth of Rudolf's castle...of Rudolf's mind! He would have found his patron in one of his many curio galleries, leaning into a cabinet to study an ostrich egg, perhaps. Or a dragon scale. There were mandrake roots, too, reclining like little men on miniature velvet cushions, and Egyptian clay figurines. Kepler would have known when the emperor had wandered into the farther gallery and stopped at the cabinet with two nails from Noah's Ark, for the glass door gave out a little frog-creak when it closed—the only sound beside the sickly scrape in Rudolf's lungs.

♦ ♦ ♦

"Audrey, for God's sake. *Stop!*"

Florian caught up to her, with Jonas dragging behind.

The three of them stood in a circle and simply regarded each other until they'd caught their breath.

"I'm sorry," Audrey said. "I don't know what got into me."

"Well, whatever it was got into us, too," Jonas said. "It's been an apocalyptic morning." He put his arm around her, but she stepped away.

"Zar's alive," Florian said quietly. "That changes everything. We've got to figure out where we go from here."

"You mean, where do we go next on this Pythagorean wild goose chase?" Audrey asked, only half-joking.

"Well, we could go for lunch," Jonas offered,

Florian ignored him and turned to Audrey. "Your intuition was right in the end," he said. "Our journey isn't over. How prescient when you said that there was something about the rosewood piano we couldn't possibly imagine." He paused. "And that Prague is not its final destination."

"No, it is not," she said, thinking: *Nor is it mine.* She considered the high crossroads to which her life had taken her. *Was the route clear now?*

She said, "With Zar alive, we must return the piano to him."

As if in answer, a fragment of Mozart piano music glistened on the air, its provenance unclear. Audrey found herself wondering how close they were to Maltese Square, and if the former Zar mansion was really empty.

"We also have to get word to Olivia," Florian said. "Tell her that Zar wants her to go to Vernet as soon as possible."

"Hang on," said Jonas. "What about those love letters she never answered? Maybe she doesn't want anything to do with him anymore."

"Jonas is right," Audrey said. "But it's a matter of urgency that we go to Vernet anyway...to warn Zar."

Florian stared at her. "To *warn* him?"

Audrey looked hard at her friends. "I have something to tell you," she said. "About that tall German with the Jack Russell terrier."

The two men hesitated.

"You mean the guy in Brussels who was watching the piano being loaded into Nero's van?" Jonas asked.

Audrey nodded. She indicated a lemon-colored establishment across the street: At the Black Comet. "Let's have lunch," she said. "I'll tell you what happened once we've fortified ourselves."

"The Black Comet," Florian mused. "A fortuitous name, don't you think? Keplerian..."

"You really can't help it, can you?" Jonas muttered.

Florian's eyes shone. "It could symbolize the dualities Pythagoras so loved. You know: light/dark; limited/unlimited; one/many..."

"How about food/beer?" Jonas added, stooping to enter the ancient portal.

CHAPTER 74

F riedrich!"

Graf was sitting alone at the back of the inn with a very tall glass of beer in front of him. The room had low, refectory vaulting, high-backed wooden chairs, and a few old weapons and etchings on the walls. Its sole occupant was the only obvious link to the present day.

"Friends!" he called, lifting his glass. "Please, join me." He regarded them wryly. "You look as if you've seen a ghost!"

"We were just speculating whether Kepler might have had lunch here," Florian joked. "Maybe you two crossed paths?"

A commotion of coats and chairs ensued, and the ordering of drinks from the hovering waitress, during which Graf went uncharacteristically still.

"There are plenty of ghosts in Malá Strana," he said, driftingly. "Did you know that a headless woman can be seen around here sometimes? And an aggrieved knight, too. At twilight. Oh, the air's positively jostling with them!"

The three musicians glanced at each other, unsure. An odd vagueness had come over Graf as if he, too, had brushed against something not of this world.

"But you must be as hungry as I am after such a monumental morning," Graf said. He proposed the traditional beef tenderloin, and everyone happily took his suggestion.

The table fell silent again as the waitress went off to fetch their food.

At last Graf said, "I've been sitting here for some time, thinking about what just happened at Karel's workshop. I mean, the fact that Zar's alive. And living in France. It's just unbelievable."

Murmurs rippled all around.

Jonas reached for Audrey's hand and gave it a squeeze. "You had something to tell us, Süsslein. Something urgent." His beard had filled out, and his eyes had a courtly gravity, and he could easily have blended in with the bearded gentlemen up at the castle discussing the universe all those centuries ago.

Audrey took a long sip of her wine. "Well…I feel as if I saw a ghost myself." She leveled her gaze on her companions. "Last night. On Charles Bridge."

The men put down their glasses and gave her their full attention.

And with that she told them about Hans Meyer.

This was not an easy task. The man had been accompanying this journey like a droning bass—a sound more intuited than heard. He'd materialized at the lake across from Olivia's house; on the tram to Schaerbeek; in Pascal's café; at Klara's.

And now in Prague.

Audrey sipped her wine and described Meyer's huge shape emerging from the mist on the bridge—the ice in his eyes, and deathly pallor. His hollow voice, and above all, his obsession with Zar. She managed to convey her terror as she'd faced this apparition alone on the already-haunted bridge.

"Why the hell didn't you tell us this before?" said Florian. "My God, Audrey! The man's obviously been tailing us."

"Meyer…*Meyer*," Graf repeated under his breath. "A common enough name. But it's important somehow." He leaned his elbows on the table and rubbed his temples. "I just can't place it."

Everyone welcomed the arrival of plates heaped with the marvel that Czechs called *svíčková*: marinated beef tenderloin with dumplings, sour-cream sauce, and wild berries. For some minutes, the only sound was the clink and scrape of cutlery.

"Why would Meyer be interested in the piano?" Jonas asked, mopping his plate with a wedge of bread.

"He's probably after the Zar inheritance," Florian offered. "And forced Klara to reveal where it was."

"That's what I thought, too," said Audrey. "But he seemed upset when I told him Klara was dead. He claimed she'd been alive when he'd left after his visit. Anyway, he seemed far more interested in Zar himself, frankly. He asked me if I knew where he was."

Graf gaped at her. "Where Zar was? He meant his grave, presumably."

"I don't think so," said Audrey.

"Maybe *that's* the information he got from Klara!" Florian said. "That Zar survived the war."

"That's it!" Graf cried, laying down his knife and fork. "Georg Meyer: that was the name of the man who attacked Klara in the Bois de la Cambre in 1942."

Everyone put down their cutlery.

"The man Zar killed?" Florian said.

"Yes."

Another stunned pause.

"Do you think there's a connection?" Jonas asked.

"Hans Meyer told me that his father died in Belgium during the war," said Audrey.

"Meyer's a common enough name, after all," Graf said, stalling.

Jonas ventured: "*Ich habe ein Kind.* Isn't that what the officer said right before Zar shot him, Friedrich? 'I have a child'. "

"Yes," said Graf. "That's correct. *Mein Gott...*" His eyes brimmed with revelation. "Hans Meyer is the son of the man Zar murdered."

Florian stared at Graf. "Meyer's looking for revenge, isn't he?"

"But after all these years?" Audrey said. "It seems unlikely."

Graf toyed with his meal. "Revenge has no limits," he said. "It can be kept alive for generations. Meyer is not a young man. Maybe he felt it was time to act—or at least, to find out if Zar might still be alive.

"He doesn't know Zar's in Vernet," said Florian. "Or he would have gone there directly."

"How did you end the encounter, Audrey?" Graf pressed her.

She stared into her wine glass. "I ran."

They all nodded sympathetically.

"We must warn Zar somehow!" Florian exclaimed. "In case Meyer finds out he's alive."

"In his letter, Zar told Klara that he has no phone in France," said Jonas. "And no internet. How can we reach him?"

"There must be some way," Florian said.

Audrey squared her shoulders, raised her chin, and said, "It's obvious: we must go to Vernet as soon as possible."

The men sat up straighter, too.

"And the piano?" Jonas asked.

"Klara wrote that she wanted it to go to the closest family member," Florian said. "Surely there's no doubt now about who that might be."

They took a moment for the name to settle over them.

"We'll have to recruit Nero again, I'm afraid," Audrey said. "Thank God for those five hundred euros we got on the bridge! And there's another thing." She put both hands on the table, as if to brace herself. "We must contact OIivia immediately to let her know Zar's alive." She paused. "And that he summoned her."

Graf shook his head in doubt. "But just imagine how the news would affect her, at her age. She never answered his letters, after all. We'll have to tell her gently. In a way that wouldn't shock her too much." He lapsed into thought. "Maybe Roland and I should go to Brussels—inform her about Zar, and offer to accompany her to France. If she even wants to see him."

"And if Meyer hasn't gotten to Zar first," Jonas added.

Graf's bright gaze darkened. "Yes."

"But how would Meyer have found out where he is?" Florian asked.

Audrey leapt to her feet. "Oh, my God!" she cried. "Karel! We never should have left him on his own. Meyer's already stopped by the workshop and frightened him half to death."

They paid for their meals and left the inn at once. No one spoke as they navigated the cobbled byways to Klavíry Náhoda. Everyone was clearly wondering the same thing: what might have happened to Karel had Meyer dropped by again to demand information on Zar.

They might have been wondering something else, too. At least Audrey was: Where did all the shades that were beginning to shift and shy along their route hide during the daylight hours?

CHAPTER 75

You've encountered some ghosts, I see," Karel said, observing their flushed faces and rapid breathing. "The Lesser Quarter is full of them, after all."

"Are you all right, Karel?" Jonas asked. He put a hand on the little man's shoulder.

Karel said nothing. He led them through the carriageway and into the workshop, his expression mask-like.

Florian remarked on the empty carriageway.

"Nero left a few hours ago," Karel said. "He's gone back to Brussels."

"But..." Graf faltered. "How will we...?"

Everyone shared a panicked look: their trip to Vernet had just been sorely compromised.

Karel ignored the conundrum. He poured plum brandy for his friends and beckoned them to the stove. Then he wandered over to Antonin's desk and looked out the window. He studied the piano relics in the courtyard—legs, lyres, struts—all reaching for the sky.

"He came by again," Karel said. His form was just a silhouette against the dying daylight.

Silence gripped the room.

"The man with the white hair?" Florian ventured.

Karel nodded. He turned on Antonin's desk lamp: Kepler's model of the universe cast its shadow over the cement floor. The bits and pieces of pianos strewn to the farthest corners of the room had taken on the aspect of cosmic junk, stuck in orbit around the tiny sun that was Zar's Náhoda.

"You know why he came back, don't you?" Karel asked, returning to the stove.

"Oh, Karel," moaned Audrey. She got up and put a hand on his arm. "I'm so sorry. We should never have left you alone." She hesitated. "He didn't hurt you, did he?"

Karel shook his head. "No. But he got what he wanted."

They gasped.

"You told him where Zar is?" cried Jonas.

"First I told him Zar was dead," said Karel. "But he didn't believe me. Then I told him as much as I had to."

"As you had to…? Audrey repeated.

"Yes. That is, I told him that Zar's in Vernet-les-Bains."

The questions tumbled over each other:

How much did you tell him?

Surely not the exact address!

Did he threaten you?

Does he know about the letters?

"Friends, friends!" Karel waved them to order. "You must understand." He smoothed the tuft of hair over his ear. "You see," he said. "He had a gun."

Dusk slunk into the room. The only illumination now was the gleam from Antonin's lamp.

"That means…" Jonas began.

Graf continued the thought: "That means that he probably intends to use it…"

Florian came to the natural conclusion: "On Zar."

"Look," Karel said, suddenly clear-eyed. "I'm no hero. I told him about Vernet-les-Bains, it's true. But not about Villa Sylvie. Anyway, Zar himself said that he'd retreated into the mountains and was impossible to find. I didn't mention Enrico, of course. And remember: Meyer will be looking for Konstantine Zar. Not for Alexandre Bergman."

"Karel's right," said Florian. "Zar's been living under a pseudonym all these years. He's a recluse. Meyer might never find him." He paused. "Hell, we might never find him."

"I would wager that Meyer doesn't know the mountains like Zar does," said Graf. "And if Audrey's description is any indication, the man doesn't seem to be in the best health."

Florian turned to Karel. "Friedrich and Roland are going to Brussels to tell Olivia about Zar," he said. "Then—if she agrees—they'll accompany her to Vernet."

"But that's wonderful!" Karel exclaimed.

"There's more," said Audrey. "We're taking Zar's piano to him."

They all turned toward the Náhoda, as if it might have some reaction to this news.

"But how?" Karel asked. "Nero's gone." He shook his head sadly. "I'm so sorry I can't help with this wonderful scheme. I can't afford a car—let alone a van. I haven't been able to move pianos for years."

"Florian, can I use your phone?" Jonas said without ceremony. "We're in need of a knight in shining armor, it seems." As the shadows deepened, and his beard seemed to thicken, Jonas was looking increasingly like someone from that epoch himself.

Florian pulled out his phone and handed it over with a smirk. "I forgot that you threw yours away."

Knights in armor were in short supply, as everyone knew. They were often not even recognizable anymore. However, the few knights that did exist still met the peerless standards of integrity and valor associated with their ilk, even if they came disguised as something else altogether.

As grocers, for instance.

"Rami has a van," said Jonas.

CHAPTER 76

It took Rami three days to arrange for emergency van repairs, close down the Casablanca General Store for an indefinite period, and make the long drive from Brussels to Prague.

Three days. It was an eternity when one feared the worst for someone—even if that someone had been presumed dead for decades, changed his name, and not one of his would-be rescuers had ever laid eyes on him. Except for Olivia, of course. *And would she even want to lay eyes on him now?* Once again, the elusive Konstantine Zar seemed more idea than flesh.

Wilmots and Graf left Prague immediately in Gloria's car. When they arrived at Schloss Helden and described their mission, the countess was so entranced that she insisted they take her own Mercedes to ferry Olivia to her reunion in comfort and style. *You can't possibly make such an historic journey in a Škoda, Friedrich dear!*

Karel offered the trio lodgings in a small studio across the carriageway that he used for storing tools and screws. He knew they'd been busking on Charles Bridge and had financial hardships. And now they faced a fifteen hundred-kilometer journey with unknown consequences. "There's not much furniture," he apologized. "But you can sleep on piano blankets—they're really quite comfortable."

Karel Náhoda blossomed into the craftsman he once was. He opened the rosewood piano with the delicacy of a master and set to work. He hardly slept, and ate little. He seemed unaware that in the course of those few days, spring had made her first appearance in Prague, and one brave blackbird had begun his yearly opera on the courtyard wall.

With reverence, Karel explored the innards of the instrument and made his diagnoses. He changed felts, adjusted hammers, replaced some of the strings and pins, and cleaned the keys with his special solvent. "This piano must be worthy of Konstantine Zar," he declared. And with that he opened the rosewood panels again, just to make sure that everything was in order.

When he'd finally finished, and called the musicians into the workshop, it wasn't only to let them admire his expertise with the piano.

But to show them what else he'd found inside it.

◆ ◆ ◆

Audrey examined the small bundle Karel handed to her.

"More letters?" Florian said, incredulous.

"Yes," said Karel. "They were wedged more deeply than the others, right at the back of that secret space under the keyboard that Antonin devised."

"They're from Zar," Audrey said, handling the squashed wad of paper. "Addressed to Madame Olivia Taverner c/o Klara Náhoda in Rue Nova." She sucked in her breath.

"Süsslein, what is it?" said Jonas.

Audrey stared at her friends. "They haven't been opened," she said.

"But..." Florian faltered. "That means that Olivia never received them."

Audrey could barely marshal her words. "Yes, it must mean that," she said. "Olivia told me that Klara had disapproved of her—that she didn't think Olivia was good enough for her brother. But to do this...to deny Olivia all knowledge of Zar's existence!"

"She was jealous," Jonas said, stroking his beard. "Zar said that he'd poured his heart out in those letters. Now we know why Olivia never answered him."

Karel let out a heartrending sigh. "Olivia doesn't even know that Zar escaped his execution—let alone survived the war. And that he's still alive, for God's sake! Klara had no business hiding Zar's letters away like that! She destroyed all possibility of love between two people—and in the process, hurt the person she loved most in the world."

"Well, not *all* possibility," said Florian. "It's not too late."

"Maybe Klara did feel some guilt in the end," Audrey said. "Because she willed the piano to Olivia if there was no one left in Prague to claim it."

"Small comfort, indeed," said Karel.

They all regarded the letters.

"Olivia must open these!" Audrey cried. "She'll surely go to Zar now! Florian, call Graf at once. We can Fedex the letters to Brussels, to Roland's place. Find out his address. That way, they can ease the shock when they give them to Olivia. We must hurry!"

Florian made the call. Then he contacted the courier service. The letters would be picked up early the following morning.

"What a deceitful woman Klara was!" Karel said under his breath. "And to think that she married into my family. No wonder the marriage didn't last."

CHAPTER 77

It was past midnight by the time Audrey finally sat down at the rosewood piano to sample Karel's handiwork. She'd left Florian and Jonas in the studio across the carriageway, wrapped in piano blankets and attempting to sleep. Karel had long since retired to his quarters upstairs, though not before he'd made sure that Audrey was comfortable, raising the piano slightly so she wouldn't jam her knees against the secret compartment. He'd also provided another lamp, and thrown a few extra logs on the stove.

She was alone in the workshop.

Trembling, she smoothed her fingertips up and down the newly-cleaned keys. The taste of cream was what she'd always loved about touching the piano—that heady crossing of the senses. She stretched her hands, sighed, and looked overhead at the distant piping and hoists under the ceiling, now the realm of cobwebs and rust. A shabby vista, indeed. *Might I catch a glimpse of her?* The lady must be somewhere nearby. Especially here, in a birthplace of her largest, most unwieldy disciple.

Her fingers rested on the simple intervals Karel had played: the harmony of Kepler's planetary ratios. They were sonorities that every musician knew—that lay at the core of everything they'd ever played. That these basic musical principles could be found in the math of the cosmos was no small marvel. Audrey recalled what Kepler had written in his *Harmonices Mundi: The Earth sings Mi, Fa, Mi [E, F, E]: you may infer even from the syllables that in this our home, misery and famine hold sway.*

She played Mi-Fa-Mi, as she had in her garret. It was a dour interval, indeed. Small and suspicious. *But did one really have to infer misery and famine from it?* She played the melancholy little waltz she'd invented in Brussels, and to her surprise, the Náhoda responded with joy and eagerness. *Could Mi and Fa suggest more uplifting words?* she wondered. "Miraculous" and "fabulous", for instance. And in several languages, too! She glanced up at the pipes and pulleys: it was obvious by now that the lady preferred such humble venues.

She played on in the night workshop, with the smell of stale coffee in the air and a century of dust on the floor, and certainty grew with each phrase she played that perhaps the Music of the Spheres really could resonate in a minuscule vessel on Earth like Audrey Nightingale.

♦ ♦ ♦

The door to the carriageway opened and someone slipped in.

Audrey glanced up. The moment yawned. It was one of those spaces between music and silence alive with metaphysics: a sliver of eternity.

"Who's there?" Audrey asked.

Just then, caught in that sliver, she could imagine only one of three people: Johannes Kepler. Emperor Rudolf. Or Konstantine Zar. The beard of her visitor strongly suggested the first two. But the height and blousy white shirt might mean it was the third one, suddenly hirsute.

Audrey stood up, faint.

Zar?

The tall man stepped into the light and she felt a twinge of disappointment.

"Audrey," he said.

She stood very still with her hand on the piano. Her heart would not slow its driving beat. Only a few days had passed since...

Since the kiss.

Jonas approached.

"What were you playing just now?" he asked.

She looked at him as if through a prism. The rake—the man-child—was gone. She smiled, and rued the twinge of disappointment. "I was playing the Earth!" she said, and hoped he would understand...especially with Antonin's Kepler corner so near. "I'm creating a waltz around Kepler's interval for the Earth," she explained. "Mi, Fa, Mi."

"Ah," Jonas said. He stepped closer. "You seem different, somehow."

"Let me guess," she teased him. "I'm no longer like one of those figures on the prow of a ship."

He shuffled, and looked at his feet. "What I wanted to say was, you're what Music would look like if we could see her."

The comment silenced Audrey at once. *Surely he'd never said such a thing to his other women.* She surprised herself by hoping this was true.

They pulled two piano benches to the stove and stoked the fire. Karel had left a bottle of cognac handy, and with a bit of searching they came up with two glasses.

"Where did you get that nice shirt?" was all Audrey managed to say. She regretted this at once. Jonas possessed a few nice shirts, in fact. Every performing musician did. How could she have been disappointed that this flesh-and-blood man—her loyal friend, seemingly transformed—had not been that other man in a white shirt, who lived only in her mind?

"It was Antonin's," Jonas said. "My concert shirts are all dirty. And..."

"And?" Audrey prompted him.

"And I wanted a decent shirt to speak with you properly."

In the light of the piano lamp, Audrey could see now that Jonas had trimmed his beard and generally taken care with his appearance. She even detected a whiff of cologne. His face was healing well from Baron Van Overberg's brutal attack.

"Süsslein," he said. "I'm not the man you think I am."

"Oh?" Audrey studied her friend. "I rather liked the man I thought you were!"

"Please, don't make fun of me. Not now. You see..." He took her hand and held it tightly. "I regret everything: the reckless behavior over the years...the women..."

Audrey pulled her hand away and got up to pace. "Why do you suddenly regret all those things now, Jonas?" she asked.

He got up, too, and answered her with another question: "Something happened at Schloss Helden, didn't it?"

"Yes," she said. "I suppose it did. Though fleetingly."

"I wanted to talk to you then. But...well, you know."

"Events intervened," she said.

They stood a few meters apart, regarding each other with the affection they genuinely felt. Around them, the piano parts in their orbits lent a touch of the celestial.

"Do you think you could ever see me in another light, Süsslein?" Jonas attempted. "I know it's a lot to ask. And it might take time. Years, even. I don't mind." He hesitated. "Look how long it was for Olivia and Zar!"

Zar...

Audrey tried to ignore the name, but it did not ignore her. There it was again: the stirring of air at her shoulder, which was probably just a draft from the courtyard. Or was it the passage of someone who'd moved through this atelier long ago, for whom she'd arrived in the same space over seventy years too late.

"Audrey?" Jonas pressed her.

She looked at him, and could see only what she wanted to see: the man she'd met in a photograph. She felt helpless before Jonas's struggle. *Had it been this difficult for Zar to proclaim his love for Olivia in the forest?*

On impulse, Audrey reached out to touch the white shirt. She had to know that it didn't feel as she imagined—coarse, woven—but was a perfectly ordinary modern garment.

In that gesture, Jonas found the courage he'd been lacking.

"Audrey, I love you," he said, now able to say it.

The kiss at Schloss Helden had been an anomaly, as Audrey recalled. A hurried meeting of lips through a car window that might never have occurred at all had one of the parties not moved his head at the last minute.

This time, though, their kiss was as hot and leisurely as the previous one had been tepid and quick. But as delighted as Jonas must have been that the evening had taken the turn he'd obviously hoped it would, for Audrey, given the history of this room, and the magic of the city outside its walls, she couldn't be entirely sure which man she was kissing.

CHAPTER 78

*Z**ar passed this way.*

Audrey observed the horizon from the passenger seat of Rami's van. She watched, spellbound, as what appeared to be clouds reclining between Earth and sky resolved themselves into mountains.

He'd also traveled to the Pyrenees in a grocer's van, on the run from the Gestapo.

She wondered if Zar had shared her awe seeing high mountains for the first time. Perhaps he'd been too ill to care; too heartsick from the memory of Olivia walking away from him forever—from the fatal hesitation that had prevented him from calling out to her, and cost him so dearly.

Audrey glanced at Rami: the gentle grocer's air of apology had been replaced by purpose. A certain zeal lifted the doleful moustache.

"*Ça va,* chérie?" he asked, smiling at her.

She nodded, and turned back to the Pyrenees. The bastion of rock stretched all the way from the Mediterranean, glittering on their left, to the Atlantic, five hundred kilometers to their right. *How would they find Zar in all that wilderness?*

Rami had embraced his knightly mission (particularly as it had been Jonas who'd proposed it). "Of course I'll help! Let's see: nine hundred kilometers from Brussels to Prague; then fifteen hundred more from Prague to the Pyrenees...hmm. And with a piano, you say? My goodness! That's a bit heavy, isn't it? Never mind. We'll find a way."

They'd left Prague at four that morning. Rami had arrived there at two, in dire need of food and a nap, which he'd managed to accomplish in only two hours. There wasn't a moment to lose: Zar had to be tracked down and warned of the danger he was in. Nor could they let up on their mission to reunite Olivia with her soulmate, even if there had been no word from Brussels that Roland and Friedrich had persuaded her to do this.

The dusty red van was facing its greatest challenge yet. Any piano would slow down a vehicle, but this piano seemed unusually heavy, somehow. Maybe it was the quantity of rosewood. Or a particularly solid frame. Or something less obvious, perhaps: Zar's papers, that Karel had returned to their secret compartment along with the jeweled brooch, making for quite some metaphysical ballast.

They were traversing an arena of desert suns, huge moons, renegades, and wine. History seemed just a continuation of countless yesterdays here. Roman chariots once rattled along over stones just meters beneath Rami's van. Later, closer to the present-day surface, pilgrims limped toward Santiago de Compostela. The young Konstantine Zar had passed here, too, not so long ago, on a road that modern travelers would recognize.

Audrey looked over her shoulder at the two forms sleeping amidst the vegetable crates. She remembered what Florian had said about the thread of music stretching back thousands of years...how as musicians they were still holding on to it.

She glanced at Jonas, and at once Olivia's story filled her with a strange synergy. In a moment of impulse, she imagined curling up beside him, as Zar had curled up beside Olivia on the night they'd rescued the injured pilot.

She shook off these thoughts.

"Florian?" she whispered, so as not to waken Jonas as well. "Have you heard anything from Friedrich?"

"They gave Zar's letters to Olivia," he mumbled. "That's all I know."

"Did she read them?"

"I don't know."

"So they haven't left for Vernet yet?"

"No."

Audrey sighed and leaned her head back against the seat. She tried to picture Olivia's reaction when Roland and Friedrich had presented Zar's unopened correspondence. How had that silvery bird, so poised and elegant, withstood such a betrayal? What must she have felt for Klara at that moment?

"You should try to sleep, chérie," Rami said. "We'll stop for lunch in an hour or so."

Audrey closed her eyes.

They'd been on the road for almost seven hours. In the flurry of departure, no one had briefed the grocer on the details of their mission. He knew only that they were transporting a piano, and that it was urgent they reach a certain elderly professor in the remote Pyrenees as soon as possible.

"The piano must be very special to that gentleman," Rami said.

"Yes," murmured Audrey. "It's very special to him." She added: "You might say that it was his first love."

"Ah," Rami nodded. "Now I understand. How lucky for him that you were able to save it!"

Audrey drifted to sleep on the guilt these words had revived.

◆ ◆ ◆

They brought in a crane on the day they demolished the gymnasium, along with a bulldozer and two containers for all the rubble.

The students were forbidden to go anywhere near the site. But they gathered after school anyway, breathless gapeseeds, peering through gaps in the barrier. They yelled with delight at the noise and drama, and also with consternation, as machines flattened the world they'd once relied on.

Audrey had already started back to her foster home. She knew a thing or two about unreliable worlds; she also knew that all the contents of the gymnasium had been salvaged except for the piano, which was destined to die with the building. She couldn't bear to watch.

But something was pulling at her. *How can you abandon your friend at such a moment?* The voice was hers...but not entirely.

She rushed back to the barrier.

The machines had already done their work: nothing remained of the gym but a large squarish object rising from the ruins. The children jostled to find peepholes. What a splendid show this was! With a whoop they watched the bulldozer roar over the rubble toward the piano, scoop it up, and trundle off, swaying under the load. There was a collective gasp as the piano was lifted high enough to clear the side of the container. The scoop remained poised in the air for a moment. *Oh, please let it down gently!* Audrey whispered, her fists clenched. Slowly, the scoop began to tip. The condemned one tumbled to the very edge and caught there, as if it might cheat death after all.

Audrey closed her eyes. But she couldn't escape the sound of it: the thud, like a mortar, when the piano fell; the severing of strings one after the other, each with its final, wrenching cry; the pistol shot as the sounding board cracked.

At last the instrument heaved onto its back and lay still.

A soul could not be so easily destroyed, however. Such a feat was beyond even divine powers, let alone such tawdry human ones. And so the thing that still trembled in that doomed box let out a sort of reverberation, solemn and majestic, as it left.

Audrey opened her eyes.

A haze of dust rose up from the container. Some of it floated back to earth, and coated the piano's remains in the gray inertia of death. A few motes lingered above the corpse, however. They caught in a beam of afternoon sun, where they danced with an almost festive air, until, transfigured, they vanished upward.

Silence reigned.

Even the children made no noise. At length they turned in unison and shuffled home like calves to the byre. No one said a word to Audrey.

She walked home alone, as she always did, and went to bed without her supper. She never spoke to anyone about what she'd witnessed. The ache from that day would wax and wane, then flare again like tissue around an embedded object. Only decades later, on the night she'd discovered the Náhoda piano, would she realize that she'd ached for all those years because she hadn't even tried to rescue her friend.

◆ ◆ ◆

A brusque shifting of gears woke her up. Something odd had happened while she'd been sleeping: a blessed painlessness had spread its warm, healing oil throughout her body.

She glanced around at the rosewood piano.

The ache had gone.

For *this* piano, she'd been able to save.

CHAPTER 79

Everyone, wake up, please!" Rami brandished a bag with coffee and croissants in one hand, and in the other, a copy of Paris Match.

He'd parked at the edge of a vast rest plaza near Dijon. There was no shortage of other battered vans parked in the vicinity, also with Moroccan drivers, plying the same route down through France and Spain to Gibraltar, and on to Tangier. Rami had driven it himself many times.

Audrey yawned and got out of the van. There was warmth in the fragile spring sun, though a mistral was blowing, persistent and tedious, and she gathered her coat against its bite.

"You shouldn't waste money on Paris Match, Rami," she said with irritation. "It's expensive. And we have so little cash as it is."

"*Exactement!*" enthused the grocer. He waved the magazine at Jonas and Florian, who were emerging from their vegetable-sack beds. "That is why I thought carefully before buying this one. Look!" The magazine pages slapped in the wind.

They all gaped at the headlines:

No Place to Hide, Even For the Superrich
Baron Aymeric Van Overberg arrested for tax evasion

Beneath this bombshell was a photograph of the baron himself, being led away by the police from his villa in Mallorca.

"What the...?" Jonas struggled into his leather jacket and took a coffee from Rami's bag.

"Yes, it is true!" cried Rami. "The baron is no longer a danger to you, my friend!"

Audrey sipped her coffee. "Well, I don't know," she said, glancing away. "We should probably still be careful."

She hadn't been able to meet Jonas's gaze since their tryst in Karel's workshop. The memory of his kiss—the bewitched, Prague one—joined the warm oil already coursing through her body after her dream. But the news of the baron had raised the likelihood that the new Jonas, no matter how transfigured, would probably fall for similar risky schemes in the future, and she wondered whether she preferred the old Jonas after all.

Rami ignored Audrey's hesitation, for the news had galvanized him. Without a word, he clambered into the back of the van and began unwrapping the piano.

"What on earth are you doing?" Florian demanded.

"We are going to have a concert!" Rami declared. He unstrapped the piano from its moorings and motioned to the two men to help him slide it toward the door of the van.

No one moved. It was unclear whether their astonishment was due to this extraordinary announcement, or to the entrepreneurial spirit that had suddenly sprung to life in Rami.

"As you say, we are short of cash," he explained. "And now we need not worry that the baron might be prowling the highways for Jonas."

"Yes, but what about Meyer?" Florian asked. "We have to get to Vernet as soon as we can, to warn Zar."

"Zar himself wrote that it would be impossible for anyone to find him without local assistance," Audrey said.

"Which Meyer will ask for," Florian added. "Anyway, he must have left Prague before we did. We have to hurry."

"Zar is Alexandre Bergman now," Jonas reminded them, munching on a croissant.

"But what if Meyer forces information from Enrico, Zar's handyman?" said Audrey.

"Friends, please!" Rami exclaimed "We will leave soon, I promise. In the meantime, I guarantee that we will drive away from this plaza being able to afford the next stage of our journey."

A look passed between the members of the former Kepler Players: a growing recognition that this event was unfolding beyond their control, and like a wave, was taking them with it.

◆ ◆ ◆

In the absence of a ramp, Audrey was obliged to play just inside the van with the doors open. Jonas and Florian set up their stands on the asphalt outside, and fastened their scores with clothespins to keep the mistral from snatching them. Everyone used vegetable crates for chairs.

It was lunchtime. The plaza was filling up with travelers stretching in the sunshine, sipping warm drinks, and chasing sandwich wrappers in the wind. Families unfolded strollers and bounced fractious babies. Cars lined up for petrol. A classical music concert had certainly not crossed anyone's mind.

The trio tuned and warmed up. A little gaggle of children pressed around the dusty red van. People exclaimed, and beckoned to their friends. A crowd soon gathered.

They began with short, lively movements: Dvořák and Saint-Saëns. (Not that anyone cared who wrote them.) Audrey's playing spilled out from the doors of the van, where Florian and Jonas bowed like demons to drown out the wind.

How exhilarating! Audrey thought, as her hands slipped about on the Nahoda's cold, smooth keys. How liberating to be freed of all that convention—of the concert temple's unbending ritual! A parallel musical universe was flourishing out here under the sky.

A man in the djellaba and sandals of the souk pulled his weary wife toward Rami's van and set out two folding chairs. Others soon joined them. Trucks roared past on the highway. The odors of diesel fumes and fried food prevailed. No one could have confused the parking plaza with the Wallenstein Palace in Prague—or with any of the other distinguished venues around the world where the Kepler Players had been invited to perform.

The throng erupted into clapping and pounding on car hoods after the Brahms. In the front row, the weary woman was drying her eyes with a corner of her headscarf.

Take your art to the humblest places. There you will make the deepest connections.

Audrey smiled at the woman. *This is what Zar meant!*

Rami worked the crowd with an empty potato sack. He bowed as he went, his hand on his heart, apologizing for any inconvenience; he smiled, and murmured his thanks in French and Arabic, and even in English, and after one hour, the gentle grocer had collected more cash in the sack than he did in his till in a typical week. And while it was safe to say that the world's great concert halls had never had to endure the wrong notes, improvisation, car fumes, and picnicking of this performance, they'd probably never known such shocked delight, either.

♦ ♦ ♦

They drove off to cheers.

"Let's see how much we earned," Jonas said, reaching into the potato sack on the floor of the van.

There were plenty of coins and smaller bills; there was also an impressive number of twenties and fifties. Jonas took a fistful out and flourished it with a grin.

"Wait a minute," Florian said. "There's something purple in there."

"What?" Audrey swiveled around in the passenger seat. A chill crept over her.

"Christ, it's another five hundred euros!" Florian cried. He pulled the bill from Jonas's hand.

Audrey turned to Rami. "Did you see who left this?" she demanded.

"No," he said.

"A tall man with white hair?" she prompted him.

"*Mais non!* Why?"

Audrey hadn't revealed her suspicions to anyone that Meyer might have left the five hundred euros on Charles Bridge—maybe even asked one of the Japanese tourists to leave it for him in Florian's violin case.

She told them her suspicions now.

"You mean he was on the bridge when we were playing?" Jonas said.

"Oh, who knows?' Audrey sighed. "The man is like a ghost."

"A ghost you talked to," Florian reminded her.

"Why would he leave so much money?" asked Jonas.

"He's playing with us," Florian said. "Making us doubt him."

"I agree," said Audrey. "It's sinister charity, that's for sure. We must hurry!" she exclaimed. "Meyer's not far away."

CHAPTER 80

Rami turned off the highway at Perpignan and headed toward the mountains. Most of the traffic carried on to Spain and points south, leaving few travelers to cross the broad plain at the foot of the Pyrenees.

They stopped briefly at dusk near the medieval village of Ille-sur-Têt to stretch their legs. A storm had passed through the valley and left a hint of bay and rosemary on the dampness. Spring had found an early foothold in the blossoming apple and pear trees, and in the sparrows prancing like tiny heralds.

"That's the Canigou massif," said Rami, pointing to distant, rounded peaks in silhouette. "You can just make out the pyramid of Canigou itself. It's an enchanted mountain, you know. Full of ancient legends."

"Zar must have found much solace here," Audrey said.

"Maybe he's already added another legend to the list," Florian mused.

Jonas leaned in to Audrey and coaxed her away from the others. "Süsslein," he said under his breath. "Can we talk, do you think? Florian can ride in front with Rami, and we can sit in the back."

Reluctantly, Audrey took her eyes off the mountains. She looked at her friend with a sad heart: at the scars Van Overberg had left on his face, and at the guileless, faithful regard.

"I don't know what to say, Jonas," she said, which was true. What wasn't true was the list of excuses she'd been inventing for herself in order to keep Jonas at bay, all of which did not hold water. Among them: *He doesn't have the depths I'm looking for*, and *It's impossible to have a romance with a good friend.*

Aloud she said, "Maybe we can talk once we reach Vernet," effectively postponing having to prop up her excuses to Jonas directly. Throwing him a crumb, she added: "You'll always have my friendship."

"Yes, of course. But..." Jonas foundered.

"*On y va!*" Rami called to them. "Let's go. It's getting dark."

♦ ♦ ♦

They pressed on through the gloaming. Audrey had declined Jonas's invitation to talk and was sitting next to Rami again. She watched the sun dip behind the foothills, leaving crimson streaks seeping into purply darkness. Distant lights pricked the hillsides, signaling ancient fortified towns.

"This must be the route Zar took on his flight from Belgium," Audrey said.

"He probably turned off here somewhere to that hamlet with the goats," Florian suggested.

"I wonder which part of the sky revealed its secrets," Audrey speculated.

"I wonder where Valerio shot Sylvie," muttered Jonas.

Audrey imagined Zar, weak from illness, pedaling his bicycle along this road in clerical disguise; she rolled down the window and for some reason, that bold, unsettled face in Olivia's photograph gave her no comfort. With trepidation she realized that their journey was transforming by the kilometer from mission to pilgrimage, and was beginning to seem so much larger than its participants: three musicians, a grocer, and a piano, bumping along in an old van toward the Pyrenean sunset.

"Did you reach Friedrich?" Audrey asked Florian.

"I left a message. They might be on their way already."

"If they managed to convince Olivia," Audrey said.

The road passed through a moribund village and at once began to snake upward. The fertile valley dropped behind in their wake and a dark mass of land reared in front of them.

"The Cathars hid from their Catholic pursuers in these mountains," Florian said. "Almost a thousand years ago."

"The Pyrenees can hide anyone and anything," said Rami, gripping the steering wheel around the switchbacks. "I knew people on the Spanish side who died in a ravine because no one could find them. The high valleys are almost impossible to reach. And there're caves, too. You can disappear permanently, if you want to." He paused. "And unfortunately, if you don't want to."

"A good place for Zar, then," mused Audrey.

The engine screamed its way up the final ascent to Vernet-les-Bains. Hairpin turns leapt into the headlights, and beyond them plunged chasms of unknown depth. Huge, mottled plane trees loomed too close to the road.

The spa town straddled the Cady River, a torrent issuing from the Canigou heights, and had always been difficult to reach. In the nineteenth century, horse-drawn contraptions struggled up the mountain to the mineral springs, and the present conveyance had no less trouble. The piano swung the van perilously close to the drop-off on each turn. Its great weight dragged them backward, and at that moment, no one could have argued successfully that the instrument's true essence was weightless.

At last they reached level ground. Rami crossed the river and pulled off the road behind a hedge. The van let out a final, dying shudder.

"It will be well hidden here," he said, and they all knew what his words implied.

The foursome struggled out. Crisp air slapped them awake. The silence was alive with rushing water and a fitful wind. Across the river, a floodlit bell tower rose from a jumble of pale, shuttered houses all crowded onto a steep foothill. Beyond the town, mountains shone in their night snows, and the vault of sky seemed more than roomy enough for Kepler's cosmic symphony.

Audrey embraced Rami. "Thank you for driving us here," she said. "You must be exhausted."

An antique bell rang the half-hour.

"Eight-thirty," said Florian, checking his watch.

"Could you try Friedrich again?" Audrey asked.

"I did," he said. "I even called Olivia. No one's answering."

"The bed and breakfast is across from the botanical gardens," Florian said, studying the map. "We're very close. The landlady said she would leave the key behind the geraniums if we arrived after eight."

They kept to the shadows, hauling their luggage and instruments by hand rather than risking the clatter of wheels. They found the house and the pot of geraniums, as well as the two rooms downstairs in which they'd agreed to double up. No one complained that Rami and Jonas had to share a double bed; or that Audrey and Florian were in a children's bunk. Like most pilgrims at the end of a long day, they were too exhausted even to dream, though if they had, their sleep would have been troubled not by the anticipation of seeing the shrine that was now so near, but by the ruthless avenger who was also planning a visit.

CHAPTER 81

The gentleman with the cello asked me to give you this, Madame," said their hostess as Audrey entered the breakfast room. "He left early this morning, on the first bus to Perpignan." She handed her guest a square piece of paper.

"Jonas Liebling *left?*" Audrey exclaimed. She examined the paper: a breakfast napkin scrawled with a few lines.

Süsslein,

I'm going back to Hamburg to my sister's. I'm confused about us. About everything.

You are so strong on the prow of your ship. So determined. I'll never be Zar. Good luck on your journey.

Jonas

Audrey tucked the napkin into her skirt pocket and wandered to the buffet table laden with fruit, bread, cheeses, cold meats, and local pastries. Jonas had clearly already helped himself. The window faced the botanical gardens around the spa buildings and forested slopes beyond, but she looked at these things without seeing them.

I toyed with his emotions, then turned away from him. Why couldn't I tell him what I really feel?

Her appetite vanished, and she took a single roll from the buffet table. *He'll disappear for good this time.*

"Oh, there you are!" Rami called, bustling through the door with Florian behind him. He noticed Audrey's distress at once. "I couldn't stop him, chérie. He was so unhappy. *Le pauvre.* So I gave him a bit of money for the trip."

"Not the five hundred euro note, I hope," Florian grumbled, pouring himself coffee. His curls were still flattened on one side from sleep, like a child's.

"Of course I didn't give him that much!" Rami said, clearly hurt.

"It doesn't matter now," Audrey said without tone. *I dragged Jonas all this way,* she thought. *And for what? For a ridiculous quest we probably have no hope of finishing...for an elderly guru and his discarded piano. Jonas deserves better.*

They ate their breakfast in silence. The men didn't mention Jonas's note, or press Audrey about why he'd left.

"Are you here for a cure?" the landlady asked as she put fresh coffee on the table. She was at least seventy, but a quick step belied her age, as did a girlish smile, giving the impression that some sort of elixir might, indeed, flow from the springs on the hill.

"We're here on a mission," Rami said. He puffed himself up in his own humble fashion, in case anyone doubted he had a role in it.

"Is that so?" said the lady.

Audrey asked: "Is there a villa around here that might have belonged to someone called Ariane Bergman after the war?"

The landlady paused, and shook her head. "Not that I know of. There's an old villa up the river road. But it's been empty for years."

The group exchanged glances.

"Just follow the signs to the abbey of St. Martin," the lady said. "There's a little bridge over the river somewhere on the right, and some high hedges. I believe there's a villa there."

"Do you think that's where Zar lived?" Florian whispered excitedly once the landlady had left. "Before he hid himself away in the mountains?"

"Maybe," said Audrey.

"We should make some more inquiries in town," Rami suggested.

"Too risky," said Florian. "We don't know where Meyer is. We should avoid the town and go directly to the villa to see for ourselves."

Audrey got up. "We should go immediately!"

Florian pulled his phone from his pocket as they went for their coats.

"There's a message from Friedrich!" he cried. "They're on their way!"

"And?" Audrey peered at his phone.

"They spent the night at Dijon, apparently. Friedrich says they hope to arrive in Vernet sometime this evening!"

◆ ◆ ◆

The van couldn't possibly have made it up the mountain road carrying a piano, so they agreed to walk to the villa.

They crossed the botanical park, keeping to the trees and dense foliage as much as possible. The three of them spread out on the steep climb above the town—Audrey first, with greater stamina and better shoes, followed by a wheezing Rami, and in the rear, Florian, woefully unfit.

The sun was brittle, the wind insolent. The paradoxes of a Pyrenean spring were everywhere: Mt. Canigou, draped in kingly snows, while far below it, delicate lilies, orchids, wisteria and bluebells already bloomed in sheltered gardens; the air, cutting on the cheeks, while the sun was warm enough to lure lizards from their walls.

Vernet soon dropped out of sight. The serpentine road enfolded them, as if they'd stepped into a zone of mystery...of concealment. The forest crowded in on both sides: oaks and chestnuts, bright in their infant green, alongside ancient pines with russet, dinosaur hides. The river was never far away, hell-bent over boulders and fallen logs, roiling in whirlpools. The wind in the crowns of the trees was indistinguishable from the rush of water.

Who came this way? Audrey wondered, stopping to catch her breath. The question kept her mind from returning to Jonas, and to how sorely she missed him. She imagined the millennia of human passage along this route. *What had they worn on their feet?* Animal hide? Sandals? Not that long ago, it had been shoes stuffed with newspaper. More efficient foot-wear, too: *jackboots.*

"That must be the bridge," Florian said, catching up to her. He pointed to a narrow wooden structure wide enough for one vehicle.

"It all looks familiar, somehow," Audrey whispered.

They crossed the bridge. On the other side towered a wall of vegeta-tion through which nothing was visible—not even light. A metal gate lolled open a crack to reveal a driveway. On one of the posts hung a carved wooden sign:

Villa Sylvie.

CHAPTER 82

Audrey held her breath and pushed on the gate.

"There must be something one should say at such a moment," Florian said. "A Pythagorean oath, maybe."

Audrey and Rami agreed.

There was a solemn pause.

Then they ventured in.

It was just as Zar had described: the villa in its bowl of land, gabled and airy…evergreens and waxy tropical trees tucked around it…two giant cypresses standing sentry at the door, and the lawn stretching to a line of poplars along a stream. But despite all the lushness, a strange vacancy pervaded the domain and the house was shuttered.

They wandered along the dirt driveway and stopped short: a jeep was parked next to the house with a trailer piled with brush.

"Looks like the gardener's here," Florian said. "It must be Enrico."

They skirted the house.

"Look!" Rami pointed to the stream.

At the far end of the lawn, a man was clearing branches from under the poplars and throwing them onto a pile. The travelers drifted toward him as if in a dream…as if they'd paid a visit to this place long ago and were trying to remember it.

Audrey halted halfway. "There it is!" she exclaimed. "The fig tree Zar talked about!"

A spreading form inclined over the stream. They approached: the tree sagged with immense age. Roots writhed across the ground like gray serpents. The fig seemed poised to return to the earth, but even so, spring still coursed through it, pushing out elfin fingers that would become its distinctive handprint leaves. The stream danced past it, and with a shiver Audrey realized that they could be standing on the very spot where Zar had listened to the water, and to Olivia's voice filtering out from the gramophone in the parlor. And somewhere here, she thought, gazing up at the beneficent regard of Canigou, Zar had convened his academy.

Florian leaned in to Audrey. "I'm starting to feel like one of Pythagoras's followers, left behind after everyone else has fled."

The gardener jerked up from his brush-clearing.

The little group waved and called *bonjour.* The man responded by tossing a log with obvious irritation. Then he bent down for something.

A rifle.

The threesome froze.

"Don't worry," Florian faltered. "It doesn't look like he's pointing it at us."

The gardener strolled toward them, the hunting rifle at his side. He stopped some distance away. "What do you want?" he yelled. "This is private property." He spoke in a rough patois.

The man had a full, dark moustache and sunken cheeks. An unlit cigarette hung from the corner of his mouth as if it were a permanent fixture. He seemed locked in the granite caution of mountain folk.

"Are you Enrico?" Audrey asked.

The man bristled. "How do you know my name?" He stared at this strange female, whose face was as refined and feminine as her clothes were baggy and drab.

"We know about you from Konstantine Zar," she said. "From a letter he sent to his sister in Brussels."

She realized at once her multiple blunders: first, that they knew Zar was in Vernet, when he was still zealously guarding his privacy; second, that they'd read his private correspondence; third, that they were probably (if the rifle was any indication) threatening Zar's exile just by being there.

Enrico narrowed his gaze. "Are you here with someone else?" he asked, his hand still tight on the rifle.

The three visitors gaped at him, then at each other.

"Do you mean an imposing man with white hair, by any chance?" Audrey ventured.

"He came here," Enrico said.

"We have nothing to do with him!" she blurted. *Au contraire*: we've come to warn Zar."

Enrico stepped closer. "Warn him about what?"

"That that man—Meyer—means to harm him."

Enrico grew agitated. "I knew he was trouble as soon as I saw him," he said. "But why?"

"He's here for revenge," Rami said.

Enrico looked at him uncomprehendingly. "That's ridiculous."

No one tried to contradict him.

"Salopard!" the gardener barked (meaning Meyer, they assumed). He took the cigarette from his mouth and spat on the ground. "Bastard! He

came yesterday. I'm sure he had a gun. He would have used it, too, to get what he wanted, if I didn't have this with me." He lifted the rifle.

"You mean you would have told him where Zar is," Florian said.

"I didn't, of course," Enrico snapped at him. "I would never betray *le Maître.*"

The Master...Enrico's honorific didn't go unnoticed by his visitors. Audrey thrilled at the title...at the closeness of Zar in this garden. She looked toward the high passes where he'd gone into seclusion. Clouds like translucent spaceships hovered in formation over the Canigou massif: a sign of the mistral, though they begged a less rational explanation, Audrey wondered how Meyer had found the villa. He must have asked for Zar around the village—gone into shops and cafes, haunted the stalls on the marketplace, several times if need be, to glean what he wanted from these tight-lipped people. He would have pressed, and insisted, until someone finally said: *Ah, yes, there was an odd musician once, come to think of it. Many years ago.* And someone else recalled the abandoned villa on the mountainside.

Enrico broke into her thoughts: "Le Maître told me never to let anyone know where he lives. Except for one person. A lady." He glanced at Audrey. "Not you, Madame. Someone older." He paused. "Le Maître's lady. I would do anything to bring them together."

A few moments passed before someone uttered her name.

Olivia.

"She's on her way as we speak!" Florian said. "Olivia Taverner is my great aunt. She received Zar's appeal to come only recently. There are two gentlemen with her: her personal assistant, Roland Wilmots. And an old friend of Zar's sister: Professor Friedrich Graf. Friedrich said they're arriving sometime this evening."

A chink opened in the granite Enrico. He offered the slightest smile—just wide enough to reveal a few cracked teeth. "But that's wonderful news!" he said, as if to himself. Then: "You can't imagine how long le Maître has waited for this moment." Enrico came into focus again, "I'll open the house at once," he said, "and put the heating on."

"You don't live here?" Rami asked.

"Oh, no. No one lives here. I live across the road. The villa still belongs to le Maître. But..." Enrico motioned in the direction of the mountain peaks. "He lives much higher now."

"Can we drive up there?" Rami asked, forgetting that his van was burdened with a piano.

The gardener shook his head. "You, *non*. I, yes," he said, and indicated the jeep. "I take him supplies twice a week." He turned to Florian. "Please tell the gentlemen to wait with Madame on the outskirts of Vernet until they hear from me. That will mean that I've brought le Maître down to the villa and they can join him there. I don't want them arriving here alone."

"I'll tell Friedrich," Florian said, and exchanged telephone numbers with Enrico.

"But Meyer..." Audrey said.

"Don't worry," Enrico assured her. "I will be on guard against him. Anyway, he cannot possibly find Zar. No one can. Not without me."

CHAPTER 83

They've been delayed," Florian said, checking his phone.

The three musicians had found a table at the back of a pizzeria in a lane tucked off of Vernet's marketplace. It was the most obscure dining they could find. They'd waited all day in the bed and breakfast for darkness to fall in case Meyer was on the prowl somewhere.

"Is Olivia all right?" Audrey asked, pouring Florian more wine from the carafe.

"He didn't say. It looks like they're planning to arrive tomorrow now. I get the impression that things are changing by the hour."

"And Jonas?" Audrey asked Rami. "Have you heard from him?" Her casualness belied the disquiet churning inside her.

"He arrived at his sister's," Rami said, observing her closely over his fruit juice.

"That's good."

"Is it?"

Audrey met Rami's gaze.

He smiled at her. "Jonas is in love with you, Audrey," he said, smoothing his moustache.

She looked away. "Yes, I know."

The men glanced at each other.

Florian turned to Audrey. "Maybe you should go to Hamburg, then," he concluded.

His comment had the effect of finishing this phrase of speculative music, though no one knew how the next one would begin.

Rami changed tonalities: "Do you think that Monsieur Zar will be safe for another night?" he asked. "With Monsieur Enrico standing guard?"

"Let's hope so" Florian said without conviction.

Audrey stood up and reached for her coat and hat. "I'll see you back at the bed and breakfast," she said.

"*What?*" Florian cried. "You can't be going for a walk!"

"Indeed I am," she said, kissing the two men on the cheek. "Don't worry. Darkness is my ally." Then, playfully, "Don't forget that I already survived a confrontation with Meyer."

Her words were of no comfort. And as she set off alone, in a rare turn of heart Audrey half hoped that her friends might deter her this time.

◆ ◆ ◆

She left the pizzeria and set off up a steep lane. Her destination was the twelfth-century church of St. Saturnin, whose bell tower stood watch from Vernet's highest point. Zar walked here when he was still living at Villa Sylvie—when snow was too deep on the mountain paths. He'd written about these ancient village byways: how they doubled back on themselves, and came to dead-ends without warning. Audrey was not so reckless as to think that Zar's presence would protect her from Meyer tonight, but she felt no fear, which was perhaps the same thing.

She stepped along culverts and irrigation canals, some of them dating from medieval times. Water ran constantly, like a sound-blanket thrown over the sleeping town; indeed, water had been spilling from the heights for millennia, and though people in the valleys had spent centuries trying to divert it, and tame it, still it ran with a splendid free will. Lush gardens dotted the hillside, some tiny and walled, others big enough for fruit trees and vineyards.

Audrey started up a precipitous alley. Houses were densely packed; stifling. She increased her pace, but even as she kept to the lit paths she would stray into a dead-end by mistake, where shadows burgeoned, and cats hissed. Somewhere a conversation lifted in a hollow wave, then was gone.

She arrived at the summit. The church of St. Saturnin abutted a small castle with a crenelated tower.

There was a bench on the little plaza and Audrey sat down.

Zar must have sat here, too. Pondering...

Silence engulfed her. At once a space widened in her mind into which thoughts tumbled with abandon. *St. Saturnin.* The church harbored the relics of the saint's left wrist. A curious body part to pray to (although perhaps not for musicians). *Meyer.* The son of a murdered Nazi. A stalker who'd become eerily like his prey: half-human, half-myth. *Olivia.* When would she get here? Audrey imagined Zar in his refuge, breathing the same air, observing the same stars, oblivious that the woman he'd enshrined for his whole life—whose response he'd waited in vain to receive—was now only hours away.

The church bell rang once. Audrey glanced up at the flood-lit belfry: nine-fifteen. The bell marked every quarter-hour. For five centuries villagers had lifted their tools and laid them down again to this rhythm; they'd opened their markets, and milked their goats, and said their evening prayers to this bell. There was an inscription on it, apparently: *May my voice be the terror of all demons.*

Silence returned.

There was no wind. No moon. The Milky Way trailed its diamonds over the church and against their light, the range of peaks was scissor-cut. The cold air already carried a trace of wisteria, and of sweet, waking soil. Reverence blossomed. It was impossible to hate, feeling this way, Audrey thought; impossible to deceive, or go to war.

She listened.

Surely this was the moment to hear it: *The Music of the Spheres.*

Pythagoras...Plato...Kepler...Zar...

They couldn't all be wrong.

Olivia...Florian...Friedrich...Karel...

Nor could they.

Certitude electrified her. If humans had been finding sympathetic resonance overhead since the time of vulture-bone flutes, then the soul must ring everlastingly.

Audrey studied the sky, unlike any she'd ever seen. Perhaps the sound of that flute was still echoing in all that vastness, along with the soul of the dark-eyed woman who'd fashioned it. Audrey shivered. *How alive it all felt!* All that spinning...shining...orbiting...She could identify Venus and Mars, and imagined that they, like the other planets, were moving through the cosmos with the glorious tones that Kepler had described.

In three-quarter time, perhaps.

◆ ◆ ◆

She leapt to her feet:

A tapping.

Definitely not of celestial origin.

The sound quickened.

Louder...closer.

The clock struck again, three times. She'd somehow missed the two strikes of the half-hour during her reverie.

Tap...tap...

Footsteps rounded the corner of church.

CHAPTER 84

Audrey dashed from the plaza and down the first darkened alley. *Why am I so sure it's him?*

For she had no doubt.

Meyer.

She couldn't shake his steps. They pursued her down Vernet's steep labyrinth and she lost her bearings. *Where was the marketplace?* Lanterns gave off only a feeble glow, meant for those who already knew their way. *Just keep descending,* Audrey told herself, for if not, she risked circling back up the hill and finishing at the church again. She glanced at the mountains, hoping they might orient her, but they'd melted into the night.

Tap...tap...

The sound stilettoed through the hush. *How close was he?*

Audrey dove into a lane with narrow façades on two sides and a garden wall on the third.

A cul-de-sac.

She was trapped.

A sly wind probed at her coat and slunk over the wall. She could hear it in the garden on the other side, lifting last year's leaves, and rattling a trellis.

The steps halted at the entrance to the dead end.

Audrey was in no hurry to turn around. How odd, she thought, that Meyer should find her again, at night, halfway across Europe. One could encounter the same misfortune anywhere, it seemed. She glanced up at the stars. One could just as well find the same providence, too, she considered. Indeed, the symbiosis of the two followed us through life, so that ideally we should be prepared to embrace one or the other at any time, and find strength in both.

The bell struck ten. Audrey waited until each ring had ridden its wave across the valley.

Then she turned.

♦ ♦ ♦

Meyer's pallor was otherworldly: a dead man propped upright. The black overcoat draped him like a shroud. Audrey had already seen his eyes on Charles Bridge—the iciest blue found in nature. But he was wearing his dark glasses tonight and the blue, when left to the imagination, suggested something even icier.

"Audrey Nightingale," Meyer said. The words had no color.

"How do you know my name?"

"From Karel Náhoda. You are the pianist of the famous Kepler Players."

"Poor Karel," Audrey muttered. "How many other bits of information did you force from him?" It was only then that she remembered Meyer was armed. She noticed that one hand was hidden in his coat.

Her comment seemed to weigh on the man. Or perhaps it was something else. Illness? *The nearness of his goal?*

"Herr Náhoda said you're a marvelous pianist." Meyer's voice moved around one tone, as it had in Prague.

Audrey stared at him. Karel must have volunteered this nugget freely. Her merits as a pianist could hardly have been of any use to Meyer's mission.

"I love music," Meyer went on. "My father loved it, too."

"Is that why you left all that money for us?"

Meyer didn't answer. Then, with a deeper hollow in his voice: "I never harmed Klara Náhoda," he said. He cleared the phlegm from his throat. "My visit must have upset her."

A twinge gripped Audrey. She sensed something still tepid beneath all that cold, ailing flesh. She recalled what Friedrich had said about Meyer's father, Georg: that he'd had a violin slung over his shoulder when Zar had tracked him down in the forest. Friedrich had said something else, too: that life was full of such extraordinary details, if one looked out for them. And that they really weren't all that extraordinary.

Meyer stepped closer. "Take me to Zar," he said. It was more a plea than a command. He labored for breath after his exertions. "I know he lives in these mountains. I think you know where."

Audrey backed against the garden wall. "I don't know where he is," she said.

"Please." Meyer loomed over her petite frame. "I don't want to force you."

She could smell him now: heavy cologne laced with an odd sweetness, as if he'd already begun to rot.

"It's revenge, isn't it?" Audrey blurted. "That's why you're looking for Zar." She pulled herself up and lifted her chin.

"Revenge..." Meyer said wonderingly. "My father was a great admirer of Konstantine Zar. My mother told me all about it."

Audrey balked. *Was the man mad as well as ill?*

But Meyer surprised her again.

"I promised my mother as she lay dying that I would find the man who murdered Father," he said. "And that I'd do what needed to be done."

"Do you know why Konstantine Zar shot your father?" she pressed him, suddenly unafraid.

Meyer hesitated. "Out of hatred for the enemy," he said.

"You didn't know that your father assaulted Zar's sister, Klara Náhoda, in 1942?" She paused. "That he raped her?"

No sound came from Meyer except the rasp of fluid in his lungs.

"Why are you continuing the cycle of revenge, Mr. Meyer, after all these years?" Audrey asked. "People often do things they regret during a war. I would wager that not a day goes by that Zar doesn't regret what he did to your father." She added, as if it were an afterthought: "How can you deny Zar the kindred soul he's been waiting for since the war—who's on her way to him now?"

"Take me to Zar!" Meyer cried, as if Audrey hadn't spoken.

With uncanny speed he pinned her against the wall. The hand in his coat pocket thrust something solid between her ribs.

"I can only take you to a man who knows where Zar is," Audrey gasped.

Meyer backed away.

"Then do that," he said. He asked for Audrey's phone, and instructed her to walk in front of him down the twisting paths. The clock struck the quarter-hour. *Only fifteen minutes.* Their encounter seemed to have lasted for hours, so utterly had the world about them changed. The harmony in that ravishing night had gone. The cut-crystal echoes...the solace...All had evaporated, making Audrey reconsider what Plato had said about the invisible world being the only real one. No doubt this was good news for a musician, toiling away at her invisible craft. But now, in the face of visible disaster, Platonic philosophy seemed to have reached its limits.

The tiny procession made its way through the sleeping town: the little woman in gray, expression defiant, followed by a sickly assassin. That other player in the drama—the wise man on the mountain—could not have known how soon he'd be facing his reckoning.

CHAPTER 85

Meyer drove Audrey up the abbey road in his slick BMW. She'd told him that the only way to find Zar was to go to the gardener's house across from Villa Sylvie. She could only hope that the mountain air would sharpen her wits and she'd know what to do when the time came, because Meyer's company was having the effect of a slow poison.

They stopped at the bridge leading to the villa. There was only one house opposite, partially obscured by trees. The jeep with its trailer was parked in front of it. There were no lights anywhere.

"That's the gardener's place?" Meyer said, motioning for Audrey to get out.

"I think so."

Meyer walked behind her to the door. Their steps on the gravel drive were lost in the rushing of the river.

No one answered Meyer's pounding.

"That's strange," Audrey said. "His jeep's here." She felt listless; robotic. There seemed no point in caring anymore. There was too much to push against, and no hope of moving it.

"Maybe he's at the villa," said Meyer.

"Oh...I don't think..."

But the man steered her toward the bridge. The river was swollen with spring melt and stampeded like a wild thing. They reached the gate and

Audrey exclaimed: the villa was unshuttered and lit up—a blazing jewel in the black velvet night.

"Obviously someone's here," Meyer said.

Audrey's mind seethed. *Why was Enrico preparing for Olivia's arrival at this hour?* She was due tomorrow, after all. Her thoughts strayed to Florian and Rami and their panic when she hadn't returned to the hotel.

The door opened as Meyer was hammering on it.

"It's you," Enrico said, with a face of stone. He said nothing to Audrey. He seemed undaunted by the sheer mass of the man standing at his door.

Audrey noticed at once that Enrico had no rifle.

"Take me to Zar," Meyer ordered.

Wind hissed through the cypresses flanking the entry.

"You must do this, Enrico," Audrey pleaded. *I would do anything to bring them together,* the gardener had said. But how would he achieve that now? He was not armed. He'd have to break his vow never to betray Zar's whereabouts, for Meyer would not let go now.

The German produced his gun and pointed it at Enrico. "Give me your phone!" he commanded. "Now, guide us up the mountain."

◆ ◆ ◆

Audrey and Enrico walked in front of Meyer across the bridge.

"She's coming tonight!" Enrico said to Audrey in a stage whisper while staring straight ahead. He didn't mention Olivia's name. His words were barely audible over the din of the river.

"But I thought..."

"That's the latest news," Enrico interrupted her.

Meyer loomed closer behind them and they could say no more.

They arrived at Enrico's and he unhitched his trailer. Meyer then ordered him to drive the jeep in front of the BMW up an unpaved ascent leading into the back country. It was the only route: Enrico could hardly have strayed from it. He did his best, however, to make the journey purgatory for the German. The BMW's suspension couldn't compete with a mountain vehicle and it was all Meyer could do to keep up with the jeep. The car plunged into craters; stones peppered the chassis. Audrey noticed the droplets on Meyer's forehead, and his hands, plaster-white, fused to the steering wheel.

She laced her fingers together in her lap until they hurt. Her journey was coming to an end, it seemed. But not as she'd imagined. *Do I really want this destination to come? Am I prepared to witness the murder of one of Music's last mystics?*

They drove for thirty minutes in bone-jolting misery. In that length of time, perhaps a skilled negotiator could have dissuaded Meyer from his mission. But trapped with him at close range, no one could have extinguished the zeal burning so hotly inside him that the unventilated car began to reek of it.

Enrico braked without warning and got out of the jeep.

Meyer skidded to a stop. His headlights picked up the man, defiant in the middle of the road, but nothing else, as the darkness around him was absolute.

Enrico waved a flashlight in Meyer's eyes and stalked over to the driver's window. "You have to walk from here," he barked.

What was Enrico playing at? Audrey wondered, trying to catch his glance.

Meyer pushed the man away with the door and got out. "Where's the path?" he said. He was already breathing hard.

"Path?" Enrico guffawed. "There's no path. Only the hiking trail to Canigou, which is over there." He waved toward the ghostly peaks. "Zar's cabin is half an hour's climb at least." He pointed his flashlight at a rise dotted with underbrush and stunted pine, then assessed Meyer. "For you, probably an hour."

Enrico pulled at Audrey's elbow as Meyer locked the car. "I'll lead him on the longer approach," he breathed in her ear. "Drop behind us somehow. There's a steep ravine near a trail marker. Go down it. You'll find a stream. It's partly underground, so listen carefully. Follow it up a valley to a meadow with large boulders. The cabin is there. If you hurry, you'll have time to warn le Maître. And please: tell him his lady is near."

♦ ♦ ♦

Audrey lagged behind at the trail marker, claiming a toilet break. Meyer, winded and suffering, ignored her. He toiled on behind Enrico with the gun extended.

When the men were out of sight Audrey plunged down the ravine. The slope was a mess of loose rocks and exposed roots, and steeper than she'd thought. Her long skirt snagged on the underbrush. The cloche hat was snatched away by a branch. Teetering, she lost control and tumbled to the bottom of the slope.

She lay for some moments where she'd come to rest. *Oh, God...I've broken my ankle.* She sat up. Her ears rang from the fall. An image rose briefly before fading: Jonas, catching her before she'd slipped into the river at Weil-der-Stadt.

She looked toward the crown of Canigou and its surrounding peaks. How aloof they seemed! Were the deities who lived up there just as unconcerned about human predicaments down below? In the starlight, she could see that the ravine widened higher up and opened into a huge arena of meadow.

Audrey struggled to her feet and tested her ankle: it was sore, but not broken. She let her breathing settle and gradually, like voices drawing closer, she began to hear it. *A stream.*

She limped toward the sound. It was just as Enrico had described: the stream coursed down a valley from the heights beneath rock and peat, bubbling up here and there only to dash underground again. Audrey had to stop often to rest her ankle, and as she did, she listened to the water. The stream trickled around a mellow, pearly D-flat that echoed from a hidden chamber somewhere. The overtones joined other, more distant ones on that vibrant night, and even in her urgent state, Audrey couldn't help but marvel.

She dragged herself up the valley over rocks and thick tufts of grass. If there was a trail, it was impossible to discern it at night. At last she reached the meadow. Remnants of snow lay all around like bedsheets. Strewn between them were boulders of all shapes and inclinations, dropped by some clumsy god. The stream ran openly here, and Audrey rested at an old yew tree bending over the water.

Where is Meyer? Her heart pummeled. The man's illness was of some comfort, to be sure. For how could he possibly make it this far—and on the longer route, too? Then came the greater question: *Where is Zar?*

The church bell sounded far down in the valley—faint, but astonishingly clear. Audrey combed the vast meadow: there was no cabin that she could see. She peered at every shadow and odd-shaped rock: there was nothing. Inevitably, her eyes lifted to the sky. How close it seemed! She could almost catch the edge of it and float away—to the very origins of Music, even...to what remained of those first raw notes. It was easy to imagine that the lady herself was abroad that night, raising her lantern. Kepler could have handily proven what he'd believed all his life: that Music was a sky-dwelling force.

Audrey recalled something Zar had said: *Music is our medicine; our peacemaker; our way forward.*

Her courage surged.

Then she spotted the cabin.

CHAPTER 86

It was the rudest of dwellings, almost indistinguishable from the huge boulder against which it crouched. The hut was made entirely of stone, including the roof, on which rough slabs overlapped haphazardly, and the result made one wonder if the hut was as old as the boulder itself.

Audrey stepped closer.

Starlight bathed the meadow. She could make out the contours of the cabin now—the dark-colored door and shuttered windows, and the weeds and brush engulfing the walls. There was a bench near the entrance, and an unhewn rock served as a doorstep. Indeed, the structure seemed to have been built around this slab.

Audrey's eyes rested on the door. A frisson passed over her: it wasn't dark-colored, as she'd initially thought. But open. With no light inside.

She studied the opening. There was something attached to the wall by the door—linear, like a rope. This pale line, waist-high, extended across the meadow as far as another bench, to which it appeared to be attached.

Audrey stifled a cry: a figure was sitting there, facing the mountains.

The camouflage was perfect: the white head, at one with the distant snows...the white shirt, indistinguishable from the icy patches on the meadow.

Nothing could have concealed the singular hush, however.

Or the identity of the figure.

Audrey made no move. Transfixed, she gazed at what Zar was studying so intently: not the mountains, but the galaxy. *Musica mundana*...cosmic music...Gradually, it seemed to her that Zar was listening more than he was observing. She wondered if he could hear the same renonance as he had as a young man during the war, at the farm with the goats not so very far from here; and if this stupendous open-air concert hall was as full of echoes for him as it was for her at that moment.

The figure stood up.

Audrey pulled back into the shadow of the yew. She watched as Zar circled the bench, sliding his hand along it until he found the rope, which he grasped.

He was facing her now.

She drank in the sight of him: the loose peasant clothing and proud set of his shoulders; his breath, drifting on the razor air. His coat hung open, and he wore no gloves. The alpine glow caught on those soaring cheekbones and time seemed to have lost its way. One would have expected his face to be ravaged—by war; heartbreak; remorse. Or at least, by old age. But none of these things were apparent.

Audrey held her breath at the flesh-and-blood Zar. She remembered what he'd written in his letters: that the mountains had released his soul, like a caged bird, and ever since, the night sky had become his natural habitat.

♦ ♦ ♦

"Enrico?" he called. "*C'est toi?*"

The voice was strong; commanding.

Audrey stepped from the yew and ventured closer.

Zar walked several paces back toward the cabin, running his fingers along the rope as he went. Then he stopped to study the sky over Audrey's head.

A fist tightened around her heart: it was obvious that Zar was blind.

"Who's there?" he demanded.

She approached him.

"Sir..." she fumbled. "Maître..."

How should I address him?

"Do I know you?" he asked. "Is Enrico with you?"

"No, sir, he's not," Audrey said. "I'm alone." She was tempted to say: *You don't know me, but I feel as if I've known you for a very long time.*

She stared at the sage. He stood tall, imposing, haughty.

"Did you lose your way?" he said.

The question startled Audrey. As did her answer:

"Until this moment, yes."

Zar thought about this. "Please," he said, intrigued. "Come closer."

Audrey did this. She looked up into the obsidian eyes, as clear and probing as she'd imagined. *How could they be blind?* It was obvious now why someone had helped Zar write that final letter to Klara. Enrico, perhaps, with an unschooled script.

Zar let go of the rope and extended his hands. Audrey clasped them without thinking. His skin felt dry and warm. Supple, like a young man's.

"Ah," he said with a wry smile. "You're a pianist. You really have lost your way!"

"But how did you know?" Her thoughts tumbled.

"Most things in life are legible," he said. "One doesn't always need eyes to read them."

Zar released her hands, and with his fingertips traced the oval of her face. Then he touched her cropped hair. "You're not much for *coiffeurs*, I think," he said, but his smile faded when he added, "There's sadness in you...doubt..."

Audrey summoned a response, but in vain.

Zar considered her carefully, and sightless though he was, the singular energy coursing through him seemed to make this possible.

"You've reached a crossroads, I sense," he said. "Don't worry. You'll know which way to turn."

Maybe words don't matter anyway, she thought, as they failed her once again. *After all, he'd already divined everything important about her.*

"I'm Audrey Nightingale," she blurted at last, mortified that she'd strayed so far from her mission. "I'm a friend of Olivia's."

Zar stood motionless. Shock suddenly aged him. He grabbed for the rope and his hand tightened on it, as if to keep himself from drowning.

"Olivia..." He spoke the four syllables with the careful devotion of someone who hasn't uttered a particular prayer for many years. "Ah, that's it," he said, an ache in his tone. "You've come as a messenger, haven't you? To tell me she's dead."

Audrey foundered. "Oh, no!" she cried. "Maître, that's not it at all! In fact, Olivia is just now on her way!"

"On her way..."

"Yes! You see, she never received your letters. Your sister, Klara..."

But there was no time to explain. A stone clattered at the far end of the meadow. Then another, closer by.

Zar tilted his head. "Are there others?" he demanded.

Audrey grasped his hands again. "Maître, someone means to harm you. He forced Enrico to lead him to you. Please...come into your cabin!"

Oh, why didn't I take these precious minutes to warn him about Meyer? she anguished.

For Zar's reckoning had come.

CHAPTER 87

H alt!" screamed Meyer.

Enrico ignored him. He strode off toward Zar and Audrey, heedless of the gun trained on his back.

Meyer stumbled and swayed over the same loose stones Enrico had traversed with ease. The heavy overcoat weighed him down; his breathing came in moans.

"Maître!" Audrey cried, "Come into the cabin!"

"But who is it with Enrico?" Zar asked. He was calm. Imperious.

Audre hesitated. "It's Hans Meyer, sir," she said. She was standing at Zar's side, as if they were welcoming visitors.

"Hans Meyer..." The handsome face drew in, bewildered.

Enrico threw himself between Zar and Meyer.

"Maître!" he gasped. "Please go inside with the lady. *Tout de suite!* I'll take care of this."

But Zar stood his ground. "Step aside," he ordered, though not unkindly.

"But Maître..."

"Step aside, please."

Audrey watched, immobile, as Enrico did what Zar asked. Even though the gardener had been forced to betray his master by leading Meyer here, he would clearly obey him to the end.

Meyer stopped a few meters from Zar. His face was waxen, and shining with sweat. He wore no glasses, and the glacial eyes revealed a strange, white fire. Though the great form wavered, he managed to hold the gun steady.

Go! Audrey exhorted herself. *Stand between them, for God's sake! Save Zar!*

But she could only watch, rooted.

"Announce yourself!" Zar said, as if this were a royal audience.

"Maître, the man has a gun," Audrey said under her breath.

But Zar seemed unmoved. Maybe he realized that he'd be leaving this world soon enough, with or without Meyer's intervention. After all, thought Audrey, observing the proud mystic, if Zar's soul resonated sympathetically with a tone in the universe, like everyone else's, then he might actually be feeling some impatience to discover the source of the sound.

Meyer took a step forward and stared into Zar's eyes.

He said, "My father was Georg Meyer. In 1942, when he was stationed in Brussels…" His lungs sighed with fluid and he had to pause. "You followed him into the forest," he continued. "And you shot him in cold blood." Meyer lowered the gun slightly, as if he lacked the strength to hold it straight.

He's dying, Audrey thought. *That's why it was so urgent for him to track Zar down.*

"I never knew his name," Zar said under his breath, as if in a dream.

The comment surprised Meyer. For a few seconds, the ailing bulk went still.

Then he lifted the gun.

"Stop!" yelled Enrico, ready to dive between the two men. But instead he froze:

Zar had extended his hand.

Everyone held their breath.

"I've been expecting you for seventy years," Zar said. He was looking into Meyer's eyes as if he could see them.

Meyer ignored Zar's gesture. He kept the gun level.

"*Ich habe ein Kind,*" Zar went on. He spoke so softly that Audrey could barely hear him. "'I have a child.' Those were your father's last words. I've remembered them, and the sound of his voice, all my life." He faltered. "The voice you would never know because of what I did."

Zar dropped the hand he'd extended. He seemed resigned to what was about to happen.

At once a wail rent the alpine arena.

Audrey glanced upward. Her pulse careened. She looked at Zar: he'd raised his head, too.

The wail sounded again, ragged and weary, as if it had travelled far.

Audrey's eyes widened. *Friedrich's flute!* Her heart surged. If the church bell was audible up here, a piercing bone flute would be as well. *They must have arrived at the villa!* Was he signaling them somehow? Or simply indulging in a bit of whimsy? (How typical of Friedrich!) In any case, Olivia and her companions could not have imagined what was about to unfold in that meadow.

Nor could the people in the meadow.

For at that moment, Meyer dropped the gun and fell to his knees.

Had he heard it, too?

He swayed as he knelt. His coat lay splayed about him over the stones like a vestment. He reached for Zar's hand, and grasped it in both of his as if to steady himself.

Audrey shot a glance at Enrico.

The German looked up at Zar and said, "I've come to…" He mustered his strength. "I've come to forgive you for what you did."

He began to sob.

Zar said nothing. Enrico came to his side and without a word helped his master pull Meyer to his feet.

"You are that child," Zar whispered to Meyer. His cheeks shone in the starlight. "Thank you…oh, thank you…"

They embraced.

The mountain night and all its players leaned in.

Audrey bowed her head. There must have been a Great Conjunction somewhere in the universe, she thought. Surely Kepler would have thought so, too. Although he probably would have agreed that no alignment in the sky could have been as miraculous as this one, here on Earth, in a forgotten corner of the Pyrenees.

♦ ♦ ♦

Audrey and Enrico helped Meyer into the cabin. "What did you mean, Audrey," he swooned. "Zar's kindred soul…coming…?"

She left the question unanswered.

Zar's bed was a narrow wooden platform with a mattress and duvet. The big German hung over the sides, but he groaned with relief as they lay him down and gave him some water.

"A rescue team can be here within an hour," Enrico said. "I can make an emergency call from up here." He felt inside his jacket. "Ah." He glared at Meyer. "You took my phone."

Meyer produced the keys to the BMW from his coat pocket and handed them to Enrico. "In the car," he rasped. He closed his eyes. "Take Zar …to his soul…"

"I'll call mountain rescue from the car," Enrico said.

"Someone should stay here until the medics arrive," said Audrey.

"No!" Meyer spoke with unexpected force. "I need nothing. Go!"

♦ ♦ ♦

Audrey left the cabin. She found Zar in the meadow, standing some distance from the guide rope.

He turned as soon as he heard her.

"Maître," she said. "We're taking you to Villa Sylvie."

"Is it really true?" he said, trancelike. "That Olivia is on her way?"

Audrey looked at the ground, trying to quell her emotion. She remembered Friedrich's flute—that it must have been announcing their arrival.

"Olivia's here already," she said, her voice catching.

Zar's aspect darkened. "I sent her so many letters over the years. But you say that she didn't receive them."

Audrey looked away, as if Zar were able to read her distress.

"No, she didn't," she said, adding, "Olivia would have come years ago otherwise." She regretted at once taking this liberty.

Zar's expression became opaque. "How do you know this?" he asked. "How do you know about the letters?" He trained his black eyes on Audrey.

"It involves a piano," she managed to say. *Olivia must have felt this way at his lecture, when he'd trapped her with his stare.*

"Ah, of course," Zar said, his mood lifting. "A piano. Pianists are never very far from their instruments."

"But Maître. It's *your* piano."

Zar stiffened. "My piano..."

"Yes!" Audrey exclaimed. "The Náhoda made the journey here, too. We found your letters inside it." She hesitated. "Klara had hidden them there all this time." She stopped herself before she'd have to explain to Zar what happened to his sister.

"Klara..." he said. A wrenching sigh escaped him: the exhale of an invalid when his illness has broken and he can finally begin to heal.

"We also found your teachings hidden in the piano," Audrey said. "Klara made sure they would be safe." Then she quoted:

"A piece of music is a journey. It begins with a single note or chord, like a first step. Music is also proof that the most profound journeys are those taken by the spirit."

Astonishment filled Zar. "My words touched you!" In a sudden, youthful rush, he pulled Audrey against him as if she were his prodigal child. "There's somewhere you still need to go, my dear," he said.

She had no chance to ask him what he meant.

"*Venez! Vite!*" Enrico called from the cabin.

And the three of them set off across the meadow.

CHAPTER 88

The gathering in front of Villa Sylvie could have been mistaken for a late-night supper party.

Florian...Rami...Roland...Friedrich... Audrey counted everyone under her breath. "Where's Olivia?" she asked.

"I don't see a lady," said Enrico. He parked Meyer's BMW next to Gloria von Helden's Mercedes.

Zar got out and stood for a moment. He hadn't spoken since they'd left the meadow. He turned his face to the house, as if he could see the unshuttered windows blazing with light, and the tips of the cypresses, fitful in the night breeze.

Audrey rushed up to the four men. She kissed Rami and Florian (*My walk through the village ended up taking a bit longer than I'd intended.*); and embraced Friedrich and Roland (*Thank God you made it! Where is she?*).

"She's here," Graf assured her. "But first, we must greet Zar."

The great musician was already shuffling toward them with Enrico at his elbow. Zar reached out to each person in turn, and everyone inclined over his hand as they took it.

"It is I who should be welcoming you to my house," Zar said, though his dour regard belied any hospitality. Audrey sensed the unrest tearing through him—the unbearable impatience.

"Where is she?" she whispered again to Graf.

He pointed toward the obscure reaches of the garden where the stream mumbled in its sleep.

"She's by the fig tree," Graf said. "She wanted to meet him outside, under the sky." He was speaking more to the others than to Zar, for clearly he'd assumed that someone would have to help the master navigate his own garden.

This, of course, would not be necessary.

Zar had already melted away.

The little gathering dared not follow. *Should they even watch?* It was as if a pilgrim had left a treasure in a shrine during his youth, and only now, in his old age, was going back to retrieve it. No one would have ventured with him into the holy place.

Audrey advanced a few meters across the lawn nevertheless. She wouldn't have dreamed of disturbing this reunion. She simply wanted to stand under a broader swathe of sky. Still, she wished she'd stayed with the group. For the dense greenery near the stream didn't provide the privacy one would have expected. And the illumination was full of sorcery.

There she was, beneath the fig tree:

Zar's lost treasure.

◆ ◆ ◆

Olivia graced the garden as she had the concert stage. She was regal in a white coat, and with her snowy hair and pale skin, she shone like a fixed point in deep space.

She spotted Zar.

"Xairetízo ti melodía mésa sou!" she called, when he was still some distance away. *I salute the melody within you.* The voice was clear, vibrant; it carried a trace of dark cherries and honey.

Had she noticed that Zar was drifting obliquely? Audrey wondered. *Had she guessed that he couldn't see?*

"Xairetízo ti melodía mésa sou!" Zar called back. Olivia's voice was all he needed for a beacon. He was striding toward her now. Anyone looking on would never have thought that this man normally had to use a rope to navigate. Or that this woman, reduced by age and circumstance, could still run as she had when she was twenty.

Audrey lingered long enough to watch the two souls fuse together under the arms of the fig tree. She'd also detected a brighter gleam in the garden just then, no doubt due to two white heads reflecting more light than one; and to the stirring of old embers into a quick, eager flame. But there were other possibilities, too—at least for those bold enough to consider them.

As Zar led his shining lady into the splendors of the night, Audrey sensed another witness to this drama: someone who carried her own illumination, and who must have been just as delighted as everyone else at the sound of these two lost melodies finally harmonizing.

CODA

Audrey rejoined the others.

The five men asked no questions. The gardener, the grocer, the Pythagorean, the professor, and the factotum with no overcoat were all gentleman at their core, and though their eyes had been glued to the shadows by the fig tree, they would never have divulged what they might have seen there—or speculated about what even now might be happening.

"They'll come back to the house, presumably," Florian said.

"I've left the door open," said Enrico. "There's plenty of food." Then, reddening, "A room is ready for them."

"What about the piano?" asked Rami.

"We'll see about that tomorrow," Roland said.

"And Meyer?" Audrey wondered.

"They've sent in a helicopter," said Enrico. "He'll be taken to the hospital in Perpignan."

"Audrey?" Rami said. "Are you all right?"

For a moment she couldn't respond.

There's somewhere you still need to go.

She looked around at everyone, as if they must have heard this voice, too.

In case they hadn't, she said: "There's somewhere I still need to go."

No one pressed her on this.

But she elaborated anyway:

"I'm going to Hamburg."

◆ ◆ ◆

They drifted to the cars.

Audrey took Graf aside. "It certainly was unique, Friedrich, signaling your arrival with that prehistoric flute of yours!" she teased. "Incredibly, you could hear it halfway up the mountain."

Graf looked at her, perplexed. "I don't know what you mean," he said. "I left the flute at Gloria's on our way to Brussels. She said she would return it to the university in Tübingen."

Audrey waited for his laugh. But he hadn't been joking.

She backed away and studied the inky tips of the cypresses. They seemed to be pointing far beyond the Milky Way to an even grander place, where there was no day or night at all, just a constant, life-affirming sound. Any student of cosmic music would have known that this sort of night was a veritable concert, though few would have speculated, as Audrey was now, that some of those echoes had actually been quivering for some time, set in motion when a dark-eyed woman picked up a vulture bone forty millennia ago.

LEONA FRANCOMBE is a pianist, author and composer living in Belgium. She studied at Yale School of Music, the *Hochschule für Musik* in Vienna, the Banff Centre, and Bryn Mawr College.

Also by Leona Francombe:

The Sage of Waterloo

Madame Ernestine und die Entdeckung der Liebe

For more information please visit:

www.leonafrancombe.com

Take a walk through the story:

NICHOLAS MAXSON-FRANCOMBE, cover artist, is Lead Artist and Concept Designer at Sandfall Interactive in Montpellier, France.

www.ingramcontent.com/pod-product-compliance
Lightning Source LLC
Chambersburg PA
CBHW061341190726
48288CB00005B/1550